The Kissing Stone

The Kissing Stone

Stone

THE HIGHLAND NIGHTS SERIES

AMANDA SCOTT

OPEN ROAD

INTEGRATED MEDIA

NEW YORK

Cover design by Lesley Worrell

ISBN 978-1-5040-5083-8

Published in 2018 by Open Road Integrated Media, Inc.
180 Maiden Lane
New York, NY 10038
www.openroadmedia.com

To Maggie Crawford,

editor extraordinaire, who inadvertently planted

the seed for *The Kissing Stone*'s secondary theme.

Thank you!

AUTHOR'S NOTE

I based *The Kissing Stone* on historical versions of an incident during the ancient feud between Clan Comyn (later Cumming/s) and the Mackintoshes of Clan Chattan. The basic plotline of the feud and its result are historical, and the major events are as accurate as I could make them, including the ending.

The following note comes from one fascinating, bestselling source on which I relied for the way we use (and abuse) intuition, and how it works:

> "Intuition is usually looked upon by us thoughtful Westerners with contempt . . . [and] often described as emotional, unreasonable, or inexplicable. Husbands chide their wives about 'feminine intuition' and don't take it seriously. We much prefer logic, the grounded, explainable, unemotional thought process that ends in a supportable conclusion. Americans worship logic, even when it's wrong, and deny intuition, even when it's right.
>
> "Men, of course, have their own version. . . . Theirs is more viscerally named 'a gut feeling,' but it isn't just a feeling. It is our most complex cognitive process and at the same time, the simplest."
> —Gavin de Becker, *The Gift of Fear: Survival Signals That Protect Us from Violence* (Copyright 1997, 2010, Gavin de Becker, Dell 1997)

GLOSSARY

For readers' convenience, the author offers the following guide:

- ❖ Catriona—Ka CHREE na
- ❖ Clachan—village
- ❖ Fain—glad
- ❖ Forbye—besides, in addition, not to mention
- ❖ Gillichallum Roy—Gilli HA lum = Young Malcolm; Roy = red
- ❖ Glen—valley, typically narrow and deep
- ❖ Glen Mòr—the Great Glen
- ❖ Hellicat—a good-for-nothing
- ❖ *Mo chridhe*—sweetheart
- ❖ Moigh—Moy (which is Loch Moy's modern spelling)
- ❖ Plaid (great kilt)—pronounced "played." All-purpose garment from a length of wool kilted up with a belt. Wearer flings excess over his shoulder.
- ❖ Stone (the)—when capitalized = the kissing stone
- ❖ Strath—broad, flat valley; typically a river runs through it (Strathnairn)
- ❖ Tables—early name for backgammon, played much the same way
- ❖ Tail—a powerful man's retinue, limited at the time according to rank
- ❖ Tocher—dowry
- ❖ Whisst—as in "Hold (haud) your whisst": Be quiet.

The Kissing Stone

Intuition (15c): n **1**: quick and ready insight; **2 a**: immediate apprehension or cognition; **b**: knowledge or conviction gained by intuition; **c**: the power or faculty of attaining to direct knowledge or cognition without evident rational thought and inference.

—*Merriam-Webster's Collegiate Dictionary, Eleventh Edition*

PROLOGUE

Scottish Central North Highlands, Raitt Castle, November 1432

"Sir, you *cannot* do this! Such hangings are not only illegal but barbaric!"

Standing outside the open main gate of the castle, twenty-three-year-old William Comyn—namesake of an ancient Lord of Badenoch—clutched his fists at his slim hips in outraged fury and faced his equally furious father with more than his usual courage. Having said, for once, exactly what he thought, Will fell silent, awaiting the explosion.

A wintry chill and gloomy sky augured a thunderous outcome for the day, too.

Nearby, men had almost finished stringing the ends of four long ropes through holes in four of the iron bars that protruded high on the stone wall framing the castle's fifteen-foot arched gateway. The other end of each rope dangled near its intended victim, waiting for Comyns to form nooses around the men's necks and haul each one up to hang until death claimed him.

The two angry men glowering at each other were both an inch or two over six feet with the same shoulder-length light brown hair, dark hazel-green eyes, and breadth of shoulder. However, Comyn of Raitt—or Sir Gervaise Comyn de Raite, as he now insisted others address him, employing the French pronunciation with emphasis on the second syllable of his first name—was a warrior of many more years' standing.

Descended from Norman knights, de Raite was also heavier in shoulders and thighs than his lanky youngest son, and his unbound hair and beard revealed more gray than brown. His temper being legendary, none of his sons—despite the Fates' originally blessing him with six—had ever so blatantly challenged his authority.

He reacted just as Will had expected.

"Nowt that *I do* be illegal!" de Raite roared, putting his face close to Will's. "I *am* the law at Raitt, from Nairn tae Lochindorb, and should be treated as such, ye impudent hellicat. What's more, them four Mackintosh villains trespassed on *my* land. For that, they must hang as a warning tae other such egregious ill-doers!"

Although Will's focus remained fixed on what was doubtless a lost cause, he knew that his father was overstating his authority, which was oft contested by neighboring chiefs and chieftains, especially the Mackintoshes, from whom de Raite had seized the castle two decades ago.

"Sir," he said, cooling his tone, "recall that after you seized Raitt from Fin of the Battles, the Regent and, later, his grace, the King ordered the Mackintosh to let you keep Raitt and commanded you both to maintain the *peace* hereabouts."

"Jamie Stewart be a feckless dafty," de Raite retorted. "He's nobbut a puppet o' the English King a-trying tae bring English notions tae Scotland. By such doing, he undermines the powers o' his nobles, most notably those of our liege lord, Alexander o' the Isles. So, I'll ha' nowt tae do wi' the King."

Having clapped eyes on the King of Scots only once, at a distance, and therefore having no set opinion of James Stewart or his notions, Will nevertheless knew right from wrong. What his father was about to do was wrong.

"That road has been a public one for centuries, sir," he said. "You have long given safe passage to travelers there, yourself. To change that practice only to hang four Mackintosh members of the powerful Clan Chattan Confederation is wrong in the eyes of the law and of God Himself. You gave them no warning and arrested them only because they were born Mackintoshes. To what end?"

"Tae what end, ye say? I'll tell ye what end. Did Alexander's forces under the command o' Donal Balloch no defeat the Mackintoshes *and* the royal army at Inverlochy? Did Jamie Stewart not imprison Alexander after Jamie's victory at Lochaber, when Alexander submitted tae him at Holyrood? Aye, he did! Alexander be free now at last but be a broken man who ha' done nowt tae reclaim his heritage!"

"All of that is true," Will admitted. "Even so—"

"Nae, then!" de Raite interjected. "We ha' sworn fealty tae the Lord of the Isles. It be our bounden duty tae bring down all o' them insolent Mackintoshes and their ilk, now and for all time."

"But—"

"Be damned tae yer prating, Will Comyn! Sakes, but ye're no Comyn at all tae be acting as ye do. So hush your gob and get ye hence, or by the Fates, I'll gie ye yer own head on a rope tae play wi'! We ha' room enow above for ye, too."

Recognizing defeat, even as his older brothers Hew and Liam grabbed him by his arms and pulled him away from their enraged sire, Will saw that their hapless victims already had nooses around their necks.

The four were proud Mackintoshes who stared stoically ahead, knowing they had done no wrong but refusing to beg for mercy. Doubtless, they also knew that Comyn de Raite made his own rules and disclaimed having done murder whenever he had committed that crime, for this was by no means his first such offense.

Although born at Raitt, Will had been home for just two years, after fostering with his granduncle in Inverness-shire for fourteen before returning at de Raite's request. Having trained as a warrior, Will had always expected to serve some noble lord, perhaps even the Earl of Mar, Lord of the North. However, his first duty, according to his granduncle, was to his own father.

Even so, Will could not bear to watch de Raite's victims' final suffering.

Instead, when his brothers released him, he strode southward around the castle and up the steep hill behind it, where he could always find solace, though it did seem as if the gathering dark clouds might begin to shed tears of rain over the villainy at

Raitt. Wishing he had time to hike to the nearer of the mountain's two craggy peaks before dark, he wondered if even that would be enough time for him to stop seeing the hangings in his mind's eye, even briefly.

Unfortunately, his fertile imagination continued to provide him with more than he wanted to see, though the storm clouds merely sprinkled a bit of rain before moving on an hour or so later.

When he returned that night, praying that darkness would hide the results of his father's evil deed until sunrise, the rising quarter moon, to his sad relief, revealed that none of Comyn's four victims still struggled against his noose.

Unfortunately, although their torture had ended, repercussions were likely to follow. How he wished his father were a more tolerant man, one strong enough of conscience to make peace with his enemies.

The reality, though, was that de Raite was chief of what remained of Clan Comyn and thus his liege lord, to whom he owed loyalty. Moreover, Raitt Castle was their home. Having agreed to serve there with his brothers, he had also assumed responsibilities that argued against leaving to seek his fortune elsewhere.

CHAPTER I

Scottish Highlands southeast of Castle Finlagh, 25 May 1433

"When one is having an adventure that is strictly forbidden, one should be able to enjoy it," eighteen-year-old Katy MacFinlagh muttered to herself as she inched her way up the almost perpendicular granite slope toward the formidable crag above it.

With an old gray kirtle hitched up under a belt to leave her bare legs and leather-tough feet free, she had been enjoying her adventure immensely.

Pausing for a breath and to see what she could see from her present position, with her head turned so that her right cheek pressed against the warm granite surface, she grinned at the sight of the vast landscape beyond.

She could see northward to the town of Nairn's harbor and the Moray Firth, four miles away, their water sparkling blue in the afternoon sun. The town sat at the mouth of the winding river from which it had taken its name. Katy could even make out the tall stone tower of Nairn's castle and could see a good portion of the river, which had its headwaters in higher mountains to the southwest.

The town, with its thousand or so inhabitants, looked smaller from where she sprawled on the peak than it did from the ramparts of Castle Finlagh, hundreds of feet below her on its own two-hundred-foot knoll above the floor of the strath.

What she could *not* see and had hoped to see was Raitt Castle, but she was still on the west side of the crag, and Raitt lay somewhere northeast of the ridge of hills. Six months ago the villainous Comyn of Raitt who lived there had illegally hanged four of her fellow Clan Chattan kinsmen for no more crime than taking the main road from Glen Spey to Nairn. A portion of that public right of way crossed Raitt land, to be sure, but Comyn de Raite had insisted the men were trespassing.

Katy's father, Fin of the Battles, controlled the west slope of the ridge and the peak she was climbing. They were part of Castle Finlagh's estate. Fin had told her that Comyn de Raite oft sent watchers to the ridgetop to spy on Castle Finlagh.

In return, her father set guards to watch for Comyns. Knowing that she would be wise to avoid meeting MacFinlagh guards or Comyn watchers alone, she had brought her mother's wolf dogs, Eos and Argus, as her companions. By keeping to thinning bits of woodland, she had walked up the steep slope to the base of the even steeper south crag and begun carefully to climb.

Aside from the awful hangings at Raitt, the area had been peaceful for nearly eighteen months. Moreover, although the west-facing slope lacked cottages, the homes of Finlagh's cottars, men-at-arms, other tenants, and families of those who worked in the castle occupied the woods west of Finlagh and much of the strath. Guards watched from the castle ramparts, too, and might even have seen her come up the slope, so if she ran into danger, a good scream would swiftly bring help.

That she had reached the crag's lower portion *without* drawing attention was a good omen, though. Likely, neither side had sent up watchers that day.

Exhilarated to have reached the exposed granite of the crag, she and the dogs had continued swiftly and agilely around boulders and over talus and scree until she had begun climbing the inviting, albeit more precipitous, stretch twenty or thirty feet below the top, where she sprawled now against its steeply angled surface.

The route had seemed to provide the fastest way with the fewest obstacles to the peak and looked easily approachable. Its southeastern section did plunge abruptly downward, but she could avoid that danger by keeping well to its west side.

That thought made her glad she had failed to persuade her twin sister to come with her. Clydia was less adventurous, though she would say more practical. She would likely insist that they avoid the smooth-looking slope altogether.

Commanding the dogs to stay and proceeding upward with caution, Katy eventually had to ease a few feet to her right to avoid a sheer upthrust looming before her. Above it, to *its* right, a vertical crevice between other upthrusts beckoned, offering a probable path onto the peak itself. Gripping a small knob with her left hand and leaning into the rock face, she stretched her right arm toward the crevice. Unable to reach it, she tried to shove herself upward with her right foot, only to feel it slip right out from under her as if it had struck ice.

A cry of annoyance and distress escaped her as she scrabbled with both feet and her flailing right hand for solid purchase . . . for any purchase.

One of the dogs—likely the male, Argus—gave a sharp bark.

"Be still, laddie," she muttered. "I can do this." The last thing she wanted was for anyone else to catch her in such an undignified position. Nor did she want to fall, but she knew better than to let panic disturb her concentration.

Finding only the unforgiving slickness of a highly polished sheet of granite that refused to provide traction for either foot, she pressed her right hand hard and flat against a bit of rougher stone that it had encountered.

The weight of her body continued trying to drag her downward. Her left hand was losing its tenuous grip on the knob. Her bare feet found no purchase at all.

Raising her head barely enough to recognize that such movement further endangered her, she nevertheless discerned a tiny horizontal crack a few inches above her right hand. By stretching that arm hard to its length and beyond, she managed to dig the tips of her two longest fingers into the crack.

Fighting now to hold terror at bay, knowing she could not hold herself so for long, she forced herself to concentrate on relaxing into the rock and tried to imagine a way, any way, to escape her predicament before sliding to her death.

Will Comyn, under orders from his father to earn his keep for once, was supposed to be keeping watch on the residents of Castle Finlagh, their enemies to the southwest, from the ridgetop. Instead, to ease his boredom and armed with only his dirk, Will had spent most of the day tracking a deer while it wandered and grazed. Aside from birds and some rabbits, the only other sign of life that afternoon had been a lone woman strolling through a clearing in the trees below him.

Having tired of tracking and long since assured himself that Finlagh had no watchers out that day, he was heading home through the forest below the southern crag when he heard a feminine cry from above, followed by a dog's bark.

Curious, he strode uphill with deceptive speed in near silence until he saw a female, likely the same one he had seen earlier, on the west side of the crag with her skirts rucked up nearly to her bottom, revealing shapely, young-looking bare legs spread far apart in a clearly futile effort to find toeholds.

The foolish lass had evidently got herself onto one of the crag's slick spots and was holding herself with one outstretched hand while the other one, like her feet, gently and carefully sought anything to which it might cling. Well below her on the slope two large, visibly nervous wolf dogs watched her.

The larger one turned its head then with a suspicious look at Will.

Well acquainted with the ridge, Will knew the danger that lay below her to the east. If she lost her grip, she could fall a few hundred feet.

As these thoughts and others sped through his mind, he maintained his silence and quickened his pace, keeping a wary eye on the dogs but fearing to speak lest he startle her into losing what purchase she had.

At least she had had the sense to spread herself out widely against the rock.

The dog that had been eyeing him began to wag its tail as though approving of his swift approach to its mistress. The other had not shifted its gaze from her.

A stone slid from under one of Will's feet and rattled downward.

Both dogs raised their ears at the sound, but if the lass heard it, she gave no sign. The dogs stayed put, apparently tense yet content to watch him.

Her legs were *very* shapely. If her skirt were to shift just an inch higher—

Briefly shutting his eyes, collecting his wits enough to speak calmly, he looked up at her and said, "I am below you to your left, lass. I'll not let you fall, so relax into the rock as much as you can and keep patient for a few moments more."

She stiffened at his first few words but did not speak. Her head was tilted upward, and she made no attempt to move it, but when he saw her body sink closer to the rock, he knew she was doing her best to relax.

"Good lass," he said. "My name is Will, and I'm climbing toward you. Soon I'll be near enough to get my right foot under your left one."

"Stop talking then, and hie yourself," she said clearly.

Will grinned, glad to learn that she had spirit.

She was muttering something else, but he could not make out her words. Nor did he care what they were. He cared only about getting one foot solidly under hers.

"Mercy, my skirts!" Katy muttered as she heard him coming closer. *"Just how much can he see?"*

The man's voice was calm, though, as if he removed impulsively rebellious young damsels from precipitous granite slopes every day. His voice was soothing, too, making it easy to relax into the rock. Even as that thought crossed her mind, she became aware of shaggy brown hair and broad shoulders a short way to her left and felt the firmness of his much larger bare foot beneath her left one.

It was warm against hers, comforting. She felt herself going limp with relief.

"Dinna move yet," he warned. "I've got only my one foot there. If you'll tilt your chin down some, though," he added with a touch of humor, "you'll see me more clearly. When I decide the best way to proceed, I'll help you come down."

"But I don't want to go *down*," she protested, now looking right at him. "Faith, sir, I've got this far, I want to see what I can see from the top."

She knew nearly everyone for miles around Finlagh by sight, and she could see him well enough now to know he was a stranger. Noting the determined look on his handsome face, and his clear, dark hazel-green eyes and thick, dark lashes, she was certain that, had she seen him before, she would remember him.

"Who are you?" she asked.

"I told you, my name is Will, and you have not yet told me yours."

"I'm Katy." She felt a tingling thrill at his wanting to know but hoped he would not ask for more, since he had offered her only one name for himself.

To her relief, he nodded and said lightly, "Well, Katy, if you do want to get to the top, I'd be fain to help you. It may even prove easier to make our way down the northwest side than to get you safely down off this slope from here. I'm coming right up alongside you now, so dinna take offense when I touch you."

"Good sakes, sir, I am not stupid," she said, wondering why the thought of him touching her had stirred more tingly feelings inside her. "If you can get me off of this devilish slippery rock, I shall be indebted to you forever."

"Nae, then, not forever," he said with a chuckle. "Lasses, in my experience—lads, too, come to that—rarely maintain any such feelings forever. You could easily decide that you want my head on a charger within a sennight."

"I could *never* be so ungrateful," she retorted.

"We may just learn the truth of that, given time," he said, meeting her gaze—nae, capturing it and warming her all through.

Even so, she was astonished that he could think such a thing of her. Various people—mostly family—had called her thoughtless, impulsive, even rebellious, but she could not recall anyone ever calling her ungrateful, even for small favors.

And, much as she would hate to admit it to anyone else, considering likely repercussions, this chap had already done her much more than a small favor.

Watching her, Will knew he had surprised her, but the plain truth was that, if he told her his surname, he was certain it would alter her opinion of him.

Her manner of speech indicated that she was wellborn and accustomed to getting her own way. Therefore, she had likely come from Castle Finlagh, but whether she was a guest or a family member he could not know. Instinct would plump for her being family were it not for one detail.

Put simply, the likelihood was small that Fin of the Battles would encourage any daughter of his to wander off by herself, let alone to climb granite peaks. However, as small as that possibility seemed, Will thought it less likely that Fin of the Battles would allow a female guest or servant to do such a thing. Nevertheless, he dared not ask for her family name lest she press him for his.

Now was no time for unnecessary talk, in any event. She seemed content with silence, so he focused on helping her reach the peak, gently gripping an arm to steady her when necessary and feeling a bit disappointed that she needed help only until they were above the dangerously polished area. She moved deftly then and with confidence up onto the craggy peak, where she cushioned herself with the hinder bits of her kilted-up kirtle and smock underneath her as she sat on a boulder and gazed raptly at the admittedly splendid panorama below.

Her bare calves were smooth and shapely, and the tops of her bare feet were, too. Their soles were doubtless as tough as his own, though.

Will scanned the area for Finlagh watchers. His cousin Dae, visiting from the Lowlands, had walked with him along the ridgetop for a short time that morning but had headed home much earlier. So, while de Raite did often keep watch on Castle Finlagh and other estates held by the Mackintosh—or "the Malcolmtosh," as de Raite and other Comyns, of Badenoch and elsewhere, called him in disdain—Will was confident that he, himself, was the only Raitt man currently on the ridge dividing Raitt lands from Finlagh's.

"It is beautiful from here today, is it not?" she said quietly, gazing eastward.

"Aye," he replied, studying her. She was older than he had first thought, at least sixteen or seventeen. Her face was smudged, her clothing tattered, but the tatters were, he thought, due mostly to the predicament into which she had got herself. She seemed remarkably composed, considering that he was a stranger.

She, or likely a maidservant, had plaited her long, thick, wheat-colored hair into two long plaits, but strands had come loose, and a light breeze across the ridge fluttered the wisps around her oval face.

She seemed unaware that she might be enjoying the view with an enemy.

Turning her head toward him, she said, "That is a lovely loch yonder, with the forested islet in it, but I had hoped to see Raitt. Do you know that castle?"

"Aye," he said, firmly controlling his tone and expression. "You cannot see it from here, for it lies farther northward," he added, gesturing. "Undulations of the eastern slopes below conceal it from us."

"Can one see it from that higher crag yonder?" she asked, pointing toward the peak a mile or so north of them.

"Likely, one can," he admitted. "But you would be a greater fool to climb that one on your own than you were to climb this one today. That other crag is both higher than this one and more precipitous."

"I am *not* a fool," she said, shooting him a fierce look. "I can take care of myself and have been able to do so for quite a long time. I know the terrain and the people around here as well as anyone."

Suppressing an urge to grin at the irony of that statement, he said, "Then you do know that, had I not come along, you'd likely have fallen to your death, aye?"

"Aye, but look at those mountains far to the west of us," she said, pointing at the still snowcapped range in the distance. "If this one had had snow on it . . ."

He shook his head, "Dinna think about that, lass. Had it been snow-covered, you would have had common sense enough to stay off of it."

Her lovely, dark-lashed gray eyes suddenly twinkled. "Art sure of that, sir?"

He wished he had nerve enough to steal a kiss, but the plain fact was that they were still precariously positioned on the rugged peak, so if he were to startle her or she resisted . . . He did not even want to think about possible consequences. However, perhaps as they walked more safely through the forest below . . . On that thought, he said, "Do you not think we should head back down now, Katy?"

Grimacing—for Raitt Castle or none, she was enjoying the view and the company—Katy looked away. As she did, she abruptly remembered Eos and Argus. "Good sakes!" she exclaimed. "Did you chance to see my two wolf dogs below?"

"I did," he said in the even tone he had used before. "They wait in that wee clearing you can see where the shrubbery ends. I hope you were not thinking that you had only to call them up that polished slope to rescue you, though."

"Nae," she said, wishing she could tell him not to be so daft and that his voice did not have that purring note in it that sent tremors through her body and irked her, all at the same time. "It would be too dangerous for dogs on that slick granite. Had I fallen, though, I do fear that they might have tried to run down to me. Come to that, I am surprised they did not bark at you."

"They heard your cry, just as I did. When I came along, the big one—"

"Argus," she interjected. "He was a huge puppy, so Mam named him after a mythical giant with a hundred eyes. He does see very well, but Mam doubts that it has aught to do with his name. Eos is named after the Greek goddess of the dawn."

"I see." He smiled as if his choice of those two words had stirred his sense of humor, and it was a nice smile, so she smiled back, and he added, "As I approached, Argus watched me rather grimly and then began to wag his tail. It might seem odd to you, but I think he knew I meant to help you."

"'Tis not odd at all," she said. "They understand much about people. My mother has trained them since they were pups. She had a wolf dog when she was a girl, and she wandered all over the hills around Rothiemurchus with him."

"Will they try to follow us if we disappear over the top?" he asked.

"If I command them to follow us, they will seek a way to do so," she said. "Not over the peak but round through the forest, until they see, hear, or smell us."

"Then you are ready to go down?"

Realizing that she had been gone much longer now than anyone would expect, Katy gave a regretful sigh and nodded. "I must," she said.

"I'll stay with you until you are safely down."

"Sakes, sir, you should go home with me. Supper will be nearly ready by then." She made the offer by habit, only to realize that although his presence might delay recriminations, questions put to him by her family would prove awkward.

His train of thought evidently followed hers, for he raised his eyebrows and said, "How would you explain me? Do you think your parents will approve of your having come up here alone, as you did, to climb such a crag?"

"But I don't mean to tell them *all* of that," she said. "To do so would only worry them to no purpose. I shall tell them we met when I was on my way back from visiting tenants I visited earlier. That is scarcely even a falsehood. That is"—she paused—"it isn't unless you deny it and tell them where and how you found me. But you are not a talebearer, are you?"

His lips tightened, sending a short but undeniable sensation through her body, warning her that she had taken another misstep.

"Do you frequently tell people only what you want them to hear?" he asked.

"But we did meet when I . . . well, *after* I took bread from our bakehouse and some other supplies to a few of our tenants. So it isn't . . ." Pausing when he raised his eyebrows, she added with a sigh, "*Do* you mean to tell them the whole tale?"

"Nae, lass, but I fear that I cannot accept your generous offer of supper," he said more gently than she had expected. "Sithee, I, too, will be late getting home."

Surprised by an unexpected surge of disappointment, she said, "How far from here do you live?"

"Some distance yet."

"Where is your home, then?"

"Nearer the Moray Firth, and we had better start down now, I think."

Agreeing, she let him lead the way, and finding the descent much easier than she had expected, she made a mental note to explore all sides of the higher peak to the north as soon as an opportunity presented itself.

When they were off the granite, she whistled for the dogs, and they soon came bounding toward them.

"I can find my way now," she said to Will, looking up some distance to meet his gaze. He was as tall as her father and her uncles. Oddly, his presence beside her felt as comfortable as her father's or one of her other close kinsmen's would feel.

"I'll walk with you until we see Castle Finlagh," he said.

"So you think you have guessed where I live, do you?"

"Am I wrong?" His gaze caught hers again.

Impulse stirred to tell him that he *was* wrong, that she lived in a woodland cottage west of the castle. But the impulse fled when she recalled that she had admitted delivering supplies to their *tenants*. Still, he could not know exactly who she was. In her old kirtle, thin already and more damaged by her climb, she could not match his likely notion of a renowned knight's daughter. Without knowing his rank, she shied away from relating hers, lest it somehow daunt him.

"I do live at Finlagh, and the dogs know the way," she said. "I have only to tell them to take me home."

"Nevertheless, I mean to see that you get there safely."

Feeling another wave of gentle warmth at the thought that he did not want to leave her, she fell in beside him and signaled the dogs to follow them.

As they walked on, they chatted comfortably, one or the other pointing out sights along the way. Bracken ferns grew taller in woodland than on the strath, and Will grinned when Katy expressed her delight at finding some delicate lady ferns, the bracken's translucent cousins, peeping from beneath their protective fronds.

Shaking his head, grinning, Will gestured toward a nearby rill, where a stray sunbeam added iridescence to the wings of three blue butterflies fluttering over two-foot spikes of tiny yellow-green woodland orchids rising from a nest of flat leaves.

"How beautiful!" Katy exclaimed.

Moments later, he put a finger to his lips and motioned toward the dogs.

Understanding easily, Katy signaled Argus and Eos to sit where they were.

Taking a few silent steps forward, Will gently parted tall wands of a chestnut stub in a hollow under the tree's outflung branches just far enough to let Katy make out the grayish brown hen pheasant staring back at them from her nest deep within its shadows. Her more colorful mate was nowhere in sight.

"How did you know?" Katy asked quietly as they moved on.

"I saw those pheasant feathers," Will said, gesturing to a few red and brown ones nearby that Katy had not noticed. "It seemed a likely place for its nest."

"The castle is just ahead," she said a short time later. "You should g—"

"Nae, lass, I must be certain that you are safe. Truly, you were unwise to come so far or to attempt to climb that crag alone."

"I am grateful to you for coming to my rescue, sir," she said, giving him look for look, "but I like adventure and often seek adventurous things to do." She saw no reason to admit that she often suffered after such adventures. Instead, she added, "Moreover, I do not answer to you. Nor do I seek your approval of my behavior."

"'Tis just as well, then," he said lightly, "that I have not offered approval but only kindly advice, because I believe that had you recognized the danger, you might have been wise enough not to go so far or climb so high."

Why did she suddenly have the odd sensation that she had

known this man for years? Collecting her wits, she said, "You should perhaps know that I dislike hearing persons I scarcely know, and who would likely do as I have just done, offer me advice about *my* actions."

"Do you?"

She glanced up to catch him smiling again. He did have a warm smile, one that lit up his eyes and made her want to smile back.

So she did smile, and met his twinkling gaze as she said firmly, "I do."

"Hmmm," he said, grinning now. "Do you know, I feel much that way, myself. I see Finlagh now, yonder on its knoll."

"Aye," she said. "I must go on alone from here. You won't want men on the ramparts to see you, I expect, so—"

"What you mean is that you do not want to have to answer questions about me," he interjected mildly. "I do understand, but I mean to linger nearby until I see you approach the knoll path and know that the guards have seen you."

"Very well," she said, having already learned that she would not dissuade him. He had been right about her not wanting to answer any questions about him, and he had not promised to keep himself out of sight.

She would also have preferred to approach the castle from the west, which was how they would expect her to come, but her companion was unlikely to agree to that. Moreover, she was too late now to risk wasting more time.

Fortunately, she saw no sign that men were searching for her.

When the forest began to thin, he stopped and said, "I'll bid you farewell here, lass. I see no one on this side of the ramparts, so I will keep watch until you and the dogs begin heading up the knoll path."

"Thank you again, Will," she said, offering him her hand and looking up into his eyes. "I ken fine that I may have sounded sadly ungrateful before. I am truly thankful that you were near, though, and quick enough to keep me from falling."

"I'm glad, too, Katy," he said with a smile that warmed her to her toes and sent more pleasant tremors through her body. "Now, get on home with you."

She took a few steps homeward then only to feel a strong urge to look back one more time. When she did, he was watching as if he had been waiting for her to do just that. He winked, and though she felt an odd temptation to stick out her tongue at him, she knew she dared not linger, so with a smile and slight nod, she hurried on down the hill, over the arched bridge of the nearer of two streams that forked around the knoll, and onto the pathway that wound up to the castle. At the top, it took her to the castle's hornwork entrance on the knoll's north side.

A guard opened the narrow postern gate in the tall double iron gates to let her in. As she thanked him, she saw her tall, dark-haired father talking to one of the other men in the courtyard. Worse, Fin saw her and began to stride toward her.

"Where the devil have you been?" he demanded when he was near enough to do so without shouting.

CHAPTER 2

Her father's expression told Katy that he wanted to shout and sent a shiver up her spine. "Your face is smudged," he added. "You look as if you've been dragged through the bushes, and that dress is fit only for the ragbag now!"

She opened her mouth, hoping to offer an explanation if she could just think of a rational one.

He stopped the words on her tongue with a slight gesture of one hand. "Go straight up to my chamber," he said, referring to the room he customarily used to deal with agents, important visitors, and malefactors. "You and I will talk there."

Hurrying inside and up the stairs to the small chamber off the first landing, she strove to collect her wits. She had to compose herself and form some notion of what she could say to him without telling an actual falsehood.

Fin entered the small chamber minutes later and shut the door.

Instead of sitting at the table where he usually interviewed persons standing before him, as Katy was, he stood just inside the room, a bit too close, crossed his arms over his chest, and glowered at her. Viking tall, he was head and shoulders taller than she was. She could stand under his outstretched arm without her head touching it. Sufficient light came through the chamber's solitary window to reveal the glint of anger in the deep-set light-gray eyes that matched her own. His dark-brown hair showed a few strands of gray, but his movements were still youthful, and she knew he was still a warrior who intimidated other warriors.

His temper seemed about to erupt.

Katy drew a breath, hoping to steady her nerves.

He said grimly, "I doubt that you have been delivering bread all this time, so just where *did* you go?"

Having decided to plump for something close enough to the truth to pass muster, she said hastily, "I finished with the bread at Granny Rosel's and then walked up to the pool and into the forest. I know I should have come home sooner, sir, but you need not worry. I did have the dogs. So—"

Cutting her off, Fin snapped, "Not worry? Just how far into the forest did you go, in what direction? No one on the ramparts saw you, my lass, which tells me that you took good care they should not see you. So now, and for the last time before I lose my temper and put you across my knee, *where* did you go?"

Swallowing hard, Katy said, "I just went up the hill, Da, mayhap farther than I should have. But I—"

"Which means that you disobeyed my orders *and* your mother's and chose to do so without concern for your own safety. So now—nae, not another word do I want to hear from you," he added when she opened her mouth. "You will first hear exactly what I think of your actions. If you are wise, you will do naught more to irk me more before I have finished."

He went on in that vein for some time before a rap on the door stopped him midsentence. "What?" he demanded in the same fierce tone.

"I beg your pardon, sir," his porter said from the other side of the door, "but ye've a visitor requesting immediate audience wi' ye."

"I'll be down shortly," Fin retorted.

"The man insists the matter be urgent, sir."

"Who the devil is it, then?"

The porter remained silent.

Drawing a deep breath and letting it out, Fin said to Katy, "You may now go straight up to your bedchamber and stay there until I summon you. I have much more yet to say to you."

Making a hasty curtsy, she fled gratefully upstairs, dashing tears from her eyes with the back of each hand as she went.

Having watched Katy until she reached the path up to Castle Finlagh and then turned on his heel and headed for home, Will let his thoughts dwell on the intriguing lass he had just met. She had shown no fear of him as a stranger, an attitude that common sense told him to deplore. Any young female ought to have wisdom enough to be wary of strangers. Conversely, their meeting had been no ordinary one and he was glad that she had seemed to know he would not harm her.

He wished that he might see her with her face washed and wearing what he assumed would be her normal attire, clean and undamaged.

Her oval face, even smudged as it was, was most appealing with its tip-tilted nose and full, sensuous lips. Her light-gray, dark-lashed eyes, their irises rimmed in black, were eyes that a man could look into forever and never grow weary.

Shaking his head at himself, he muttered, "Put her out of your head, my lad. That one is likely nobbut trouble."

Will moved at a good pace up and along the slope of the ridge, and by the time he approached Raitt Castle, from the southwest, the sun had sunk below the ridge behind him, casting Raitt into shadowy depths.

Two decades ago, de Raite had seized the castle from the Mackintoshes—specifically from Fin of the Battles, while Fin was away, fighting in the Battle of Harlaw. That seizure took place during the young King's English captivity, and Scotland's Regent, the Duke of Albany, ordered the Mackintoshes to keep the peace and let the Comyns keep Raitt and its estates of Meikle Geddes.

On his grace's return nine years ago, he had issued a similar order to de Raite to keep the peace, which de Raite oft chose to disregard. However, thanks to heavy winter setting in soon after the illegal hangings, the area had been quiet since then.

Although most people thereabouts called Raitt a castle, Will had seen real castles and knew that Raitt was no such stronghold. True castles were fortresses, protected by their settings, as Finlagh was by its knoll some two hundred feet above the base of the ridge's west slope. Finlagh's massive hornwork, curtain wall, ramparts, and outer deep-ditch defenses provided yet more protection.

Raitt boasted excellent stonework, a tower that could serve as a siege tower, if necessary, and a fine stone hall house, which, with its impregnable undercroft and a solitary entrance ten feet above ground level, had stood for over a century.

However, the wall surrounding the castle and its courtyard was only eight or nine feet high. Outside it, in woods to the east, stood a clachan of tenants' cottages with smoke curling from three or four of them. Their residents would expect to shelter inside the hall house during any attack.

Approaching the southwestern angle of Raitt from above, Will noted that weeds and grass had overgrown the defensive ditch between the wall and the slopes above it, nearly concealing the ditch. Likely, it had acquired more dirt from runoff over the winter, too, but if he were to suggest that someone ought to clear it, his father or an older brother would likely assign the thankless task to him.

The hall boasted two towers and a high-pitched roof with short corbelled parapets at each gable end. A round three-story tower with a vaulted, conical roof projected from the southeast corner, and a square tower containing the garderobe projected more than a dozen feet from the hall's long, northwest-facing side.

The walls of the hall house were nearly six feet thick and topped with a wall walk accessed only from the attic above the great hall. An ancient chapel—Raitt's oldest structure—and other outbuildings stood in the courtyard southeast of the hall.

Raitt lacked a proper gatehouse, but its imposing gateway boasted red sandstone facings similar to those of the hall house's arched entrance and the unusually large arched and traceried windows of its upper floors. The Mackintoshes his father had hanged by the tall iron gate had long since been unceremoniously buried in the nearby forest.

Nodding to the guard who opened the gate to admit him, Will crossed the courtyard to the timber bridge that stretched from a low, central knoll to the hall's main entrance, ten feet above the ground. In an attack, the porter could raise the last few feet of the bridge from inside and lock that portion against the hall doorway in much the same way as a drawbridge over a moat.

When he was near enough to the tall door to see the teeth of the portcullis peeping out from above and just in front of it, he saw the porter peering through the squint beside the door. The door opened, and Olaf, the plump, gray-bearded porter, said, "A good even tae ye, young sir," as Will passed him into the entry hall.

Separated from the huge hall, as the entry was, by a massive wood screen stretching three-quarters of its length, Will could hear enough from the hall as he replied to the porter's greeting to know that most of the men had already come in.

"I kent fine that ye'd be home for supper," Olaf said, shutting the huge door.

"Has someone been looking for me?"

"Just her ladyship," Olaf replied, moving to peer through the squint again. "She'll still be in the solar, for Himself has nae come in yet. But Masters Hew and Liam must be peckish, for they be on yon dais wi' your Lowland cousin, the noo."

"Thanks for the warning," Will said dryly. "I must wash before supper."

"Our Tam just took a basin and jug intae the inner chamber for Himself," Olaf said. "If ye be quick, ye can use that and tell Tam tae refill the jug after ye."

Taking his advice, Will went around the screen into the long hall, noting as he passed under the minstrels' gallery that men had already claimed most of the places at the two trestles stretching from the dais at the other end of the chamber. No one had taken a seat, nor would anyone do so before de Raite or his chaplain—if that gentle man joined them, which was rare—had said the grace before meat.

A fire roared in the handsome hooded fireplace near the south-corner entrance to the round tower. Framed with red sandstone like the windows, the fireplace corbels carried a lintel and formed the flue. Two elaborate iron sconces flanked the opening on either side, each holding a large candle, which would soon be lit.

Daylight was rapidly dimming outside.

Stepping onto the dais, Will strode toward his father's private inner chamber, nodding to Hew and Liam, the two eldest of his four remaining brothers, and his cousin Dae as he passed the high table. His eldest brother, Rab, had died at the Battle of Lochaber, killed by a Clan Chattan warrior, Sir Àdham MacFinlagh.

The inner chamber furnishings consisted of a writing table, a washstand, and a great sword de Raite had inherited from his father, which hung between two narrow lancet windows on the wall to Will's left. Young Tam was filling the washstand basin. Washing quickly, Will said, "Empty this, lad, and fetch more hot water for Himself." Recalling the porter's words, he added, "Is her ladyship in the solar?"

"Aye, sir," Tam replied. "That is tae say, I havena seen her come doon."

Thanking him, Will took the narrow stairway from the inner chamber's passageway to the solar on the next floor of the tower, saying as he neared its doorway, "It's just me, Aly. Art within?"

"Aye, Will," was the soft reply. "Come in."

Katy's bedchamber was empty when she entered, but Bridgett, the curvaceous, dark-haired maidservant who attended her and her twin sister and whose mother, Ailvie, served Lady Catriona, came in while Katy was washing her face.

Handing her a towel, Bridgett greeted her in a tone that told Katy the young woman knew she was in disgrace.

Thankful that Bridgett had not seen her tears and hoping her father would not come in while Bridgett was there, Katy accepted the towel and turned away as she patted her face dry. Then, draping the towel on its rod, she said, "Prithee, fetch out a fresh kirtle, Bridgett. I must change for supper."

"Bless ye, m'lady, I see that much for m'self," Bridgett said, glancing at each of two cupboard beds that flanked the window wall as if to be sure no one had mussed them since she had made them up. Only then did she open the woven willow kist in the alcove between the door and the bed on the left, which contained Katy's fresh clothing. "Wherever did ye go tae get yourself in such disarray?"

"I'd liefer not answer that question, for I have heard all I want to hear on the subject," Katy said, adding with a grimace, "I expect I'll hear more anon, though."

"Aye, sure, an' ye will, too, for I did hear that ye were gone so long as tae put your da in a fret. Certes, but ye should ken better nor *that*, so I'm puzzled as tae what . . . or *who* might ha' held your interest so long."

"And, pray, who has been carrying such tales to you?" Katy demanded.

With a shrug, Bridgett said, "'Twas that Lochan as told me, that's who."

"Faith, Bruce Lochan, our captain of the guard?"

"Certes, he be the only Lochan as either of us has ken, is he no?"

"I expect so, but he should not be prating about me to you or to anyone else."

"Then ye'll no want tae hear aught else he said," Bridgett said lightly as she tucked a stray lock of dark hair back into her cap and bent to the kist. Extracting a pink kirtle with white lace edging at neckline, sleeves, and hem, she gave it a snapping shake and held it up to waning light from the window.

"I don't want *that* kirtle," Katy said. "'Tis my best one."

"As I ken fine," Bridgett said, her blue eyes gleaming. "Ye'd best take that clout from the basin, though, and wash your face again, *and* your hands. Ye've still got smudges on 'em. There be a dab by that wee scar on your forehead, too, and others on your cheeks. I'll wager ye didna get *them* a-visiting me granny, neither."

Wetting the towel and scrubbing her forehead, both cheeks, and her hands again, Katy said, "What else *did* Lochan tell you?"

"I thought ye didna want tae hear aught more that he said."

"Marry, but I wish Cousin Àdham and Fiona had taken you with them to the Borders for their annual visit with her kinsmen," Katy said grimly. Her cousin, Sir Àdham MacFinlagh's lady wife, hailed from the Scottish Borders and had married Àdham two years ago, at the King's behest, in St. John's Town of Perth.

"Ye ken fine that Sir Àdham and Lady Fiona had nae need o' me," Bridgett said, hands on her curvy hips. "Forbye, I'd nae wish tae leave Finlagh, nor tae travel so far, and so I did tell her ladyship."

"But you've not yet told me what else Lochan said to you," Katy reminded her. "You take too many liberties, Bridgett, and so I do not hesitate to tell *you*."

"Nae, then, why should ye?" Bridgett replied with a warm smile that revealed twin dimples in her cheeks. "Ye've had ken o' me since me Granny Rosel brought ye intae this world, and this be how I were then and how I be the noo. I say what I think, just as ye do. Ye should be accustomed tae me by now, and I learned long since that them as speaks plain must be able tae bear plain-speaking in return."

It was on the tip of Katy's tongue to remind Bridgett that *she* was a servant, but her better sense intervened. Not only would Bridgett laugh at such a reminder, but it might also stir her to recall *and mention* more of her mistress's faults.

In any event, the chamber door opened then to admit Clydia in her favorite blue kirtle, laced over a cream-colored smock. Despite likely having spent much of the afternoon in her kitchen garden, she looked as neat as could be.

"Oh, good, Bridgett, you *are* here," she said, shutting the door. "Lochan told me you might be, so I came straight upstairs to warn ... That is—"

When her gaze met Katy's frown, she stopped and pressed her lips together.

"Nae, then, Clydie," Katy said with a sigh, "do not hesitate to speak plainly. As Bridgett has just reminded me, I do so, and so does she. Come to that, most of the women we know speak plainly. You are more tactful, but tact and I have small ..." Her sense of humor stirred then, and she grinned ruefully.

Clydia chuckled. "Small acquaintance, aye, we know. You speak or act first, and *if* you think, it is usually long afterward."

"So of what did you hope to warn me?" Katy asked. "If it is that Da is vexed with me again, you need not. He has made that plain to me already."

"I expect he has," Clydia said. "However, although Bridgett is holding your best kirtle, you do not seem to know why she is."

"I said I don't want it, but she will not heed me."

"Nor should she. Da sent me to tell you that we have a visitor and that you must dress nicely for supper with him."

"Him? Who?" Katy's thoughts flew to the mysterious Will. Surely, that too-sure-of-himself gentleman was not so daft as to—

"Gilli Roy," Clydia said, banishing the image of Katy's stalwart rescuer and leaving dismay and the image of her slightly built, redheaded kinsman in its stead.

She gaped at her twin. "Gillichallum Roy Mackintosh? Our *cousin*?"

"Aye, sure," Clydia said, taking the pink kirtle from Bridgett and holding it up. "Take off that dreadful rag you're wearing and wash any other bits that need washing. You cannot want to look like what young Rory calls a 'middenraker.'"

Despite herself, Katy laughed at the image of the outspoken scamp her cousin Àdham had brought home with him after the Battle of Lochaber. Turning back to the basin, she said on a lingering gurgle of laughter, "If Da heard you quoting our Rory, and using *such* a word—!"

"Da is not here," Clydia pointed out. "But if you do not hie yourself, my dearling, he soon will be. Then you, not I, will be the one ruing his presence."

Bridgett helped Katy take off her tattered kirtle and soiled smock and handed her a clean linen smock to put on.

As Katy donned it and tied the strings gathering it at its neck, she said, "Is that the other thing Lochan told you, Bridgett, that Gillichallum Roy had come?"

"Aye, it is," Bridgett admitted.

"Sakes, has everyone been talking about me?" Katy demanded. When neither of the other two answered her, she said, "But why is Gilli here? And *why* should I put on my best kirtle to greet him? No one has ever told me to do *that* before."

"This time is different," Clydia said.

"Plainly so, but why?"

"Because, evidently"—Clydia exchanged a look with Bridgett,

who rolled her eyes—"he has come to offer for your hand in marriage."

Katy stared at her. "Gilli? He *wouldn't*! He does not care a pin for me."

"Apparently, he does," Clydia replied in her usual calm way.

"Well, he must be daft, and I *won't* have him!" Katy retorted.

Will entered the tower's round solar from the stair passage to find his sister, fifteen-year-old Alyssa, curled against pillows on the cushioned seat created by the splayed embrasure of two tall, open windows. The solar overlooked the castle's rear wall to the forested south hillside beyond it, so the light was dim despite narrow lancet windows on the east and north faces of the encircling wall.

Alyssa smiled at him. Slender and small, she had well-defined features and alert, quick-moving hazel eyes that twinkled when she smiled. A white veil covered her neatly coiffed blonde hair, and she wore a pale yellow kirtle and had wrapped a dark-green wool shawl around her shoulders. She had needlework in her lap.

The breeze drifting through the windows behind her was chilly.

"They will serve supper soon, Aly," Will said, returning her smile. "Would you like me to go downstairs with you now?"

"Sit here for a few minutes first," she said. "I have scarcely seen you for two whole days. Have you been out on the ridge again?"

"I have, aye," he said, pulling a stool near the window seat for himself.

"Did you see aught of interest?"

He shrugged. "Squirrels, birds, two deer, a few hawks overhead, a hen pheasant on her nest." *And a pretty, young madwoman who required rescuing when she foolishly tried to climb a tor,* he added silently. *A madwoman with a most alluring manner about her, one that I'd like to know better, in many ways.*

"I wish I could go with you sometimes when you walk along the ridge."

"Sakes, lassie, I'm supposed to be guarding against enemies. What if you were with me and we came upon some?"

"Have you ever come upon one?" she asked him.

"None to concern me," he admitted. "But I'd wager that if I did take you along, de Raite would have my head on a charger."

"I wish you wouldna call him de Raite," she said. "It sounds disrespectful."

"I cannot call him 'Father,' lass. His uncle Thomas was more of a father to me than de Raite has ever been. Nor can I call him 'Gervaise' unless I pronounce it in the French way as he does, which I think foolish, whilst the Scots way could make people think I refer to our brother Jarvis, instead of de Raite. I *like* Jarvis."

"I know," she admitted. "I also know that you are still angry with Father over those dreadful hangings." When he grimaced, she added, "I agreed with you, you know. He ought never tae have hanged them. Why, now he will not even let me accompany *him* into Nairn, let alone go with Meggie and two guardsmen as I did before. He fears I might hear more than he wants me tae hear about the hangings."

"I know you agreed with me, but you are wise to keep silent," Will said. "He would react badly if you shared that opinion with him or others."

"I know," she said sadly. "You are the only man here who does talk with me. Do you not wonder if our menfolk treated Mother the same way they treat me?"

"I scarcely remember her," he admitted. "I was just seven years old when you were born and she died. De Raite sent me off to Inverness-shire then to live with our granduncle. He *said* it was because he believed that wee lads should have little to do with womenfolk before we are grown."

"And 'tis when you began calling him Comyn of Raitt—and now de Raite," Aly said. With a sigh, she added, "I have scarcely been outside the castle wall since he hanged those men."

Will frowned. "Has he forbidden you to go beyond it? Surely, you and Meggie still pay visits in the clachan. That is one of your chief duties, is it not?"

"Aye, and we used tae walk in the woods, as well. After the hangings, I feared the Mackintoshes might retaliate, so Meggie tended to those duties until recently, and nae one complained of aught that she could not resolve by herself. In troth, Will, without Meggie's guidance and that of other women in the clachan, I should never have known *what* my duties entailed."

"You ought to have friends of your own station, Aly. Mayhap you should ask de Raite to let you visit some of our kinsmen."

"Would *you* ask him? He pays nae heed tae me. In troth, I think he dislikes me, so I cannot think how I am ever tae marry and have a household of mine own."

Will knew that de Raite paid little heed to Alyssa unless she irked him. However, he assumed that such neglect was due more to de Raite's ignorance of womanly things than aught else. Aly had been a biddable child, and she was now a biddable young woman. Although Will had disagreed with de Raite more often than not, he did agree with him that Alyssa, at fifteen, was too innocent and childish yet to marry, despite being three years past the marriageable age for girls.

He also knew, however, that if de Raite decided he could build a strong alliance by offering her to the son of another powerful laird, he would seize the opportunity. "I doubt that he dislikes you, lass," Will said. "He just thinks more about his own goals than he does about other people's."

"I ken fine that he has more important matters tae consider, but he looks on me more as a servant than one of his children. For my part, having had naught tae do with women of mine own station, other than a rare visit tae Nairn's kirk of a Sunday, I ken more about *being* a servant than about acting as a lady should."

"It must be hard, Aly. I cannot teach you such things myself, but I do know that Aunt Eubha, Granduncle Thomas's daughter, offered to come to look after you. De Raite refused to have her."

"Aye, he said she would try tae rule him and he'd no have that," Aly said. "I doubt any woman could rule him. I do know that married ladies have many responsibilities beyond caring for children, though. Someone once told me that daughters of noble lairds oft live with noble kinsmen tae learn proprieties and how tae run a household when they marry."

"Who told you that?"

Alyssa shrugged and looked away. "I canna recall who. Is it not so?"

Will thought about that. Perhaps Katy was not a daughter of Sir Fin of the Battles but a niece or cousin sent to foster with his lady wife.

"*Is* that true, Will?" Aly demanded, leaning forward. "Were you no listening tae me, sir?"

Regaining his wits, Will said, "Aye, sure, I was, lass. They call it fostering, and I expect daughters of the great lords do foster with kinsmen or other lords' families. But de Raite is not a great lord. Sakes, even if he were, I doubt it would occur to him to arrange a fostering, especially if you have not asked him to do so."

Alyssa grimaced. "How could I ask for a thing of which I knew naught, and how would I dare ask him tae send me elsewhere? He never even took me tae visit Granduncle Thomas Cummings and our cousins near Inverness whilst you were living with them. Nor has he invited them tae bring their lady wives tae meet me when those cousins have visited Raitt."

"They would not bring their ladies if he did invite them, because Raitt is known to be a male household," Will said. "In troth, Aly, I've known since I returned here that you have been unhappy. I ought to have given thought to how unusual your life is, for a lass."

"I do not blame you, Will. The best times of my life are moments like this, when I can talk tae you." She drew a deep breath and let it out before adding with a rueful look, "But you can do naught tae aid me, for 'tis as Meggie says: 'Life be what it be, and one lives as one lives until one dies.'"

CHAPTER 3

Silence reigned in the twins' bedchamber for nearly a minute after Katy's furious declaration that she would not have Gilli Roy Mackintosh as a husband.

At last, reluctantly, she met Clydia's patient gaze. "How am I to handle this? You know as well as I do that Gilli Roy does not want to marry me any more than I want to marry him."

"I do," Clydia said, glancing at Bridgett, who had moved to tidy the washstand and bundle up the ruined kirtle for mending or the ragbag. "However, you cannot tell Father that you refuse to see Gil, can you?"

Katy winced, knowing that she dared not test her father's patience more than she already had—not, in any event, until Fin had time to regain his normal equanimity. "Do you think that such a match would please him?"

"Gil is not as fine a warrior as our father or Cousin Àdham," Clydia said. "But he is the son of the Captain of Clan Chattan."

"Malcolm's *youngest* son," Katy said sourly. "And doltish, withal."

"Nevertheless . . ." Clydia glanced again at Bridgett and then back at Katy.

Katy shrugged her indifference. Bridgett knew nearly all that anyone could know about the two of them and had never been a talebearer. However . . .

"Even Bridgett would warn me against marrying a man I don't want to marry," Katy said.

Bridgett grimaced. "Aye, that I would, though the one I married were a rogue wha' talked more wi' his fists than wi' his mouth. Had it no been for the Battle o' Lochaber, I'd still be married tae him. I ken fine that the rest o' ye thought it were a dreadful battle, but tae me own mind, 'twere a bless—"

"We know," Clydia interjected. To Katy she added, "Mam will know how you feel about Gil and will stand your friend if you cannot stomach him. However, you must dress suitably and treat him civilly, even warmly. I agree that he has never shown interest in a closer kinship with you, but you have little choice in the matter now and will have none if you irk Da more than you already have today."

Grimacing, Katy sat on a tall stool in her smock to let Bridgett brush and arrange her long hair into a thick coil at her nape. Lulled by the rhythmic strokes, Katy reflected on what an odd day it had been, first to be rescued by a so-intriguing stranger, then to face her angry father, and now . . . a proposal of marriage from her doltish cousin? It was as if the Fates were toying with her!

A too-short time later, wearing the pink, lace-trimmed kirtle and the plain white veil that she usually wore in company, she went downstairs with her twin, leaving Bridgett to tidy their room.

The great hall at suppertime was a lively place, because nearly everyone who worked in or near the castle was welcome to take supper there. Many of the castle guardsmen slept in the hall when off duty, so after supper, they would dismantle the trestles and lay pallets out for sleeping. Most of the women and the off-duty men with families would return to their cottages in the nearby west woods to sleep.

Katy saw her father and Gilli Roy from the foot of the stairway, for both men stood together near the large fireplace directly opposite the great-hall entrance. They had doubtless been watching for her to come downstairs.

Fin still looked stern, and Gilli Roy seemed uneasy, even apprehensive.

At least, despite the occasion, he had dressed simply in a fresh tunic and a muted red-and-green plaid. Just two years ago, he had visited St. John's Town and returned with curled hair and foppish clothing. His nose and chin still jutted out as if one were trying to outdo the other, but the curls were gone and his hair was neatly tied back with a plain black ribbon.

He met Katy's gaze briefly before his own slid away toward Clydia.

"Is he trying to discern which of us is which?" Katy muttered.

"He can tell by our clothing and your wee scar, as well you know," Clydia murmured with a look that told Katy her sense of humor had stirred. "Do recall, for your own sake, that you agreed to be civil, or your scowl will terrify the poor lad."

Accepting what she knew to be excellent advice, Katy raised her chin and strove to pin a smile on her lips.

Fin's stern expression relaxed, proving that her choice was a wise one. He greeted them almost cheerfully and said, "As you see, Katy-lass, your cousin Gilli Roy has come to visit."

"Aye, sir," Katy said, turning to Gilli and making her usual slight curtsy. "We bid you welcome, cousin. Do you make a long stay?"

"Nae more than a fortnight and mayhap less," he replied quietly. Then, glancing at Fin before meeting Katy's gaze again, he added glumly, "The length o' me stay must depend on the success o' me venture . . . or its lack o' success."

"Marry, sir, what is this venture of yours that so much must depend upon it?" Katy asked, brushing what felt like a hair from her cheek.

Gilli Roy paled, but Fin said, "We'll discuss that after supper, Katy-lass. Your lady mother is on the dais now, so we will join her there."

Gilli Roy turned toward the dais, while Katy glanced at Clydia and collided with her direct gaze. "What?" she muttered as they followed the two men. "Was I not civil enough?"

"Aye, sure, you were," Clydia said. "But you let Gil think that you have no notion of why he is here when, in fact, you do."

"Aye, but you did not want me to blurt *that* out, did you?"

"You know I did not, but you used the word *marry*. We may both find ourselves in the suds if Da learns that I told you so much."

"How did you find out, then? I thought Da himself must have told you when he sent you upstairs to fetch me, but Gilli Roy's demeanor and words belied that. So, who did tell you?"

"Rory did," Clydia said. "That scamp evidently overheard as much and could not bear to keep it to himself. Da told me only to fetch you and tell you to dress for a visitor. I'll own, though, that I am glad the laddie did tell me. Had he not, and had I not warned you, you would have pressed Gil to tell you exactly why he has come. You know you would."

Katy acknowledged the truth of that statement with a nod.

At the high table, she sat in her usual place, at her mother's left, with Clydia at her own left and her father and Gilli Roy at Lady Catriona's right. Thus, Katy did not have to concern herself with the men as she helped herself from platters of meat and a pottage of chicken, leeks, and cabbage that gillies offered her.

Lady Catriona, with a bit more than fifty years behind her, still had the tawny, sometimes unruly hair that her daughters had inherited in a slightly lighter version. At present, her own long tresses were confined in a plain white coif, and she wore a simple golden yellow gown that made her eyes look golden too. At a distance, people often mistook her for one of the twins, and she could still occasionally outshoot her husband with a bow and arrow.

"Did you enjoy a pleasant afternoon, dearling?" she asked Katy after they both had begun to eat.

"More pleasant than Da thought was wise," Katy replied frankly. "I finished taking the bread and such to the cottars in less time than usual. Then, I wandered from Da's pond onto the southwest hillside." Blinking away Will's image when it leaped into her mind, she added, "In the end, I was gone too long."

"That was unwise, which you know as well as I do," Catriona said. "But I expect your father has made that plain to you."

"Aye, Mam, he did, and you are right to say that I'd ken as much if he had not," Katy said with a sigh. "Even Bridgett scolded me."

"I shall say no more about it then," Catriona said. "It is good to see our Gilli Roy, though, is it not? We have not clapped eyes on him in months."

Looking more closely at her, Katy saw nothing to make her suspect that Catriona knew the true reason for Gilli's visit. Also, since he had been standing with Fin when she and Clydia came downstairs, the likelihood was strong that Fin had had no chance yet to inform her mother of Gilli's intended offer.

Spreading mustard from a small pot onto her meat with her eating knife, Katy said, "Gilli likes to come to Finlagh, I think. Although Moigh Castle lies some twenty miles from here, he visited us several times last year before the snow grew too deep in the mountains between Finlagh and Loch Moigh."

"I'm glad that spring has come at last," Catriona replied.

"I saw a pheasant hen on her nest today," Katy told her.

Conversation meandered gently through such subjects until Fin stood to give the grace after meat, thus bringing the others in the hall to their feet.

Then, turning to Catriona, he said, "Gilli Roy and I will join you and the twins shortly, up in the solar, my love."

As Katy turned away, she caught the eye of the young urchin her cousin Sir Àdham had brought home with him from the Battle of Lochaber four years ago. His fair curls more tousled than ever, Rory raised slightly darker eyebrows in query, but with her back to her parents, Katy dared not respond to the boy's curiosity, lest they note the exchange with their keen archers' eyes and demand explanation.

No one, including Rory, knew exactly how old Rory was. Àdham had guessed he was eight or nine at the time of Lochaber, which would make the boy eleven or twelve now, at most. He bore some connection to their villainous Comyn neighbors, though, for he had lived with them for a time. Even so, Àdham believed Rory's insistence that his presence at that horrific battle site had been much against his will and that he wanted no more to do with any Comyns.

Since Àdham believed him, everyone else at Finlagh did, too.

Following her mother upstairs to the solar and aware of Clydia's reassuring presence behind her, Katy drew a deep breath and wondered just how Gilli would proceed with his offer of marriage.

"Leave the door open for your father and Gilli Roy," Catriona said as she took her usual place on the cushioned settle near the window embrasure. "I am eager to hear the news from Loch Moigh. I hope all is well there."

Katy's keen ears had caught the sound of footsteps on the stairway, so she said only, "I hear them coming, Mam."

The two men entered shortly thereafter, and Fin shut the door behind them. Without a pause, he said, "Sit ye down by your mam, Clydia. Gillichallum Roy has something he wishes to say to our Katy."

Gilli Roy looked from one woman to the others, his blue-gray eyes widening, his cheeks flaming above his sparse, pale-orange-red beard. Then, turning to face Katy, he waited only until Clydia sat down and Fin stepped back before saying hesitantly, "I want . . . that is, I thought that mayhap ye might be willing tae . . ."

Noting her father's tightened lips and twinkling eyes, and her mother's open mouth, Katy felt unexpected pity for Gilli Roy. When his pause lengthened until she feared that Fin would intervene, she said more sympathetically than she might have, "What is it, exactly, that you want to ask me, Gilli?"

Licking his lips, he said, "Just if ye'd be willing tae consider taking me as a . . . well, that is, tae live . . ." Glancing around when Catriona clapped a hand to her mouth, only to meet Fin's grim gaze next, Gilli shook his head. "I told 'im I'd make a right mull of it, and so I have. What d'ye say, though, Katy?"

Quietly, she said, "I think you ken fine what I *would* say if you could manage to finish your question."

"Aye, sure, but ye mustna say nowt afore we talk first, the two of us."

Fin began shaking his head, but Catriona stood, turned to him, and said mildly, "I think we should let Gilli Roy explain what he wants of Katy without an audience, do not you, my love? You come, too, Clydia, and show me what progress you have made with the quilt you have been making for Granny Rosel."

"I do not think we should leave them alone yet," Fin said.

"I disagree, sir," Catriona said firmly, giving him a direct look. "They are cousins, after all, and have oft been alone together since they were bairns."

Fin's lips twitched, but he nodded and said, "Defiance, that's what it is."

Chuckling low in her throat, Clydia said, "Aye, sure, sir, for we all ken fine that you live ever under the Cat's paw."

Even Katy smiled at the familiar phrase.

Gilli Roy looked vastly relieved when Cat tucked her hand into the crook of her husband's elbow and leaned gently against him, urging him toward the door.

Clydia stepped ahead of them to open it, and when they had shut the door behind them, Katy was alone with Gillichallum Roy.

Silence in the solar continued until the footsteps on the stairs faded away.

Katy waited with what she considered extreme patience until she could stand it no longer. "Well?" she said at last, sharply.

Gilli Roy eyed her bleakly.

"Gilli, this was your notion, after all. Are you not going to speak to me?"

Frowning, he drew a breath and said, "I ha' nae notion o' how one does this business properly, Katy, for I ha' never heard any man do it. Ye'll ha' guessed, though, that I ha' come tae offer for yer hand."

"You might at least have brought me flowers or a love token," she said.

"I didna think o' flowers or aught else, though I expect I'll ha' tae get ye a ring. I did see bluebells in the woods west o' here, but bluebells by themselves . . ."

"Aye," she said when he paused. "They look their best whilst rooted in the ground. In any event, flowers or none, though I like you as a cousin, Gilli, I do *not* want you for my husband."

"I ken that fine, and so I did tell my father, but he be that set on us marrying. He thinks ye'd be a grand match for me."

"Did you ask *my* father what he thinks of the notion for *me*?"

He nodded. "I dinna think he looks fondly on it. He said he thought ye be a mite young for marrying, despite being well past the age o' consent, but he did say I could ask ye. Methinks he doesna want tae irk me da by refusing tae allow that."

"Then this notion is wholly the Mackintosh's," Katy said.

Gilli Roy nodded again. "He said ye'd come wi' a fine tocher, as ye be Sir Fin's elder daughter." With a sigh, he added, "I like ye fine, too, Katy, but I dinna want tae marry ye, neither. Still, I doubt we'll ha' much say in it, though, if your da wants tae avoid irking mine."

"Prithee, stop playing the dafty," she said. "We will just tell my parents that we have decided we do not suit each other. I am sure—" Breaking off because he was shaking his head, looking more doleful than ever, she said, "Why ever not?"

"I canna do that," he muttered. "If I go home straightaway, me da will be gey wroth wi' me. He'll say I must ha' muddled the asking or given up too soon, 'cause wi' him being Captain o' the Clan Chattan Confederation, and me being his son, I should be able tae persuade anyone I'd like tae become me wife."

"But you are his youngest son, Gilli," Katy protested. "He has two others who are older, so you cannot possibly possess enough wealth yet to offer a wife."

"'Tis true, that, which be why I must marry a lass wi' a good tocher," he explained. "Still, as ye may ken fine, me da outlived his own four older brothers tae become Chief o' Clan Mackintosh and Captain o' Clan Chattan. So, he believes I may well succeed him. But, Katy, I dinna want tae do that!"

"Nor are you the first to feel so," Katy said in what she hoped was a soothing manner. The impatience she frequently felt with Gilli had returned, though, and she suspected that he could detect it in her tone. More softly, she added, "You must know that Malcolm followed his brother, my own great-grandfather Lachlan, as head of Clan Chattan only because Lachlan's only son rejected the position."

"Aye, sure, I do, but that does nae matter tae me da. He has ever thought that Cousin Ferquhard be nobbut a coward. I dinna want Da tae think that o' me, though he does ken fine how I feel about fighting and war. Everyone does."

Sternly, she said, "Do you mean to say you expect *me* to let my parents think we *would* suit each other?"

"I dinna want ye tae lie," he said earnestly. "But mayhap we can tell them ye'd like more time tae think about it. I could stay here whilst ye do that."

Feeling a new stirring of vexation at that suggestion, she said, "'Twould be as much a lie as saying that we might suit each other. I am nearly certain, too, that Mam would not believe it. Let me think a bit, though," she added.

"Think as long as ye like," he said with a sigh. "I can tell ye, though, that I thought all the way here and didna think o' nowt save that ye might agree tae it."

"Which is not what you want me to do, though, aye?"

He spread his hands and said dismally, "If ye say aye, we'll ha' tae do it. If ye say nae, then I'll be handing me head tae me da for washing."

"Or a good clout," Katy said sympathetically. "If you are right about my father's reaction to the idea, though, we may persuade him to let us both to think more before I have to give you an answer."

"How long d'ye think?"

"Marry, how can I know? First, tell me this: Art certain that my father was less than delighted to learn that the Mackintosh wants us to wed?"

"I canna be certain o' nowt, Katy. All I ken is what I said afore. Fin told me he thought ye were too young yet for wedding. Even so, he said I could ask ye and he would think on it."

Katy sighed, aware that her father must know just as her mother would that such a match held no appeal for her. But would Fin accept a refusal?

In any event, Gilli was right in saying that Fin would be reluctant to go against Malcolm's will. After all, the Mackintosh was Fin's liege lord, clan chief, and the confederation captain to whom he had pledged his loyalty. He would most likely decide that her wishes were less important than the Mackintosh's.

She would have to take good care, though, in how she discussed the matter with him. She could not lie to him, not in *any* way.

At last, she said, "I will try to say only that I think it would be unfair to you, Gilli, even rude, to decide so important a matter without taking due time to think first. You must be aware, though, that Da may declare an hour or so long enough."

"Then ye must urge him tae let ye think longer," Gilli insisted.

"I' faith, Kate, I canna go home tomorrow or the next day, either. Only think how that would look! I'd liefer enjoy a long visit here afore ye must decide."

"We will just have to see what my father says."

Grimacing, Gilli said, "We ken fine what he will most likely say, so we'd be fools tae hope he willna say it."

"Mam will not let him force me into any marriage," Katy said. "Of that I am certain . . . or nearly certain," she added when a shade of doubt crept in.

Supper, or any other mealtime at Raitt Castle, was a noisy affair.

With young Alyssa and her plump, gray-haired maidservant, Meggie, the only women ever present and de Raite caring little about proprieties after he had said the grace, his men snatched food from platters, bellowed across the room at one another, and often upset platters or jugs if more than one man reached for an object at once.

Will was certain he was the only male at Raitt who noticed how Aly winced when someone—a gillie or one of her own brothers—snatched a platter or sauce bowl or swiped fingers or food into the bowl nearest her as she was reaching for it.

Their father never paid any heed.

Alyssa and Meggie sat far to his left, for the five or six seats at that end of the high table were not just for ladies, as they were in most noble houses. Will sat next to Alyssa with their older brother Colley between him and their father. The three eldest of Will's remaining four brothers, Hew, Liam, and Jarvis, along with their cousin Dae from the Lowlands, sat at de Raite's right, Hew beside him.

Men were still coming into the hall that evening when Will escorted Alyssa to her place. Meggie stood beside it, awaiting her.

As they moved to join her, de Raite said abruptly, "Ye, there, Alyssa! Where ha' ye been all this day?"

Curtsying to him, she said, "I walked tae the clachan with Meggie, sir. The women had collected nuts, herbs, and such, so we helped sort and bundle them."

"Ye should tell Olaf or someone when ye go out, for I dinna like ye away so long. Ye should be here tae supervise the kitchen and the household servants."

Will nearly spoke up to defend Aly but held his tongue, knowing from experience that he would likely make things worse for her if he spoke.

Rising from her curtsy, she said, "I do see tae my duties, sir, and I did today, as well. Since then, I have been upstairs in the solar, mending."

"Aye, well, I've a notion ye've been a-going out more oft of late. Worse, I suspect ye' may ha' been a-meeting someone or t'other. If I learn that I'm right about that, I'll make ye gey sorry."

"I ken that fine, sir," Alyssa said submissively. "I met only with our women in the clachan. Nor have I given you cause tae doubt my obedience tae your will."

"Just see that ye don't, that's all," he snapped as he turned away, gesturing as he did for everyone to sit and sitting himself without bothering to say the grace.

With a sigh, Alyssa sat by Meggie, and Will took his seat at Aly's right.

Menservants began setting platters of food on the high table and the long trestle tables in the lower hall. The noise level increased.

Aware that Aly's relief seemed greater than her frustration with de Raite and tempted to ask her more questions, Will decided to wait until they were alone again.

She was talking quietly with Meggie, so he let his thoughts drift to his morning encounter with the lass, Katy, and wondered what she was doing now.

Perhaps her father—if Fin of the Battles was her father—had been as suspicious of her activities as de Raite was of Aly's. Surely, Katy's father, whoever he was, had greater cause for concern than de Raite did. Aly was ever obedient and would never think of trying to climb one of the high crags, let alone to do so alone.

He wondered if he would meet Katy again and what she might be up to then.

❖ ❖ ❖

Bidding Gilli good night in the solar, Katy went downstairs, aware that her mother, her father, and Clydia would be awaiting her in the inner chamber, a smaller private room behind the great-hall dais. Much as she wished she could storm in and tell them exactly what she thought of Gilli's so-called offer, she knew that such behavior was fraught with peril.

Fin never reacted well to storming; and Catriona—while perfectly capable of creating storms of her own—nearly always condemned other people's outbursts.

Katy's imagination provided myriad opening statements as she left the solar and descended the stairs. Seconds later, recalling Clydia's earlier accusation, she decided she would be wise to think before saying a word. She would have to think fast, though, in the short time it would take to reach the inner chamber door.

The strongest point Gilli had made was that her father would be reluctant to go against Malcolm's wishes. In fact, unless she or Gilli could present valid reasons to reject any notion of marriage between them, Fin would likely insist that they do as the Mackintosh demanded.

On the other hand, she was nearly certain that neither her father nor her mother would expect the idea to please her. Her best hope was that Catriona would understand her aversion to it. To that end, she would present her thoughts calmly, clearly . . . and without prevarication.

"They are always pressing me to be tactful," she muttered.

Considering that thought, she wished that she knew the exact difference between what people called "tact" and just plain lying. Perhaps tact lay in Gilli's desire for more time, whereas if she were to say that *she* needed time . . .

The inner chamber door loomed before her.

CHAPTER 4

Will kept an eye on Alyssa throughout supper, hoping to learn what might have stirred de Raite's suspicion about her activities. He discerned easily that she was more nervous than usual.

Although she chatted with Meggie for a time, the increasing din in the great hall made it hard to hear what even the person next to one said, and she soon shifted her attention solely to her trencher. Noting then that she pushed food around but ate little, he leaned near enough to mutter into her ear, "Art ailing, lassie?"

Starting, she muttered back, "My head aches from the noise, Will. I dare not ask tae be excused, though, when Father is vexed with me."

"Has he cause for vexation?" Will asked, persuaded that their words would not carry past him through the din to Colley's ears or beyond Aly to Meggie's.

Aly shrugged. "Da always fears that I'm in mischief if I am out of his sight, though Heaven kens why he should, Will. I take care tae give him nae cause. Except for being the death of our mam," she added matter-of-factly.

"Don't talk blethers, Aly. You did not kill Mam."

"Birthing me killed her, Will. You canna get from that. And you canna pretend that Da ever wanted a daughter, can you?"

He could not, for de Raite had often said he had hoped for an army of sons. Instead, he said firmly, "He'll be glad he *has* such a pretty daughter when he seeks an alliance for her with some nobleman's marriageable son."

Flushing, Aly fixed her gaze again on her trencher.

"Well?" Will said, laying a hand atop hers where it rested on the table.

Turning her hand palm upward, she squeezed his. "I am glad you think me pretty, sir. If anyone has offered for me, though, I am unaware of it."

"Perhaps de Raite hopes our cousin Dae will offer for you."

Aly wrinkled her nose and pressed her lips tightly together.

"Do you dislike Dae?"

Looking past him toward Colley and evidently satisfied that their discussion was as private as it could be at such a time, she met Will's gaze and said in a voice just loud enough for him to hear, "Cousin Dae be nobbut Hew's lackey, Will. Nor do I believe that Father wants me tae live as far away as a town in Perthshire."

"True," Will admitted. "But would you dislike living in a town?"

"How can I know how I would feel?" she asked reasonably. "The only town I know is Nairn. I wouldna mind living there if I like the man I do marry. But I'd be daft tae decide where I want tae live afore anyone offers for me. Where would *you* like tae live after you marry, Will?"

He grinned. "Sakes, Aly, I ken little more than you do about places beyond Inverness, Nairnshire, and Badenoch. I've heard tales of other towns, but men say that disasters such as the plague run rampant in Lowland cities, so I'd liefer stay in the Highlands. I stay here because I owe duty to de Raite and to you, too, and I'm content enough whilst I can spend my days in the woods and nae one troubles me."

"I wish I were a man," Aly said wistfully. "They always have choices."

The incessant clamor faded noticeably then, and Will saw men in the lower hall getting to their feet and beginning to dismantle the trestles. Others fetched dice or playing cards, laid out pallets for sleeping, or simply left the hall.

Guards on the wall walk changed shift at midnight, so their

replacements, and the men who would replace those at dawn, would sleep in the great hall.

Will and his brothers preferred sleeping in the attic behind the minstrel gallery, because it had access to the roof, and on hot summer nights it was cooler there. In winter, heat rising from the great hall fireplace kept it warm.

As Will stood, he realized that Alyssa and Meggie were waiting for de Raite to dismiss them.

When he did, Will began to follow them as they made their way behind his father and brothers toward the tower stairway.

"Hold there, lad," de Raite commanded as Will neared him. "Ye'll come wi' the rest of us intae the inner chamber. I've a matter I want tae discuss wi' the lot o' ye. Ye must come, too, Dae," he added. "Ye ha' well nigh become another son and can make yourself useful tae me."

"Willingly, sir," Dae Comyn said, shoving a hand through his tousled dark auburn hair before planting a tattered gray cap atop his head.

Darker-haired Hew, beside him, clapped Dae on a shoulder.

With a sigh, Will watched Aly disappear up the tower stairs toward the solar and her bedchamber above it. Then, moving to stand before the great sword hanging between the lancet windows and glancing at the other men, he returned his thoughts to his father and what devilry the man might be up to now.

He had not long to wonder, for as soon as his sons and nephew were in the chamber, de Raite shut the heavy door separating it from the tower stairs and hall.

Moving toward the large south window, he stood before it with his feet apart and looked searchingly from one young man to the next. Then, apparently satisfied with what he saw, he said, "As ye all ken fine, Donald, Thane o' Cawdor, despite being royal Constable o' Nairn Castle, does liefer live at Cawdor than keep close watch on his castle as he should. The town o' Nairn itself and all o' Strathnairn and Badenoch were long afore him controlled by Clan Comyn, as they should be, and . . ."

Will's inner voice urged him to remind de Raite that such

Comyn control had ended soon after the reign of King Robert the Bruce began, more than a century before. The Bruce, offended by fierce Comyn opposition to his claim to the Scottish throne, had done his best to destroy their power by revoking their castle warrants and officially expelling them from Badenoch and other parts of the Highlands.

Common sense reminded Will of the futility of such intrusion, given de Raite's success in seizing Raitt Castle and its estates—which had rightfully belonged to the Mackintoshes—*and* gaining the King's permission to keep them.

As he was assuring himself that silence was his safest option, de Raite went on to say, "Since the Thane clearly prefers Cawdor tae living in Nairn Castle, I'm thinking we should take steps tae point out the error o' his irresponsibility."

Unable to keep silent any longer, Will said mildly, "Do you not think such steps might incur the King's fury, sir? After all, his grace's decision to let us keep Raitt relied on your promise to maintain peace hereabouts, with everyone."

"Faith, be ye such a feardie yourself that ye think I fear Jamie Stewart?" de Raite demanded. Before Will could reply, he added, "I ha' nae use for your opinion. The Bruce took our lands, but 'tis Stewarts and royal arse-lickers like the Malcolmtosh and the Thane as seek tae control them. We owe Jamie nowt, nor the others neither! That fool Cawdor keeps but a token guard at Nairn Castle, so . . ."

As she opened the door to Castle Finlagh's inner chamber, Katy heard her mother say, "Here they are now," so one or both of the wolf dogs had sensed her approach and warned Catriona. Her words also told Katy that the human occupants of the room had expected Gilli to be with her and were discussing them.

A glance at Clydia, in the window embrasure looking up from her needlework with a smile, reassured Katy that her twin had said naught to discomfit her. As she shut the door, she noted with relief that no one other than her parents, her twin, the two dogs, and one small black-and-white cat was present.

Fin, standing near the embrasure, said, "Well, Katy-lass, I trust you have news of import now to tell us, but what have you done with Gilli Roy?"

"Mercy, sir," Catriona protested. "Let your daughter enter the room and make herself comfortable before you quiz her."

Expelling the too-hasty breath she had inadvertently inhaled, Katy relaxed, certain now that she had two allies in the room. "Thank you, Mam," she said. With a wry twist of her lips, she added, "I ken fine, though, that you must all be eager to learn what Gilli had to say to me."

"But what have you done with him?" Fin demanded again. "I expected . . . that is, *we* expected him to accompany you so that you might tell us together."

"Did you, sir?" Katy said evenly. "You did not tell us that that was your expectation, so Gilli stayed upstairs. In fact, I think he meant either to seek his bed or to walk outside for a time, to think."

"What the devil is there for him to think about?"

Katy met his stern gaze without a blink. "Marry, sir, are you not the same father who is ever warning me against making any decision hastily? You talk now as if you had no notion of what Gilli would say to me." Noting his gathering frown, she added as calmly and yet as firmly as she could, "But you do know, sir . . . That is to say, you *did* know exactly what you expected him to say."

"Now, see here," Fin began, only to catch his wife's raised eyebrow and hesitate. Turning his gaze to Clydia, who looked down at her needlework and showed no intention of aiding him, he returned his gaze ruefully to Katy. "You are right to take me up so, lass," he said. "I expected you to want to express your delight in the honor that Gilli Roy does you but to share that special moment with him as well as us. Sakes, I expected you both to want that."

"Did you, sir?" Katy wanted to shout the words this time, nae to shriek them at him and more besides, but she knew better than to behave so disrespectfully.

Catriona said, "Are you going to tell us what Gilli Roy did say and how you responded, love?"

"He told me the truth, Mam," Katy said. "I agreed only with his notion that we should take more time to think and mayhap to know each other better before we decide whether to take such an important step in our lives."

"By Heaven," Fin said curtly, "would you insult Malcolm so?"

"How can taking time to think be an insult to anyone, Father? We are asking only to do what you have so frequently recommended that *I* do before making much less important decisions. In fairness, you must admit that you have scolded me time and again for making decisions too hastily. Have you not, sir?"

Catriona was silent, her lips pressed so tightly together that the skin outlining them had paled, but Katy suspected that the tightness was due more to her mother's sense of humor than to her displeasure.

Fin glanced at Catriona, grimaced, and looked his daughter in the eye. "There are times, my lass, when parents and other adult kinsmen expect their offspring simply to heed their sage advice."

"Indeed there are such times, sir, because you have explained such to me before, as well," Katy said. "You told Clydia and me then that we would have a strong say in our marriages and that it is against Scottish law for anyone to try to force a woman into marriage against her will. Is that not so for men, too?"

"I did, and it is," he admitted. "Nevertheless . . ." He paused.

"I ken fine why you are irked, Da, because you have made it plain that you do not want to offend the Mackintosh."

Fin raised his eyes to the ceiling for a long moment.

Realizing that he was controlling his temper with effort, Katy kept silent.

At last, he looked at her again, sighed deeply, and said, "Just tell me that you did not refuse Gilli Roy outright."

"Nae, sir," she said. Catching her twin's quick glance upward, Katy nibbled her lower lip briefly before adding, "I did want to. But I feared it would be rude."

"You were right," he said. "You are also right about my desire to avoid offending Malcolm, and about our Scottish laws. They do pertain to every Scot. If you and Gilli Roy decide that you cannot abide each other, despite your years of friendship, then I'll do what I can to soothe Malcolm. But you must promise me that you will not dig in your heels, Katy-lass. Gilli Roy has offered you the great honor of becoming good-daughter to the Mackintosh, Chief of Clan Mackintosh and Captain of Clan Chattan. It would be most unwise to reject that honor out of hand."

"You should know then that it was Gilli who suggested that we should take time to think before making any announcement. Although we have known each other as cousins and friends, neither of us has ever considered marrying the other."

"But now you will both *carefully* consider that opportunity," Fin replied.

Meeting her twin's gaze again to see Clydia give a slight shake of her head, Katy understood that she advised silence and reluctantly agreed.

Catriona said lightly, "I must say that I had not expected you to marry so soon, my dearling. I ken fine that you are past the age of consent, but I fear that I still think of you and Clydia as my bairns. It will be much harder for me to part with you than it was to part with our sons."

Clydia chuckled. "Certes, but we can understand *that*, Mam."

Katy smiled, and when Fin opened his arms, she went to him and hugged him as tightly as he hugged her. "I do not want to disappoint you, Da," she murmured against his chest.

"You won't, Katy-lass. We did spring this matter on you, so I suppose we should be grateful that you did not hurl a stool at poor Gilli Roy's head when he put the question to you. How long do you think you will need for thinking?"

"Marry, sir," she said, gazing up at him. "I don't know. Must we set a time?"

"Nae," Catriona said, moving to stand beside them and laying a gentle hand on Katy's shoulder. "Take the time you need, dearling. Gilli Roy is welcome to stay here with us for as long as he likes."

"He will be glad of that, I know," Katy said with certainty.

When she and Clydia went upstairs to their chamber, they found Gilli sitting on the landing outside it.

He got hastily to his feet. "What did they say?" he demanded. When Clydia chuckled, he seemed to collect himself and said, "I ken fine that Kate told you all about it."

"Faith, Gil, I was there," Clydia said. "She told all of us about it."

His eyes widened, and he turned back to Katy. "Ye told them everything?"

"Nae, I did not," Katy said. "I told them you were the one who suggested that we needed more time but that I agreed, and—"

"How much time did they give us?" Gilli demanded.

Katy grinned. "Mam said to take all the time we need and that you are welcome to stay here until we decide."

"That be a good thing, then," he said. "I be a dreadful slow decider."

The next morning, Gilli Roy left the castle before Katy and Clydia came downstairs to break their fast. Returning in time for the midday meal, he brought a visitor, a mendicant Dominican friar— wearing the customary cream-colored, ankle-length tunic, black cape, and capuce or hood of his order.

Since mendicant friars and monks brought news from all over Scotland and the world beyond, they found a warm welcome wherever they stopped.

"This is Brother Julian from Blackfriars at St. John's Town," Gilli said. "We met just as we approached the knoll. He speaks both Scots and the Gaelic."

Handing Fin letters from the Borders and Perth, Brother Julian said, "I have learned that, thanks to the many ships passing through the harbors of Nairn and Inverness from distant ports, many people hereabouts also speak both languages." Then, moving to the place offered him beside Fin at the high table, he obliged his request to say the grace before meat.

As everyone took seats, Katy heard Fin ask how far the man had traveled.

Pushing his capuce back from his tonsured head, Brother Julian said with a grin, "Hither, thither, and yon, but I ken fine that, letters tae read or none, ye'll be wanting tae hear as much news from the Borders and your kinsmen there as I can give ye. I can tell ye straightaway that Sir Àdham, Lady Fiona, and her family were all well at Ormiston Mains despite a new outbreak o' the fearful plague in some Border parts."

"I do not like to hear that," Fin said, signaling to the carver and his gillies to begin serving. "New outbreaks must pose risk to them."

"The trouble lies well westward yet and south into England," Brother Julian assured him. "Your lot will likely stay at Ormiston for the nonce, though, especially as a self-styled wise woman—one Janet Fortune—has predicted that the end of the world is nigh. 'Tis proven, she said, by the pestilence doing its all to wipe out whole populations in Europe, England, and much of our own Lowlands."

"Mercy!" Catriona exclaimed.

"Prithee, brother," said Fin, "do not speak widely hereabouts of such a pestilence. 'Twould stir panic in many quarters."

"Aye, sir, I ken that fine," Brother Julian said. "Forbye, ye should ken that a daft Polish preacher blames the Kirk for the recent outbreaks and agrees wi' Janet Fortune that plague does mean the end is coming. In fact, the two say it will occur on the seventeenth day of June, just over a fortnight from now. Such warnings are common whenever the plague strikes, though. And, as we all ken fine, God will determine the world's end, not yon Janet Fortune or her outlandish preacher."

Katy exchanged a startled look with Clydia but relaxed when Catriona said with a sigh, "You are right about the plenitude of such prophecies, Brother Julian. We hear dire predictions after any disaster or violent storm, as well as outbreaks of the plague as far away as southern England or even France."

"One does well to pay small heed to any prediction," Fin said. "The world has survived for centuries now and will doubtless do so for many more."

"You may have heard such predictions, Mam, but we have not," Katy said, unable to stop the words from flying off her tongue. "What if the woman is right?"

Brother Julian said mildly, "If it is the will of God, it will happen, and not all of the King's powers or prayers from the rest of us could stop it. But I do not believe that God created this earth and the multitude of splendid creatures on it merely to destroy them all on a whim."

Gilli Roy, who had been silent for some time, said, "That

woman, Janet Fortune, sounds daft. If she continues tae rattle her tongue so, 'tis likely that someone will accuse her o' witchery."

"She could even be burned at the stake for heresy," Brother Julian said.

Katy gasped.

Catriona said calmly, "I think the sensible thing is to say little about this prophecy. Word of it would spread fast and doubtless terrify many people."

"I regret to tell you, my lady, that news of plague and prophecy has spread to the Highlands already," Brother Julian said. "Many Highlanders have kinsmen in the Lowlands, after all, and many of those kinsmen evidently decided to move north upon learning that the plague had struck just a few miles south of them."

"I'll tell you what I think," Fin said. "We must encourage any of our people who express concern about what Gilli rightly calls a daft prediction to recall how many such they have heard that failed to come true. I will wager anything you like that this one is just another such wheen of blethers."

No one debated his conclusion.

Gilli disappeared again that afternoon without waiting to hear what was in Sir Àdham's letter, but Katy noted that he did so without drawing her father's ire.

She had no desire to draw Fin's attention to herself, so after learning that her cousin still considered his young son perfect and that his wife, Fiona, was enjoying their visit to her childhood home, Katy spent the rest of the afternoon sorting herbs from Clydia's kitchen garden for drying in rafters above the bake ovens.

When she found herself wondering how soon Fin would start pressing for an answer from her and Gilli Roy, her thoughts shifted, seemingly of their own accord, to the intriguing man with the engaging smile she had met on the peak. Will was much better looking than Gilli and provided more interesting conversation. She wondered what he would think of the wise woman's dreadful prophecy.

As the twins prepared for bed that night in their chamber, Katy said, "Do you think Da is right about that prediction, Clydie, that it is just daft?"

"He usually is right about such things," Clydia said. "Brother Julian seems sensible, too. In any event, I will not disturb myself about it without more evidence than the word of two Lowlanders. What are you going to do about Gilli Roy?"

"I have not decided," Katy said, unwilling to declare again to her twin that she did not intend *ever* to marry Gilli. She would say so only after she had formed a plan to persuade her parents that she *should not* marry him.

In bed, with the candle snuffed out, after a few minutes of silence, Clydia said, "I mean to walk up the south hillside tomorrow and gather some new herbs to replant in the garden. Do you want to come with me?"

"I would, but I think that Gilli and I should show at least some evidence of trying to know each other better. He has shown no interest yet in doing so."

"Did you ask him where he went today?"

"Aye, sure, but he said only that he likes the solitude of the woods for thinking. He knows as well as I do, though, that Da will not let him keep wandering about, nor is he likely to let us wander off together."

Clydia chuckled. "You are right about that," she said. "I'll wager that Gil hopes Brother Julian will stay for at least a sennight."

Katy chuckled, aware that she would welcome any distraction that kept her father from pressing them to marry. However, Wednesday morning, while the family and their guests were breaking their fast, Brother Julian thanked Fin for his hospitality and said he would be on his way as soon as they rose from the table.

"So soon, Brother?" Catriona said, leaning forward to speak across her husband. "You are welcome to rest here for as long as you like."

"I thank ye kindly, m'lady, but I have promised to visit Nairn and travel on into the mountains to the west to perform a wedding. Sithee, a couple has married by declaration there, but her parents insist that there must be a kirk ceremony, too."

"Marriage by declaration?" Gilli Roy said, staring at the friar. "I have heard of such, but I do not know exactly what it means or how it is done."

Astonished that he would express interest in such a thing, Katy wanted to shake him for extending talk of marriage at all.

"'Tis an ancient and legal form of wedding in Scotland," Brother Julian said. "'Tis gey rare, though, to hear of it amongst nobles and others of higher society, who view marriage as a religious sacrament after parental negotiation and consent. However, Scottish law predates the Kirk in a number of areas and, I believe, has always allowed one member of a couple to declare before witnesses that the two are married. Unless the other party denies it, they are thereafter legally wedded."

"Sakes," Gilli Roy said, "I had not heard *that*. Does it happen often?"

"In many areas, aye," Brother Julian said. "Although the Kirk does frown on such unions and prefers that priests or chaplains perform all marriages, in kirk when possible. Many communities lack priests, though, and winters, especially Highland ones, can be long, with travel difficult. So it oft becomes a matter of convenience, even necessity," he added with a wry smile.

"I think it sounds dreadful," Katy said. "I want all of my friends and family at hand to see me married, with a proper celebration *cèilidh* and *lots* of music."

"I do, too," Clydia said.

Gilli Roy was silent.

CHAPTER 5

That same Wednesday morning, Will followed the ridge of hills southward, obeying de Raite's orders to make certain that naught was occurring to indicate Clan Chattan's having somehow learned of de Raite's intent to seize the castle stronghold of Nairn.

He would do it, too, Will thought. His father always did what he said he would do. The seizure of Comyn lands, though it occurred over a century before, gnawed at the man as if it had happened just days ago and before his very eyes.

The only excitement that day, though, occurred on Will's return when his sister, wide-eyed, informed him that some priest had predicted the end of the world.

"What do you mean by prating such a thing, Aly?" he demanded with a grin.

"'Tis true, Will. A mendicant friar from Blackfriars Monastery in Perth took his midday meal with us today, because he'd heard we have a chapel and desired tae see it and meet Father's chaplain. He was going tae Nairn and then tae Cawdor and southwestward intae the high mountains, but he told us that a fearful plague has spread from France all the way tae Scotland and that's what is causing the world tae end. A Border wise woman even predicted the date, just a fortnight from now!"

"Come, come, Alyssa," Will said. "No one can predict such a thing."

"But she did, Will! A friar is like a priest. He would not lie. You just *hope* it does not happen," she added. "'Tis easier tae hope than tae worry or even tae pray hard that it does not, Will, and you often take the easy ways!"

Realizing she was distraught, Will tried to reassure her but feared his efforts were useless. Although she admitted that this Brother Julian had given them all the same assurances, she still seemed worried that the world's days were numbered.

Following de Raite's orders, he spent Thursday on the ridge but saw no sign of Katy or aught to suggest that the residents of Finlagh suspected any impending trouble in Nairn. The fact remained, though, that they were strong allies of Cawdor.

Will had known the Thane of Cawdor's son, Wilkin, in Inverness, where Cawdor had a house. Wilkin was three years older than Will and lived primarily at Cawdor, but they had met when Will was ten and had enjoyed fishing and hunting together whenever Wilkin stayed in Inverness, until Will returned to Raitt. Learning then that de Raite despised the Thane, Will had not seen Wilkin again. Nor had he visited Cawdor, although it was just a few miles west of Raitt on the Inverness road. He wished now that he could warn them of de Raite's intent, but he could not do so without drawing the enmity of every man in his family, and likely Aly's, too.

It occurred to him that she might deem both decisions the "easy way" for him, but a good clansman supported his own people, whether he liked them all or not.

Friday, having awakened betimes from a dream of shapely legs, he took his usual route but followed a barely discernible track well below the ridgetop, taking care to leave no sign of his passage for others to detect.

In the years he had lived with Granduncle Thomas and his Inverness-shire cousins, along with reading, writing, and numbers, they had taught him much of swordsmanship, archery, other weaponry, tracking both game and humans, and how to conceal himself as he traveled through woodland in enemy country.

Even as a child before his mother's death, he had learned that, in the Highlands, a friend in April could be an enemy by May. It was wise, Thomas had said, always to look after oneself and prepare for the worst.

Returning to Raitt as a young warrior of one-and-twenty, having fought Islesmen in protection of Inverness before and after the Battle of Lochaber, where his brother Rab had died, Will had expected his four older brothers to boast skills similar to his own but had not expected them to be so eager to prove that their abilities outmatched his. Fortunately, his granduncle and cousins had taught him well enough to hold his own with the brothers he scarcely knew, and he continued to hone his skills with regular practice.

His return to Raitt had preceded the Battle of Inverlochy, but no one at Raitt had fought there, because de Raite had decided to stay and protect the castle, lest the Mackintoshes take advantage of their absence to seize Raitt, just as de Raite had done when Sir Fin and many of his men left Raitt to fight in the Battle of Harlaw.

Not long after the defeat at Inverlochy, an incident occurred involving Sir Àdham MacFinlagh that caused de Raite to send Hew to live with Cousin Dae's family. According to the others, de Raite had refused to speak Hew's name and his temper was utterly unpredictable then, likely to ignite in a breath. Its volatility had not lessened with Hew's return, although he had been home now for a year.

Their cousin Dae had been visiting them at the time of the incident and had returned to Raitt a fortnight ago for his second visit.

Soon, birdsong, squirrels' chatter, and the brief sight of a slinking wildcat cheered Will's thoughts, but he paid no less heed to his surroundings and eased silently into the shrubbery when he heard voices ahead. When the two men, unaware of his presence, passed him lower on the hillside, he delighted in his ability to watch and listen to their aimless conversation as they went.

They would also be keeping watch, he knew, but he was nearly certain by then that they were the only Mackintosh or Finlagh watchers nearby. He had likewise seen no travelers about, lone or otherwise, so unless a woodland creature surprised him with unusual behavior, he expected to enjoy an uneventful day.

❖ ❖ ❖

"I vow, cousin, you ha' the fiend's luck with dice," Gilli Roy complained after Katy made her cast across the table in the solar and beat his throw again.

They were alone but had left the door to the landing wide open.

"My luck holds only because we are playing for pebbles," Katy assured him. "I beat everyone at dice unless we play for something I care about."

"Well, we canna play for more than pebbles without rousing your da's ire," he said as he gathered up his few pebbles and her many more. "Come to that, I'd liefer be out in the fresh air than in this chamber or any other."

"We're supposed to be learning more about each other," Katy reminded him, which instantly flung Will's image into her mind again. Her thoughts of him and how comfortable she felt with him had kept her awake much of the previous night.

"Faith," Gilli said, "we ken each other fine enough tae ken we shouldna wed, and this play-acting be tedious. I'd liefer walk in the woods or go wi' ye whilst ye take things from Clydia's garden tae Granny Rosel and them in the wester forest."

Katy wrinkled her nose and Will's image vanished. "Clydia and I did that yesterday, so I have no excuse to go again so soon. Clydia would not want to go, either, because she says the weeds are taking over her garden rows. She would welcome our aid pulling them out, though, if you do want to go outside."

"I dinna want tae pull weeds," Gilli Roy said petulantly. "Nor do I want tae stroll about yon wee courtyard again wi' ye. People who ha' shown nae interest in our doings afore stare at us now. I vow, Kate, your father's captain o' the guard and his chief assistant, that MacNab, never take their eyes off us."

Katy grinned. "The two Bruces, we call them. But their taking such interest suggests that our Bridgett must have told Lochan that you offered for me. That likely means everyone else knows it, too."

"Why would she prate o' your affairs, and *mine*, tae Lochan?"

"Because she likely thinks he would make *her* a good husband," Katy said. "She talks about him often but never says a word *to* him when I am nearby."

"Does he pay heed tae her?"

Katy shrugged, amused. "She says he is daft, but sometimes, she admits, he sends strange thrills all through her by just looking at her. But, she says, he is shy."

"Shy!" Gilli rolled his eyes. "How could Lochan ever ha' become captain o' the guard for Sir Fin if the man be so diffident a mere female thinks him shy?"

"Bridgett is *not* mere, though I expect I should have said Lochan is shy only around females. He rules men with an iron hand, and Da says he does a fine job."

"It sounds as if your Bridgett talks nobbut blethers," Gilli said severely.

"Well, do not let her hear you say that," Katy said, grinning. "She says what she thinks, so I doubt she would suffer criticism from you without replying in kind."

"Then, I wish she *would* marry Lochan. He'd soon put a stop tae that."

When Katy continued grinning, he shook his head at her and said, "See here, Kate, I need tae get outside these walls. Methinks I'll walk tae yon pool your da created on the hillside above us. D'ye want tae come wi' me."

"Da might dislike it," she said, certain that Gilli would rather be alone, because he had managed to take solitary walks every day since his arrival as he said he did at Loch Moigh, and had not suggested before that she go along.

"I'll walk out with you, though," she added. "'Tis a fine spring day, and I can help Clydia with her weeding."

Deciding by midafternoon that he had gone far enough without seeing aught of interest to de Raite, Will turned toward Castle Finlagh and home. An hour later, when Finlagh's tower came into view, he studied its ramparts and saw only one guard who seemed to be eyeing the wooded slope further north.

Motion below on the hillside drew Will's attention when what appeared to be a pale blue skirt whisked through the woods near the bottom of the slope.

Standing still, imagining fine, shapely legs beneath that skirt, he watched, hoping he was right and wondering how far she meant to walk. Noting long wheat-colored hair tied back with a white kerchief and a slender body that he recognized easily, he knew that his initial instinct had been correct.

Moving quickly yet stealthily, he made his way through the forest toward her, taking care to keep trees and shrubbery between himself and the lass. He knew he would likely startle her, but she would deserve it if he did.

"By my troth," he murmured, "she must learn to take better care of herself, for this area may soon turn much less peaceful than it has been. She ought not to wander about unguarded as she so plainly does."

Senses alert to the slightest sound or sight of her passage, he followed easily. Deducing that she headed for the southernmost of two streams careering down on each side of the knoll, he timed his arrival to step out in front of her as she arrived.

She stopped in her tracks. Then, tilting her beautiful, now clean face up to look into his eyes, she gazed at him silently and more solemnly than he'd expected. She carried an empty pail and had doubtless come for water, although she might more safely have fetched it from the same stream nearer the castle.

"As you see, you should take more care to be wary of your surroundings," he said evenly. "I might have been an enemy or even a wildcat."

"Might you?" she said with astonishing calm and no hint of their having met before. Could she have forgotten him in just four days' time?

Nae, *not* possible, he decided. Even if she continued to insist that she had not needed rescuing, he *had* saved her life. Yet she behaved as if awaiting a response from a stranger. His lips tightened with annoyance but also with a surge of regret.

She cocked her head slightly, and a ray of the lowering sun gilded wisps of hair that had escaped her kerchief. Her long-lashed, so-beautiful light-gray eyes remained steady. Her skin, from her hairline to her chin and throat, was so smooth that his fingers itched to stroke it.

"You are trespassing," she said. "This is Castle Finlagh land."

"Your father's land, in fact," he said, though he was still uncertain if she was Fin's daughter or a maidservant. On the tor, she had shown more confidence than any maidservant he knew; but, in truth, he had known only his sister's Meggie and the women who served his Inverness cousins. Yet, here young Katy was, calmly confronting a man she had met once and fairly challenging him to take her to task.

"Do you *know* my father?" she asked serenely.

"Now, see here," he said, stepping closer. "Do you mean to pretend we have never met? Because if you expect me to do the same—"

Her gaze narrowed, but she said as calmly as before, "We have never met. Certes, I would remember you if we had."

"You must be daft if you think I'll accept such pretense!"

"Prithee, do not use that tone to me," she replied. "I dislike incivility."

"Incivility?" He reached for her, but she eluded his hand, and when he stepped closer, keeping his eye on the pail, lest she swing it at him, she slapped his right cheek hard enough with her free hand to make it sting. "What the devil—?"

"Do not touch me," she said firmly, still maddeningly calm. "I fear that you have mistaken me for someone else, but if I scream, men will come. A guard on our ramparts saw me come this way and by now must wonder what keeps me, so you would do well to leave. You got this far without alerting them, so I expect you took care to stay hidden. That was wise of you. Our people can be surly with travelers who do not show and identify themselves when they come into view of the castle."

He almost believed her, but when she turned away as if she meant henceforth to ignore him and simply fill her pail, his cheek began to burn like fire. He shook his head and decided to see just how far she would carry her pose.

"Would you like me to fill that pail for you?" he asked with gentle mockery, hoping she would reveal her true self with her infectious, even mischievous, grin.

Instead, she glanced back at him and said bluntly, "'Tis unnecessary. Please, go." Then, scooping water from the stream with a deft gesture, she straightened, turned her back on him, and strode off out of the woods toward the castle.

Stunned, still disbelieving, he followed her to the edge of the woods but took care to do so quietly and with a wary eye on the castle so he would not inadvertently show himself to anyone on its ramparts.

The lass was so trusting that she did not bother to look back.

As she stepped into the clearing that wrapped around the base of the knoll, he saw her wave to someone. Moving to a tree trunk wide enough to conceal him, he watched her cross the clearing to the path leading up to the castle entrance. As he watched, a second lass came down the path toward her, wearing a pink kirtle trimmed with white ribbons. She was grinning.

"By the Rood," Will muttered, "they've got two Katys!"

"I came to help you pull weeds," Katy said when she was close enough to her twin not to shout.

"You are too late for weeding," Clydia replied with a thoughtful frown as she came to a halt. "I just went to fetch this pail of fresh water from the stream."

"You don't always go clear into the woods."

"I was hot from the sun, my plants are thirsty, the woods are shady, and so I do take water from the stream there more often than not."

"Why do you look at me as if you'd liefer speak elsewise than of water?"

"Because I am curious about something, but I'm not sure that I want you to explain it to me."

Shaking her head, Katy said, "You must know that, having said that much, you must now tell me what has happened to make you feel so."

"I suppose I must," Clydia said thoughtfully. "You know the feeling one gets sometimes, as if you feel another person's gaze on you or an odd sense of danger?"

"Aye, sure, and though our brothers used to say we were daft when we would tell them so, we were often right." Katy frowned. "Do you mean to say that someone may be hiding in our woods . . . now?"

"He was not exactly hiding."

"Clydia, what are you saying? Is someone there? Someone we don't know?" Looking up toward the ramparts, she saw no one looking their way. "We should—"

"*We* do not know him," Clydia interjected with emphasis. "But he thinks he knows me. In fact, Kate, he seemed certain that he did."

Katy's mouth dropped open, Will's image instantly leaped into her mind, and heat rushed into her cheeks at the thought that he had been watching for her. Closing her mouth, thoughts racing, and cheeks still burning, she looked ruefully at her twin. "He must have frightened the liver and lights out of you!"

"Nae, for though I did have that odd sense briefly, it passed before I could feel fearful. I think that may have been because I noted that birds and animals were behaving normally and not as if a predator had entered the woods. By the way that he spoke to me, I knew you had met him. When was that, Kate, and where?" she demanded. "Why did you not tell me about him?"

"There was nothing to . . ." Faltering when Clydia shook her head, Katy said hastily, "By my troth, I met him only the one time."

"Was it Monday, when you were away so long and said you had gone onto that slope and stayed longer than you had intended?"

"Aye, it was, and . . ." Nibbling her lip, she tried to think how best to explain what had happened.

"So he was sneaking about then, too, was he?" Clydia said. "Good sakes, Kate, Da will want to know that such a sneaksby makes himself free of our woods."

"Nae, Clydia, we cannot tell him that. Will is a good man, not an enemy and certainly *not* a sneaksby."

"How can you judge any man properly after just one brief meeting, especially when I've just found him sneaking about in our woods?"

"Our meeting was not so brief," Katy admitted. "In troth, he may well have saved my life, Clydie, though I do not mean to admit as much to him, ever."

Looking heavenward, Clydia grimaced and then said, "That does explain why he felt he had a right to scold me for being, as he thought, quite alone in the woods, but we have drawn notice from one of the lads on the ramparts. Also, it must be suppertime, so we must go in, but I want the whole tale after supper."

"Not until we are in bed and Bridgett has gone," Katy said firmly. "If she hears a whisper of this, Da will shortly hear it from Bruce Lochan. Moreover, I see Gilli coming now yonder from the north. We can all go in together."

Later that evening, abed in the chamber the twins shared, each with her own narrow cupboard bed and a solitary, currently unshuttered window between them, Katy had settled in and decided that Bridgett did not mean to return when Clydia said, "Now, Kate, tell me all that you know about that man."

"His name is Will," Katy said, turning onto her side so she could watch Clydia's reactions. "I know little more about him than that he aided me when I did need help." The sun had dropped behind hills west of them, but dusky light through the window revealed that her twin lay supine, quiet and staring upward.

Katy's right plait tickled her chin, so she flipped it back over her shoulder, but when Clydia's visible eyebrow quirked, she said quickly, "I expect I went a bit farther than I may have let Da believe."

"A bit?"

"I stayed south of the castle and on our own side of the ridge," Katy said, attempting to sound virtuous but mentally adding, *mostly*.

Clydia said, "Then why am I recalling, when you admit that much, how often of late you have wondered if one might see Raitt Castle from the top of that ridge? Exactly where were you when you met him?"

"On the craggy south peak," Katy said. "And one can*not* see Raitt from there."

Sitting upright, Clydia swung her legs out, gathered her quilt about her, and looked narrowly at Katy. "*On* the peak? At the *top*?"

"Not *atop* the top. The granite slope below it became unexpectedly slippery."

"So you slipped."

"Aye, but I did catch myself. Only I could not gain purchase with my feet, because the slope was gey steep there and like ice or wet slate. I must have cried out. I did hear Argus bark, so Will came and helped me reach the top. Naught more came of my adventure, save a fine view of a loch with a forested islet in it."

Clydia was quiet long enough to make Katy wonder if she was waiting for her to say more. Instead, Clydia said, "So, you had Argus and Eos with you."

"Aye, sure, but they could not get to me safely."

"They let that Will-person get to you, though."

"Aye, he said they looked as if they were pleased to see him."

"And he likely saved your life," Clydia reminded her. "How far might you have slipped had he not come along?"

"Too far, and onto de Raite's land. Da would *not* have liked that."

"He would have cared much more about you, though," Clydia said. With a sigh, she added, "No wonder the man felt he had a right to take me to task today."

"He should not have done that."

"Aye, but he thought he was talking to you, of course, so one cannot blame him. Did he not tell you from whence he comes?"

"Nae, but when we reached the peak, I was disappointed not to see Raitt Castle, so I did ask him if he knew it, and he said that he had heard of it."

"Everyone hereabouts has heard of it," Clydia said. "What else did he say?"

"When I said I'd be indebted to him forever, he predicted that I would want his head on a charger within a sennight. I can tell you, though, that his taking you to task, for any cause whatever, nearly does make me want his head."

"An empty threat," Clydia retorted. "If he said naught of where he had been, did he say aught of where he was going?"

"Aye, sure, he said he was going home. Oh, and I did ask him then where that was. He said it was nearer the Moray Firth so he likely lives in Nairn or one of the fishermen's clachans along the firth.

"So, he came from the south and was heading north. I wonder why he came so near Finlagh today."

"I don't know," Katy said. "I am sorry, though, that he scolded you."

"Likely, so is he," Clydia said with a wry look. "I smacked his face for him."

Katy's eyes widened, "He must think I'm daft to have behaved so to him."

"Nae, for I expect he watched long enough to see us meet," Clydia said. "He will likely know that there are two of us and no longer think that it was your fault."

Katy was quiet, wondering what Will was thinking.

"Will, are ye deaf?" Hew snapped, startling Will out of the reverie that had repeated itself on his way home and throughout suppertime. De Raite had adjourned alone to the tower's inner chamber afterward, but Will's brothers and cousin had been entertaining themselves at the table while he tended his gear near the fireplace. The fire, untended, had reduced itself to embers.

Turning toward his eldest brother, he said, "Sorry, Hew. What is it?"

"I asked ye if ye saw aught o' interest from the ridge today," Hew retorted. "Ye came back later than usual, after all."

Chuckling and tugging an ear, redheaded Colley, next to Hew, said, "Hoots, mon, mayhap he had tae vanquish an enemy o' some sort. Were that it, Willy-lad?"

"Leave him be, Colley," Jarvis said, shifting an errant brown curl from his forehead. "He's taken duty none of us wants, whilst Liam and ye did nowt save ride intae Nairn wi' Hew and Da today. Whilst there, ye seem only tae ha' studied the women ye saw in Nairn's market square. Be ye seeking a wife, then, one o' ye?"

Liam said, "Mind your own affairs, Jarvis, and keep yer nose out o' ours."

Although grateful to Jarvis for the diversion, Will ignored them and kept his attention on Hew. "I saw the usual watchers but naught to vex us, and Castle Finlagh seems peaceful. People come and go, women and men, but merely to attend to chores and such. The cottars in the woods west of them seem to keep to themselves, but I would take notice if aught were to change there."

"Just keep yer mind on what ye're doing," Hew told him. "It

may be vital tae ken what them Mackintoshes be up to sooner than ye think. Da has a plan."

"What is it?"

"When he wants ye tae ken, he'll tell ye, hisself. Meantime, I'm tellin' ye tae see tae your duties, practice your archery and your swordsmanship, and report aught that seems new or unusual when ye walk the ridge."

Deciding that Hew was just trying to make himself important, a tactic he used too often for Will's taste, and knowing that Alyssa was likely in bed by that time, he soon bade the others good night and took himself up the ladder at the other end of the hall, to the minstrel gallery and the attic behind it where his pallet lay.

Access to the wall walk being achieved from that attic chamber by another ladder, he decided to enjoy some fresh air before retiring. Climbing to the access door, he stepped out onto the walk, waved at the nearest guard, and noted that light still glowed from the south-facing window of Alyssa's tower room, as well as from the inner chamber window two floors below hers.

The hall had been smokier than he realized, and the air was fresh and crisp, so he breathed deeply. Strolling to the northern side of the walk, he leaned on the parapet and stared toward the lights of Nairn and the vast darkness of the firth beyond while he let lingering images of the two Katys walking away from him replay and wondered what it felt like to have a sibling exactly like oneself.

The situation fascinated him. One thing he knew for sure was that he wanted to see them both again, to find out if he could tell the real Katy from her twin. He bet himself thousands of farthings that he could, if only because her twin seemed so different in personality from Katy. Likely, she had nice legs, too, though.

Due to Lady Catriona's having decided to take advantage of clear skies to begin her spring cleaning and preliminary measures for shearing their sheep, the twins spent Saturday morning gathering bed curtains, coverlets, and blankets to shake for airing on lines in the courtyard, while the housekeeper and maidservants turned out storage bins and took inventory of everything in the larder, kitchen, and bakehouse.

Others cleared rushes from the great hall and replaced them with fresh ones that had dried in the kitchen rafters over the winter, while still others swept the cobbles of the courtyard and began cleaning and tidying the several outbuildings.

At midafternoon, Catriona excused the twins and Gilli, suggesting that they had helped enough for one day and should take themselves off to walk or swim.

They opted for a walk to the pool that Fin had created by damming a stream above the knoll, but the twins had no sooner stepped into the cold water, holding up their skirts, than Gilli said, "I need some time tae m'self, so ye'll ha' tae excuse me for the nonce. If ye still be hereabouts when I return, I'll find ye."

"Now, where do you think he is going?" Katy muttered, watching him vanish downhill into the forest west of them. "He is unlikely to visit Granny Rosel or any of our other people in those woods."

"I have asked him where he goes," Clydia said. "He will say only that he rambles about in the woods, watching the creatures and such."

With what her father would call an unladylike snort, Katy said, "I like to ramble, too. Have you not noted, though, that when Gilli returns, he nearly always does so from the path to the north, as if he had come from the path into Nairn?"

"Art sure of that?" Clydia asked with a thoughtful frown.

"We saw him come from there yesterday, and I have noticed it before. He has wandered off during his visits these two years past at least. Before then, when he visited on his own, even stayed for a month, he did not walk out alone as often."

"I do recall Bridgett saying that Lochan had wondered if Gil had friends at Cawdor or some such place," Clydia said thoughtfully. "Cawdor is northwest of us, so mayhap he does. The Thane of Cawdor has a son near his age, after all."

"Aye, sure, Wilkin," Katy said. "Gilli has never mentioned him or Cawdor, though, or said much about his wanderings. There, look, Clydie! He's cutting round through those trees below the knoll. I want to see where he goes. This water is still too cold to take off our kirtles, let alone swim in our smocks unless we want to freeze," she added, stepping back onto dry grass. "Moreover, if we slip through our woods yonder to the east, I wager we'll catch up with him on that Nairn path."

"Aye," Clydia agreed, stepping out, as well, "but we are not supposed to go beyond sight of the ramparts that way, and we might easily do so if we follow him."

"Blethers! Gilli and I are supposed to be getting better acquainted, Clydia, so I try to come out when he does so people can see us. But today he left without inviting either of us to go along, so he *wants* to be alone. I want to know why."

"But—"

"Just come with me," Katy said urgently. "No one is watching us from atop the wall." Gripping Clydia's arm, she drew her downhill toward the woods. "If we hie ourselves, we may hear his footsteps. Look," she added minutes later, pointing, "You can see his red hair. This area has been peaceful for months, so—"

"We will both end in the briars if Da catches us," Clydia muttered. "What if we meet with a villainous Comyn or some other rogue?"

"Sakes, Clydie, though we oft see or hear of travelers from Nairn or one of the clachans near the firth coast walking along the ridge top or even below it on their way to the Monadhliath Mountains or the high path eastward into Glen Spey, have you heard aught of our men catching lone Comyns or any other rogues this close to Finlagh?" Katy demanded. "I have not. But, in troth, I think the only members of our family who would recognize a Comyn are Mam, Da, and Àdham."

"But we do know they oft set watchers above, and our brothers…"

"Pish tush," Katy replied. "Neither of our brothers is here. As for watchers, Da's men watch them, too. Look yonder, though," she added. "Gilli has turned off the path by that tall beech tree."

"Mayhap he is going to Cawdor then. He may know a shorter route, one that does not require meeting the Inverness road first, as we do."

"Hush now, and move faster," Katy urged. "We must not lose sight of him."

They did lose him, but the path he followed, despite being as faint and narrow as a deer trail, was clear enough for Katy to see. Leading, with Clydia close behind, she eased through the thick flanking shrubbery, taking care to move quietly.

The breeze dropped, and woodland creatures quieted, so she easily heard Gilli's voice when he exclaimed, "Thank the Fates, ye were able tae get away!"

Stopping where she was, Katy raised a hand to warn Clydia and heard her twin whisper, "Aye, he has met someone, but we must go back now, Kate."

Turning to face her but listening for more from Gilli or his companion, Katy muttered, "I must see who is with him. He just proposed marriage to me, after all."

"'Tis most likely another man," Clydia whispered back. "In any event—"

"Hark," Katy snapped, when she heard another male voice that she identified as easily as Gilli's. "That's Will talking. What can he and Gilli have to discuss?"

"Whatever it is," Clydia muttered back, "your Will sounds angry."

"He is not mine," Katy retorted, taking care to keep her voice low. "I mean to see what they are doing, though."

"We must *not* go any farther," Clydia warned.

"You stay here. I'll just see what they are doing and come right back."

Moving forward before Clydia could argue, Katy could hear Will doing most of the talking. However, the two men kept their voices down, so while she detected tension between them, she could not make out their words.

The discussion stopped abruptly, and hearing someone fast approaching from their direction, she tried to get off the path before she saw that it was Gilli Roy.

He was in a hurry, and though he could not help seeing her, he looked furious and pushed roughly past her without a word.

More curious than ever, Katy kept going, telling herself she needed to be certain that the other person was Will.

Abruptly hearing his voice again, still scolding, she increased her pace until she saw him looming over a beautiful if tearful blonde girl of somewhat more than her own height. The two stood beside a massively tall gray stone, and Will was scolding her in much the same manner that he had scolded Gilli.

The girl saw Katy first, stiffened, and quickly brushed tears from her cheeks.

Will whipped around, his gaze colliding with Katy's. Saying something sharply to the girl, he strode toward Katy as if the shrubbery were not there.

She stood still, her heart pounding and an odd thrill shooting up her spine, but she met his angry gaze, silently challenging him to dare to scold her, too.

CHAPTER 6

When Will caught sight of the Finlagh twin watching them, he snapped, "Go straight home, Alyssa. I will follow you anon, and we *will* talk again."

"Who is she, Will?" Aly asked.

"Never mind about that," he said. "Just go, now!"

She turned obediently away but looked back over her shoulder to say, "You willna seek him out tae hurt him, will you?"

Having fixed his gaze again on the lass watching them, he did not reply but strode swiftly toward her. He was as certain as he could be that she was Katy and not the other one, although he could not have explained how he knew. He just did, and seeing her there, watching them after he had caught Aly with the unknown redheaded scoundrel, set his anger aboil. He felt an uncharacteristic, likely even unfair but nonetheless strong urge to give Katy a good shaking.

She did not look away or step back, but when he got close, she caught her lower lip between her teeth and moved her head slightly back away from him as if she were frightened but striving mightily to conceal it.

He stopped where he was and said sternly, "What are you doing here?"

She hesitated, drew a breath, and said in much the same tone as his, "I could ask the same thing of you, sir, for we stand on Castle Finlagh land. Who is that girl and why were you scolding her?"

"If you heard me scolding, you must know why I did."

"I heard only your tone, not the words. Who is she?"

"My younger sister," he said. "I scolded her because I saw from above that she had come too far from home for her own safety, just as you have. Moreover," he added hastily when he saw her lips part, doubtless to debate that last point, "if you know that upstart who just stormed past you, you may tell him for me that he is to leave my sister alone or answer to me for his insolence."

"I expect you told him that yourself. You have not even told me her name or exactly who *you* are, so to demand that I tell him any such thing is . . . is . . ."

"Is what? You were unwilling to tell me much about yourself when we met," he added, since she seemed unable to find words strong enough to suit her feelings. "You might at least have warned me that you have an identical twin."

"I do not share such information with people I do not know," she said.

When he raised his eyebrows, her lips twitched into a near smile. "I suppose you are as reticent as I am," she said. "But you do know who I am now, aye?"

"I suspect that your father is Fin of the Battles," he admitted. "Look here, Katy, I am not angry with you. If I sounded so, 'tis because . . . mayhap because I saved your life on the tor and feel now as if I have known you much longer than I have. Sithee, I care about your safety as much as I do about Al—about my sister's."

"Sometimes, I have to get away," she said with a little sigh. "I feel safe in our woods, and although I am not supposed to climb to the top of the ridge as I did when we met, I felt safe there, too, because the dogs were nearby."

"They could not help you when you needed it, though."

"I know. I *am* glad you were there when I slipped, Will."

He felt warmth spread through him at her words. Without considering his own words, he said impulsively, "If you should need rescuing again or want to see me for some other cause, mayhap you could let me know . . . somehow?"

Her eyes widened. "How?"

"I don't know," he admitted, feeling foolish, even guilty to have suggested such a thing to her. Nevertheless, now that he had, he hoped there might be a way.

"Do you come this way often?" she asked.

"I do roam through the area, but I usually keep near the ridgetop to avoid trouble with anyone who might take offense at my passage."

A twinkle lit her beautiful eyes. "That is wise of you if you roam often there and have not made yourself known to our people," she said.

"I tend to prefer my solitude unless someone requires rescuing," he replied, scanning the nearby woods as he spoke. The area remained eerily quiet, as if even its customary denizens were treading cautiously.

Evidently discerning his wariness, she said, "My sister awaits me yonder, sir. She is likely worrying about me, too. If the creatures can sense her concern . . ."

"They worry, too, aye, and this place is well concealed," he said when she paused. "You should go, though, if your sister worries."

Eyeing him thoughtfully for a long silent moment, she said, "Do you know the pool, where our south stream is dammed above the castle knoll?"

"I have seen a pond there, aye."

"If I were to drape a cloth, a kerchief, atop shrubbery there, could you . . . ?"

". . . see it from the ridge?" he said, catching her thought.

When she nodded, he said, "I do see the pool now and now whilst I'm on the ridge, so likely I'd see a bright or white kerchief. Others may see it, too, though."

She nodded. "But if anyone questioned me, I could suggest that a gust of wind had caught it and blown it beyond my reach, could I not?"

"Aye, you could, lassie," he said gently. "But I hope you will not make a habit of avoiding the truth or telling me only what you think I want to hear."

She cocked her head. "Sakes, sir, do you always tell the whole, exact truth?"

He chuckled then. "Katy, if anyone ever tells you that he never lies or even shades a truth, you may be nearly certain that he does and likely does so often. My own feeling is that I'd like always to be able to walk into a room knowing that no one in it is likely to distrust my word or accuse me of acting dishonorably."

Brushing a hair from her cheek and with a smile that revealed intriguing dimples on each side of her mouth, she said, "Then I won't do it with you."

Forcing himself briefly to ignore the dimples, he said, "'Twill be better so, lassie. Friends must be able to trust each other."

She nodded then, soberly, so he hoped he had made his point, because truth was important between friends, loved ones, and even between enemies.

Thomas had taught him that habits of truth led to trust, which was important because a trust, once broken, was nearly impossible to rebuild. Hard on that thought, though, came another, more discomfiting one, that while he had not lied to Katy, neither had he told her the whole truth about himself.

Doubtless, Aly would say he had taken the easy way instead, but the plain fact was that he had never met anyone, male or female, who intrigued him more than Katy did, and he was certain that she would want no more to do with him when she learned who his father was. Given time enough before that happened, he hoped he might prove to her that he was not at all like de Raite. Then, perhaps . . .

Noting that she was staring at his chest, he gently tilted her chin up, smiled, and held her gaze.

It was as if he were trying to see right into her head, but his smile was contagious, erasing any lingering tension she felt, so she grinned back at him.

"What is that tall gray stone yonder, behind you?" she asked. "It is at least a yard taller than you are and nearly as wide as you are tall. Yet, it stands so deep in these woods that I have never seen it before."

"'Tis what one calls a standing stone," Will said. "I have seen other such stones but never one so deep in a forest. Usually, they stand in fields or large clearings or in circles of such stones. I do not know how they stand upthrust as they do. But your sister still awaits you, does she not?"

"Most likely she does, so I must go."

"I suspect that I should address each of you as 'my lady,'" he added.

"Aye, perhaps," she said, grinning again. "People do call me Lady Katy, because many hereabouts still call Mam 'Lady Catriona,' rather than Lady Finlagh. So, if you were to ask for me as Lady Catriona . . ." She shrugged.

"I see, so you are named for your mother."

She nodded. "You know, if I should leave a sign—that is, if I should need rescuing or to tell you aught of import—how would I know where to meet you?"

He grimaced. "I should not be agreeing to meet you at all. I am as certain as I can be that your parents would strongly disapprove of any such plan."

"But you suggested it!"

"I did," he agreed with a sigh. "I meant it, too. By my troth, though, I do not know why I let myself submit to so hypocritical an impulse, especially after chasing that upstart away from my sister. I do *not* want to anger Fin of the Battles."

Before he could continue and possibly decide not to be party to the plan, Katy said, "Da would understand your wish to keep me safe, sir."

"Aye, sure, he would," Will said with a touch of mockery.

Fearing that his next words might be to forbid leaving such a sign, she said hastily, "I do need to go. You should return the way you came, too, so that you run less risk of our men finding you here and demanding to know your purpose."

"Wait," he said quietly. "I do have a notion."

Turning back, she said, "What sort of one?"

"How we might meet if you do want . . . that is, need my help again."

The thought of such a tryst with him shot an unfamiliar thrill through her. "Have you thought of a place?"

"Not an exact place, but if you do leave a kerchief on shrubbery near your pool before midday, the chance is good that I might see it that same day."

"Marry, sir, do you cross our land every day?"

"Nae, but I can see that pool from the ridge when I do chance to come this way. You may have to look for me more than once, but I will engage to meet you midafternoon the day after I see the kerchief, if you walk into the woods on your east slope—say, to the stream where I met your twin. If I must leave before you arrive, I can pile a small cairn of stones near the stream to let you know that I'll return the next day. But, lass, think carefully about this. You are safe with me, aye, but you must know that roaming about alone as you do is more dangerous for a woman or girl than for any lad."

She nearly declared that she knew she was safe with him but decided that such an admission would convince him she was *too* daring. Instead, she agreed to think about what he said, took her leave, and found Clydia where she had left her.

"I thought you might have returned to the castle with Gilli," Katy said.

"Gil did not even pause to speak to me. He just pushed past me as if I were another shrub. I thought he must have done the same to you, so I waited. I did not expect to wait so long, though. I was about to come in search of you."

"I'm glad you did not."

"You were talking to him," Clydia said flatly. "I suspected as much."

"To Gilli?"

"You know I did not mean Gil," Clydia retorted with a frown.

Chastened, because her twin rarely frowned or spoke so to her, Katy said, "There was a girl with Gilli Roy. Will told me that she's his sister and he caught them together. He sent Gilli away with what Da calls a flea in his ear."

"That explains why Gil did not want to talk," Clydia said. "I called to him to wait for us, but he ignored me. Your Will's fury must have upset him badly."

Knowing that to object again to the "your Will" would be

fruitless, Katy said, "His sister looked two or three years younger than we are, Clydie. Gilli should not be meeting so young a lassie in secret."

"I agree, but I like Gil, Katy, and I think he feels as if no one does. In troth, I feel sorry for him."

"If you want him, you are welcome to marry him," Katy said.

"I don't feel that sorry," Clydia said with a reassuring chuckle.

Will's thoughts raced between his delight at seeing Katy and his anticipation of seeing her again now that they had a plan for future meetings. However, before he reached Raitt, he knew that, despite the way he felt about the scoundrel Aly had met, he could not in good conscience scold her further for doing what he had just agreed to do himself.

"What *was* I thinking?" he muttered, but the question was moot. He knew that pure desire had stirred the impulse. Sir Fin's Katy fascinated him, and he *wanted* to see her again. He had never known a lass of her age and standing who possessed her confidence, let alone one with a love of adventure that might match his own, albeit with evident disregard for even her powerful father's commands. In one breath, she was nearly childlike, in the next an enticingly attractive young woman.

His mood vanished when his father met him in the screens passage as he entered. "There ye be," de Raite said, scowling. "Where the devil ha' ye been?"

"You ken fine where I was, sir," Will said calmly. "You sent me out yourself this morning, after you sent Hew into Nairn."

"Aye, but Hew were back afore midday," de Raite said.

"If you expected me to return by then, you would have said so."

"I didna expect any such thing, but it be nigh on tae supper-time, and I ha' just told yer sister she's tae go without, because she came in nobbut minutes ahead o' ye. Did ye see aught worthy o' tellin' me this day?"

"I saw the same two watchers I oft see above Finlagh and another two lads betwixt Finlagh and the westerly track that crosses our ridge well south o' here, where it passes over the hills eastward from Loch Moigh to Glen Spey."

"That be as usual, too, then. Ye saw naught else, though . . . naught tae make ye think they ha' ken o' me plans for Nairn?"

"Nae," Will said. "In troth, though, short of an army on the march northward from the southwest, I do not know what activity I should—"

"Ah, bah," de Raite snapped. "Ye'd see Fin gathering men at Finlagh and more such men making their way there from Moigh or heading intae Glen Spey tae reach Rothiemurchus, where, as ye ken fine, the Malcolmtosh's war leader abides."

"I do ken that," Will said. "I saw naught to suggest such movements, naught at all of Rothiemurchus men or that Sir Fin has gathered men. I will say, though—"

"That ye dinna approve o' me plans, aye," de Raite cut in sharply. "I dinna want tae hear it, nor will ye take part in the raid tae seize Nairn Castle. The last thing I need there be a nae-sayer wha' dinna ken nowt. When we leave Monday morning, ye'll tend tae your duties here, keep watch on yon ridge, and ye'll keep your roving sister inside these walls. She tried tae tell me she missed her way back from yon clachan, 'cause she were a-thinkin' o' folks' troubles there. I call that blethers, so I'll no have her walking out and about on her own whilst I'm away. Ye're tae see that she minds that, Will. Ye ought tae be able tae do that much."

Will's own unpredictable temper stirred, but he managed to tamp it down. With de Raite in the mood he was in, anything Will said would likely stir the man to fury. When that happened, only God could predict the outcome.

Katy waited until they were leaving the dais after supper to confront Gilli Roy. "We are going to talk," she said firmly.

"Aye, sure, but not here in the hall," he said. "Tell Clydia we be going up tae watch the sunset from the ramparts. She can tell anyone else who asks for us."

Taking the stairway to its upper landing and the ladder there to the roof, they emerged atop the castle near the crenellated west parapet. Its higher portions were eight feet high, but its shooting positions were three or four feet lower.

The parapet walkway emphasized the oval shape of the castle, and since gently rising hills that surrounded the knoll's east, south, and west sides obscured more distant views in those directions, Katy and Gilli Roy moved to the north end, where they could look over the hornwork guarding Finlagh's entrance at an uninterrupted prospect of Strathnairn and lower portions of the river, all the way northward to the town of Nairn, its harbor, and the Moray Firth.

Although the sun hid behind western hills, its light still glimmered on the harbor and firth, on Nairn's kirk steeple and castle towers, and on unshadowed bits of the river Nairn as it flowed northward to its confluence with the sea.

Two Finlagh men-at-arms strolled back and forth on the long sides of the parapet, keeping watch. Waving at them, Katy received waves in return.

After scanning the area when they reached the north parapet, Gilli folded his arms to lean atop the wall at one of the shooting positions and made room for Katy beside him. "Those two lads willna trouble us, I reckon," he murmured. "I ken fine why ye want tae talk, Kate. Ye must ha' heard that chap a-ringing a peal over me."

"I could hear naught of what the two of you said, but I did see the girl you met, Gilli. So, do not be offering me a wheen of blethers. Just tell me who she is."

He gave her a long, measuring look. Then, evidently realizing that denial or argument would be futile, he said, "Her name is Aly."

"Aly what? Where does she live?"

"I dinna ken, exactly," he said. "Sithee, we met wholly by chance."

"When?"

"Some two years ago," he admitted. "Dinna be shooting questions at me like arrows, though, Katy. If ye want tae hear this, let me tell it in me own way."

Nodding, she pressed her lips together.

"I were in one o' me moods whilst I were a-visiting here, though I dinna ken why I were that day. I just didna want tae talk tae anyone, so I pushed off the main track into them dense woods till I came tae that old standing stone and heard her crying. Someone had been mean tae her—her da, I think she said. We talked for a time, but she didna say naught o' kin or clansmen. We talked

as if we had met as bairns intead o' that very day. Sakes, I talk wi'
Aly easier than I talk wi' anyone else, even our Clydia or yourself."

"If she lives near enough to know that tall stone and be out on
her own as she was, her family is likely from Nairn or from one of
the clachans in the area," she added, remembering what Will had
said about living nearer the Firth.

"Aye, that be logical, I expect," Gilli said, idly stroking his thin
beard and looking northeastward as if he might see through the
hillside and beyond.

Affecting a casual air, she said, "Who was it that caught you
with her?"

"I ken only that he must be kin tae her," Gilli said grimly. "He
tore in tae both of us, her for straying too far from home and me
for 'accosting' her, he said. As if I'd harm a hair o' that lassie's pretty
head, as sweet and gentle as she be!"

Katy stared at him. "Marry, Gilli, you must know her well to
say that about her. How often have you met her?"

Eyeing her more warily, he said, "Once but usually two or three
times, mayhap four, during each visit I ha' paid tae ye these past
two years or more."

"Then how could you offer for me if you care so much for her?"

"It be nowt o' the sort, Katy! I tell ye, I dinna ken aught save
that I can talk wi' the lass. She's just a *friend*, one who feels as I do
about things. Lest ye be unaware o' the fact, I ha' few friends. Forbye, me da says I must marry ye."

Feeling a strong urge to smack him for the tone in which he
had spat the last sentence at her, and a stronger urge to tell him
that she had met his Aly's brother, Katy managed to control both
her twitching hand and her all-too-unruly tongue.

"But why have you not learned more about her home or family
even if you fear you cannot offer for her hand?"

"Because I dinna care a whit who her kin may be. I like the lass
and she likes me, and I can talk tae her without worrying about
who her kinfolk are."

Katy did not press him further, though she suspected he knew
more about his Aly than he claimed. To be sure, *she* knew no more
about Will, but she had met Will only twice and had not quizzed

him because he seemed more interested in talking about other things than about himself. Nevertheless, she suspected that in a span of two years, Aly would likely have revealed her clan affiliation or surname, if no more. Had she not, surely even a feardie like Gilli Roy would have mustered enough courage at least once to follow her home.

However, and more importantly, Katy did not intend to mention Will to Gilli, for she doubted she could trust him to keep her brief acquaintance with Will to himself, especially if he thought it might serve his own ends to betray that trust.

Another, more niggling instinct stirred, that she might not *want* to know Aly's surname, since it would also reveal Will's. After all, if Gilli did know who Aly was and would not say, he must have strong reason to keep it to himself. Maybe their father was a shopkeeper in Nairn, or a fisherman from one of the clachans.

She smiled then, unable to imagine the woods-loving Will in a shop or how she would explain any of it to Clydia. She did *not* look forward to that.

Will noticed that Aly remained unusually silent during supper, paying heed only to her trencher. Beside her, Meggie was also quiet. When the meal was over, Aly made a curtsy in de Raite's general direction, unnoted by de Raite, and whisked herself and Meggie off toward the tower stairway.

In the clamor that always accompanied that moment, with men leaping to their feet and beginning to dismantle trestles, attend to other chores or, having none, to find ways to amuse themselves, Will heard de Raite shout to Hew and Liam to join him in his chamber and then order Jarvis, Colley, and Dae to follow them. "Look after the lads in the hall, Will," he added. "I dinna need ye within."

Nodding, Will waited only until his brothers, cousin, and de Raite had shut themselves in de Raite's chamber. Then, he headed upstairs to the solar.

When he entered, Aly looked up from her favorite seat in the window embrasure and said to her woman, "Meg, prithee, await me in my chamber. Will wants tae speak with me."

The older woman nodded, and Will stepped aside to let her pass him.

Without waiting for her footsteps to fade on the stairway above them, Alyssa said, "If you mean tae scold me further, sir—"

"I do not," he said quietly. "Sithee, I was angry, but I should not have talked to you as I did with that lad standing there."

"Father is angrier than you were," she said. "Come, sit by me, or pull up yon stool," she added. "I shall have a stiff neck if I have tae keep looking up at you like this. I know you saw that young woman, too, for you were heading that way when I left you. She is pretty."

"I did see her," he said, moving the stool closer and straddling it. "I wonder about something, though. Have you heard aught of twins living hereabouts?"

"Certes, for we had two sets born in the clachan these past few years. Twins be rather common, Will, though frequently one twin does die soon after birth. Why, you must ken fine that their graces, the King and Queen of Scots, lost one of their own twin sons soon after they were born. That made me so sad."

"Aye, but do you know others hereabouts besides the ones in our clachan?"

"I did hear that they have twin girls at Finlagh. I have never seen them, though, so I ken naught else tae tell ye about them."

Will considered telling her she had seen one of them that day.

Alyssa was watching him, though, and her eyes suddenly lit up. "Faith, sir, was *she* one of them?" she demanded. "Be it true that her sister looks exactly like her, so much so that gey few can tell them apart?"

"I thought you knew naught else about them," he said. When she could not meet his gaze, he added gently, "Who told you about them, Aly? That lad you met? *He* told you?"

"You will keep your promise?"

"For the nonce, aye," Will said. "If he annoys me again . . ."

"He won't," she said sadly. "Father has forbidden me tae go outside our wall unless Meggie is with me. Even then, we are tae go only tae the clachan and back."

"What else did that lad tell you about the twins at Finlagh, and how does he know them?" Will asked grimly enough to make her eyes widen.

"He is their cousin. His name is Gil, and he said he is one of the few who can tell them apart. They do take pains, though, he said, never tae wear similar clothing, especially when they go tae town. Then, the lady Clydia nearly always wears blue with a formal caul and veil, whilst Lady Katy prefers other colors and wears only a veil with her long plaits twisted intae a knot at her nape beneath it."

"He told you much about them, then, if he even told you their names," Will said. "But, lassie, you do know that you cannot see him again, especially if he is kin to Fin of the Battles. What de Raite would do if he finds *that* out—"

Alyssa reached out and gripped his forearm tightly enough to leave a bruise and said urgently, "You must not tell him! Prithee, sir, swear that you will not!"

Putting a calming hand atop hers, he said, "You know I won't. But you need to make me a promise, too, that you will not see him again."

She nodded, saying gruffly, "Thank you, Will, for if Father should learn even so much as that he is kin tae them at Finlagh . . ."

"What do you mean, *even so much*?" he demanded. "What else—?"

Tears filled her eyes, and when a sob followed, he could not bear it. Rising from the stool, he pulled her up into his arms, wrapped them around her, and held her close while she let her tears and her sobs flow freely.

When the storm passed and she had collected herself, he said, "Now, lassie, what is it you fear to say? You know you can trust me."

She stared at him, tears welling again, but he set her back on her heels and waited silently. At last, she eyed him mistily and said, "Ye promise ye willna tell?"

"I promise."

"Aye, then, I'll tell ye. Gil . . . Gil is the youngest son"—she flicked another searching look at him, which he met calmly—"of the Mackintosh."

Will stared at her, stunned to silence.

"Ye ken fine what Father is like and how much people fear

him," Aly said. "You have oft heard him accuse me o' secretly meeting someone, too. Faith, but he's made such accusations since I was twelve, Will, and until I met Gil I had given him nae cause. I suspect one reason I did linger tae talk tae Gil that day was that Father *had* accused me so often. I wanted tae see how it would feel tae do it."

"But meeting him secretly was gey dangerous, lassie."

"That just made it more intriguing, even exciting, and we share many things in common. He also feels like a misfit in his family. Sithee, his older brothers are much older than he is, just as mine are much older than me. And he, too, has few friends. He says it is because most men he knows are warriors, whilst he believes that people should employ civil discourse rather than war tae settle their disputes. I agree that civility is more sensible than resorting always tae arms."

"Likely, it is more sensible," Will said, surprised that a son of the Mackintosh would feel so. "Unfortunately, though, Aly-love, such a position requires that all sides agree to discuss things peaceably."

With a heavy sigh, she nodded, and her tears spilled over again. She turned from him toward the door, but he caught her, put his hands gently on her shoulders, and kissed her forehead. "I'm sorry, Aly," he murmured, "and I'm sad for you."

Not until she had vanished up the stairs did it occur to him that she had given him only her nod as a promise that she would not meet the lad again.

CHAPTER 7

De Raite did not leave on Monday as he had planned, having learned that the Thane of Cawdor was in Nairn overnight. Instead, he seized the opportunity to send for reinforcements from kinfolk near Lochindorb, who arrived late Tuesday. They all set out for Nairn together at last on Wednesday morning after breaking their fast.

Alyssa had kept to her own chamber in the meantime, and Will had kept busy practicing his archery and swordsmanship with some of the other men who wanted to keep their skills well honed while waiting for their departure.

When the others had gone, he waylaid Meggie as she carried Aly's tray toward the tower stairs and said, "I would speak with her ladyship in the solar as soon as she has broken her fast, Meggie. Prithee, tell her she is to come down to me there, or I will go to her bedchamber."

He had broken his fast at dawn and informed his father's steward directly afterward that he would walk the ridge that day, as usual. The steward did not question his decision, which was, Will thought, just as well for the steward.

After three days of worrying about Aly, suffering nights full of too-invigorating dreams of Katy, and days of de Raite's carping, he felt ripe for murder.

When he went up to the solar, Aly kept him waiting only minutes before she entered, eyeing him warily. "Art vexed with me again, Will?"

"Nae, lassie," he said, standing and holding out his arms to her. When she walked into them and hugged him hard, he added, "In troth, I owe you another apology for quizzing you so fiercely the other day about your friend. I, too, have secrets, lass, that I'd liefer de Raite not learn."

"Do you? Will you tell them tae me?"

"Secrets are best told to no one else," he said gently. "I'll say naught of yours, though. Dinna fear that I will."

"I canna see my friend again, so you will have naught tae say."

"Aly, I know you are sad and also lonely. You said some days ago that you wished you could walk the ridge with me. Would you like to do that today?"

"Aye, sure, but what if Father finds out?"

"If he does, I shall point out to him that he gave me contradictory orders, because he commanded me to tend to my usual duties but also to keep you penned inside the wall. Now, how can I be sure you will behave yourself if I do not see to you myself? I cannot do that if I walk the ridge alone."

Lips atwitch as she struggled not to smile, she muttered, "Faith, but Father would say you should do both easily, but I do want so tae go with you. I expect the men on the gates must know of father's orders, and likely Olaf does, too."

"You leave Olaf and the men on the gates to me. We should easily return before the others do, in any event. Do you know why they went to Nairn?"

"Aye, sure, for Meggie said she heard that Father means tae seize the town and its castle, because he dislikes the Thane of Cawdor as its constable. Father says the sheriffdom of Nairn and the constabulary of its castle are rightfully his."

"Others disagree, but in any event, the castle seizure will take time, so I expect the earliest anyone will return would be tomorrow. If I am wrong, and he does return, I'll take the blame. So, now, art willing, Aly?"

"Aye, sure," she said, her eyes shining.

"Then fetch your gray cloak, and ask Meggie to stay in your chamber and tell anyone who might come seeking you to say you are with me, or sleeping."

"'Twould be a lie tae say I were sleeping, and they would still expect her tae fetch my midday meal."

Will realized that he did not care a whit if Meggie lied to protect Alyssa, that he might even lie himself in such a case. Lightly, he said, "I have food enough for us both, Aly. Meggie can eat your midday meal herself if she likes."

Raising her eyebrows, Aly fell silent again and then nodded. "She would do that for me." With that, she turned and ran up to her bedchamber, returning minutes later with her gray cloak. "Meggie said I must relish the day," she said.

"Good for Meggie!" Putting an arm around her shoulders and giving them a gentle squeeze, he added, "Now, behave as if you have no fears, and I will, too."

As Will expected, Olaf offered no more than a quizzical look before opening the door for them. Aly had tucked a hand into the crook of Will's elbow, and her grip tightened on his arm as they crossed the timber bridge to the steps at its end.

"Courage, Aly," he said as they descended and turned toward the heavy iron gates in the wall's arched entryway. "I won't let them bite you."

He nodded to the gatekeeper, who opened the gate without hesitation.

"There, you see," Will said when they were outside and he heard Aly expel a sigh of relief. "We'll go up yonder hill into the woods, and I'll teach you how to conceal yourself from an enemy, if you like."

She nodded with a smile.

"If we should chance to meet anyone, do not tell them who you are. In fact, say naught unless I give you leave. We do have enemies hereabouts, as you must ken fine."

Still busy with the annual cleaning, Katy had found few opportunities to watch the slope east of the castle for any sign of Will and had not dared to leave a signal at the pool for him to meet her, either. Not only did she not control her own time on such days but he might have had second thoughts about meeting her.

Clydia and Bridgett were still supervising maids dealing with the increasing pile of mending, including featherbed tickings that had lost feathers. All featherbeds required shaking and airing twice a year, and laundering at least once a year.

Catriona having declared Monday that the time had come for the laundering, Katy had been helping with that ordeal. Fortunately, only the twins' beds, their parents', and Àdham and Fiona's had featherbed tickings, for each could require up to fifty pounds of feathers. Two more existed for honored guests or to replace any needing mending. The entire castle bustled and hummed for two days with the laundering.

Catriona's Ailvie saw to it that the thin mattresses underlying each featherbed also received a good beating and airing, while men hauled water from the streams to the sunny courtyard, heated it over fires there, and filled tubs in the yard for scrubbing the tickings with lye soap.

Maidservants washed and rinsed the feathers, then spread them on screens in the hall, kitchen, and courtyard to dry, while men and lads waxed the well-scrubbed tickings after they dried. When the feathers were dry, women stuffed them back into the tickings with dried herbs and lavender to scent them and carefully restitched each ticking. Throughout the process, the reek of drying feathers permeated the castle and would linger for days, despite the herbs.

When the time came at last for Wednesday's midday meal, Katy was glad to think she might sit still for a while. After tidying herself, she hurried downstairs.

Clydia greeted her at the high table with a sympathetic grin. "My fingers ache from pushing needles through ticking, but I'd liefer sit and sew than deal with musty wet feathers or watch over other folks with a critical eye."

"I'd prefer to see others doing both tasks," Katy muttered.

Catriona and Fin joined them, and when they had taken their seats, Cat said lightly, "I'd wager that you are both longing to get away for a walk or a swim."

Katy said, "Have we much more yet to do, Mam?"

"We will be nearly finished when the last of the tickings and feathers are dried and in their proper places. Your father and some of the men are rearranging stores in the undercroft, but you and

Clydia need only see to your usual chores now. I will need your help again when we start shearing the sheep. But, until then . . ."

Katy looked at Clydia. "Do you want to swim?"

"Aye, perhaps, for 'tis a fine day and warm enough, I think."

"The water will still be cold," Catriona warned them. "Take your cloaks to warm you afterward. Take Rory and Argus, too, to watch for passing strangers."

They left as soon as they had collected towels and Rory. With Argus ranging ahead along the stream that spilled southward down the west hillside, from the fork well above the castle knoll, they made their way up to the pool.

It was chilly, as Rory, sticking his toes in, announced to the twins. "Ye can ha' your swim," he added. "I'll keep a watch out from yon sunny rock, and I swear I willna peek. Argus, ye stay wi' them, so if they try tae droon, ye can pull them out."

"If I had not seen that that laddie can outswim most fish, I would call him a feardie," Clydia said with a chuckle as the boy climbed his rock and turned his back to them, and Argus lay down a short distance away and sleepily watched the twins.

"Rory has more bones than flesh," Katy pointed out. "Mayhap it feels colder to him than it does to us."

In the event, neither of them stayed long in the water, but when Clydia suggested returning to the castle, Katy said, "I want to stay a while longer. I'm warm enough, so mayhap I'll walk over to Granny Rosel's or into the woods."

"Then keep Rory with you as well as Argus," Clydia said.

"Nae. I do enjoy Rory's chatter, but I'd liefer be alone for a time. I'll keep Argus, though, if you like."

"Aye, you should, and dinna do aught to irk Da."

Grinning wryly, Katy said, "I do *not* want to do that."

By the time Clydia and Rory were out of sight, Katy had dismissed the notion of visiting Granny Rosel, for Clydia's warning had reminded her that she had not seen Will since Saturday. If he had followed the same pattern today that he had described the day they met, he might be heading back northward by now.

On the thought, she jumped up and walked briskly around the curve of the wooded hillside toward the slope east of the castle, taking care to stay south of the crags. Argus trotted ahead of her, looking back occasionally to keep her in sight. As the woods thickened, he slowed and looked back more often.

Katy moved as quietly as the wolf dog did, listening carefully to the forest sounds. Even so, she saw Argus perk his ears before she heard any warning that someone might be nearby.

"What is it, laddie?" she murmured.

The dog stopped, glanced back at her, and then perked its ears southward and wagged its tail.

Delight surged through Katy. "Show me," she whispered.

Argus moved forward, and she followed. Moments later, closer than she had expected, she heard a murmur of voices, barely recognizable as male and female.

Tail wagging faster, Argus looked at her hopefully.

Raising her hand, palm out, and dropping it to touch her thigh, she signaled him to stay with her. Obediently, he turned to walk beside her, and she moved forward at an angle that soon brought her within sight of her quarry.

Her heart began pounding in her chest, and she knew she was grinning from ear to ear.

"What is it, Will?" Alyssa demanded, moving closer to him. "What do you see?" By then, though, she could see for herself. "It be that same lass I saw in the woods yonder the other day, and she looks gey happy; so, you do ken her, aye?"

"I do," he replied, keeping his voice low. "Just remember what I said earlier, Aly. Give away no information unless I say you may."

"I remember," she said. "But if that dog be as friendly as it looks, a-wagging its tail as it does, I want tae meet her."

Will's body had reacted instantly the moment he recognized the lass who, for nights, had haunted his dreams, and he was eager to talk with her. It could prove awkward, since Alyssa was with him, but walking the ridge over the past few days, he had watched for Katy or some sign that she needed or wanted to see him.

He had been disappointed to see none.

In truth, he was not sorry to have suggested meeting her again, though they were taking a dangerous path. Even so, her lure was strong, strong enough to send heat surging through his body and make him yearn to touch her. He did *not* mean to miss this chance to speak with her if only to be sure she had suffered no harm after meeting her cousin the day he had caught the scurrilous red-headed scruff with Aly.

"Stay here, Alyssa, whilst I see what she wants."

Moving forward on the words, sure that Aly would obey, he strode down the hill, capturing Katy's gaze as he did, without a thought for careless step or unseen root, seeing only how her expression softened and how beautiful she was.

Movement drew his attention long enough to Argus to see the dog's tail still wagging. It went on doing so when Argus shifted attention to a point behind Will. Only when Katy's gaze did the same did he see that Aly had followed him.

Looking past Katy then and noting that no part of the Finlagh ramparts showed through the dense foliage, he felt some relief. They were still too close to the castle for comfort, though, so he would have something to say to Aly later.

Katy, grinning, extended a hand to Aly, who grasped it with both hands and with a wider, more joyful smile than Will had seen from her in months. "I'm Katy," Katy said. "I think I we saw each other in our north woods the other day."

"We did, aye," Aly said. Then, looking at Will, she waited.

Katy, too, eyed him and made no effort to free her hand from Aly's grasp.

Will wondered what she would say if he asked if her scapegrace cousin "Gil" had taken himself off yet or not. He could not ask that, though, not with Aly there.

Katy raised her eyebrows at him. "She is your sister, is she not?"

Will said simply, "Aye, her name is Aly."

Smiling again, Katy said, "I am pleased to meet you, Aly."

"Me, too, tae meet you," Aly said. "You are so beautiful!"

"Marry," Katy said with a chuckle, "we have been cleaning for days, so I feel as if it will be months before I am even tidy again. You must know how that is."

"Aye, sure, I help with cleaning, too," Aly said, then cast a hasty glance at Will, which he read with ease as fearing that she had said too much.

He gave her shoulder a reassuring touch, but he knew they dared not linger.

"Mayhap you might visit me sometime," Katy said, shooting Will a quizzically challenging look that he read as easily as he had read Aly's.

"Mayhap, one day," he said.

Then his irrepressible sister blurted, "Oh, how I would like that! I expect you saw that I know your cousin, so mayhap we can be friends. Sithee, I have never—"

"Aly," Will interjected quietly.

Flushing, she looked at him, eyes flashing, lips pressed together. He held her gaze, but her lips tightened. She said, "'Tis true, Will. You ken fine that it is."

"That is enough," he said. "We must go."

Tears sprang to her eyes, but she collected herself and turned back to Katy. "I am glad tae have met you, my la—"

"Just Katy," Katy said gently. She looked at Will as if she might say more, but before she could, he caught sight of movement in the woods beyond her.

A half-breath later a boyish voice called just loudly enough for her to hear. "Lady Kate! Sir Fin wants ye!"

As Will grabbed Aly by an arm and whisked her back into the shrubbery with him, Katy turned swiftly, calling back in similar tones, "I'm coming, Rory!"

"Aye, good, but hie yerself," the boy replied. "Yer da has visitors!"

More quietly but with a gesture of her right hand, she added, "Argus, go to Rory. And, you, sir," she said in a normal tone, turning and peering into the shrubbery as the dog trotted away toward the boy, "art still there?"

"Aye," Will murmured.

"Mayhap tomorrow, at yonder stream of the pail and smack," she said with a mischievous grin. "Do you think you can meet me there?"

"I'll try," he replied, smiling at the reminder of his first and only, surprisingly painful meeting with her twin.

CHAPTER 8

"Who is it?" Katy demanded when she met towheaded Rory and Argus moments later. The boy was ruffling the dog's ears. "Who has come?"

"Donald, Thane o' Cawdor, and his son, Wilkin," Rory said, straightening to face her. "They rode a pair o' fine bay horses and had four men-at-arms wi' them. They rode them horses right up yon steep track tae the castle entrance, too."

"Donald must have business with my father," Katy said with a frown. "Do you know why Da sent for me?"

"Nae, but I heard him ask the lady Clydia where ye'd be," Rory said. "She said ye'd lingered at yon pond and might ha' gone tae see Granny Rosel. Only then she tellt me I should come intae these woods here and call tae ye." He cocked his head. "Does her lady-ship ha' the Sight, d'ye think?"

"She does not," Katy said. "You know that the Sight does not provide information about other people's locations. She just knew I wanted time to myself after days of cleaning amidst many people, clouds of dust, and noisy, nosy boys."

"Aye, that would be why, I'd wager," Rory said with a cheeky grin. "I'm thinking now that I should say nowt about where I found ye, though."

Katy smiled. "I think you have shown that you know when to speak and when not to speak, my laddie."

When they reached the castle courtyard, Katy saw more men there than usual, but the visitors were orderly and quiet. In the hall, she found her mother overseeing arrangements for their guests with her usual calm and steady eye.

Looking up, Catriona said, "There you are, dearling. Do not linger now but run upstairs and don a fresh kirtle. Bridgett is there now with Clydia."

"Rory said Da had sent for me, and that the Thane of Cawdor has come," Katy said. "Is aught amiss?"

"Aye, for Donald says that Comyn de Raite has seized the castle of Nairn and claims to be taking over the sheriffdom there, as well. Your father wants us all to stay inside the castle until the matter is sorted out," Catriona said.

"Mercy, were many people hurt?" Katy asked.

"I don't know, love. I expect we shall hear more at supper. Hurry, though, for Donald came only to bring us the news. He will depart after we eat. Sithee, he has sent running gillies to Inverness to raise men-at-arms and another to Loch Moigh," she added, glancing toward the huge fireplace on the far side of the hall.

Looking that way, Katy saw Gilli Roy standing by the fire, peering down into the flames. He glanced up then, his solemn gaze meeting hers.

"Gilli looks sad," Katy said.

"His father will want to know what the two of you have decided," Catriona said. "We'll talk later, though, after Donald and Wilkin leave. Go now and change your dress. Then, mayhap you will have time to talk with Gilli Roy."

Stifling a sigh, Katy cast another glance at Gilli before going up to her bedchamber, where she found her twin with Bridgett.

Clydia twitched the skirt of her favorite blue kirtle into place, smiled, and said, "I see that Rory found you."

"Just where you said he would," Katy said dryly. "He asked me if you have the Sight."

"Good sakes," Bridgett said. "That boy kens as well as we do that the Sight happens but rarely and usually during some horrible disaster. Ye'd best be washing yourself quick, though, m'lady. I ha' put out that yellow gown that ye like, and Lady Clydia threaded new green-ribbon lacing intae the bodice for ye, too."

Moving to the basin, Katy said, "Thank you both. I expect that you heard what Comyn de Raite has done now."

"Aye, Mam told us," Clydia said. "That man—sakes, that whole clan—is horrid. I hope no one was killed or badly injured."

"Mam told me that Cawdor has sent a runner to fetch Malcolm."

"Certes, he would feel obliged to," Clydia said. Then, frowning, she looked at Katy and added, "I have not seen Gil for some time. Have you?"

"Just now," Katy said. "He was staring into the fire, looking miserable. That poor laddie does not want me any more than I want him."

Clydia began to speak, cast a look at Bridgett, and fell silent.

Katy said, "Bridgett does not repeat the things we say, Clydie."

"Nae, I do not," Bridgett said bluntly, "but neither do I wish tae ken all about other folks ye might discuss. A body can hold only so many secrets, and them what concern others be the hardest tae keep, 'cause they pile up, as ye might say, till it be possible that one might spill out o' a body's mouth—unintended, o' course."

"She is right," Clydia said. "It is unfair of us to speak of things involving others that she should not repeat. Bridgett is loyal to us, not to others we know or to whom we may be kin. But you must talk frankly with Gil, Katy."

"Aye, Mam said much the same thing. She also said that Cawdor and Wilkin will depart after supper. I'll talk to Gilli then."

Fin and the Thane of Cawdor dominated the supper conversation at Finlagh. Other than polite responses when her mother or Clydia asked her to move a sauceboat closer or pass the bread, Katy was barely aware of the men's voices or anything else at the table. Her thoughts had riveted themselves on Malcolm and how soon they could expect his arrival and his demand for news of the betrothal.

She knew both of their visitors, for Cawdor sat just a few miles west on the strath. Donald, the burly, white-haired fifth Thane of Cawdor, was fifty-five, two years younger than Fin; and Donald's son—lankier, dark-haired William, who would become the sixth Thane—was twenty-six and known familiarly as "Wilkin."

While exchanging greetings with the two notable warriors before the grace, Katy had noted that both were more solemn than usual.

Comyn de Raite had murdered the fourth Thane nearly three decades ago and they were angry with him now and concerned about the well-being of the people of Nairn, but she knew they confidently expected to oust the Comyns from the town.

Just then, she heard Donald say in his deep voice, "My runners are swift, and Malcolm won't delay."

"We expect he'll take but two or three days to arrive," Wilkin said, his hazel-brown eyes twinkling. "Then we'll see some fine sport as we rout the devils."

Shaking her head at him, Katy stifled a sigh but reminded herself that two or three days were better than Malcolm arriving sooner, especially since she hoped to see Will the next afternoon. Gilli had to come first, though, so after bidding their guests good night at the table she hurried after him when he walked away.

"Gilli," she said quietly but firmly when she caught up to him, "we simply must decide what we are going to do before your lord father arrives."

"The ramparts again?" he muttered.

Since the hall was clamorous with men amusing themselves or preparing for bed, and her parents would retire to the inner chamber after escorting Cawdor and Wilkin to the courtyard, she said, "I think so. We will have more privacy there."

Atop the castle, the night was dark enough for stars to be out. No moon had appeared the night before, so Katy doubted they would see one tonight.

The air was crisp, and she had not bothered to stop at her chamber on the way to fetch a shawl because, instead of following her as gentlemen usually did going up a steep spiral stairway, Gilli had hurried on ahead. Also, since he tended to be dramatic in both speech and actions, she was unsure that she should trust him not to do anything foolish.

When he began to stride across the rubble-strewn roof instead of keeping to the walkway, she paused by the south parapet. "Gilli, we can talk here. No one else will come up before the guards change at midnight."

He stopped where he was and stood, slumped. When she kept silent, he straightened, turned, and walked slowly back to face her.

"What are we going tae do, Katy?" he muttered. "I ken fine that ye dinna want tae marry me, and ye ken fine that I care much more for Aly. I canna tell me father about her, though, so . . ." He spread his hands. She could hear his distress in his voice; and, even in the dusky starlight, she saw it in his face.

She said softly, "Gilli, I know you care about Aly, and we both know that Malcolm will not want to hear that, especially when you claim not even to know her clan affiliations."

Gilli said despondently, "I tell ye, Katy, the only thing my father will want to hear be that ye've agreed tae marry me. Every night I dream I've fallen intae an icy river that sweeps me away. I just let it happen, too, because that fate doesna seem so dire now. Me father be that set on making us marry each other, and your father will do whatever mine tells him tae do."

Gently, certain now that she had only one obvious course before her, Katy said, "But I will *not* do that, Gilli. I doubt that you have any chance of marrying your Aly unless you are willing to steal her away and declare yourselves married to each other. In any event, though," she added hastily, "Malcolm *can*not force me to marry you. In troth, I doubt he can legally force *you* to marry someone you do not want, but I ken fine that you fear to defy him. So I must do it for both of us."

Gilli Roy stared at her, his mouth agape. Then, forming his words carefully, he said, "What was that ye said afore, Kate, about us declaring ourselves married?"

Thursday morning, Will awoke with a smile on his lips, recalling that he would see Katy that afternoon. De Raite had not returned; nor had anyone who had gone to Nairn with him. Even so, Will knew he could not risk taking Alyssa on his patrol again and was relieved when she did not ask to go.

The morning passed slowly, but he saw no indication as he headed north that Fin of the Battles was gathering men-at-arms at Finlagh, so he made his way back earlier than usual, ostensibly to check again for such activity. Finding a place of concealment from which he could watch the spot on the stream where he had met Katy's twin the day he had mistaken her for Katy, he settled in to wait.

He had not been there long before he saw one or the other of them heading straight for him, pail in hand. Instinct told him the lass was Katy, but he waited until she stopped by the stream and peered expectantly into the shrubbery, first in the woodland on the slope above and then at shrubbery on either side of her.

When her mouth twisted in disappointment, Will said, "I'm here, lass. I wanted to be certain which one you were."

"Art so sure you know?" she asked, grinning when he showed himself.

"I am," he said, emerging from the bushes. "Your sister is more dignified."

"Aye, she is," Katy agreed. "Is Aly your only sister?"

"Aye, but I did not come here to discuss sisters. I came because you asked me to come. Is aught amiss?"

"Marry, sir, you must have heard that the wicked Comyns have seized the castle in Nairn. Comyn de Raite is now calling himself its constable and Sheriff of Nairnshire. My father even gave orders for us all to stay inside Finlagh's walls until de Raite comes to his senses, but the men on our ramparts can see all the way to Nairn, and people have been coming and going from our castle to our west woods and back all day, so no one paid me heed. That was good, too, because I was in no mood for confinement just because of that man!"

Feeling instantly villainous himself, Will squirmed inside, but if he told her that "Comyn de Raite" was his father, she would walk away in anger. It would be much easier to explain things to her after matters settled down again.

"I did not hear about that," he said, reflecting that the words were true, since no one had bothered to inform them at Raitt that the attack had succeeded.

Stepping closer to her, he added, "I expect that with the attackers four miles away you are safe enough at Finlagh. Since violence has erupted, though, it may spread. In troth, lass, you ought not to have come outside your walls alone."

"As I said, our men are on the watch," she repeated, avoiding his gaze as she did. "We will have good warning if any enemy heads this way," she added lightly. "I wanted to see you, Will. I like talking with you. We have become good friends."

"Sakes, lass, we have met only three times," he said.

Smiling, she said, "Aye, but I feel as if I have known you much longer."

Putting two fingers under her chin and tilting her face up, he said rather hoarsely, "When you look at me like that, I want . . ." He paused guiltily. "Nae, I should not say what I want. 'Twould be gey wrong of me."

Her eyes twinkled. "Say it. If I were Bridgett—she's the maid-servant who looks after Clydia and me—I would say that you want to kiss me and that a person should just say what he or she wants. It saves time and avoids confusion, she says."

"Is that what she says?" he asked, bending closer. His body urged him to take her at once and make her his own. Steeling himself, he resisted that urge.

"Well?" she said, raising her eyebrows. "Will you or will you not?"

"By heaven," he replied, cupping his hand to the back of her head, "I will."

She did not resist, so he put his free arm around her, pulling her closer. She was so small, so slender, and just holding her so was lighting fires all through his body. Stroking her back and shoulders and moving himself gently against her, he moaned in his throat, raised her chin a bit more, and watched her expression as he kissed her.

His lips were warm against hers and Katy's feelings threatened to overwhelm her. Certainly, nothing that Gilli Roy Mackintosh had ever said or done had stirred anything remotely akin to the fascinating sensations that Will's kiss shot through her.

She pressed closer to him, on tiptoes now, wishing that the heated feelings racing through her body could last forever.

Will suddenly gripped both of her shoulders and set her back on her heels.

"This is madness," he muttered. "Nae, lassie," he added when she gaped at him in bewilderment. "I do *not* mean that the feelings you have or that I have are madness. In troth, you captivated me from the start. I've thought of little else since that day. Even so, this, now and *here*, is madness. Your father or one of his men could come along any moment and see us. We must not meet here again."

"Do you mean that you do not *want* to meet again?"

"I do not mean that!" he retorted. "We must just think of a safer place, one that is safe for both of us but especially for you."

"The gray stone," she said without a thought. "It rises from Finlagh land well off the path to Nairn, and we both ken fine how to find it. I can even find it from the woods west of the castle knoll and avoid the Nairn path altogether. The woods there are dense, too, until one gets to the clearing below our knoll, within range of arrows from the castle. It should be safe for kissing," she added with a wry look. "Of course if my cousin and your sister should return—"

"Nae," he interjected, shaking his head. "My sister will not dare to return there, and your cousin had best not dare, either. So, leave your signal when you want to meet me, and I'll see you there at midafternoon the next day. If you cannot linger, leave a cairn for me. If I get there first and cannot stay, I'll do the same."

"Then, if *you* want to meet me, you need only leave a cairn near the pail-and-smack stream, and I'll know to meet you the next day at the stone."

"Aye, then," he said. "It would be as well, though, not to meet at all until the conflict within the town of Nairn ends and matters return to normal."

"Aye, sure," she agreed, wondering if matters would ever be normal again.

❖ ❖ ❖

Friday, when de Raite, Hew, Liam, and Cousin Dae returned at midday, they were full of themselves and gloating over their success.

"Ye should ha' been with us, Will," Hew said, chortling. "Even ye, on your own, could ha' taken yon castle. I vow, nae one in that great stone pile expected attack or had prepared tae defend against one."

"Aye, that be so," Dae said, shaking his head. "Cawdor's men had grown so complacent after months of peace that we just marched in and your father informed them that he was taking over as rightful Constable of Nairn Castle."

"So nae one was injured then," Will said evenly.

"Almost nae one," Dae said, casting a humorous look at Hew.

Liam chuckled. "Some dafty told us we couldna take the castle because it belonged tae the Thane of Cawdor. Hew knocked him flat, and that was the end of that, because our da made it clear he was not only the new constable but rightful Sheriff o' Nairnshire, as well."

Will looked at de Raite. "Then you will return straightaway, aye?"

De Raite shrugged. "I'll move intae town in a few days, when it suits me. Raitt lies closer to town than Cawdor, and I left Colley and Jarvis wi' a hundred men tae hold the place until Hew and Liam return Sunday or Monday tae aid them."

"I thought your objection to Cawdor was that he does not live in town and keep a close eye on his castle."

"Be ye daring tae question my decisions?"

"Nae, but what if Cawdor wants his town and castle back?"

"He kens fine no tae challenge me when I ha' the upper hand," de Raite growled. "Ye must ken that his father challenged me once, tae his regret."

Will knew that de Raite had murdered Andrew, fourth Thane of Cawdor, but he had better sense than to engage him on that subject. Instead, he said, "Cawdor will send for reinforcements from Inverness and Loch Moigh, will he not?"

"Aye, sure, and the Malcolmtosh and others may come, but he's twenty miles away and it'll take time for them all tae raise men.

Ye'll take yourself tae yon ridge these next days, though, tae see what ye can see. Cawdor won't move hisself without reinforcements, so nae one be likely tae enter Nairn afore Tuesday afternoon or Wednesday. I'll be ensconced in Nairn Castle m'self long afore then, and our lads will spread out and about. So, we'll ha' warning if aught goes amiss."

Dae said with a smile, "I heard that you killed Andrew Cawdor yourself, sir."

Giving him a sour look, de Raite said, "If ye heard it were murder, it were nae such thing. 'Twas a fair fight."

"Aye, sure, if you say so," Dae said hastily.

"I do." De Raite watched Will, as if he were daring him to add his mite.

Will remained silent, knowing that if his father had persuaded himself the fight was fair, he was the only man in the north Highlands who believed it.

Will had heard the story from Granduncle Thomas, who expressed no doubt that Comyn of Raitt—as everyone had known de Raite at the time—had murdered the fourth Thane of Cawdor by drawing a dirk without warning and stabbing him to death. An armed man fighting one without a weapon in hand was not a fair fight.

As Granduncle Thomas had put it when describing the incident to Will, who was born four years after the incident, "Your sire possesses a thoughtless, impulsive nature. When his temper erupts, his good sense deserts him forthwith."

Having met Cawdor's son, Wilkin, while living with Granduncle Thomas, and liked him for his ready sense of humor—though Wilkin's admittedly prankish nature had gotten the two of them into trouble more than once—Will would have liked to press de Raite to tell the truth. However, he knew that he himself could speak and act impulsively, too, especially in a rage, so he took advantage of Thomas's stern lessons, paused to consider potential results, and stifled the urge.

De Raite rarely took time to think.

Will was certain that Cawdor and Wilkin would rouse their neighbors, including Fin of the Battles, and that the Mackintosh, as Captain of Clan Chattan, would surely view the seizure of Nairn as cause to take lawful vengeance. With two of his own sons at Nairn, de Raite ought to have considered that.

Will's concern eased as they were finishing their meal and de Raite ordered Hew and Liam to return to Nairn the next day to take charge at the castle. De Raite would join them, he said, when he heard that Cawdor was raising an army.

During supper that evening, one of de Raite's watchers arrived from the southwest mountains, exhausted, with a warning that the Mackintosh had gathered his men and would likely be heading north at dawn.

De Raite nodded. "'Tis as I expected then, lads. It will take them at least two days if it doesna rain, and they'll need tae rest then afore any fight."

Suppressing a sigh and thankful when Liam drew de Raite's attention, Will quietly withdrew himself from all temptation to point out that de Raite was assuming too much, and went to bed.

CHAPTER 9

She was walking by herself in lush green woodland filled with violets
and bluebells. She was alone because no one had ever wanted to
marry her, and now her hands and body were dry and more wrinkled than Granny Rosel's. She had given up the one offer of marriage
she had ever had, just tossed it away on a gentle breeze, and now
here she was, alone, lonely, and too old for any man to want.

The woodland flowers were beautiful, though, and she heard
birds singing, distantly. But, nae, they were closer now, and there . . .
a robin on a branch.

It was not chirping or tweeting that she heard, though, but
whistling.

Looking into the shadowy woods ahead, she saw Will coming
toward her as if her ancient mind had conjured him up out of the distant past, except that he was still young. Even so, when he smiled, her
body reacted with odd thrills much as Bridgett had described how
she felt when she was near Lochan. Doubtless, though, the oncoming
chap was Will's grandson, as stalwart as his grandsire, and how foolish she felt as an old hag to be responding in this strangely exciting
way to such a handsome young man!

Sakes, she hungered for him. She wanted him to touch her, to kiss
her, and not to stop wanting her as Will had. The younger version
of him was closer now. A bouquet of violets appeared in his hand
and grew larger as he came nearer. She was smiling and wondered

at herself, but her body tingled youthfully, so she reached out to take the flowers.

Smiling himself now with delight, he extended the bouquet to her and said in very un-Will-like tones, "Lady Kate, for mercy's sake . . .

. . . *wake up!*" Bridgett exclaimed. She stepped hastily back when Katy sat bolt upright in her bed and looked around in open-mouthed bewilderment.

"But it was so real," Katy said, feeling absurdly disoriented to find herself in her bed. "What a strange dream!"

"What did ye dream then?" Bridgett asked.

"That I was an old woman in a greenwood, and no one except Gilli had ever offered for me. Then a man appeared . . . someone I . . . I knew . . . and . . . and I don't recall the rest," she added hastily, thinking she had already said too much.

"Did he give ye aught tae take away wi' ye?" Bridgett asked archly.

"Aye, he was handing me a bouquet of violets when you woke me."

"Then, I'm thinking me granny would say ye're in love, m'lady."

"Marry, how could I be?" Katy demanded. "I'm *not* in love with Gilli Roy! Nor have I known anyone else long enough to have such feelings for him."

"Ye ha' better sense than some, then. That big dafty Lochan did say he loved me almost the first time he talked tae me. I told him right then that he were daft."

Katy stared at her. "Lochan said that? Sakes, I could never . . . One simply does not . . . cannot fall in love like that."

"I dinna ken aboot that, but ye're blushing. Also, if that dream laddie gave ye violets and ye do love him, me granny would say he'll be faithful tae ye."

Feeling enough heat in her cheeks to know she was blushing, Katy said defensively, "Whoever he might be, if I don't meet him till I'm your granny's age, I cannot see what good *that* will do me. Mayhap the dream was just warning me of how foolish I would be to turn down Gilli's offer. If that was its meaning—"

"Nae, nae, for I had such a dream o' bein' an old lady when I were nae more than a bairn, and Granny laughed when I told her aboot it. She said it meant I'd ha' good fortune, and that verra same day,

I went intae Nairn wi' me mam and Lady Catriona, and when we were just leaving the hall here, Sir Fin give me a farthing tae spend. So, dinna fear; ye'll soon see that me granny has the right of it."

"I doubt I shall enjoy good fortune, though," Katy said. "The Mackintosh is likely to arrive before long, and . . ."

Pausing, she realized she had said nothing to Bridgett or anyone, except Clydia, about the decision she had made with Gilli. Clydia had understood why she wanted to refuse his offer but had doubted that Fin or Malcolm would let her do so.

When Katy had reminded her of the law making it illegal to force women into unwanted marriages, Clydia said, "Aye, but if Malcolm wants this betrothal as badly as Gil says he does, they will likely both press the two of you until you obey."

"I shan't let them do that, because I promised Gilli I would not," Katy told her twin firmly. "Nor do I think Mam or Da will let Malcolm force me, because Da keeps his promises, and I will keep mine to Gilli."

Nevertheless, Gilli Roy watched her uncertainly all day, in visible fear that she would not act as she had promised him she would. Neither of her parents mentioned the betrothal, so by the time Malcolm and his men arrived at suppertime, Katy's nerves were taut and her courage had waned.

Malcolm entered, frowning, with two men-at-arms following him.

When he saw Katy, his frown vanished and he strode across the hall to her, smiling, his hands extended. He was a small man, barely a head taller than she was, with gray hair tied back at his nape and bright, twinkling blue eyes.

"I'm pleased tae see ye, lass," he said, giving her a kiss on each cheek. "I vow, ye get prettier every time I clap eyes on ye."

"I thank you, my lord," Katy said, making her curtsy, conscious that Gilli was watching more nervously than ever and that Clydia had come downstairs. "Did not my parents meet you in the courtyard?"

"They did, aye, and will be in directly. But why is our Gillichallum Roy standing yonder by the fire when he should be beside ye, presenting ye tae me?"

"He has no need to do that, sir. You know me well already."

"Aye, sure, but I'm thinking that the pair o' ye—"

"Forgive me for interrupting you, sir," Katy said, squaring her shoulders and meeting his gaze. "I fear we must disappoint you."

"Nae, nae, lassie, 'tis a good match. I be gey pleased with it."

"There is no match, my lord. I should more truthfully have said that *I* must disappoint you, because Gilli understands his duty and tried hard to persuade me. But, though I love him as a cousin, I do not want him for my husband."

"Art promised tae someone else, lassie?"

"Nae, sir, but—"

"Then there be nae obstacle tae the match," Malcolm said.

Katy's temper stirred, but seeing her parents appear in the hall entryway behind Malcolm, she controlled herself enough to say firmly but civilly, "I do not think of my own feelings as an obstacle, my lord."

"I warrant ye'll do what your father tells ye tae do, even so," Malcolm said tersely, "just as any other well-bred young woman must."

Stiffening, with a surge of defiance struggling to leap from her tongue, Katy saw her mother, beyond Malcolm, shake her head and put a finger to her lips.

Tightening her own lips, Katy inhaled a shaky breath and let it out slowly. Though she could see that Malcolm was angry and was sure he understood Scottish law, she was not the one to remind him of it, and Fin had just come into the hall.

He joined them, saying, "I've told your lads outside that they and the rest of your men can bed down in here, in the courtyard, or in the clearing below the knoll, Malcolm. We have pallets to ease the hardness of the hall floor or the courtyard paving stones. And, if you like, you may have the solar to yourself."

"I'd like that fine, lad, but most o' me men will keep tae the forest west o' here, near yon cottages, so as not tae alert any Comyns wha' may be watching Finlagh from your east ridge tae the number o' men we have."

"You sent to Rothiemurchus for Sir Ivor, too, did you not?"

"Aye, sure, and told him tae come in from the west as we did, so he'll be on Clan Chattan land all the way. I mean for our men tae rest tomorrow, for I'll no attack any town on the Sabbath whilst innocent folk be a-going tae kirk. But we hied ourselves here so the men can rest and be ready tae leave afore dawn on Monday, just as we did today."

"Your men, with mine and Cawdor's, may be enough to take the castle."

"I canna trust tae that, though, for we dinna ken how many men Comyn de Raite left tae hold the town, and I dinna want war wi' the man."

"I doubt that de Raite wants war, either," Fin said.

"Perhaps, but I dinna plan for what he may or may not do," Malcolm replied. "I try tae plan for all that the villain *could* do, and this fight be between de Raite and me. When he hanged four of our Mackintoshes six months ago, afore winter set in so hard, I honored me promise tae Mar and his grace, the King, and took nae vengeance. But I'll be hanged m'self afore I let that devil take all o' Nairnshire."

"How many of my men will you need?" Fin asked.

"We'll ha' enough without 'em, for Sir Ivor will bring many and Cawdor and his lot from Strathnairn and Inverness will join us as we go. Ye're tae stay here whilst we head out as quiet-like as we came from your west woods. After all, de Raite likely has watchers and may ha' designs on Finlagh. Meantime, there be one other wee matter we must discuss," he added, looking pointedly at Katy.

Scarcely daring to breathe, she shifted her anxious gaze to her father.

Fin said mildly, "You refer to this notion of yours that Gilli Roy should marry our Katy, aye?"

"Aye, sure, and Gillichallum Roy be willing enough."

"Is he, though? In troth, Malcolm, I have long thought that he and Katy behave more like a brother and his younger sister than young lovers."

"Bah," Malcolm said. "'Tis a close kinship they have is all, and tae my way o' thinking, good friends make good marriages. Forbye, their union will bind our two families more tightly together."

Katy shut her eyes, sent a brief but urgent prayer aloft, and opened them again to watch her father.

"I understand your wishes, Malcolm," Fin said with a slight nod. "Still, Katy is young yet and not, I think, eager to marry. She is also aware of our Scottish laws as they relate to marriage. Had she and Gilli Roy shown tender feelings for each other, I would not stand in their way. But I have told each of my daughters that she will have a strong say in choosing her husband. I cannot ignore that promise now."

Katy relaxed, and her thoughts flew again to Will. She had not told him that the Mackintosh wanted her to marry Gilli, not only because she had been dead set against the notion from the outset, but also because she supposed that Will would tell Aly. She wanted no part in giving such news to the girl for whom Gilli so plainly cared, perhaps loved, and who might even love him.

Malcolm had not yet replied to Fin, but his displeasure was plain to see.

Will awoke Sunday morning wondering how far the Mackintosh might have traveled the day before and how large his army would be when he reached Nairn.

He had heard much about the Mackintosh, the reputedly small and ancient Captain of Clan Chattan, from Granduncle Thomas, and nothing that Thomas had said of Malcolm, as Thomas had always called him, suggested that the man had lost any of his skill. He had, after all, survived not only the Great Clan Battle of Perth four years before the turn of the century but also Harlaw two decades ago and the terrible defeat at Inverlochy less than two years ago. Such a man, aged or not, would not waste time once he knew that Cawdor needed him and his men.

Even so, Will had seen only normal activity the last couple of days, and his father's other watchers had reported no sightings by suppertime that day of aught suggesting an army.

Nonetheless, he remained uneasy. Much as he had disapproved of de Raite's seizure of Nairn, he could not wish disaster on his kinsmen or their men.

Waking at his usual time Monday morning, Will dressed and went downstairs to break his fast before heading back to the ridge. A glance outside had revealed clear, sunny skies, and the morning seemed peaceful.

De Raite, who had beaten him to the high table, even greeted him in a friendly way, so it was a shock to them both minutes later to hear a brief clamor in the courtyard before Colley and Hew strode into the great hall.

"They attacked us and wrested the castle from us afore dawn!" Hew shouted. "Them devils even put four o' our leaders tae the sword!"

Will leaped to his feet. "Where are Jarvis, Liam, Dae, and the rest of our men?" he demanded.

Colley said gruffly, "Jarvis be dead, as well as Fergus Niven o' Badenoch. That old bastard Malcolm killed Jarvis himself when Jarvis challenged him."

Swallowing hard, Will blinked away sudden tears. Jarvis was the one brother who had made any effort to be friendly to him. His sorrow swiftly turned to anger.

"Be damned tae ye, Hew!" de Raite snapped. "Bad enough that ye've lost another o' your brothers. What be ye a-doing here if we still ha' men in Nairn? Ye be their leader, for I put ye in charge! Ye should be wi' them!"

By then, Will had all he could do to avoid turning on his father in pure rage to remind de Raite that he had warned of just such an outcome.

"Gi' me peace, Da," Hew retorted. "Had the castle no had a sally port, Malcolm would ha' killed us, too! We barely escaped. Did ye want us tae die, too?"

When de Raite looked about to erupt, Colley said, "Cousin Dae were in town somewheres wi' Liam and a troop o' our men, a-telling folks ye were claiming the sheriffdom. Liam's nae fool, sir. He'll bring that lot home safe."

"I hope he does," de Raite said grimly. "Not that it matters much now that we've lost the castle, but this will *not* be the end of it. By heaven, I shall inform the Malcolmtosh—aye and Fin of the Battles and Sir Ivor of Rothiemurchus, too—that I mean tae report their defiance o' the agreement that Jamie hisself made betwixt the lot of us tae maintain the peace. But how did ye let this happen, Hew?"

Fists clenched, Will did not stay to hear Hew's excuses. If de Raite could not see the irony in his last few words and his complaint against the Mackintosh for breaking the peace, when de Raite had done the same thing and done it first, Will could think of naught to say to him or to Hew that either would want to hear.

Instead, he headed onto the ridge and had another look at Finlagh Castle from above on his way south. Seeing naught that stirred him to think he might earlier have misrepresented its peacefulness, he continued his usual patrol.

On his way home, the castle still looked undisturbed, but a carefully spread white kerchief decked a bush near the pond above it.

Katy and Clydia had nearly finished preparing for supper Monday evening when Catriona entered their bedchamber to tell them that Malcolm and Cawdor had routed the Comyns and that Malcolm had returned from Nairn with his men.

"Mercy," Clydia exclaimed, "that was quick!"

"Aye, but they did leave here well before dawn," Catriona reminded them. "Now that Cawdor has reclaimed his constabulary and gathered more men to guard the city until he can be sure that all is safe again, Malcolm has decided to go home."

Looking at Katy then, she added, "He will take Gilli Roy with him, love, so you need fret no more about that."

"Is Malcolm still vexed with me?" Katy asked her.

"Not any longer, but be kind to Gilli Roy, for I do think that Malcolm does believe that he ought to have persuaded you."

Although Katy was tempted to tell her about Gilli's Aly, because Catriona usually knew all their secrets, she did not. That secret was Gilli's. Glancing at Clydia, she saw that her twin had evidently found a knot in her lacing.

Downstairs, as the twins crossed the hall toward the dais, Gilli hurried after them and called out Katy's name loudly enough for her to turn to see that he was holding out her kerchief. "One o' ye must ha' dropped this above by yonder pond," he said. "It had blown on tae a bush there."

"Oh, you found it," Katy said, stifling her vexation. "That is mine, Gilli. It got wet, so—" Breaking off when Clydia caught her eye, she shrugged.

"Aye, sure, I see," Gilli said, catching up with them. "Ye forgot it when ye came down from there. I'm glad I saw it, then."

"You have been away all day, Gil," Clydia said. "Where did you go?"

"I didna want tae go wi' the men intae Nairn, as ye might understand," he said. "So I just walked here and about."

"To the Stone?" Katy asked him quietly.

"Aye," he said with a sigh. "I hoped I might ha' a chance tae say good-bye tae Aly, but she wasna there. By me troth, though, it fair gave me a chill tae think about her whilst I were standing there. 'Tis likely I'll never see her again."

Gently, Clydia said, "The Fates may be kinder than that, Gil."

"I hope so," he said. "She says her da's a right villain, though, that he'd likely kill her, did he ever learn she were a-meeting wi' me."

"Then we must pray that he is not so wicked or that he never finds out," Clydia said practically. "In any event, fathers rarely kill their daughters, Gil."

"Some do, though," he said. "Me own cousin slapped his eldest daughter so hard that she hit her head against a stone wall and died."

"Who is Aly's father?" Katy asked him.

Gilli Roy's cheeks reddened. "I dinna ken," he said. "Dinna think I never asked," he added defensively when the twins looked at each other and raised their eyebrows. "I did ask her, but she started a-weeping and said it were best that I knew nae more than what she had told me, which was nobbut her name being Aly. I couldna force her tae tell me, could I?"

"Did you never follow her home?" Katy asked.

He stared at her. "Nae, for she said I must not, and I trusted her word."

Diplomatically, they agreed that he had behaved properly. Katy thanked him again for returning her kerchief, with the unspoken hope that Will had seen it before Gilli retrieved it, and they joined the others at the high table for supper.

Malcolm, Gilli Roy, and Malcolm's men left the next morning for Loch Moigh after breaking their fast with the family.

Malcolm's visit had placed extra demands on the larder at Finlagh but also on the generosity of the cottars in the west woods, who had felt obliged to share aught that they had with the men-at-arms who had slept there. Accordingly, Catriona ordered more baking, and Katy promptly offered to deliver bread to the forest folk that afternoon after the fresh-baked rounds had cooled.

Catriona gave her a searching look that vanished when Clydia offered to accompany her. "Thank you both," she said then. "Give Granny Rosel a hug from me, and tell her I look forward to a visit with her later this week and that I'll bring Ailvie with me. Come to that, you two ought to take Bridgett with you."

Katy bit her lower lip to avoid protest, but Clydia said, "I think Bridgett would liefer stay here, Mam. She told me that Lochan has scarcely spoken to her for days, and she means to find out if he has gone dumb or is just being difficult."

Catriona grinned. "She will catch that man, I think. Bridgett knows her own mind, and I have seen the way Lochan watches her when she crosses the courtyard."

"When she swishes across it, you mean, teasing him with her hips," Katy said with a chuckle. "I have seen that, too."

Laughing then, Catriona left them to their usual chores. While Katy tidied the solar, Clydia made a list of yarns she needed and what fabrics she wanted to inspect on their next visit to the town draper, assuming, she said, that Nairn remained peaceful now that Cawdor was back in charge.

While Katy attended to her chores, she tried to imagine how best to let Clydia know that she wanted to be alone for a time that afternoon, so she could visit the Stone and see if Will was there.

He had said he would try to meet her in midafternoon, after all.

Hours later, as the twins walked from the castle to the woodland cottages with the fresh bread, Katy remained silent, still wondering just what to say.

"What are you scheming now?" Clydia asked with a note of humor in her voice. "Nae, do not look at me as if I were a witch, Kate. You wear your thoughts on your face, as I have oft mentioned before. 'Tis also why I believe you did not accidentally leave the kerchief Gil found yesterday at the pond."

Gritting her teeth, knowing of no way to avoid confiding in Clydia but knowing, too, that her twin would honor her confidence, Katy said, "I want you to let me have time to myself later and not tell anyone else."

"It must be that Will again then, aye?"

"Aye," Katy admitted with a sigh. "I like him, Clydie, more than I can put into words, and I trust him, too."

"Good sakes, Kate, his father, Aly's father, is a villainous man, according to Gilly Roy. As I have been pondering that, disturbing possibilities have been stirring in my mind. Just now, as I thought of you meeting Will on the peak, I realized that he likely heard you or saw you from the ridge. What if he is a Comyn of Raitt and was watching us?"

Katy felt a chill but quickly rallied. "He *cannot* be, Clydie. If he were, he would have captured me just as those Comyn villains captured Àdham shortly after he returned from Inverlochy two years ago. Will is too kind to do such things."

"So you think, but how can you trust someone you barely know, Kate? That sounds as daft as Lochan telling Bridgett he loved her when he scarcely knew her."

"Mayhap it does, but I do," she insisted. "Not only did Will save my life, but my trusting him seems to be much the same thing that you mentioned when you said it scarcely surprised you when he stepped out from behind the tree that day, because you'd had that odd feeling that someone was nigh, but felt no real fear."

"Trust is much different, though," Clydia replied. "The other seems more of a warning sense to make one wary of whatever one is about to do. Trust is—"

"—trust," Katy interjected. "One trusts or one doesn't, that's all. One feels safe, and I feel as safe with Will as I do with you or Mam or Da."

"Do you not think that we should ask Da about these feelings, then? He must have them, too, so he is likely to know more than we do about what causes them."

"Then, ask him if you like. I still want time to myself this afternoon. I mean to take a walk, Clydie . . . alone."

"Where will you meet him?"

"I shan't tell you, because if Da or Mam asks you where I am, you would have to tell them. This way, you can honestly say you don't know."

Clydia gave her a long, measuring look and nodded. "Aye, then we will begin our visits at the farthest cottage. But if you are not back before supper . . ."

"I will be," Katy promised. "I do not mean to go more than a short distance from the knoll, not beyond hailing distance."

Clydia still looked doubtful, but Katy knew the words were true. After all, if the dense canopy of trees did not conceal the Stone, men on the ramparts would see it. So if Will should be so daft as to threaten her, those men would hear her scream.

CHAPTER 10

Fearing that he might miss Katy and hoping it was as safe for her to meet him at the standing stone as he thought it was, Will had abandoned the ridge much earlier. He had been waiting for over an hour at the Stone, his ears alert for the faintest sound of her approach or that of anyone else. The woods were alive with songbirds and other creatures, all behaving normally.

He even heard the shrill, repetitive *kee-kee-kee* of a kestrel, though he could not spot the bird. Its chestnut-brown and gray coloring would match the trunks and branches of most trees in that dense woodland.

The familiar sounds, scents, and feeling of peacefulness relaxed him. The day was warm, and he did not mind sitting on the flat rock he had found amidst thick shrubbery a short way from the huge stone.

He could see it easily through the foliage, so he would see her when she approached. So sure was he that he would hear her coming that when his thoughts drifted again to Jarvis's death, he forced his attention abruptly to a pair of baby gray squirrels chasing each other, flinging themselves from branch to branch of the trees.

Moments later, though, his mind's eye presented another image of Jarvis with the doubtless bloody sword plunging into him. Emotion struck so strongly then that he scarcely knew it as grief, making him wince and shut his eyes. When he opened them,

Katy—in a pink kirtle, with her thick wheaten plaits reaching over her bosom to her waist—stood silently by the Stone, peering into nearby bushes.

Feeling better at once, Will raised his hand and stood.

"Good, you *are* here," she said, smiling as she pushed first one and then the other dangling plait back over her shoulders and moved to stand before him, her beautiful eyes alight with pleasure. "Have you waited long?"

"Nae," he said, though he knew he had been there at least an hour, perhaps two. Now that she was here, though, smiling as she was, it did not seem to have been long at all. Studying her face, he seemed bereft of words, so he said the first thing that came to mind, "I never noticed that wee scar before. How—?"

"Stairs," she said, "when I was four. My parents kept telling me not to run up them, but I always did, and so . . ." She shook her head. "I don't want to talk about that. I . . . I wanted to see you and . . ." She looked at him so hungrily that without a thought he opened his arms. When she walked into them, gazing up and raising her arms to rest her hands gently on his shoulders, he needed no further invitation.

Her lips were warm and soft against his, and she kissed him back, igniting the same fires that just holding her had ignited in him before, plus new ones. When her right hand moved to his cheek and stroked it, his body stirred immediately He touched her lips with his tongue and then pressed it gently between them.

To his surprise, she opened them.

For a pleasant few minutes, as his tongue probed the velvet softness of her mouth, he thought of nothing but Katy and the rightness of holding her in his arms. She fit as if God meant her to be there. He wanted to hold her forever.

When a squirrel chattered loudly nearby as if it had heard his thoughts and disapproved, he heard Katy chuckle low in her throat. She tilted her head back and looked up at him with her infectious grin.

"I have never before been kissed like that," she said. "Nor did I ever suppose that I'd let a man put his tongue in my mouth or that it could feel so right there."

"I'm glad you've not done it before," he said, smiling. "I like knowing that I'm the first to do it."

"Do it again," she murmured, and he was happy to oblige, so for a time, they kissed and stroked each other, murmuring soft words and urging each other on, until Will began to feel a different, stronger urgency for something more dangerous.

Forcing himself to stop, he kissed her one more time, gently, and held her a little away from himself. "We should stop now, I think, and perhaps talk more."

"Aye, then, but I'm glad I found you here," she replied. "It has been a fine day altogether, for you must have heard about the Mackintosh and Cawdor taking Nairn Castle and the town back from the wicked Comyns who seized it."

"I heard," Will said, as the appalling image of Jarvis and the bloody sword leaped again to his mind's eye. "They put four of the leaders to the sword."

"Aye, perhaps, but if it is so, it was a kinder fate than when Comyn de Raite hanged four innocent Mackintoshes by the neck from his gateposts and watched them strangle to death. Those Mackintoshes had broken *no* law."

"That is true," Will said with a sense of foreboding.

She looked narrowly at him. "You seem suddenly . . . unhappy. Nae, you look sad, or . . . Mercy, did you *know* them?"

Meeting her astonished and then wary gaze, he felt tightness in his throat. Nevertheless, knowing he could no longer keep silent, let alone defend his behavior, he said gruffly, "One of the men they put to the sword was my older brother Jarvis."

She stared at him long enough for him to note that the forest had fallen silent.

"Do you mean that you are *one* of them, one of those wicked Comyns?" she demanded. "But you cannot be! I ken fine that you were not with them, for I saw you myself on our slope with Aly the day they seized the castle in Nairn. You are *not* one of them! Prithee, Will, tell me that you are n—"

"My name is Will Comyn," he interjected bluntly. "De Raite is my father."

"Nae!" She turned abruptly away, seemed to hug herself, and

then whirled back, flinging out her arms. Without shrieking, keeping her voice low but hurling the words at him as if they were stones, she said, "I *trusted* you! God-a-mercy, but I defended you! And now . . . *now* you tell me that you are one of those . . . those devilish Comyns! How *could* you?"

With the last three words, control fled. Her right hand flew up, aiming hard and fast for his left cheek, and although he knew he deserved her scorn *and* her fury, he caught her hand before it made contact and held it tight.

"Nae, my lady," he said. "I have let only one person, your twin, strike me with impunity since I was twelve, and I'll not let it happen again even for you."

When Katy tensed, as if she meant to try again anyway if he were foolish enough to give her the chance, he gave her a stern but silent look.

After a tense moment, with a sigh, her hand in his relaxed and he let it fall back to her side. "You are wiser than I thought," he said, meeting her gaze again.

"I am not a fool, so I won't test my strength against yours, Will, but I will *never* forgive you for this."

"Sakes, lass, I cannot help that I was born a Comyn, nor does my being one change the strong feelings I have had for you since the day we met."

"It changes mine, though," she retorted, "because I trusted you, and you betrayed that trust." Twisting her hands together, she glowered at him as if she expected him to defend himself.

But, although he had never lied to her, by concealing his full identity he had deceived her. Knowing of no acceptable defense for that, he kept silent.

With a sound more akin to a beastly growl than any he had ever heard from so small a female, she turned on her heel and stormed away back toward Finlagh.

He did not try to stop her.

"He does not even *care* that he betrayed me," Katy told herself as she forced her way through the dense underbrush and back through the forest the way she had come. "He stood there. How could he not say *something*? How could he have been a Comyn all along and not *told* me? Why did I never *guess* that he was, even when Clydia suggested it?"

Recalling moments when she might have pressed harder—in truth, when she ought to have demanded that he reveal his family name and clan, she grimaced. "How could I have been such a fool?"

She knew what her mother would say about that, aye, and Clydia, too—that she had not *wanted* to know, that she had likely resisted every chance that arose to demand the information. They would be right, too, and this, now, was her reward.

Tears welled in her eyes, but she dashed them away angrily with the backs of both hands. Shrubbery tugged at her clothing, branches whipped her arms, and one narrow, leafy branch brushed right across her face. She ignored them all.

"By the Rood, he ought to have said *something*," she insisted. "He did not even apologize. He just stood there, looking sad or hurt or . . . or— Sakes, what will Clydia say when I have to tell her that he is a wicked Comyn? What if Da finds out? At least Gilli is gone . . . Mercy, poor Gilli Roy!"

Malcolm would flay Gilli if he learned that he had been secretly meeting Comyn de Raite's daughter. "And, despite all Gilli had said to the contrary, he *must* know who she is," Katy decided, awed by the thought. She had never thought of Gilli Roy being at all brave.

At least Clydia was not one to crow, and she would be pleased that Katy was keeping her promise to be back before supper. In fact, she had scarcely been away long enough for anyone else to note her absence. Skirting the clearing below the castle knoll from east to west, she crossed it from the west side as she would have had she merely visited Granny Rosel and her neighbors.

Entering the hall, she saw both Argus and Eos curled by the fireplace and men setting up trestles for supper in the lower hall. Looking toward the dais, she saw her mother step out of the inner chamber behind it and catch her eye.

"Oh, good, you've returned, dearling," Cat said. "Prithee, come into the inner chamber before you go upstairs. Your father and I want to talk to you."

A shiver shot up Katy's spine at those words. What if her parents had learned where she had been and with whom? Clydia would not have betrayed her, but Fin and Catriona had oft seemed to be all knowing.

Seeing no help for it, she went to the dais, where Cat waited for her to enter the chamber first. Katy nearly sighed in relief at seeing Clydia there with Fin.

Oddly, Bridgett and her mother, Ailvie, were there, too.

When Catriona had shut the door behind her, Fin said, "I'm glad you are back, Katy, because I've had news that affects all of us. You may sit if you like, all of you," he added. "But this should not take long."

The women took seats, watching him with varied degrees of wariness.

"I have had a message from Comyn de Raite, signing himself as 'Sir Gervaise Comyn de Raite,' as we know he now styles himself. The message is formal warning that he is sending word to his grace, James, King of Scots, charging Malcolm of Clan Chattan and Donald, Thane of Cawdor, with transgressing his grace's explicit order that they maintain the peace in Nairnshire."

Katy said, "But *he* is the one—"

"Nae, lass," Fin interjected with a wry smile. "Everyone here sees the irony in de Raite's charges, so let me finish what I have to say. Then you may add whatever you like. I have sent a runner after Malcolm to warn him of Comyn de Raite's threat, but I'll wager that Malcolm pays it less heed than I do, because we both know that most people in Nairnshire will support Malcolm's actions, and Cawdor's. After all, Jamie himself confirmed Cawdor's constabulary. He is unlikely to pay Comyn's charges much heed, if any."

"Marry," Katy said when he stopped. "I should think his grace would charge Comyn instead with breaking the peace."

"I think Jamie would like to clap him in irons, but he has said that he prefers to keep him at Raitt, where he is farther from other dissident but still scattered Comyns, rather than go elsewhere to wreak his havoc. Sithee, de Raite would like to reunite his clan and gain more territory for himself, and though Malcolm upset this recent foray, de Raite has a short temper and may try other attacks."

"What are you going to do, sir?" Katy asked, fearing that he would confine them to the castle. Despite Finlagh's strategic location, the castle was ill suited for siege conditions. Though it looked large, it was in truth too small to contain the cottars, other tenants, and all the men-at-arms who would seek shelter within its walls. Poultry and sheep required shelter, too, because everyone had to be fed.

Fin smiled as if he were reading her thoughts. "I am going to ask you all to be more cautious. We are well situated to see an impending attack from any direction. I will add more watchers, but I'd like those of you who enjoy solitary walks"—he looked directly at his lady wife before shifting his gaze to Katy—"to take more precautionary measures, such as walking in pairs or taking the dogs with you. I would also ask you to let others know exactly where you mean to go and how long you mean to be away. If you cannot agree—"

"We will," Catriona said. "Will we not, *everyone*?" She looked right at Katy.

"Aye, Mam," Katy said, thinking it would not matter, because she was no longer speaking to Will. The thought stirred an unexpected but strong sense of injury and sadness that threatened to overwhelm her until Clydia spoke.

"Da, you have made me remember something I wanted to ask you."

"Aye, sure, Clydia-lass, what is it?"

"Katy and I were discussing the odd feeling, sometimes a chill that one gets now and now, as if someone is watching us or danger lurks ahead, though one seems to have little reason to suspect such a thing. Do you know what I mean?"

"Aye, sure," Fin said. "That feeling has saved my life—and if not my life, then surely my reputation as a knight—a number of times. Such sensations are mental warnings to which you should pay heed."

"But what causes them?" Katy asked.

"I can tell you what I learned as a lad at St. Andrews when I was there with your uncle Ivor and others that the bishops had agreed to educate. Bishop Traill called the sensation 'intuition,' which derives from the ancient Romans and refers to an instinct that one might define as a flurry of thoughts, facts, common sense, experiences, and random incidents noted over time, coming together in a blink and giving one pause. Traill said that such intuition can fling itself together so fast that your body sometimes reacts without thought. Always, though, it is cause for reflection, such as paying more heed to your surroundings. Each one is a warning, though it can produce anything from a mere pause for thought right up to a jolt of true terror. That last one is the sensation that he advised us always to heed and *instantly* obey."

"But how?" Clydia asked.

"In my own experience, by changing one's intended action or direction as swiftly and sensibly as possible."

"But how does one know the difference between just being wary or wondering and true fear?" Katy asked.

"I don't know that one stops to measure such differences," Fin said. "I can tell you that once, when I had such a jolt in the midst of a battle, I flung myself aside without a thought and just missed losing my head to a chap behind me already swinging his sword. I'd had no warning, but I knew instantly that I had to move, so I did. I didn't *feel* as if I'd merely blinked. I felt as if I'd had time to recall my exact position, which way to go, and how fast. It was as if all the action around me had slowed, though of course it had not. Traill told us similar tales of other warriors."

"Did he explain how one might know everything that one must know to act sensibly in such a case?" Clydia asked.

"He explained that things others have said, myriad facts, seemingly innocent warning signs, and other knowledge acquired from birth onward collect in one's mind and push themselves forward as one thought when they are needed. He could not explain how the process itself works. It just does, he said, and one should always trust and heed such instincts if one desires to live a long life."

Katy sighed. Clearly, such instincts did not include the one that had told her she could trust Will Comyn.

❖ ❖ ❖

Will had kept an eye on the direction in which Katy stormed off in her fury and listened for sounds of her return or an unfortunate result of her impulsive flight. Hearing only the sounds of shrubbery being thrust aside, he turned gloomily homeward.

He had taken just a few steps when an indignant young voice behind him said, "Ye should ha' told her straightaway who ye were, ye dafty!"

Turning sharply, Will saw a fair-haired lad of eleven or twelve in front of the Stone, glowering as if he resented not being big enough to strike him down.

"I thought I kent all o' ye Comyn villains, but I dinna ken ye," the boy went on, looking scornful. "If ye be brother tae Jarvis, ye must be the bairn what the auld laird sent away tae grow up wi' his ain kin near Inverness."

"You seem extraordinarily knowledgeable about my kinsmen," Will said.

"Aye, sure, for I bided wi' them for a time till I grew sick o' them," the boy said. "Sithee, old Rab . . . ye'd ken Rab fine, I warrant," he added, cocking his head.

"I knew him when I was much younger than you are, but Rab is dead."

"Aye, sure, at Lochaber, for I saw Sir Àdham kill him when Rab tried tae kill Sir Àdham first. And that feardie Hew . . . he ran off, so I stayed wi' Sir Àdham, and he brung me tae Finlagh. Did yer Inverness kinsmen grow sick o' ye, then?"

"Nae, my father sent for me after Rab died."

"Did ye no fight at Lochaber, then? I were there, wi' Rab and them, 'cause Rab and Hew made me fetch and carry for them. But they were vile tae me, and their da be a fair demon hisself, so I stayed at Finlagh, and I like it fine."

Will frowned. "What's your name, and where did you spring from now?"

The boy jerked a thumb at the Stone. "I were standin' ahind yon great rock."

"So you were listening to us, the lady Katy and me."

"Aye sure, for I followed Lady Katy, 'cause she didna take the dogs, so I heard all that the pair o' ye said tae each other. Ye made her gey angry, and I dinna wonder. Why did ye no tell her who ye were from the start?"

"Because I wanted to know her better, and I feared she would hate me if she knew I was a Comyn," Will said frankly. "Sithee, lad, I am not like the others."

"Talk dinna mean nowt, though. Ye'll ha' tae show us ye're no like 'em."

"You're right about that, but you owe Lady Katy an apology, too."

The boy grimaced. "Ye dinna think I should ha' stayed quiet ahind yon rock. I didna think I should interrupt ye whilst ye talked, though, either o' ye, and when ye started a-kissing her, I—"

"Nevertheless, you must tell Lady Katy that you heard us," Will interjected firmly. "If you do not and she finds out some other way that you did hear and see us, you will be in for it, my lad. I want to know your name."

"I'm Rory," the boy said. "I were just a-looking out for our Lady Katy."

Will raised his eyebrows and waited.

"Aye, then, I'll tell her," the boy said in a rush of words. "Like as not, she'll be wroth wi' me, but she never stays angry long, though."

Will was glad to hear those last words but feared that Katy would remain true to her own word and never trust him again.

"What do you mean, he betrayed your trust?" Clydia demanded after she had dragged the tale out of Katy as they prepared for bed. "However did he betray it?"

"Good sakes, by not telling me at the outset exactly who he is, of course."

"But you told me you trusted him completely, right from the start."

"I did!"

"Did you tell *him* you are Katy MacFinlagh, daughter of Fin of the Battles?"

"Nae, but I never—" Katy stopped, pressing her lips together.

After some thought, she said, "You mean I did not trust him enough to tell him all that, but you know we never give more information to people we meet than we must, so I expect you think Will likely acts the same way when he is on land other than his own."

"Just so," Clydia said. "I think the feeling that you could trust him had more to do with your sense of safety than with his name or kinsmen. You trusted him not to harm you, Kate, and that trust *does* seem to have been well placed, aye?"

Katy hesitated, pondering the thought. "I do still believe he would not harm me physically, but that does not ease my anger with him."

"Nor should it," Clydia said. "He deserves your anger."

Katy nodded but wondered if she could trust even her thoughts about Will. However, images of him and thoughts of what they had been doing before she had mentioned Nairn kept flowing through her mind, and she could not stop thinking about him. Right before she finally slept, she realized that she wanted to see him again. That thought lingered and leaped into her mind again when she awoke Wednesday morning to find that the shearing of their sheep had begun.

Although the twins had little to do with the shearing, they did help with the resulting wool and with supervising the washing and carding of it. The ensuing chaos—with lambs and sheep bawling and shearers and other helpers shouting out orders, needs, and replies, and often arguing about whether the world would end or not in less than a sennight—was such that Katy knew she would not get away that day. Nor did things settle to a normal rhythm until midway through Thursday.

Even then, their parents kept the twins too busy to think of escape. They did not trouble their heads about the prophecy, though, because Fin had said it was daft.

Accordingly, as soon as Katy had broken her fast early Friday morning, she told her mother she was going out to walk with the dogs while the day was still chilly and would return in an hour or so to finish her chores. Then, collecting Argus and Eos, she headed out into the courtyard and met Rory striding toward her.

"I been a-looking for ye," he said, stopping in front of her. "I ha' tae tell ye summat, but I ha' scarce clapped eyes on ye, and I dinna want ye a-ringin' a peal over me till I finish the tellin'. So, keep hold o' your temper that long, if ye can."

Amused, and curious as to what mischief he had created this time, she said, "Tell me quickly, for I mean to walk about the hillside, and I have chores yet to do."

"Aye, well, I can be quick enough. See you, I saw the way ye was a-heading t'other day, and I feared ye might run intae trouble by yourself. So, I followed ye, and when ye came tae that great tower o' rock a-sticking up out o' the earth as it does, I slithered in ahind it, like, tae wait and see where ye'd go next."

"You should not have done that, Rory, not without telling me. I might have liked to have your company."

"I ha' me doots about that," he said with a grimace. "I were just a-looking out for ye, as ye might say."

Knowing from experience that she was unlikely to hear more to excuse his behavior by pressing him, Katy said bluntly, "How much did you overhear?"

Just as bluntly, he said, "Near all that ye said tae the man, and he tae ye. Afore ye rip me head off, though, I can tell ye that he kens what I did, and he kens what I think o' his keepin' such a secret from ye. Then, he said I owed ye an apology, too, meaning— I think—that he kens fine that he owes ye one, hisself."

Katy stared at the boy, her thoughts racing. Will's expressions, tones, and demeanor had been easy for her to read from the start. Could a child read him as well? And how much could she trust the child?

"Have you said aught to anyone else about this, Rory?"

With a look indignant enough to tell her she had offended him, he said, "I wouldna do that, no tae your ladyship or tae anyone in your family. I owe much tae Sir Àdham for a-rescuing me when he did and tae Sir Fin for letting me stay, so unless Sir Fin asks me straight out . . ."

"I know," she replied with a sympathetic smile. "No one hesitates then."

"Where be ye a-heading the noo?" Rory asked her.

"Just for a walk," Katy said airily. "Mayhap up to the pool

or a bit further. I'm taking both dogs, though, just as Da said I must."

"Good, then," Rory said. "I'll just tell anyone who asks me, direct, that that be where ye be a-going and that ye've took the dogs along."

Something in his manner, perhaps his own airiness, gave Katy to understand that he suspected exactly where she might be going.

Dismissing him, she wondered if she might intercept Will on his way south for the day. If he wanted to apologize, she would give him that chance, but she also wanted to apologize for losing her temper. Clydia had been right about the manner of her trust. She did still trust Will not to harm her physically, and to have blamed him so fiercely for doing something she had done herself was unfair.

Accordingly, she signaled the dogs to accompany her and went out the gate and up to the pool, pausing there long enough to splash her hands and feet in the water before entering the woods and making her way to the eastern slope.

Argus ranged back and forth ahead while Eos stayed beside her. She knew that both dogs would alert her to anyone approaching from any direction, so she aimed a bit uphill and a little southward to make up for Will's longer stride.

However, when the dogs perked their ears and changed direction slightly northward, their tails were not wagging as they would have been for Will. Clicking her tongue and patting her thigh, she drew them back to her and slipped into thicker shrubbery with them to see who it was before the person approaching saw her.

CHAPTER II

Katy gasped when she saw Aly striding along above her in a simple pale green kirtle without so much as a light cloak over it to ward off the chill in the air.

She was about halfway between Katy's position and the ridge crest, with her attention firmly fixed on the way ahead of her, so she failed to see Katy and the dogs emerge from the bushes. Katy hurried after her until they had gone far enough for her to call out without fear that anyone at Finlagh would hear her.

When she did, Aly started and clapped a hand to her mouth as she turned, but when Katy smiled and waved, the younger girl waved back and hurried to meet her.

Katy wore her favorite pink and tawny-gold-striped shawl over a dun-colored kirtle with yellow lacing. Despite the shawl, she felt ice in the morning air.

"You must be chilled through," she said as Aly drew nearer.

Aly was warily watching the dogs, but when both of them lay down a short distance away, she said, "Nae, I have been hurrying, so I be warm enough, and I didna take a shawl out, for my father was at home when I left. He'll be away by now, but he thought I meant only tae go with my maidservant, Meggie, tae the clachan near Raitt where our tenants abide."

"But it could be dangerous for you out here, alone as you are."

"Aye, but you be alone, too, save for yon great dogs," Aly pointed out. "Moreover, my father kens fine that your people wouldna hurt a lone lassie. Sakes, even he wouldna do that."

"But you might . . ." Katy began, only to stop with a wry grimace. "Just listen to me telling you not to do the very thing I love doing myself," she said. "I must learn to think more before I offer advice to other people."

"'Tis a common failing," Aly said, nodding. "My brothers oft tell me no tae do things they do theirselves. I canna be away long, though. Meggie willna return till I do, but I'd hoped tae catch up with Will, though I have me doots now that I can. He'll likely be fashed an I do catch him, but . . ." She shrugged.

Recognizing a kindred spirit, Katy wanted to know more about Will. "Has he a favorite track that he follows?"

"I think so. He seems oft tae come this way, though mayhap higher up on the ridge. I ken fine that he be trespassing—me, too, now—but when my father says tae do summat, my brothers do it. I shouldna be talking tae you as I am, but I like you. You be a canny lass, I think. Be it true that your sister looks just like you?"

"Aye, though we are not as much alike on the inside as we are on the outside. Clydia is more practical and possesses a calmer nature than mine."

"Clydia be a fine name," Aly said. "After the river Clyde, aye?"

"Aye," Katy said, adding quickly, "How long before you left home this morning did Will leave? Do you think he is far from here by now?"

"I fear so," Aly said with a sigh. "I didna wait tae see him go, for I feared my father might guess I wanted tae follow him. I try never tae fash my father."

"'Tis always unwise to do that," Katy agreed. "I had hoped to see Will, myself. I . . . I was angry and a bit unfair with him the other day, I fear."

"That explains his moods then," Aly said, nodding wisely. "He has been sad these past two days. Whatever happened, I suspect he regrets his part in it."

Impulsively, Katy said, "Would you give him a message for me?"

"Aye, sure, if I see him alone. If he doesna ha' tae practice his weaponry wi' the others, he does oft visit wi' me in the solar afore I seek me bedchamber."

"Then tell him . . . tell him we are shearing our sheep, which will take a few more days to finish, but to watch the shrubs again by Tuesday or Wednesday."

"I dinna ken which shrubs you mean."

"Just say that that's my message to him."

Looking puzzled for a moment, Aly said, "Och, aye, then it must be a secret message. I'll tell Will, but I do wish our fathers could be friends, m'lady."

"Just Katy," she said. "*We* are friends now, Aly, you and I. I ken fine that you would rather be meeting Gilli Roy than me, but he has gone home. Even so, if ever you need me, come to Finlagh and ask for me. Come to that, if you walk this way and chance to meet one of our men, just tell him that you are my friend."

"I would like tae see Gil again," Aly said wistfully. "Are you going tae marry him? He did tell me his father wants the pair of you tae wed."

"We are not going to, though," Katy said firmly. "Gilli is my cousin, and I like him, but I do not want to marry him, and so I did tell his father."

Aly's eyes widened. "Ay-de-mi, you said that straight tae the Mackintosh?"

"I did," Katy said, realizing from those innocent few words that Aly did know who Gilli was, which meant that he had known all along that she was Alyssa Comyn. "We must not linger any longer," Katy added. "Will may oft cross our land with impunity but only because he walks alone and is therefore no threat to us. Safe as you are here, it would be best if none of our men sees you. If you had to reveal your name, word of that might spread to town and one of your own menfolk might hear of it."

"I'll keep out of everyone's way, and I'll tell Will what you said. You're no still angry with him then, aye?"

"Not as angry as I was. I'll know better how I feel, though, when I see him."

As she watched Aly walk up the slope, heading northward,

Katy could think only of Will. Her thoughts returned to him frequently that day until she went to bed.

Would he be glad to learn that she wanted to meet him, or irked?

The following Tuesday afternoon, with the shearing done, Katy washed seven kerchiefs at the pond and spread them on nearby shrubs to dry.

The next morning, realizing it was the seventeenth of June, the day the wise woman Janet Fortune had predicted the world would end, and hoping that no one would order her to stay inside, Katy rushed through her morning chores, finished her midday meal in haste, and slipped away from the castle to the standing stone.

The day was warm, the sky clear and bright with sunshine. As she passed through the shrubbery, she felt more aware than ever of the cheerful birds, the buzzing of bees over flowering shrubs, and the aromatic small yellow flowers that newly carpeted the ground beneath the forest bracken. Soft whispers, above her, suggested stray breezes stroking leaves in the green canopy. Honeysuckle grew in a few open spaces, drawing more bees, until the woods seemed alive with chirps, buzzes, chatter, and more raucous birdcalls. The world, she thought as the Stone came into view, seemed too much alive to be ending today.

Will, wearing the familiar plain linen, knee-length tunic under his brown-and-green plaid, was waiting when she arrived and held out his arms to her.

She ran right into them and hugged his warm, muscular body without a word, breathing in the herbal scent of the soft wool plaid as she let him hold her even closer for a long few moments of pure relief. She had not known before then how much she had feared she had destroyed the friendship that, in such a short time, had come to mean more to her than she had realized.

Looking up at him, noting that he had not shaved in days and that his scruffy beard was darker than his sun-streaked light brown hair, she murmured, "I am deeply sorry, Will. When anger seizes me, I forget to think, let alone to listen."

"Nae, lassie," he replied gently, still holding her. "You have no need for apologies. You were right, because I should have told you who I was as soon as I even suspected who your father might be. I own, though, I feared you would walk away if I did, so your fury came as no surprise to me when you did find out."

"But I never told you exactly who I was, either. You just guessed, and I don't want to talk more of that, so prithee tell me that you did not scold Aly for coming into our woods by herself on Friday. She was trying to follow you, you know."

"I do know, and she ought not to do it, so she deserved scolding. She brought me a message, though, that was too important for me to do aught but thank her."

Katy smiled, wishing she could stay in his arms for hours. "Don't talk then, Will," she said. "Kiss me again, instead. This is our kissing stone now, after all."

"Aye, sure," he said, and did so until she moaned with pleasure, when he spread his plaid on the dry leaves of the small clearing before the Stone and drew her down to sit on it beside him. Then, leaning against the Stone and embracing her again so that she leaned against him, he said lightly, "Did that wee rascal Rory chance to tell you he followed you here and witnessed our last meeting?"

"He did," she said, stroking his beard and finding it soft to the touch. "He also said he scolded you. In fact, he said you told him that he, *too*, owed me an apology. And that, he said, was how he knew you were as sorry as I was about our fratching. So, kiss me again, sir."

Obeying, he made a good job of it and soon eased her down to lie beside him. She had a feeling that she ought to protest when he moved a hand to her waist, letting his thumb stroke the side of her breast along the way, but the sensation he stirred was too pleasurable for her to object. As he continued to stroke her in this and other ways, excited by his efforts and striving to please him with similar touches and strokes, she wished they could go on so forever but knew they could not.

Just at that moment, as if he had heard her thoughts, he shifted himself to lean against the tree again and said quietly as he drew her back into the shelter of his arms, "I may have to be away for a time soon."

"Why?"

"Because de Raite wants to meet with Comyn factions from Badenoch and Inverness-shire, and some of our other allies in Glen Mòr. He says it is useful for us to make regular contact and conference with all of our allies to assure that we can depend on them if we need them. I would agree that such is of import, but I cannot recall his having any such meeting since my return to Raitt."

"You have not always lived there?"

"I left when I was seven and returned less than two years ago," he said. "Sithee, I'm much younger than my brothers. So, soon after Aly was born and our mother died, de Raite sent me to live with his uncle, Thomas Comyn. Thomas refers to himself and his close kinfolk now as Cummings rather than Comyn, because he disapproves of de Raite. He rarely talked of him to me, other than to tell me I would eventually have to return to serve my duty to de Raite as his son."

"Do you always call your father 'de Raite'?"

"Aye, for 'tis how he calls himself now, and it seems daft to call someone 'Father' whom I scarcely knew as such. Before Mam died, I rarely saw him, so I felt no love for him, but I did know and love my mother. I miss her to this day."

"I cannot imagine how hard that must have been, to lose her as you did," Katy said. "My father can be stern and has a quick temper, but we always know that he loves us. As for Mam . . ." She stopped, unable to put into words how she would feel if anything happened to take Catriona from them.

"I think you will likely be a fine mother one day, like your own mam, who is a lady much respected hereabouts." He looked into her eyes. "You will think me daft, lass, if I say what I'm thinking now."

"Say it, anyway," Katy said, her breath catching in her throat.

Her body seemed to hum. Never had she felt such an attraction, let alone such a strong bond, to anyone. She had thought she could read her mother and father well, but at times with Will, despite their short acquaintance, she felt as if she knew his thoughts before he spoke them, because the man wore his feelings on his face and in every line of his body. If this was such a time . . .

"You *will* think me daft," he said then. "But I feel as if I have known you all my life, and I have wanted you for my own since the day we met. I just wish we could magically create peace between our clans, so that we might somehow marry, because I do think you would make me a fine and fascinating wife and our children a wonderful, loving mother. Even if it weren't such a daft idea, though—"

"But it isn't," Katy said, squeezing his arms tightly in her excitement. "I know just how we can do it."

Will shook his head. "Nae, *mo chridhe*, it cannot be, and I am a villain for suggesting that such a match could ever take place between us. Even if your father were willing to let you marry a Comyn, mine would likely have me flogged if I suggested such a marriage to him, or hang me himself."

"But if we married, you could live at Finlagh," she said. "Or we could build a home of our own in Nairn or Inverness . . . or somewhere else. In any event, sir, if you meant what you said, I do know a way, because the mendicant friar, Brother Julian, explained it all when he visited us."

"The same Brother Julian who brought news of the plague in the Borders and that crazy woman's prophecy that the world will soon end?"

"Aye, and come to that, Will, you must know that today is the day she predicted it *would* end. Da says she is daft and that the world has survived many such predictions. But suppose she is right? If you meant what you just said to me, we need only declare ourselves married to *be* married. Then," she added, "if she is right, we will die together and be together for eternity."

He shook his head. "How can that be, Katy-love?"

"'Tis what Brother Julian called 'marriage by declaration.'"

Will grinned. "That sounds even dafter than my yearnings."

"Aye, well, I believe Brother Julian. I am certain that it is a legal form of marriage, so I hereby declare us married, Will Comyn. Will you deny it?"

Still amused, he said, "Nae, sweetheart, I'll not deny it, but neither will I agree to consummate such a union on the mere possibility of its being real."

"Consummate our union?"

"Aye, you do know how bairns are made, do you not?"

She had been gazing at his chest, but she looked up then, her eyes widening as she said, "Aye," making it difficult for him to restrain his increasing amusement.

"Never mind that now, lassie mine," he said. "We—"

"Will?" Her tone was wary, even concerned, and her eyes had widened more than ever.

"What is it, Katy-love? You know I will do naught to harm you."

"I do know that, but it is getting colder, Will, though the sun still shines. The birds have quieted, too, and so have the bees." She scrambled to her feet. "Mercy, Will, but I no longer *see* any bees or hear any forest creatures. The light seems dimmer, too, although there are no clouds and 'tis only midafternoon."

Realizing she was right, he stood, too, and picked up his plaid. In mere minutes, the temperature had dropped and shadows were paler, as if thin clouds obscured the sun.

"Faith, sir, look up through the leaves! The sun is vanishing! I can see but a narrow curved edge of it left, as if all the rest had darkened!"

Following her gaze as well as he could through the canopy, he saw that she was right. The orange edge of the sun had narrowed under a dark, round shadow. As he tried to make sense of it, he noted that the once hushing breeze through the trees had grown stronger, as if it were striving to become a strong wind. Leaves kept obscuring his view. The woods had darkened, too, as if night were fast coming on.

Distant screams sounded then from east and west, echoing eerily.

Whispering as if she feared being overheard, and clinging tightly to him, Katy said, "It *is* the end of the world, Will. Marry, but Janet Fortune *did* predict it. Just pray tell me it is not my fault for being so undutiful to my parents in my feelings for you or my declaration of marriage in defiance of our usual custom."

Although the disappearance of the sun behind what was now clearly a round black shadow was an unusual and worrisome event, possibly even an omen of disaster, Will had heard Thomas talk of similar events and managed to force calm into his voice as he said, "Even if the world does end, Katy, it would not be your fault or mine. Only God has such power."

It occurred to him, though, that in view of all the violence of late, the event could well be an omen direct from God. Perhaps the Almighty was annoyed with the behavior of his mortals on Earth and had decided to give them strong warning.

He thought of the forthcoming meetings with other Comyns and wondered if de Raite had more than mere talk and strengthening comradeship in mind.

A halo of wispy white, like a smoky crown, surrounded the blackness above. The wind increased. The forest creatures remained silent.

"Don't leave me," Katy muttered.

"Nae, I won't," he said. "In troth, I do not believe that the world is ending, for I once saw a similar shadow, myself, covering the moon. My uncle called it an 'eclipse.' 'Tis an awesome, fearsome sight, though. Doubtless many are terrified."

"What if it *is* a sign that God objects to our marriage?"

"Then our marriage will not come to pass, Katy-love."

"But it has," she insisted. "Brother Julian said such a marriage is legal."

"Nevertheless, we are still standing and alive, Katy. If we were to blame for aught of this nature, do you not suppose God has power enough to destroy the two of us without terrifying everyone else?"

He felt her relax a little, but she still held him close.

The once clear and sunny day had darkened to night, which continued for long minutes. Even so, he could see no stars through the branches above them. It was a strange event, indeed, but the earth around them was still.

Surely, the end of the world would be more tumultuous.

Then, at last, to Katy's cry of delight and Will's profound relief, a thin, dark-orange edge of the sun began to emerge on the other side of the shadow. The odd semi-darkness and chill persisted for a minute or two more before enough of the sun emerged to make it unbearable to watch it, even through the leaves.

The wind in the trees dropped back to a light breeze. The creatures kept silent, but Will saw a nightjar, like a small hawk, flit through the branches above them with the churring sound it usually made only at night.

Slowly, the sky grew sunnier, a squirrel chattered, the air began to warm again, and the world seemed to be returning to normal.

"'Tis safe now, Katy, and you must go home at once," Will said firmly. "Your people will soon be missing you if they have not done so already."

"You must go home, too, sir," Katy said, "because Aly will be as frightened as I was. Sakes, though, I wish I had brought the dogs with me."

"Aye, but I will keep near until you reach the path to the knoll," Will said.

"You must not do that," she countered urgently. "The guards will be more alert than ever. What if they catch you?"

"Nae one will see me, but 'tis true that you should have brought your dogs."

"Aye, she should have, but I be here with her," Rory said quietly behind them, adding hastily, "I'll keep her safe, sir, and she'll help me keep safe, too. I'm gey glad the sun came back, but how did Auld Clootie snatch it away as he did?"

The two of them stared at him in stupefaction, but Will found his voice before Katy did. "It could come and go by itself, because it did," he said grimly. "I do not know the how of it, but I doubt the devil had aught to do with it. I do know that if you continue to follow her ladyship without her knowledge as you have, you will answer to me, my lad. I can promise you a good skelping if it happens again."

"Aye, sure, and that be why I didna say nowt afore now. But when I saw that Lady Katy had no taken Argus and Eos with her after Sir Fin said she must take some'un or both o' the dogs, I followed so I could tell him she had me if he should learn that she'd forgot. I did stay back, mostly, but . . . Be ye truly married, then?"

Will gave him a stern look. "Never mind that, but I want your sworn word now," he added. "Is that tale you just told me the truth?"

"As true as that I still be a-standing here after Auld Clootie stole the sun out o' the sky. God Hisself must ha' put it back, 'cause nae one else could do it."

"So you concealed yourself behind the Stone again, did you?"

Eyeing him more warily than ever, Rory swallowed, squared his shoulders, and said, "Aye, then, I did. I didna ken how else tae keep sight o' her."

"Then hear me well, my lad. Henceforth, if you follow her lady-ship for any reason whatsoever, you will announce your presence to her and to anyone she might meet. If you do not, and I catch you at it—"

"Aye, aye, I ken fine what ye'll do. Nae need tae keep a-pratin' on it."

"Get along with you then, both of you," Will said.

When Katy hesitated, clearly yearning for another kiss, he said, "You should have brought the dogs, lass. Do not forget them again."

She made a face at him, and he smiled, then shooed them off and followed them, turning back toward Raitt when they left the woods for the knoll path.

He reached home in good time to seek Aly out before supper, but as he crossed the hall, Hew shouted, "Ye're back early for once, so unless the sun's brief disappearance scared ye witless, get your gear together. We mean tae be away at dawn toward Inverness. Take your weapons and aught else ye might need should we meet wi' trouble on the way."

"What trouble might we meet talking with kinsmen?"

"Devil snatch ye, Will! Just do as I bid ye for once in a way. Da wants ye on this trip, with your weapons. Ye may even get your chance tae show him that ye're worth summat after all."

An icy trickle slid up Will's spine, giving him pause to wonder at Hew's choice of words, and to recall his own thoughts about omens as the sun disappeared.

Ignoring his feelings and the memory, he went to find Aly.

❖ ❖ ❖

Katy entered the hall to see her father on the dais talking to Clydia. Fin saw her, too, and said in an even tone that carried nonetheless chillingly to her ears at the other end of the hall, "Where have you been?"

"In the woods, sir," Katy said, fighting to keep her voice calm. "Below the castle knoll and I think a bit northeast of here."

"You did not take the dogs."

"Aye, but she did take me, Sir Fin," Rory said, stepping past Katy.

"I see," Fin said. "Did the vanishing sun frighten you, laddie?"

Rory shrugged. "I dinna ken where it went, so it did seem strange, but I didna think the world were ending, like some folks did. Who were a-setting up such screeches everywhere then?"

"Many people were frightened," Fin said. "Doubtless, because of the rumors arising from that Border woman's witless prediction."

"Aye, that's what I thought about it, m'self," Rory said, nodding.

Katy doubted that he was telling the truth, but she was not about to say so.

"You have chores yet to do, laddie," Fin said. "I thank you for keeping an eye on our Katy, though," he added when Rory looked about to speak again.

The boy nodded and turned away, and Fin gestured for Katy to step nearer.

With a sigh, wondering how much trouble she was in, she obeyed and cast a glance at Clydia as she approached the dais.

Her twin gave no hint of what lay ahead, but Fin had folded his arms across his chest, which was never encouraging. Suddenly, despite her assurances to Will, she did not feel at all like a married lady.

Her father waited until she stood right in front of him before he said, "Did you truly believe that that twelve-year-old laddie was the sort of escort I meant for you to take walking with you?"

Since she could not admit that she had not known Rory had followed her, she was glad for once when Fin gave her no chance to reply before adding grimly, "Because if you did think that, you were much in error. From now until I tell you otherwise, you will confine your activities inside this castle's walls."

Katy stared at him in dismay, managed to curb her urge to shriek, and said with what she thought was admirable calm, "I am not to go outside the wall at all, sir? Not even to take bread to Granny Rosel or visit others in the woods?"

"I am not punishing you as severely as I might, Katy, though you surely deserve something more for defying my orders. The truth is that I have heard from several people that de Raite has been quietly meeting other Comyn factions since he lost control of Nairn Castle. I sent word of his activities to Malcolm this morning, so we'll know more anon, but since I cannot trust you to look after yourself properly, until we have a better understanding of de Raite's plans you will stay inside our walls unless your mother or Clydia is with you."

Recalling Will's warning that he might have to be away for a few days, Katy wondered with a shiver if he was involved in whatever de Raite was plotting. Even so, she breathed more easily after Fin's last few words until a second glance at Clydia gave her pause. Her twin looked nearly as stern as Fin did.

"There you are, my dearling," Catriona said from behind Katy, having apparently just entered the hall. "Were you as stunned by the sun's disappearance as the rest of us were? I vow, I have never seen anything like it, and chaos erupted in the woods. Nearly everyone fell down to his or her knees, praying for deliverance. I'll admit that I sent up a few prayers, too."

Fin said lightly, "Young Rory just informed us that he was unimpressed. Did he speak truthfully, Katy-lass?"

"I don't know," Katy replied, trying not to recall how calm Will had been, lest she somehow reveal his existence or her feelings for him. Hastily, she added, "Rory did not shout or scream, as some did—for I heard them, too—but I was too stunned myself to heed his reaction. What caused that, Da?"

"Although I have never witnessed one before, I believe it was a phenomenon known as a solar eclipse," Fin replied. "Bishop Traill explained that, as the Earth goes around the sun, sometimes the moon gets between them so that its shadow darkens the land below. The Earth can move between the sun and the moon, too.

When it does, it causes a lunar eclipse. I have seen some of those, one that totally eclipsed the moon and others that partially did so. Lunar eclipses are more common to see."

So Will did know what he was talking about, Katy thought fondly.

"I can recall your telling me about such things," Catriona said. "Mayhap that is why I did not fear that the world would end. I do think we must have a *cèilidh* to celebrate the end of our shearing, though, *and* that the world did *not* end today. I have been out amongst the cottars, shepherds, and crofters, calming those who were terrified and inviting everyone to join us here tomorrow with food, drink, and entertainment to share. If you will send word at once to Cawdor, sir," she added, smiling at her husband, "I am sure they will be delighted to participate."

"If we are all still here," Katy said with a grin. "After all, Mam, the day is not over yet."

CHAPTER 12

"Och, Will, I was so frightened!" Aly exclaimed when he entered the solar. Leaping from her window seat, she cast herself into his arms. "Do you ken why the sun disappeared and the night came and went?" she demanded. "Meggie said it were the end o' the world, but then it were nae such thing. We are all still here."

"Aye, we are, Aly, and you are safe."

"I am when you are here," she said.

He could tell that she was still nervous, though. She had evidently heard more news than he had, too.

"Meggie said all the shops in Nairn were closed today," Alyssa said. "Everywhere one went, she said, people were on their knees a-praying."

"Then God heard their prayers," Will said gently.

"Aye, perhaps," Aly said doubtfully.

"Do you not think he hears our prayers?"

"Mayhap he does, but so many at one time? How does he sort them out?"

With a chuckle, Will said, "Granduncle Thomas told me that God is all-powerful and can work miracles, so one does not ask how he does it. If you are hungry and ready to go down to supper now, I will go with you."

De Raite had not yet stepped onto the dais, but most of the men were at their trestles, and Liam and Colley had joined Hew at the high table, so Will escorted Aly to her place. Meggie hurried in moments later and stood at her place beside Aly.

De Raite emerged from his tower chamber scant seconds later, and Will heard Meggie breathe a sigh of relief.

De Raite paid the women no heed.

When he reached his place, he looked out on the lower hall and said grimly, "As ye all ken fine, I meant for us tae leave at dawn tae meet wi' clansmen from Badenoch and then tae talk wi' others in Inverness and the Great Glen.

"However," he went on, "after this afternoon's startling event, I'll be putting that business off for a day. We'll give them who feared the world's end had come, due tae a brief darkening o' yon sun, time tae recover their senses. Certes, every man here had better do so, unless he wants me tae make him an example for the rest. We leave at dawn on Friday."

A rumble of conversation ensued until de Raite pounded the table with a fist. When silence fell again, he looked at Will. "I expect that our Hew told ye that ye're tae come with us now that Jarvis be dead. We'll be talking wi' clansmen about how the Malcolmtosh be too fond o' having his way in affairs of import tae us. Donald o' Cawdor, likewise. I'll no stand for any o' yer nonsense in these talks, though. If ye canna speak sensibly, ye'll keep your mouth shut, or we'll fall out, me laddie."

Beside Will, Aly drew a breath as if to speak but caught it and kept silent.

"Did ye ha' aught tae say about this, lass?" de Raite asked in a too-silky tone. "I canna think what it might be, so dinna keep us all in wonder. Speak yer mind if there be a thought in it worth sharing."

Paling, she said cautiously, "With respect, sir, I just wonder if mayhap some in the Clan Chattan Confederation, even the Mackintosh, might be friendly enough tae join you in seeking peace. Surely, they canna all be evil."

"And what would *ye* ken o' them villainous snakes?" de Raite demanded in a near snarl. "Ye ha' nae business meeting wi' any o' them on the sly. Forbye, if ye ha' done such a thing, I'll soon sort them out, and ye, too, Alyssa."

"Nae, sir!" Aly exclaimed. "You asked me what I thought, and that thought had come tae me. I just obeyed your command tae tell you what it was."

"She does make sense, sir," Will said mildly. "It might serve us well to seek a mutually peaceab—"

"Shut yer gob!" de Raite snapped. "I dinna want tae hear that trittle-trattle from ye now or when we meet wi' clansmen. The Malcolmtosh and others in that damnable confederation o' his ha' been enemies of our clan for more than a century. Such soft talk be nobbut treachery tae your own."

Having succeeded in drawing de Raite's attention from Aly to himself, Will nodded to the gillie who had waited to set a platter of sliced beef and pork on the table before him to go ahead and do so.

The usual pandemonium reigned thereafter in the lower hall. Colley began talking with de Raite, and beyond them Hew and Liam suddenly burst out laughing.

Beside him, Aly stared at her trencher. She had scarcely moved since de Raite's rebuke, so Will speared a slice of beef and set it on her trencher.

"Eat something, lass," he murmured close to her ear. "De Raite's words are only words. Although they can hurt, we can use our own good sense to lessen their pain. Someone once told me to imagine hurtful words as birds lighting on a branch in your mind. Then imagine them spreading their wings and flying away. The sooner you let them fly, the sooner you will feel better."

"I be afeard of him, Will. Ye ken fine that he doesna use only words in his anger. Was it Granduncle Thomas who told you about turning words intae birds?"

"It was, aye."

"I wish you had taken me with you when you went tae live with him. He doesna sound near as fearsome as Father."

"Thomas talked about fear, too, lassie. Fear can be useful, he said, because it helps keep us alive. We should heed it when it rises but never let it control us. You know you can speak to me of anything. Mayhap I can help ease your fears."

"Aye, you be a wise man, Will. I dinna think you can banish my fears with talk, though. They ha' been with me too long.

Sithee, saving yourself and Meggie, I live in a household of violent men."

"How would you like to get away for an hour or two?"

"Tae do what?"

"I thought we might walk toward Nairn. The air outside is fresh from the firth and cool. It might help to banish your megrims."

"Father willna let me go."

"I'll see if I can persuade him. It will be light out for several more hours."

"Oh, Will, if you could. I feel smothered in this hall. All the noise and smoke make my head ache."

"Eat some bread and the meat I gave you. I do not want to have to carry home a lady who has fainted from starvation."

She smiled, and that was enough for Will. He got up and moved toward de Raite, who regarded him with a glower. "What d'ye want?"

"Alyssa is still frightened about today's strange event, sir. I'd like to take her out into the fresh air and show her that she need no longer concern herself with the unusual darkness this afternoon or the predicted end of the world."

"Are ye telling me it didna scare the liver and lights out o' ye, then?"

"It was intriguing," Will said frankly. "Though I did once see the moon disappear so into the earth's shadow, I had thought that only in folktales was it possible for the moon to cast *its* shadow on the Earth. However, I could not imagine such an eclipse would scare you, nor had I put any faith in the word of an unknown Border woman that the world would end today. So, nae, sir, I was not frightened."

"Then mayhap ye've got more in your cockloft than I thought. I, too, found the event interesting, though it may still be an omen of some sort," de Raite added with a grim smile. "I'm thinking it portends coming trouble for the Malcolmtosh."

"Then, may I take Aly out for a time, sir? I thought we might walk toward the firth and back. We'll take Meggie, too, if you think that would be wise."

"Aye, it would; just dinna get lost," de Raite said. "Try tae learn if Alyssa's been a-meeting anyone, though. I dinna like her walking about where I canna see her, and I ken fine that she's done that more than a time or two."

"I think Aly has too much respect for your temper to attempt any such daft venture on her own, sir," Will said without a blink of guilt. "I have known her for barely two years, but she seems as meek as a nun's hen to me."

"Aye, she is that," de Raite said. "Get along then, and dinna forget ye'll be a-going with us on Friday."

"I won't," Will said.

Before de Raite could change his mind, Will plucked Aly from her stool, sent her to fetch her cloak and Meggie, and hurried them through the hall and outside, pausing only to tell Olaf that they were going beyond the gate.

"Is Himself feeling more the thing, then, sir?"

"More the thing, Olaf?" Will asked, looking right at him.

The women stopped in the open doorway.

"Aye," Olaf said. "He were all of a tremble earlier, like the rest of us. Pale as a ghost he were when he stumbled in after that pernicious black hour."

Suppressing his amusement, Will assured the porter that de Raite had recovered himself and might dislike further talk of that momentary weakness.

"Aye, ye've the right about that, sir," Olaf agreed, nodding.

Their exchange had an unexpected, beneficial effect on Aly.

"Father was frightened, too?" she exclaimed disbelievingly as they crossed the timber bridge and descended to the flagged courtyard.

"Evidently, he was," Will said with a smile.

The sun was approaching the western horizon when they set out northward from Raitt, and they soon saw the towers of Nairn's kirk and castle.

Will let the women choose the way and followed them. Hearing his name shouted, away to his left, he turned to see who had recognized him from the distance. When he saw the rider heading toward him on a sleek bay horse, he shouted to Meggie and Aly to keep going, adding that he would catch up.

Turning back, he waited for the horseman.

"I recognized your walk," Wilkin Cawdor said, grinning down at him from the saddle. He wore breeks and a jerkin of dark leather. "I was thinking o' ye, too, trying to imagine a safe way to pass on a message to ye from Thomas."

"You've been in Inverness then," Will said. "How fares the ancient one?"

"Still full of pepper and fond of good whisky," Wilkin said. "Might that be your sister, Alyssa, yonder?"

"Aye, but do not get any notions about her," Will warned him. "It is doubtless as much as my life is worth to talk to you in the open like this."

"In troth, I'm surprised ye've kept your head on ye. Likely Thomas will be, too. He sent greetings and said to warn ye to keep out of the trouble as be brewing now. Said he never managed to stop ye, himself, so he expects me to fail, too."

"Have you any news of worth?" Will asked dryly, recalling that Wilkin had initiated much of the past "trouble" to which he had referred. "Sithee, de Raite was wrong to take Nairn and is furious now, but I have no influence with him."

"I thought ye'd say summat like that," Wilkin said with a grin. "But if ye'd like to learn more about de Raite's enemies, Father and I had an invitation from Finlagh today to attend a *cèilidh* tomorrow, celebrating the end of shearing and the evident survival of the world. Father will be engaged elsewhere, but I'm laden with dozens of cousins and could take a 'cousin' along if ye'd enjoy the escapade. Forbye, since I ken fine that ye took nae part in the seizure of Nairn, I'd wager that nae one at Finlagh has ever clapped eyes on ye."

"You would lose your wager," Will said, giving his childhood friend an oblique, even mischievous, look. Casting a glance to be sure the two women still strolled amiably on, he added, "We must discuss the matter more, I think. Sithee, two lasses at Finlagh *have* clapped eyes on me. For the sake of one of them, though, I'd risk it if I thought we could get away with—"

"Sakes, Will, 'twill be easy to fool them," Wilkin interjected with his merry laugh. "For entertainment, I shall play the lute and you can sing. Now, tell me which two of their maidservants saw you, so I can be sure we avoid them."

Fin having approved of Catriona's *cèilidh*, the usual bustle required for such an event ensued that evening. Every guest would bring food or drink and be willing to provide entertainment. As hosts, Finlagh's residents had only to put meat on spits to roast and bring casks of ale and wine from their undercroft storage. People would wander from courtyard to hall and back, so they would have fires inside and out.

The twins helped Catriona make her lists of chores for everyone. Usually, such activity led to an exchange of news and gossip. However, Cat banned talk of what people were calling the Black Hour, and Katy had no impulse to say she had declared herself married to a Comyn just before the event, so talk was desultory.

Just thinking of her declaration gave Katy the shivers. She had to remind herself several times of Will's certainty that the darkness had been none of her doing. Fin's explanation of the event was also reassuring. Even so . . .

Recalling that Will would be away for a time and that de Raite was likely plotting mischief, she wondered if Will had already gone. If so, would he take part in that mischief? His demeanor had never suggested so, she reminded herself.

She slept fitfully that night, but by morning, with bright sunlight beaming through the narrow window between her bed and Clydia's, she felt like her usual self. The day passed swiftly, because Catriona kept everyone busy in the great hall or kitchen and bakehouse, or outside in the courtyard.

Despite her insistence that a *cèilidh* was the simplest amusement to organize, Cat always assumed that her guests might fail to provide enough food and drink for everyone and strove to predict and avoid any lack.

"Moreover," she said as she explained one flurry of activity to her husband and daughters at the midday meal, "we have lambs aplenty and poultry, *and* wood, so roasting extra meat will be no trouble at all. Anything left over, should there be any, will soon grace our table and go to those who have less."

Guests began arriving by midafternoon, mostly cottars with their families, shepherds and other tenants from the strath, and friends from Nairn or nearer. The party from Cawdor arrived shortly before the normal hour for supper, while Clydia was changing her dress and Katy stood beside Catriona and Fin helping to receive their guests in the dusky, torchlit courtyard a short way from the main gate.

The group then passing through the gateway included the Thane's son Wilkin and a string of Cawdor tenants, most of whom were familiar to residents of Finlagh. The Thane was not with them, so they streamed behind lanky Wilkin, who had his lute, and a second man, slightly taller than Wilkin, who wore the red, tight-fitting hood of a jester with bells attached to the three points of the fool's cap on his head and the points of the dagged red cowl over his shoulders. Beneath it, he wore a thigh-length blue tunic, belted at the waist. When Katy's gaze met his, she nearly cried out in shock, instantly recognizing him.

How had Will Comyn dared to come to Finlagh?

Katy had all she could do to keep her jaw from dropping, but his eyes danced as if he were delighted to have stunned her.

"What have you done with your father, Wilkin?" Fin demanded then, jerking Katy's attention from Will to pay heed to Wilkin's response.

"He had another obligation," Wilkin explained glibly. "I am to relay his regrets to you all, as well as his felicitations on having survived not only the end of the world but also what everyone hereabouts seems now to be calling the Black Hour. Frankly, I do not think the black part lasted nearly so long."

"Nor do I," Cat said, smiling. "But the unusual darkening and slow return to normal light lasted much longer than an hour. Our bees even went to bed. But you have not yet presented your friend, sir, and I do not think we have met him."

"Och, aye," Wilkin said, clapping a hand to his forehead. "Forgive me, my lady, and ye, too, Lady Katy," he added with mischief in his hazel eyes when he looked at her. "This unfortunate chap chances to be my cousin, William Calder, from Inverness. As ye know, our lot is rife with Williams, and he is another such. Forbye, he was visiting and I knew ye'd welcome him, so I brought him along with me."

"Indeed, he is welcome," Catriona said as she turned, still smiling, to extend a hand to the supposed jester. "We are pleased to meet you, William Calder."

Katy held her breath, ignoring Wilkin, as she watched them.

"Pray, m'lady, call me Will, for I'll likely not answer to William," Will said gruffly, as he shook hands with Fin. "I am honored to meet you, as well, sir."

"Although he has little else to recommend him to your ladyships, he *can* sing," Wilkin added lightly. "His ballads are most amusing."

Trying to maintain her countenance, Katy shifted her gaze back to Wilkin and caught a look of unholy glee on his face. She knew he was delighted with himself for introducing a member of the enemy Comyn clan into Castle Finlagh and hearing Fin and Catriona welcome him there.

Aware then that her father was watching her, she felt a tingle of alarm.

Mercy on us, Da will have my head for this. And what Clydia will say when she sees Will, I do not want to imagine!

Her twin would be outraged and was unlikely to believe that she had had naught to do with the young men's prank. Surely, it was just a prank, too, because although Wilkin was heir to the Thanage, he had played pranks before. Moreover, she thought grimly, he would not want to brew mischief against his family's closest ally. But, if he was their friend, how could he also be Will's?

Would Clydia recognize him?

To the best of Katy's knowledge, no one else at Finlagh, except Rory, had seen him before, and she could only hope that if Rory recognized Will, he would not give him away. In a jester's ridiculous close-fitting cap and cowl, with none of Will's hair showing, and the scruffy, darker beard—

"Katy, where are your manners that you have not yet spoken to our guests?" Catriona demanded quietly beside her, bringing a flush of heat to Katy's face.

"I beg your pardon, Mam," she said hastily. "And yours, Wilkin. My wits must have abandoned me. Does your jester tell jokes and turn cartwheels, sir?"

Wilkin shot her an approving grin but said, "Ye'll have to ask Willy, Kate."

Her eyebrows flew up. "Willy?"

"Aye, sure," Wilkin said. "For so I have called him since we were lads together in Inverness town, where my father has a house, as I think ye know."

She did know that, but . . .

"Greetings, Wilkin," Clydia said from just behind Katy, having evidently approached while her own senses were still reeling. "'Tis good to see you, sir."

"Thank you, m'lady," Wilkin replied, suddenly looking uncomfortable. "May . . . may I present my cousin, William Calder of Inverness."

To Katy's relief but not much to her surprise, Clydia said without a blink and with her usual poise, "Welcome to Finlagh, sir."

Despite the red lacing at his throat, or perhaps because its bow shook, Katy saw Will swallow before he said, "It is indeed an honor to meet you, m'lady."

"Show your cousin around, Wilkin," Fin said, clapping him on the back. "We look forward to your music, as we always do."

"It will be our pleasure, sir," Wilkin said. Taking Will by an arm, he guided him toward the fire now burning brightly in the center of the courtyard.

Clydia said nothing until the flow of guests ebbed to a trickle. Then she said, "Come with me, Katy. I want a private moment with you."

Half expecting their father to say he wanted to talk to her first and relieved when he did not, Katy went meekly back into the hall with her twin.

Eyeing the gathering crowd, and people trying to claim space on benches at the tables by setting belongings on them, Clydia said, "We'll go elsewhere."

"We can talk later," Katy said hopefully.

"Nae, we'll talk now, in the inner chamber," Clydia said, leading the way to the dais and then into the chamber behind it. When she had shut the door behind them, she said, "How could you do such a thing, Kate?"

"You did recognize him then?"

"Aye, sure, how could I not?"

"I promise you, Clydia, on mine honor or anything you like, that I did not invite him. His presence here is Wilkin's idea of an amusing hoax."

"It is *not* amusing. It could be dangerous. We should tell Mam and Da exactly who that man is."

Katy drew a breath and tried to think, but with Clydia glowering at her, it was hard to concentrate. Her twin's temper could be as fierce as Katy's own if she lost it. Katy's belief in Will remained strong, though. "Let me talk to Will first," she said as calmly as she could. "I do believe that this was all Wilkin's idea. Will would not play such a trick on his own, nor would he harm me or anyone in my family. You met him, Clydie. Did you dislike or distrust him?"

"Nae, but we do not know him, Katy. Even if we did, he is still a Comyn and therefore is as much our enemy as any other man in his clan."

"He is not like them," Katy said, struggling not to raise her voice. "He was born a Comyn, aye, but so was Aly. They are unlike the rest, and I think we should encourage them to know us better. Also, Wilkin is friends with Will despite being our ally and despite de Raite's seizure of Nairn. But, if I tell Da who Will is, here and now, surrounded by men and women who will doubtless see him as just another enemy to kill . . . I can*not* do that, Clydie, and if you do I will never forgive you."

Clydia's eyebrows shot upward, but her expression eased. "You care about him that much, do you?"

"I do," Katy said flatly, "more than I can say." She nearly told Clydia then that she had married Will by declaration the afternoon before, because she had always shared her thoughts, actions, and opinions with her twin. This time, though, she could not bring herself to do it. Not now, not during the *cèilidh*.

"Very well," Clydia said. "But we must not linger here, because someone will soon be looking for us and demanding to know why we vanished."

She opened the door to the dais, and the two stepped out of the chamber.

Katy shut the door and turned to see Wilkin striding toward them, as people in his path swiftly made way for him.

"Art vexed with me, the pair o' ye?" he asked ruefully as he stepped onto the dais to confront them. "I vow, I meant nae harm to either o' ye."

Clydia said curtly, "Why did you bring him here?"

"Never mind that," Katy interjected. "How do you even know Will?"

"Ah, so ye do ken who he is," Wilkin said. "I was uncertain o' that, but I've known him since he was a bairn of ten years and was living with de Raite's uncle, Thomas Cummings, near our Inverness house. Father is friendly with Thomas, who is a town burgess. He rejected the Comyn name and has called himself Cummings for years now. He is usually peaceful, though he did take a hand in defending the town of Inverness when Alexander of the Isles attacked the castle and burned the town. Will had a hand in the town's defense, too. Sithee, he learned the arts o' war from Thomas and his sons, who are older than Will is. He's a fine warrior."

"Then why did he not stay with Thomas Cummings and call himself Cummings, as well?" Clydia asked him.

"Because de Raite had entrusted Will to Thomas only on the agreement that when he wanted him, Thomas would send him back. I expect you recall when de Raite hanged four Mackintoshes some months ago?"

"Aye, sure," Katy said.

"Will opposed their hanging until de Raite threatened to hang him as well. He would have done it, too. Will would likely have fought more, even so, had it not been for his sister, Alyssa. In that household of heathen bullies, Will feels responsible for Aly, so he stays and tries to choose his battles. I ken fine that I ought not to have brought him here tonight, and he came only because he wanted to see you in your own home, Katy. If you can forgive us enough to let us stay until we have taken our part in the entertainment, I vow I'll whisk him away then."

Wondering if that would be soon enough for her to elude her father's wrath, but unable to say no, Katy looked at Clydia.

"Aye, sure," Clydia said after a brief pause. "What could go wrong in so short a time after the world was supposed to end? To be sure, though, that prophecy might have been a day off, might it not?"

Having abruptly found himself bereft of his companion in the courtyard crowd, Will scanned the area and saw Wilkin's broad-shouldered back filling the castle entrance just as it disappeared inside. Making his way as fast as possible for a man in the better part of a jester's costume with bells tinkling, through a raucous crowd, Will reached the doorway just as Wilkin reappeared in it.

"Where the devil have you been?" Will demanded. "Don't abandon me like that again, you dafty," he added in a lower tone. "Recall that it is worth my life to be recognized within these walls. Sakes, if Fin of the Battles did not hang me, it need only for word of my being here to reach de Raite's ears for him to do so."

"Calm yourself, laddie," Wilkin said. "I'll not let anyone hang ye. If worse comes to worst, ye'll seek sanctuary for yourself and Alyssa at Cawdor."

"As if your father would welcome us, knowing well that de Raite would try to bring the walls of Cawdor down around our ears."

"He might not like it," Wilkin said seriously. "But, if such a time should come to pass, we will do all we can to aid ye."

"I know you mean well, and I cannot deny that I'm glad to see Katy, but this was a devilish dim-witted escapade."

"Certes, the lady Clydia thinks so," Wilkin said with a sigh. "I ken fine that ye said she had seen ye and would recognize ye as easily as Katy would, but I hoped Clydia would see humor in it."

"You are lucky that she did not slap you as she did me."

"Aye, well, I like her as much as I like Katy, mayhap more so. I did promise them that we will depart after we have performed our songs, though. My people know to follow us or stay here, as they choose."

"Minions have set up a platform yonder," Will said, gesturing. "Does that mean the entertainment will take place out here?"

"'Tis likely. They were shifting trestles about in the hall, so there may be dancing there before or afterward. Do ye no want to dance with your lass?"

Will yearned to dance with Katy. There would be only ring dances at a *cèilidh*, but he enjoyed dancing and had not done any since returning to Raitt. His Inverness cousins had entertained often, and he missed that at Raitt. "Can we do it without irking anyone?"

"Sakes, laddie," Wilkin said with a grin, "ye're dressed to act as daft as ye please, unless ye think the lass herself would spurn ye."

"I don't know how she will react," Will said with a dawning smile. A jester *could* get away with much at such an affair, perhaps even steal a kiss.

"Look yonder," Wilkin said minutes later. "That chappie on the platform is a famous bard. If he begins a tale . . . ah, yes, I hear strains of a piper inside. Let us see if they are preparing for a ring dance. Ye may thereby get your chance straightaway. If we were to wait till after we perform, we'd be breaking my promise to the twins."

Accordingly, they went back inside. Others were heading the same way, too, so Lady Catriona's *cèilidhs* likely followed a known pattern. An Irish whistle had joined the piper's tune, and another man banged a tabor in time with it. A third played a fiddle, so Wilkin took out his lute and strummed along with the tune.

Dancers were forming a ring, so Will made his way toward Katy and saw her watching for him. As he approached, another lad grabbed her hand and drew her into the fast-forming ring. She saw Will then and held out her free hand.

He hastily accepted her invitation, though doing so put him and another man together. To Will's surprise, Lady Clydia quickly stepped into the breech.

Because of his greater height, she had to turn her head to look up at him. She muttered nonetheless sternly, "You and Wilkin should be flogged for this foolery. I'd be doing no more than my duty if I introduced you properly to my father."

"Would you, m'lady?" Will said with a warm smile, leaning closer so she could hear him as the music grew louder and the ring of dancers began slowly to move. "Certes, but we would both be well served if you did, especially Wilkin."

"Despite your ridiculous costume, you have no need to tell me that it was his idea," Clydia retorted. "He is known for such, sir. But to put you in danger as he has is not being a true friend, and so I have told him. He says, however, that he has known you since childhood and that you are utterly unlike the other men in your family. He also says that he thinks you are in love with my sister. Is that true?"

Her first few words had made him feel as much a fool as he looked like one, but the rest gave balm to his heart. As the circle of dancers spread itself larger, he found himself trying to believe in Katy's marriage by declaration.

It had to be nonsense, though, because why would such a tradition even exist near such civilized towns as Inverness and Nairn? Each had a fine kirk.

He was still gazing at Clydia when Katy squeezed his hand sharply and he looked at her with a warm smile. "What would you, m'lady?"

CHAPTER 13

He has the most endearing smile, Katy thought, as he bent nearer to hear her reply. "I heard Clydia say you look ridiculous in that costume and you do," she said, speaking just loudly enough for him to hear her. "I'm glad you came here tonight, though. I only wish I could present you properly to my parents."

He shook his head with a wry grin, making the bells on his cap jingle. "Your twin made the same wish, lass, but she made it sound like a threat to expose me."

"She won't do that," Katy assured him. "She will tease Wilkin in much the same way, if she has not already done so," she added, looking toward the musicians.

The music changed to a faster pace, so she soon needed every breath for dancing. By then, the circle was awhirl. Spectators clapped their hands and stamped their feet in time to the music as they cheered the dancers on.

There being no way now to converse, she saw that Will was also paying heed to the dance. The leaders had broken the circle to turn in a new direction, weaving in and around, under arms, and then turning back on the rest of the line until they connected with the last dancers in a circle again.

Will's hand felt warm, wrapped around Katy's, and reminded her of how he had held her hand on the crag the day they met. She squeezed his again, and whenever he looked her way, she grinned.

She was enjoying herself hugely. He smiled, and everyone who saw his smile, even Clydia, smiled in response to it.

When the ring broke and turned on itself again, Katy saw Bridgett dancing between the two Bruces, MacNab and Lochan, laughing and flirting with Lochan. When he did not respond, she turned to MacNab and pulled him close enough to kiss his cheek. Katy grinned but then saw Lochan eye the two with a heavy frown.

By the time Bridgett looked his way again, big, blond, square-built Lochan was staring at his feet as if he were afraid of making a misstep.

Katy looked at Will then to see if he had seen them, but his gaze captured hers, sending waves of pleasure through her body, making her wish they could slip away somewhere more private together. *That* was clearly impossible, though, since everyone there knew her.

However, Will must have had similar thoughts, for when the music ended, to Katy's stunned surprise, he tipped his fool's cap toward her and planted a big, warm kiss right on her lips in front of everyone. Then clapping the cap back into place, he made her a grinning, bobbing bow.

The crowd around them began loudly cheering and applauding.

Her lips were still warm from the kiss and she was still laughing when MacNab came to claim her hand for the next dance. At *cèilidhs* and other such casual diversions at Finlagh, everyone danced with everyone else, so she accepted, only to see Wilkin usher the still grinning Will hastily back outside.

Katy's spirits fell, but she took good care not to let MacNab or anyone else see aught but a smile on her face.

When Wilkin and Will appeared in the courtyard again, shouts rang out for Wilkin to play for the crowd. Pulling Will with him, he stepped onto the makeshift stage and began to play a popular bawdy tune. Easily recognizing the tune, Will began to sing, and soon the crowd was singing with him.

Energized by their enthusiasm, he encouraged more with jesterlike antics, larking about so that his fool's cap points danced and jingled until the song ended.

Wilkin played a second tune then, more mournful but just as well known. With shouts for more, the pattern continued until they had done five songs, when both men bowed and left the stage to a pair of pipers, who played a raucous martial tune as they mounted the stage. The crowd cheered approval, and someone threw more wood on the fire, shooting sparks high into the air.

"We leave without the usual farewells, I think," Wilkin said.

"I do thank you for dragging me here, despite the danger," Will replied. "I'm off at dawn to Badenoch and Inverness-shire, to visit fellow clansmen with de Raite and the others. This is the best time I've had since I returned to Raitt, though."

Wilkin gave him a searching look. "Ye have more ken of Katy than I knew," he said, leaning closer and adding quietly, "I think ye're in love wi' the lass!"

"I may be," Will admitted. "In troth, I feel as if I have always known her, though I cannot tell you why that is. We met by chance on the ridgetop between Raitt and Finlagh, and I . . ." He paused, trying to think of how best to explain.

"Ye neglected to explain that de Raite is your father, I'll wager."

Will nodded. He nearly added that she had declared them married just before the eclipse, but he decided that should stay strictly between himself and Katy. Wilkin was not a man to talk of such, but he might tell Cawdor or some other trusted friend in confidence, which, in Will's experience, was exactly how rumors spread and changed and could ruin people's reputations if not their very lives.

"'Tis early for you to be leaving, Wilkin," a voice said behind them. They turned to find Fin approaching them. "I am sorry that Donald could not come, because your music and songs delighted our guests. I wanted to thank you both for participating as you did," he added, offering Will his hand.

Shaking it, albeit with a rueful sense of being gravely in the wrong, Will said sincerely, "It was a great honor to meet you, Sir Finlagh. I've heard tales of your past and know you to be a valiant warrior."

"I have heard the same tales, and some are even true," Fin said. "I prefer peace to war, but I must not keep you. Donald is likely expecting the pair of you."

"Aye, sir," Wilkin agreed without hesitation. "'Tis a fine *cèilidh*, though. Pray extend our respects and felicitations to Lady Catriona."

Departing, they strode together down the torchlit path to the foot of the knoll. Reaching the much darker, narrow path to Nairn, they noticed at once that there was no moon. The heavens were ablaze with stars, though.

Although Will felt guilty about deceiving his host, he was glad that Wilkin had persuaded him to go. More than that, he was delighted to have seen and danced with Katy, and if the kiss he had stolen was not as warm and wonderful as those they had enjoyed before the eclipse, he had enjoyed it enormously nonetheless.

Returning the jester's belled cowl and fool's cap to Wilkin when they parted at the intersection of the path with the public road, Will bade him farewell.

"Have you seen Bridgett?" Katy asked Clydia from the washstand as they prepared for bed. "She has been here, because our cresset is alight and the water in the ewer is warm. However, she seems to have taken away the towel that was here."

"I last saw her dancing between the two Bruces in the ring. She was flirting dreadfully with MacNab and ignoring Lochan."

"Not ignoring him, exactly," Katy said. "I saw her, too, and though she did flirt with MacNab, she kept a close eye on Lochan. He seemed to be aware—"

The door opened and Bridgett hurried into the room. "Ah, good, I see ye've managed well wi'out me," she said with a wary smile. "I came up whiles ago tae put hot water in yon jug, but I'd forgot fresh towels, and when I went doon again, Lochan were waiting for me. Seems he were irked aboot summat I didna do."

Clydia shook her head. "He was irked because you were flirting with MacNab, aye? We saw you, Bridgett. You were."

Bridgett's chin came up. "If I were, 'tis me own business and none o' Bruce Lochan's. The man acts as if he canna see me at all and then has the impudence tae take me up for summat like that. If MacNab, who will likely be knighted one day, cares tae smile at me when he chances tae find hisself a-holding one o' me hands in a ring dance, 'tis naught tae do wi' Bruce Lochan, and so I did tell him."

Katy's sense of humor stirred. "What did Lochan say to that?"

Bridgett gave an elaborate shrug. "I paid his daft ill-words nae mind, but when he were done talking, I told him I be me own person. I do what I do and say what I say. This be how I am, I said tae him, and if he means tae have aught more tae do wi' me, let alone tae be flinging me orders, he'd best get used tae that."

"What of MacNab, then?" Clydia asked her.

"Och, he's a bonny lad and a fierce warrior, but the man has *ambition*," Bridgett added on a note of strong disapproval. "He wants tae see more o' the world than Nairnshire and will likely settle nearer Perth than here, 'cause he has kinsmen there. That wouldna do for me. All o' me ain folk be right here."

"But mayhap Lochan thinks you *care* for MacNab," Clydia said. "He does not seem the sort to fight another man for a woman, but I may be wrong about that."

"Ye're not," Bridgett said. "Lochan can be fierce as MacNab and fiercer in the fighting, for he's got the biggest forearms I ever did see. He didna become captain o' the guard without he can wield every weapon better 'n most, neither. But the man be so shy that I likely scared him off. See you, I meant tae say summat soft tae him afore leaving it be, but he went off wi' Sir Fin and didna give me a chance tae say nowt, because Sir Fin came tae tell him Malcolm wants him tae send a score o' men tae Moigh tae help watch the nearby hills. Why d'ye think that be?"

Katy's gaze met Clydia's, and she felt herself shiver.

"What?" Bridgett demanded. "What be the two o' ye a-thinking?"

"If Father is sending Lochan with men to aid Malcolm at Loch Moigh, it must be because Malcolm thinks de Raite is stirring trouble again," Clydia said.

"He did say tae Lochan that Cawdor be going tae send a score, too," Bridgett said, her eyes widening. "Och, what'll I do if Bruce Lochan gets hisself kilt afore I can tell him I didna mean nowt by *all* I said." She wrung her hands together, adding softly, "Most of it, aye, I did mean. But the man seems able enough tae look after hisself and a good woman, too, if the almighty lord spares him tae do it."

"Then you must remember him in your prayers," Clydia said gently.

Katy nodded, but her realization that if de Raite *was* plotting mischief near Loch Moigh he might somehow involve Will drove all other thoughts away.

When Will went downstairs to break his fast Friday morning, he saw that his brothers all carried enough weapons to be going to war.

Turning to Hew, he said with a nod toward de Raite at the high table, "Has he got more in mind than just talk?"

Curtly, Hew said, "He'll be ready, that's all."

De Raite, evidently overhearing them, declared that he never went into a negotiation without preparing first for any occurrence that might arise.

"What sort of negotiation is it, then, sir?" Will asked.

"'Tis me own business the noo, but I'll tell ye when I ken more," de Raite retorted. "We'll meet wi' our Badenoch men and some Glen Mòr Comyns, and I dinna want any o' them tae fear that we willna be ready for aught that occurs."

He was too glib, and Will did not care for such an attitude from a man in whom he placed little trust.

"Will Thomas Cummings meet them with us?" he asked.

Giving him a look that told him de Raite disliked being questioned about his plans or anyone else's, Will nevertheless held his gaze and waited.

At last, with a sigh, de Raite said, "Ye should ken fine by now that me uncle and I differ on many matters, and when it comes tae essential Comyn affairs, I'd liefer confer wi' men who be more of a mind wi' me. Sakes, he nae longer even calls hisself a Comyn!"

"So, Granduncle Thomas knows naught of this conference," Will said. "He is a canny man, sir, and a wise one. We should at least hear his opinions."

"He's nobbut an ancient wi' daft notions," de Raite snapped. "I dinna like him. Sending ye tae him were a grand mistake, so we'll nae talk more o' this. Ye'll do as I bid ye without comment or complaint, me lad, or I'll see ye rue the day."

Hew smirked at Will, which increased Will's concern. Whatever de Raite and Hew were up to, he doubted that it would entail only talk with fellow Comyns. It would do him no good, though, to pursue his suspicions with Hew, Liam, or Colley, because all three men habitually supported de Raite.

They departed an hour later, taking the main road west toward Inverness, but well before then, they turned off onto a track that led southward and followed the course of the river Nairn uphill through woods on the east face of hills that Will knew formed part of Glen Mòr's steep eastern slopes.

He was still trying to imagine what de Raite had in mind when his cousin Dae approached him that night as they made camp on the south shore of a narrow loch in yet higher hills where he had hunted with Wilkin, several miles southeast of Inverness. Clouds had gathered all afternoon. Some had burst into brief pelting rain; others produced a continued, annoying drizzle. The air was now damp and heavy. They had scouted but found no one else in their vicinity, let alone Comyn kinsmen.

Will welcomed his cousin, saying, "Art hungry, Dae?"

"Starving," Dae said. He was about Hew's age, ten years Will's senior, but having grown up in the Lowlands of Perth, Dae tended to regard Highlanders with awe. Hew had oft called him a "Lowland feardie." As Hew's man, Dae had never been more than polite to Will, but compared with Hew or Liam, he was affable.

Men were spreading out in the dusky light to forage for food before full darkness fell, because they expected another moonless night. None paid heed to the damp, nor would they if it rained harder. Only a fierce thunderstorm on high ground would put de Raite off whatever plan he had or make his men seek shelter.

They were still in Clan Chattan country. So, although Glen Mòr was home to other clans, including several that supported Clan Comyn, camping on what amounted to the back side of its northeast slope rather than taking the main road through Inverness to the western side, where most of their allies dwelt, made Will sure that de Raite was up to no good.

Most clans on the east slopes supported the King. Those to the west favored Alexander, the Lord of the Isles, who, since his release from imprisonment the previous year, had shown no interest in resuming hostilities and kept uncharacteristically silent.

However, in the months following the royal defeat at Inverlochy, Alexander's allies, including Comyn factions, had joined his Islesmen under his cousin Donal Balloch and done all they could to stir trouble for the King's allies in Glen Mòr and surrounding areas. The Highlands had been quiet for a time since then, though, and Will doubted that any in Glen Mòr would cheer if de Raite stirred trouble again.

Dae murmured, "I'm thinking there be more tae this than what yer da has said, although Hew said only tae keep m'self ready for trouble, and all will be well. But de Raite sent Liam and two o' his men on southward for summat. What it be, I dinna ken 'cause it be devilish hard tae get aught out o' Hew. But if I'm going tae get kilt in a row that yer da has wi' some other clan, I'd like tae ken the why of it."

"I have had such feelings all day," Will said grimly. "I have little to explain them, though, other than our failure to meet yet with fellow clansmen. Has Hew chanced to mention *who* is to meet us?"

"He says nowt tae me o' nowt," Dae grumbled. "I ha' seen the man prepare for battle afore now, though, and that be what he's a-doing. All he'll say is that we ha' tae be prepared for aught that may come."

Will nodded. "Then more lies ahead than they want to say. Whatever it is, we'll soon find out, so we should sleep. Dawn comes early this time of year."

As it was, they slept only a few hours before Hew and Liam crept about under a black, drizzly sky, rousing their men. Before Will was fully awake, he knew that de Raite planned to attack someone, but he knew naught of where they were going or how many men, if any, would join them when they arrived.

Then, Hew said, "Our way up tae Loch Moigh lies a quartermile ahead. Allies be coming from all directions tae surround the castle afore dawn, so it will mean the end for the Malcolmtosh. Da says Jamie Stewart willna mind, 'cause we can prove Malcolm broke the peace when he stole Nairn back from us."

"Has de Raite *sent* word to the King?" Will asked as he finished arranging his plaid and adjusting his baldric to lie diagonally across his back and chest with his sheathed sword's hilt ready to draw with his right hand. Slipping his dirk into its own sheath, he added, "I ken fine that he *talked* of complaining to Jamie, but—"

"Sakes, man, he's been a-planning this attack since then," Hew said as if that should have been obvious and answered Will's question.

It was not obvious to Will, for though de Raite had seized Raitt Castle while Sir Fin was off fighting for the King, he had attempted little truly warriorlike since.

Malcolm, meantime, had steadily enhanced his own near-legendary repute with skillful handling of matters from the King's Parliaments to the royal victory at Lochaber and the Mackintoshes' meritorious actions and few losses at Inverlochy.

"But to attack Loch Moigh!" Will exclaimed. "That's just madness. Does it not sit much higher in these mountains, in the midst of Clan Chattan territory?"

"Aye, it does," Hew said with a smirk. "That be the glory of it. Sithee, they dinna ken we're a-coming. And, when we take it, we'll hang the wee Malcolmtosh from his own gatepost. But Da will explain it all tae ye, or tae Jamie if he must. Fact be that Malcolm be a gey old man wha' doesna listen tae reason. Da says he should ha' been hanged long since, so wi' luck, we'll attend tae that afore day's end."

Before Saturday's dawn broke two hours later, de Raite's men and their allies, from all directions, had crept up and over the steep, rocky slopes surrounding Loch Moigh and hidden themselves behind boulders, natural rises in the terrain, and in rocky declivities nearer the loch and the dark stone castle on its islet.

The night had remained moonless, damp, even muddy, and as dark as such a night could be, but the clouds were beginning to break. Stars peeked brightly between them, providing light enough to make out dark shapes of men moving here and there, but only, Will suspected, if one knew the men were there.

They had come quietly, making no more sound than the stirring of a pebble or the hushing of a leafy shrub or slight splash of a puddle as they eased themselves into concealment, less noise than night creatures might make while doing the same.

By Will's reckoning when he had topped the northwest end of the rockbound oval in which the loch's calm water mirrored the stars, Loch Moigh was over a mile long and nearly a half mile at its widest point. It lay northwest to southeast amid higher peaks of the Monadhliath Mountains. Its islet was much the same shape as the loch and perhaps one-fifth of its length.

The towering dark shadow of Moigh Castle dominated the islet.

At de Raite's order, Will led the way to the south shore with Dae and others behind him, keeping low to the muddy, broken ground and far enough above the water to be invisible to men in the castle or on its ramparts. Cautiously, he and Dae led the way eastward amid rocks and shrubs until they neared the loch's outflow.

There, its water spilled noisily into a shrubbery-flanked burn flowing steeply downhill. If Will reckoned right, it likely joined the river Erne, which flowed northeastward from the mountains and emptied into the Moray Firth ten miles northeast of Raitt, near a village called Invererne.

He soon got himself settled on mostly dry granite where he could see that the castle and loch remained peaceful. It was so peaceful in fact that, despite the glow of dawn from behind him that now lit the castle, he saw no hint of movement on its ramparts. Was Malcolm so confident of himself that he did not even post lookouts above? And where were his boats?

That last thought no sooner occurred to him than pandemonium erupted above them. Men seemed to erupt from the rocks and shrubbery there, trapping the Comyns between their attackers and the loch.

Leaping up, snatching his sword from its sheath, Will whirled to see an attacker rushing at him, his sword already aimed to knock Will's away from its central, protective position and likely slit his throat with its backswing.

Opting for closer quarters, Will stepped into the attack with his right foot and began shifting his sword toward center, as his opponent would expect. As quickly as the man brought his sword up and back to strike, Will dipped the tip of his under the other man's blade near its hilt, causing that blade to glide up along his own sword and bringing the two men closer together.

In a flash, his opponent's blade slid to the hilt of Will's sword and Will spun at once to his right, watching the end of the other blade pass left to right in front of his eyes as both blades closed and arced up together. Knowing he now had leverage, Will forced the other sword to the ground and stepped on it, anchoring it there.

As his opponent tried frantically to tug his weapon free, Will swiftly raised his sword tip skyward and struck the man's left jaw hard with the hilt.

The man dropped at his feet and lay still.

Will was bending to see that he still lived when another man challenged him.

Hoping to deter the second one with a wide swoop of his blade that slammed into the advancing sword with a clang that jarred his shoulders and nearly knocked him off his own feet, Will watched with almost as much dismay as his attacker did when the latter's sword crashed to the rocks, its blade shattered. The man turned away, his right hand seeking wildly, likely for the dirk sheathed beneath his plaid.

Action to his left then drew Will's eye briefly to Dae fighting someone. In that glance, beyond them, he also saw Malcolm's boats lined up safely on the islet shore, and swimmers in the water, heading toward them.

Comyns, likely still hoping to take the castle, he thought as he edged swiftly through an open space to Dae's side, just as Dae's opponent tried to behead him with a wave of his sword. Jerking Dae backward by his plaid with his free hand, Will engaged the driving sword, knocking it upward and away from Dae.

Its wielder was made of sterner stuff than the others, though, and retained control of his weapon. Aware of Dae scrabbling low behind him, doubtless having dropped his weapon, Will kept his attention on his opponent and tried to ignore the screams, shouts, clanging of steel, and general chaos around them, sounds to which until then he had been deaf. He was nonetheless aware that he and his opponent were moving too near the outflow of the loch for comfort.

With more light now, he saw that his opponent was tiring. As they circled each other, feinting, he also noted men on the ramparts, raining arrows down on the swimmers in the loch. By then, Will had determined that he could control his opponent's movements with his own, because the man was clearly more interested in killing him than in heeding the ground beneath their feet.

Granduncle Thomas had taught Will early on to avoid letting his opponent establish the ground. He had made Will practice not only such tactics but also how to control movements of almost any opponent in subtle ways. The trick generally required one to know the ground and gave an edge to men fighting on their own land. Will had practiced on every sort of terrain that Thomas could find, though, until rocks and declivities, shrubbery, and other such details of a landscape had become his friends. When he had spied out a path for himself, he worked his opponent toward the burn and then up onto the slope down which it plunged.

Seeing Dae duck behind bushes below the outflow, he realized that the men around him were so engaged in life-and-death struggles of their own that they paid no one else heed. Taking the first chance he saw to close with his man, he whipped his own dirk from its sheath and put its sharp point through the man's sword arm.

Snatching the weapon from his weakened hand, Will gave him a shove, growling, "Hide yourself in the rocks or under a bush. Ye've nae need tae die here."

Then, without pause, he dashed toward the place where he had last seen Dae and found him below the rise, cowering in a thicket of willows beside the burn.

"Ye see now that I be a feardie, just as Hew said," Dae grumbled.

"Hold your whisst," Will said curtly. "I mean to see us both safely home, but we must first follow this burn for a time, unseen. I'm unwilling to die in support of de Raite's daft notions, and not only did we know naught of this, but everyone up there is trying to kill an enemy with whom I have no quarrel. Nor do you. Sakes, we do not even know where de Raite and our other men are."

"From what I ken o' Hew," Dae muttered morosely, "for all that he calls me the feardie, when things go awry, he disappears. I ken fine that he, Colley, and Liam stayed well north o' the loch. As for yer da, he seems tae be the sort o' leader as would liefer lead from behind, as ye might say, so I'd wager he's somewheres on that side, too, high enough tae see the fighting without taking part in it. Neither o' them gives a man much confidence."

Silently, Will agreed with Dae's assessment of both men. He said firmly, though, "We have no time for talk if we're to get away from this place alive."

"Right, then, which way?"

"The sun is still behind those peaks east of us, and we are below the action here," Will said, thinking aloud. "Even so, we must move quickly to avoid notice, so you go ahead of me, straight downhill. Keep to shrubbery if you can. I'd liefer meet no swordsmen if we can avoid it. I don't even know most of the Comyns de Raite recruited, and every man here looks much the same as another to me. However, we must also take care to cross this burn before it joins the river Erne . . .

". . . if it does," he added silently.

"Art sure ye ken how tae get us out o' here?" Dae asked minutes later.

"I hope so. I do know the river Erne flows east of Raitt to the Moray Firth, so we must keep west of it and head north. In time, we will cross a path that runs from Moigh eastward to Glen Spey, where Malcolm's war leader lives at Rothiemurchus. My route along the ridge from Raitt has been to follow it to that path and back whilst keeping watch for groups of strangers or odd events."

"That may be a place tae ford, yonder," Dae said a short time later, pointing to an area below them where a number of boulders sat well above the water.

"Good," Will said. He could not hear the battle any longer over the sounds of the river, so he hoped it was over and that Colley and even Liam had had the good sense or good fortune to evade death. He was nearly as certain as Dae was that de Raite and Hew would emerge unscathed.

Just as the thought crossed his mind and he started to step from one boulder to another, he heard a rumbling crash above him and turned to see two boulders careening down toward them. His forward foot slipped, and knowing he could not save himself from a fall, he let himself go limp to minimize the damage.

He landed awkwardly, pain shooting through his right ankle, his head banging a rock. He heard Dae say distantly, "I think some'un ha' seen us."

CHAPTER 14

The days following the *cèilidh* passed slowly for Katy and other inhabitants of Castle Finlagh. On Malcolm's orders, received Friday, Fin had stayed home to be sure the castle did not become a target if things went amiss at Loch Moigh.

The twins knew their parents were uneasy, because their two older brothers, with holdings in Glen Spey, would have responded to Malcolm's call. Reports from several sources indicated that Comyn de Raite had assembled an imposing army.

The first news from Loch Moigh arrived late Sunday evening, when MacNab returned alone. Katy, Clydia, and Cat were with Fin in the inner chamber when MacNab arrived. When he smiled, showing that his news was not dire, Fin let them stay.

"I came as quick as I could, nigh running most of the way, but Moigh Castle be safe, for the knaves never got nigh it," MacNab said. "Malcolm sent runners out as soon as he got your warning, sir. He had a fine response, too, from every clan in the Confederation. From others, too, including your brother, Ewan Cameron, and his lot from west of Glen Mòr. I tell ye, it were a fine thing tae see.

"As Malcolm got word of Comyn de Raite's routes," he added, "men on our side hid themselves all around, well back from Loch Moigh. We let the Comyns move in and surround it, giving them glittous hellicats tae believe they could force unsuspecting Malcolm tae surrender. Instead, we ambushed them. We did lose some men in the battle but none as I know of from Finlagh, Glen Spey, or Cawdor."

"'Tis good news, then," Fin said, as Catriona expelled a breath of relief.

"Aye, Malcolm's plan worked, and de Raite's failed. We never even caught sight of him. He seems tae be one as avoids a fight by keeping hisself safe and sending others tae do the fighting. 'Tis no my way of leading, nor yours, Sir Fin, or Lochan's, or the Mackintosh's, either."

Katy's stomach had clenched when he said that de Raite sent others to fight. Certain as she was that Will must have been one of those he had sent, her throat closed so tightly she could barely breathe, let alone speak.

Although she was aware that Clydia was watching her, Katy kept her gaze on MacNab, hoping for more specific information.

Clydia said, "If de Raite avoided fighting, he likely survived the battle, aye?"

"Aye, m'lady," MacNab replied. "We'd heard nowt of his death afore Lochan sent me here tae report. Someone did say one of his sons was injured, but that were nobbut a rumor. Nae one could say which son it might be.

"For de Raite tae attack Moigh was daft," he added. "Sitting high in those mountains, in the midst of its loch, the castle be nigh impregnable. Its lookouts can see for miles; but de Raite thinks he can do what wiser men deem impossible."

"He *must* be daft," Katy muttered, her mouth so dry since his mention of de Raite's injured son that she could barely form the words. Aware that she had drawn her parents' notice, she kept her eyes on MacNab and said no more.

She shared her feelings only with Clydia after they were in bed that night.

"I know you disapprove," Katy said, "but Will did save my life that first day, so I cannot wish him ill. In fact, I'm in dreadful terror for him."

"I know," Clydia said softly from her own narrow bed. "Until we learn more, though, all you can do is pray that if Will is safe now, he keeps safe."

"He can*not* be dead," Katy said fiercely. "God would not be so cruel."

Will's injuries were neither severe enough nor painful enough to incapacitate him. They were enough, though, in Sunday's waning daylight to make him glad that despite their earlier scare with the boulder, no one seemed to be pursuing them.

His head, indeed most of him, ached. He had twisted his right ankle badly, and he was bone tired. Though his injuries irked him and Dae tried his patience, Dae had been kind enough to fashion a crutch out of a downed tree limb for him.

From a vantage point atop a rocky ridge west of the river Erne, thanks only to the red woolen cap Liam wore when he did not wear his helmet, they had seen what Will believed to be Hew, Liam, and Colley returning with de Raite by much the same way they had come. A ragtag score of men followed them, likely the few warriors from the Badenoch and Raitt contingents who had survived.

Will and Dae had followed the west bank of the river Erne for a time before climbing to the ridge above the river to let Will get his bearings.

Since then, they had seen no one else.

In Will's opinion, the Black Hour had been an omen of the failure to come. Likely, though, de Raite would be furious and blame everyone except himself for the defeat. Such was his usual reaction to loss or a thwarting of his expectations.

Hew and Liam would bear the brunt of his fury. As Will had seen, though, de Raite had badly underestimated the army Malcolm had raised in the short time he had had. By surrounding them all *and* the loch, his men had easily ambushed them.

Will remembered how de Raite had crowed that he would be close enough to see the dismay on Malcolm's face when the man awoke at dawn to find himself and his precious castle surrounded.

Shoving that image aside, Will tried to focus on putting one foot in front of the other and getting himself and Dae back to Raitt. Then, Katy's image intruded, looking as furious as she had been when she discovered he was a Comyn.

Doubtless, she would now deny ever having declared them married.

He expected to run into trouble at least once as he and Dae wended their way through the rugged mountains back toward Raitt, so they kept out of sight as much as possible. Although they had to move slowly, they managed to evade detection and found plenty of water. However, wary of building a fire, they ate mostly berries, raw nuts, and roots they found along the way.

By day's end Monday, Will was certain that the other Raitt men would be home long before them and wondered if anyone had even missed them, let alone searched for them. They camped that night by a burn and reached the track that led east to Glen Spey near day's end on Tuesday.

When forested slopes came into view as they headed north, they felt safe enough when they reached the trees to wash off the worst of their dirt in the first rill they saw. Will also soaked his still-angry ankle again for a while before moving on.

That night, they slept soundly in dense shrubbery and followed Will's patrol route on Wednesday, keeping below the ridgeline of the hills, where he knew from experience that they could elude watchers. He thought they must be two days behind de Raite and the others by then.

"You should go on ahead of me now, Dae," he said. "I've slowed you down for days and can make it from here easily, so—"

"Nae, then," Dae interjected, wide-eyed. "I'd no be able tae sleep nights did I let aught happen tae ye after ye saved me life as ye did. 'Twere bad enough that ye had tae do that, though I did warn ye that I'm nae good wi' a sword."

"Blethers," Will said. "You fought as hard as anyone and have naught for which to apologize. I helped at the last only because *I* wanted us to get away."

Dae shook his head. "I'm nae warrior," he said. "Never could be. I like visiting Raitt, but I didna expect tae end up in any battle, let alone agin such a warrior as yon Mackintosh. I ha' nae wish tae say aught agin yer da, but . . ."

When he hesitated, Will said bleakly, "I feel as you do, Dae. De Raite seeks to control all the land that our ancestors held and refuses to see that his hopes are futile, because he will never persuade wiser men like my granduncle Thomas to join his cause. Without them . . ." He shrugged.

"Aye, and wasna that what I were a-telling m'self, whiles ago?" Dae replied. "I believed he meant only tae talk wi' clansmen and come tae agreement wi' them. He never asked me did I want tae *fight* for him."

"Nor did he ask me," Will said. "The others must have known, though. I'm surprised Hew did not warn you."

"He thinks little o' me skills as a warrior," Dae said with a grimace. "Nae more do I think better o' m'self, though. Sithee, it be rare these days tae find oneself at battle in the Lowlands. In the Borders, aye, for men turn on each other there like tomcats in mating season and most times wi' less warning. In more peaceful places, like our village nigh St. John's Town, a man forgets what it be like tae take up arms and fight for his life. I *like* peace, m'self."

"Certes, I'd like to see more of it hereabouts," Will said grimly.

At last, Thursday at midday, he caught sight of Castle Finlagh through the trees ahead and, aware that Katy must suspect where he had gone and know what had happened there, he watched for a view of the pool above it, uneasy about what he might see. To his deep relief and delight, white kerchiefs decked the shrubs.

Having laundered her kerchiefs at the pool on Monday, Katy had walked to the Stone with Argus and Eos each day since then without seeing Will. Failing again Thursday afternoon, she wended her way home by way of the south stream to find Clydia on one knee beside it with her skirts rucked up, filling her pail.

Looking up with a sympathetic smile, Clydia said, "I've not seen him either, Kate, or heard anyone mention his name. Da did hear that de Raite returned late Tuesday with some of his men, so yesterday he sent more of ours than usual to the ridge. If Will tried to return through our mountains instead, he may have seen our men and changed his mind. Forbye, if he took part in that attack, he likely fears that you will no longer welcome him here."

Again, Katy nearly told her that she and Will had married by declaration, so she could hope he had *not* taken part in the raid, but honesty banished the thought. If his father ordered him to fight, Will would have obeyed him.

She remembered something else, too.

"He told me they were going to confer with allies in Glen Mòr, Clydie, so I think de Raite lied to him, for I am as certain as I can be that when Will said he would have to be away for a time, he did not expect to be going into battle. Had he so much as suspected it, he would not have been so casual about leaving."

Especially since I had just declared us married, she added to herself. *Even if he didn't believe me!*

"Then he is simply not home yet," Clydia said. Straightening with the full pail, she shot a shrewd glance at Katy and added, "Do not fear for him until you have cause, Kate. Recall how long it took our Àdham to get home after Inverlochy."

"Aye, but Inverlochy is much farther from here than Moigh even if de Raite went by the longest route, and—"

"Nae, then," Clydia interjected. "Do not borrow trouble, Kate. It usually comes quick enough on its own. Help me carry this pail."

"Aye, sure," Katy said, suppressing a sigh. Carrying the heavy pail between them, they went back to the castle to water Clydia's garden. When they had finished, Clydia gathered her tools and put them away in a nearby shed.

Katy saw Bridgett across the courtyard, talking with Lochan. Just then, Bridgett threw her hands in the air, turned, and strode into the castle through the kitchen door, slamming it shut behind her so hard that the sound echoed in the yard.

Looking again at Lochan, Katy saw the big man, arms akimbo, staring at that door. One blond eyebrow quirked up, but his lips were pressed tightly together.

Emerging from the shed, Clydia said, "What was that noise?"

"Bridgett slamming the kitchen door. She is irked with Lochan."

Clydia grinned. "Then I expect she told him so. He does look a bit stunned."

"She has likely been as worried about him as I am about Will," Katy said quietly. "Remember what she said after the *cèilidh*?"

Clydia blinked. "I do. She was afraid he might die before she could tell him that she had not meant everything that she had said to him that night. She did have time before they all left, though, to say whatever she wanted to say to him."

"Aye, perhaps," Katy agreed. "One often feels, though, as if one has lots of time ahead to speak. Even Bridgett, who prides herself on speaking her mind, might have hesitated to tell Lochan she worried about his safety."

Clydia nodded thoughtfully. "I love our cousin Àdham dearly, but I admit that I would hesitate to tell him such a thing. Men can be touchy about a woman's concern. 'Tis as if they fear we don't trust their skills."

"I think they fear that such words could linger in their minds and undermine their ability to protect themselves," Katy said.

"That sounds wise," Clydia said. "Art sure you are still my twin, who rarely thinks such thoughts about herself, let alone about others?"

With Will's image prominent again in her mind's eye, Katy said solemnly, "I am learning, Clydie. I remember Mam saying once when Da was away, years ago, that 'tis hard not to worry and harder still not to let them know that you do. I had not thought about it since that day, but when you said men could be touchy, it jumped right into my head again."

"Then I expect you mean to go to the Stone again tomorrow," Clydia said.

"Aye, tomorrow and the day after and the day after that, if I must."

CHAPTER 15

Will and Dae barely stayed awake long enough Thursday night to eat supper and were asleep before de Raite and the others returned from Nairn. When Will awoke Friday morning all alone in the attic, he knew that Dae and the others who shared it had left him to sleep and was grateful.

Despite his attempt to dismiss Alyssa's belief that Katy had worried as much about his safety as she had, he could not let it go. Katy filled his first thoughts just as she had filled his dreams for days. He looked forward to meeting her again as soon as possible to let her see for herself that he was safe.

His head no longer hurt unless he touched a spot that had made solid contact with a rock. His ankle was another matter. It still ached, but when he stood it seemed able to bear his weight.

Bending to pick up his pallet and add it to the stack against the nearby wall, he ignored the makeshift crutch. He could walk without it, although that might become less bearable if he took his usual route. He could get to the Stone, though, if he could think of a way to justify leaving Raitt without doing his patrol.

Finding Dae alone at the high table, Will realized that the hour was later than he had thought.

His cousin eyed him with a grin. "I thought ye might sleep all day. I could have, and I didna ha' tae bear wi' your injuries."

"Is de Raite here?" Will asked.

"Yonder in his chamber, but the man's mean as a badger wi' sore feet today. When Alyssa and her woman come doonstairs earlier, he told Aly tae get herself back up tae her chamber and told Meggie tae take *all* her meals up tae her. Said he were in nae frame o' mind tae stomach females at his table today. I were thinkin' it might be a kindness for me tae marry that lass and tak' her home wi' me."

"Do it," Will said tersely. "I'd give you my permission, not that it will matter if de Raite refuses. I doubt that he would, though."

"But he would, aye," Dae said. "Thinks o' her as part o' his chattel, he does. Forbye, the lass doesna see me for nowt, and I'm none so certain o' me own dad. He's been after me tae wed a townswoman, which be one reason I came tae Raitt."

Nodding thanks to the lad who hurried in with a platter of beef, a bowl of boiled eggs, and a basket of hot rolls, Will took an egg and cracked it on the table.

"D'ye want mustard, sir?"

"Aye," Will said as he peeled the egg. Then, to Dae as the gillie trotted back toward the screens passage and kitchen, he said, "Where are Hew and the others?"

"De Raite sent them intae them east woods tae gather wood and bring home meat. Said that though they hadna done much tae aid him at Loch Moigh, mayhap they could find game such as rabbits, quail, or pheasant, for supper tonight."

"Ouch," Will said, glancing toward the inner-chamber door to be sure it was shut. "It sounds as if the man fails to recall that he ordered them to stay with him, in safety, to oversee the battle."

"Aye, his memory has always seemed tae be more convenient for him than for truth," Dae said. "I'm thinking o' takin' m'self off, afore the lion emerges from his lair. Ye'd be wise tae do the same, nae?"

"That is good advice," Will said. "I may head over the north slope of our ridge and down into the woods on the other side."

"D'ye want company?"

"Nae, I'll just find a place in the woods, sit for a spell, and enjoy the solitude. I'm still too achy and tired to put up with everyone here, or to walk far. So, if de Raite expected me to walk the ridge today, he'll be disappointed."

"Aye, he will, for I willna do it either. Me feet still hurt, and he didna say nowt about the ridge. Come tae that, he didna say nowt tae me o' nowt. So, if ye dinna want me, I'll take me bow and seek game in yon woods south o' here."

Will wished him good luck and decided that the sooner he, too, was gone the less chance there would be of a clash with de Raite. On the thought, he put a roll and a second egg in a small cloth sack to tuck under his belt, rolled up two slices of beef, added a bit of mustard when the lad came pelting back down the hall with a wee pot of the stuff, and minutes later, was outside the wall.

Pondering as he chewed his meat, he decided that for once the Fates had been kind. With his brothers in the east woods, his best and safest course was to head northwest, which was exactly the way he wanted to go.

Heading over the lowest part of the ridge to the main road, taking his time to ease strain on his ankle, he followed it to its intersection with the path to Finlagh. A glance at the sun then told him it was nearing midafternoon.

Will quickened his pace.

Hearing someone coming through the woods from the northeast and doubting that Will would announce his presence so noticeably, Katy hastily scattered the small cairn she had been leaving each day by the Stone and quietly stepped behind it. She had left Rory and the dogs far enough away that the boy would not overhear anything she and Will said if Will did come, but near enough for Rory and the dogs to hear her shout.

The boy had promised that he would stay put, and she was sure he would. He had told her himself that he knew Will was a man who kept his word.

Cautiously peeping through branches, and despite the dense woodland, she could see enough of the approaching figure to feel reassured. She waited, though, until he stepped into sight and she saw that he was limping.

Rushing from behind the Stone to cast herself into his arms, she sighed with relief when they closed warmly around her.

"I am glad to see you, too," he murmured, kissing the top of her head. "Look at me, lass. I want a proper kiss."

She looked up then, meaning to ask how he had gotten hurt, but his lips found hers before she could, and his arms tightened around her.

Responding with eager willingness, she dismissed the rest of the world and enjoyed his kisses and caresses, hugging him, and reveling in his presence. When he moved to spread his plaid on the ground near the Stone again, she helped and immediately noted his injury again. "Why are you limping?"

"I was clumsy, turned my ankle," he replied, moving gingerly to sit on the plaid and patting the place beside him. "It can happen to anyone."

As she nestled in beside him, she said curiously, "Do you mean to say that you did *not* take part in the battle at Loch Moigh?"

"Nae, lass, for I did."

"Then, why did you not warn me that the Comyns meant to attack there?" she asked reasonably. "The Mackintosh is our liege lord, after all."

"But I had nae ken of that plan when I saw you. By my troth, lass, de Raite said naught of his scheme to me or to anyone who might have warned me until shortly before the attack. I did begin to suspect some such plan, but—"

"Would you have warned us if you *had* known?"

He hesitated.

"Well, sir?"

"Lass, I don't know what I'd have done then. I feel dreadful that I took any part in it at all. I am a Comyn, and I ken fine the history of the feuding betwixt our clans, but my cousin and I could scarcely tell one side from the other and left the field as soon as we could. He, too, had followed de Raite's orders unknowingly."

"I don't care about him. But you profess to care about me, and we are—"

"I do care about you," he interjected. "In fact, I—"

"Then you should . . . Faith, I know that one's clan is one's clan,

Will, but it irks me that you cannot tell me what you *would* have done. I hate this feud!"

"I, too," he said, with a sad sigh. "I dinna want to fratch, Katy-love."

Giving herself a shake to cool her temper, she reached up to stroke his cheek as she said, "I don't want to, either. I just wish we could run away to a place where clans do not feud, where we could live peaceably. We are married now, after all, unless you mean to tell everyone you do not believe me when I say that it is legal."

"I would not contradict you or abandon you, *mo chridhe*," he said with his warm smile. "Whatever I may believe, and though we did depart the battle since we had no quarrel with either side, I am not a man who customarily runs away.

"Sithee, de Raite had sent us and the others to surround Loch Moigh and its islet castle, gloating that he would be near enough to see Malcolm's dismay when he awoke that morning. Instead, the Mackintosh's men let us place ourselves before moving quietly in to ambush *us*, trapping us between themselves and the loch. Dae and I both had to defend ourselves, but, by my troth, lass, I know not if the men we fought were Mackintoshes or Comyns, because everyone was wet and muddy from the rain and from creeping about as we were doing. Come to that," he added as if it had occurred to him only then, "many on our side did not know me. Any one of them might have mistaken me for a Mackintosh— and Dae, as well."

"That would have been horrid," she said, hugging him again.

"Aye, it would," he agreed. "As for running away with you now, I'd like nothing better than to be with you always. But I ken better than most how it is to be torn from people one loves. You'd be miserable if you had to leave your family."

Wanting to deny those words, to make clear to him her certainty that she had fallen in love with him and would be happy anywhere he was, Katy managed for once to hold her impulsive tongue long enough to try to imagine a way to make such a declaration credible.

Instead, she realized that Will was right.

Will could see Katy's thoughts in her expressive face and recognized the moment she knew he was right.

Drawing her closer, he held her, inhaling the sweet herbal scent of her hair.

"I built a cairn by the Stone, so you would know I'd been here, and scattered it only today when I was not sure it was you I heard coming," she murmured against his chest. "I . . . I came yesterday, too, *and* Tuesday and Wednesday as well."

"Alone?" he asked, raising his eyebrows and holding her a little away to watch her expression but trying to avoid an accusatory note.

Apparently, he failed, for she looked up at him with a mischievous smile. "I, too, keep my word, sir. I promised my father I'd not walk about alone, but I left Rory and the dogs far enough from here that, although they will hear if I call to them, Rory cannot hear what we say. He promised he would stay there, and he does not break his word, either."

"You are sure of that?"

"I am. I would remind you, too, that when I heard you coming from the north, rather than the south, I stepped behind the Stone until I could see through the shrubbery that it *was* you. I expected you to come your usual way, and silently."

She was learning to think more carefully, which was good. Chuckling, he said, "My ankle still betrays me, so I am a bit clumsy. If young Rory and the dogs are waiting for you, though, mayhap you should go."

"I don't want to go yet," she said. "I was gey worried about you, Will. I know you will say I should not worry, and I am sure you are a fine warrior, but I cannot help it. My father is Sir Fin of the Battles, known as such throughout Scotland, and I still worry about him if he has to fight."

"I know what it is to worry, Katy-love. I cannot be vexed with you for caring about my safety."

"I like you to call me that," she said, smiling. "Do you love me?"

"Wilkin told me that I do, right after the *cèilidh*," he said with a teasing look.

"That does not answer my question."

"Even if I tell you that he told your twin that I do?"

"She did not mention that to me, however."

"Aw, lassie, you must ken fine that I do. But we both know that no one in our families will want to hear that I do," he added soberly.

"But I do love you, too, Will, so we can worry about all that and sort it out later. When will I see you again?"

"We cannot meet every day without leaving trails for others to see, but I'll watch for your kerchiefs and cairns and you can watch for my cairns at the stream."

"The pail-and-smack stream," she said with a grin. "Aye, good, but you should not walk our ridge so often for a time, I think, sir. Not only has Da put more men out, but you should also rest your ankle. Art sure 'twas your only injury?"

"I have a few bruises, too," he admitted. Pulling her close again to kiss her and making an even more thorough job of it this time, he realized that his head was no longer aching and decided she was good medicine for him.

There was one thing that still worried him, though.

"Look here," he said, holding her away again, "you haven't told your parents about that declaration of yours, have you?"

"Nae," she said with a sigh. "I am not brave enough to do that alone. If you were willing to stand with me, I could tell them."

"Aye, perhaps, but we cannot do that without talking more first, and planning," he said. "The way things are now . . ."

"Aye," she said, nodding when he paused. "But I should tell you, sir, that I never understood love until I realized how much I feared for you, knowing that you were likely in the battle at Loch Moigh. If only you could come to us and take shelter at Finlagh. We could tell my parents then, together."

Will shook his head. "I cannot, Katy. I would be deserting Aly, and like it or not, I still owe duty to de Raite."

"No one would blame you for leaving him, though, and you can bring Aly with you," she said impulsively. "I mean it, Will. You would both be welcome."

"Do you think so? I do not, because de Raite would declare war on Finlagh."

"Aly says your father does not care about her. Also, she could marry Gilli Roy."

"I ken fine who you mean, because she told me about him, but that would make everything much worse. I know Aly thinks de Raite does not care about her, but she is his daughter, lass, and I can assure you that he would wreak havoc if she ran away and tried to marry a Mackintosh. As for what Malcolm would do—"

"But surely, de Raite would not test Malcolm's strength again? Not now."

"Perhaps, but with all that has happened, tempers are too high on both sides for reason to prevail. I want you more than I can say, Katy-love," he added. "We *will* find a way, but it will be through wisdom and patience, *not* by running away."

Argus and Eos met Katy some yards from where she had left them, but Rory had kept his word and stayed put. His curiosity was evident, and he waited bare seconds after spotting her before demanding to know if she had seen Will.

"Aye, he is safe," she said quietly. "But do not ask more questions, because I do not want to talk. We will go back to Finlagh."

"Sakes, were he vexed wi' ye? He shouldna—"

"I told you to ask no more questions, Rory. I mean it. I need to think."

"Aye then, I'm mum, but ye must ken fine that it be nearly time for supper."

"I know, so we must hurry."

Parting from the boy when they arrived in the courtyard, Katy went inside and found Clydia upstairs in their bedchamber with Bridgett. That they had been talking was evident when both turned to her and then looked at each other.

Recalling Bridgett's reaction to Lochan earlier and having no wish to discuss Will in her presence, Katy said to Clydia, "Have you asked her why she stormed away from Lochan and slammed the kitchen door?"

"I have," Clydia said. "However, you arrived before she told me anything more than that she is furious with him."

"We saw that much ourselves," Katy said, beginning to untie her kirtle laces, thereby releasing dry leaves that had caught in them while she'd crouched in the bushes behind the Stone. "What did he do now, Bridgett?"

"I hung your russet-colored kirtle on yon hook for ye," Bridgett said with a gesture toward the garment, looking askance at the leaves. "As tae Lochan, the man must be mad. Ye ken fine that his mam kens Granny Rosel and me own mam."

"Everyone for miles knows Granny Rosel," Clydia said. "Most of them also know that Ailvie is Mam's attire woman."

"Aye, that be true, and ye ken fine that Lochan's mam lives nigh them, aye?"

Impatiently, Katy said, "We know them all, Bridgett. What did *Lochan* do?"

"The dafty asked his mam does she *like* me."

Katy rolled her eyes, and Clydia said, "But what is wrong with that, Bridgett? I should think that any man would want his mother to like the lass he might . . . that is, to like any woman that he liked."

"Aye, sure, but that isna Bruce Lochan," Bridgett said, adding indignantly, "The dafty told me his mam said she were a good friend o' mine. I dinna ken that I'd call her a *good* friend, being as she's years older than what I am. She speaks kind tae me, though, and I ha' always been courteous tae her."

"I still fail to see why you are angry with Lochan," Clydia said.

"Then I'll tell ye plain, m'lady. The man straight out told me that he doesna *like* his mam's friends!"

"Oh," Clydia said, and though her mouth was still open, she left it at that.

Katy bit her lower lip hard, wanting to laugh but knowing she would hurt Bridgett's feelings if she did. Then thoughts of Will swept back, making her wish she could talk as openly with someone, just to say everything that she was thinking and feel safe doing so. It was the first time in her life that she had not shared every thought with her twin. But at the thought of seeking Clydia's advice about Will Comyn, a cloud of doubt swirled into her mind.

Clydia disapproved of her meetings with Will. She would likely react just as their parents would to news of Katy's declaration of marriage to him.

Sakes, her inner voice muttered, *the one who knows more about all of this than anyone else is that scamp Rory. I certainly cannot discuss it with him!*

De Raite was waiting for Will, clearly furious. "Did ye think tae avoid me again, sir? Where the devil ha' ye been keeping yerself since ye got home?"

Will knew that his anger was more about how long it had taken him and Dae to get home from Moigh than anything that happened afterward. He listened quietly to what de Raite said and apologized when it seemed appropriate. He explained his injuries and how he had acquired them, and when de Raite began to repeat himself, Will asked him pointedly about the outcome for the rest of their men.

"We lost nigh two-thirds o' them, thanks tae them treacherous Mackintoshes. Ye and Dae were nae help tae us either, it seems," de Raite added snidely.

"No man can do more than his best, sir. None of us expected them to ambush us as they did. They must have placed themselves at a distance long before we drew nigh, but none of our own lads or our allies reported such movement as there must have been for Malcolm to have gathered such a force and got them into place."

"Aye, but someone *ought* tae ha' seen it," de Raite snapped. Will did not rise to bait so plain but let him rant until de Raite added, "Come tae that, ye be one o' them who ought tae ha' seen them. I ken fine that Fin sent his man Lochan wi' a host o' men. Ye must ha' missed their departure from Finlagh. Tell Liam I want him tae take your patrol for the nonce. Ye'll stay here tae rest your foot and mayhap think on keepin' your useless opinions tae yourself for a time."

No one commented on Katy's afternoon absence, so she hoped to avoid discussing it at all. However, she and Clydia had no sooner gotten into bed and seen Bridgett depart than Clydia said, "Did you see him? Is he safe?"

"Aye, he is," Katy replied, fluffing up a pillow.

"Is that all you mean to tell me? Was he wounded?"

"He hurt his ankle and has a few bruises."

"So he did fight with the Comyns against our people."

"He did not know that de Raite meant to attack Malcolm," Katy said flatly. "No one, let alone de Raite himself, told him where they were going."

"Or so your Will says," Clydia said mildly. "He is bound to be loyal to his clan, Kate, and to fight whenever his father or brothers say he must."

"He said neither he nor his Lowland cousin knew de Raite's intentions until they reached Loch Moigh. Malcolm's men had laid an ambush. Will is lucky to have escaped death."

Clydia was silent.

"You think he is lying to me," Katy said at last. "He would not do that, for he dislikes lying or even shading the truth, Clydie. Moreover, he cares for me—deeply—and I . . . I love him."

"You think you do," Clydia said. "You scarcely know the man, Kate. Moreover, he began your so-called relationship with a lie."

"He did *not* lie," Katy said, her tone sharpening. Striving to sound as calm as Clydia was, she added, "He did not admit that he was a Comyn straightaway, but you know why he did not. Despite that, I felt then and I feel now as if I have known and loved him forever. Sakes, Clydie, the man saved my life, and the truth is that I hope to spend the rest of it *with* him."

"Katy, you know you cannot do that. Da will never allow it."

"He cannot stop it. I . . ." Realizing what she had nearly said, she fought to think of words that would make it sound logical or at least—

"Just what do you mean by that," Clydia demanded, silencing Katy's thoughts. "Our father would do *anything* he had to do to stop such a wedding."

Tears welled in Katy's eyes, and her throat tightened so she could not speak.

"Well?" Clydia said. "You know I'm right."

Swallowing hard, Katy said, "'Tis too late. Do you recall Brother Julian?"

Sitting upright, her anger visible in the moon's pale light through the unshuttered window, Clydia exclaimed, "Do you mean to say that Will Comyn declared you marri— But nae," she said, correcting herself dryly. "He would not know of Brother Julian unless you told him. You did it yourself, did you not?"

Katy's voice failed her again, but Clydia's did not. "Have you gone mad, Kate?" She went right on from there, giving free rein to her anger.

Unlike Katy, Clydia rarely lost her temper, but when she did, it was fiery, even explosive, and often loud. Katy nearly always tried, unsuccessfully, to defend herself. This time, she did not try.

She knew that Clydia was right in many ways. She should not have acted as she had; their parents would be angry; and worst of all, she did not know what Will's father might do in response to her declaration of marriage. Come to that, if de Raite found out and forbade it, Katy did not know if Will would support the declaration.

Nevertheless, she listened until her twin had had her say.

Even then, she was quiet.

"Have you naught to say?" Clydia demanded.

"I love him, Clydie. I know you think I'm daft or even mad, but since that first day I have felt as if, next to Da, Will is the best and kindest man I know. I trust him and I want him. If I cannot have him, I will refuse to marry anyone else."

CHAPTER 16

De Raite's sour mood continued for several days while messenger after messenger arrived from his erstwhile allies to report their losses.

Finally, into a long silence at the midday meal on the last day of June, Hew said, "It has occurred tae me that, wi' so few allies left tae us, if the Malcolmtosh decides tae attack us, he might just snatch Raitt back for hisself."

De Raite rounded on him with a snarl, saying, "That will never happen, Hew Comyn. Not whilst I be alive tae prevent it!"

Softly but nonetheless daringly, Alyssa said, "Mayhap the Mackintosh will offer us a more peaceful solution, Father. 'Tis likely that he and his allies lost many men, too. He may want to seek—"

"Leave the table!" de Raite bellowed, half rising from his two-elbow chair. "This be men's talk and none for witless females!"

Flushing deeply, Aly jumped up from her back-stool and fled. Without a word, Meggie followed her.

Forcing himself to speak calmly, Will said, "If Aly should be right, sir, surely you would not spurn such an offer."

Livid with fury, de Raite surged to his feet, shoving the heavy chair over behind him. "This meal be over," he snapped. "All o' ye, every last man o' ye, get outside and get back tae your chores. I dinna want tae see your faces again today."

Two evenings later, a full moon had no sooner risen above the eastern horizon than a dark shadow began slowly but surely to creep across it, covering nearly all of it and stirring many residents of Raitt to express concern over this newest astronomical event. It took more than two hours for the shadow to pass.

Most folks had seen a partial lunar eclipse before, but as Meggie told Will, "'Tis gey ominous, sir, coming so soon after the sun disappeared. Folks still be frettin' about the end o' the world."

De Raite loudly insisted to everyone that he had seen many such events before, but he became more irritable than ever.

By then, a week had passed since Will's return, and his ankle no longer troubled him, but Liam had insisted on continuing the patrols southward. As much as Will wanted to see Katy again, he did not want to draw de Raite's fire by arguing with Liam and had not dared risking a signal until he could be sure it was safe.

Then, Friday morning while nearly all who took meals in the great hall were still breaking their fast, de Raite stood abruptly to announce that he had decided upon a new course of action.

Will stiffened, fearing that he meant to attack somewhere else, even Finlagh.

"Sithee, our Will and Alyssa dinna be wrong tae want peace," de Raite said, glancing down the table at them. "Our Hew were right, too, tae say that without peace, the Malcolmtosh and his damnable Confederation might try tae seize Raitt from us. Still, I ha' decided that we canna wait for the Malcolmtosh tae request such peace, for I dinna think the man has the wisdom tae do it.

"So, though Liam already be on the ridge and this goes against me own nature and good sense," he said, "I sent a running gillie tae Moigh nobbut an hour ago wi' a message tae Malcolm. I told the man that our losses ha' been so great—as, in troth, they have—that I be willing tae bury animosities and establish friendly relations wi' him and his Confederation if he will agree tae such. Tae that end, I ha' invited him, his two knights—Sir Fin o' the Battles o' Finlagh and Malcolm's war leader, Sir Ivor Shaw-Mackintosh o' Rothiemurchus—along wi' their lawful tails, tae celebrate our agreement here at Raitt a sennight from tonight wi' a grand banquet. We must seal such an agreement wi' proper ceremony, aye?"

The hall remained silent, as if everyone had stopped breathing.

Then, Colley said, "Is that no too soon tae expect the man tae come here, Da?"

"It is not," de Raite retorted. "God created the world in *six* days! I also said that Malcolm must send his reply tae me by me own gillie, for I didna want tae give him time for plotting schemes o' his own. He need only command Sir Ivor tae meet him at Finlagh. We just had a full moon, so they will still ha' a good half-moon tae return tae Finlagh after the banquet. I ha' also decreed that, since it is tae be a celebration o' peace, nae one is tae bear arms."

Again, silence followed his words. Below the dais, men were looking from one to another, making Will wonder if they were thinking as skeptically he was.

That de Raite would not only entertain a peaceful solution but offer one to Malcolm seemed so unlike the man as to be almost humorous. He could think of nothing to say, though, and he was certainly not going to laugh.

Abruptly, Alyssa clapped her hands together and exclaimed joyfully, "Oh, Father, what a splendid notion! How wise and generous you are to think of it!"

A cheer sounded, then another and another, here and there, until everyone was cheering and clapping.

De Raite beamed, accepting the ovation as his due.

Will told himself firmly to be grateful and to do all he could to see that de Raite followed through with his offer.

"Will, is it not wonderful?" Aly exclaimed. "Now we can—"

Leaning swiftly closer, he muttered, "Whisst, lassie, whisst! Say naught more of this now. We'll talk of it later."

Some of the light went out of her eyes, but he could not help that. Even if de Raite did mean to make peace with Malcolm and the Clan Chattan Confederation, he would never agree to a marriage of his daughter to Malcolm's son—especially his youngest one, who, as youngest, had little to recommend him—or, come to that, to one between his own youngest son and a daughter of Fin of the Battles, no matter how beautiful, desirable, and incredibly lovable she was.

That last thought tied a knot in his chest and erased what little was left of the brief surge of hope he had felt after de Raite's announcement.

The fact was that de Raite was not only deceitful himself but distrusting of others, all of whom, he chose to believe, were as dishonorable as he was. By comparison, the Mackintosh was a prime example of honor.

A notion stirred then that de Raite might be counting on that trait for some scheme of his own.

Will felt desperate to see Katy, but what he might say to her and how they could safely meet if Liam continued to claim his patrol he did not know. Just then, as if the thought had conjured him up, Liam strode into the hall, looking grim.

De Raite snapped, "What the devil be ye doing back here so soon? Ye canna ha' been gone longer than an hour or so."

"Two great wolf dogs tried tae attack me is why!" Liam snapped back.

Beside Will, Aly started and turned to him, but when he put a warning hand on her arm, she settled back in her seat and pressed her lips together.

"Did ye kill them?" de Raite demanded.

"Nae, I did not, for I were just above Finlagh. They appeared of a sudden right before me. Then, a woman some distance back o' them saw me, so I shouted doon tae call off the dogs. She just stared at me, so I shouted that I'd lost me way, a-heading for Nairn. When she pointed northward, I hied m'self back here."

"Seems tae me ye should ha' been much farther south by then," de Raite said. Without giving Liam time to reply, he looked at Will. "Has anyone ever caught ye on yon route, William?"

"Nae, sir," Will replied firmly. "I expect I've had more training than Liam, though, in moving through woodland without raising an alarm."

Liam glowered, but de Raite ignored him, saying, "Then ye'll return tae that duty, Will, at once. I want as much news as ye can glean from there. Keep watch over paths tae the south, too, where Malcolm or Sir Ivor might travel."

"Aye, sir, willingly," Will said with deep sincerity.

Katy felt as if she had tiptoed through the week in near isolation from the rest of her world. She had neither seen nor heard from Will and feared he might have suffered more injuries than he had admitted.

She had left her kerchief on a shrub near the pool after a visit to Granny Rosel two days ago and could recall nothing now that the two of them had discussed.

Leaving the kerchief in place, she had twice visited the Stone, hoping to find Will waiting for her, but she had not left a cairn there and had retrieved the kerchief earlier that Friday morning, because she dared not return three days in a row. As it was, she had risked Fin's discovering her absences and demanding explanations she would prefer not to give.

Clydia, having had her say, would not betray her. Her twin's anger had evaporated once she had expressed her opinions and Katy had listened to her.

Katy had made her no promises, though. Nor would she.

She had spoken the truth in declaring her love for Will, and she wanted to believe that her declaration *had* made them lawfully husband and wife. She was sure that her parents would object to such a union nonetheless and that Fin, who knew the King of Scots personally, would find a way to nullify it even if it was just as legal as Brother Julian had said it was.

As for de Raite, she did not want to imagine how he might react if he found out about her declaration, or what he might do to Will for knowing her.

What she wanted, more than anything, was to see Will and hear his voice.

She was deep in such thoughts during Friday's midday meal, wondering how she could love a man so and fret herself nearly sick over him, when she had known him for such a short time and seen him so few times since meeting him.

"Who the devil was he?" Fin demanded so abruptly that his question pierced straight through Katy's thoughts and drew her startled gaze.

He was looking at her mother, though, as Cat turned calmly

to nod at the manservant holding a basket of apples for her to select one.

Leaning close to Clydia, Katy muttered, "Who was who?"

"A man Da just heard that Mam saw yesterday in the woods, above . . . um . . ." Lowering her voice, she leaned closer and breathed, "the pail-and-smack—"

Her interest suddenly intense, Katy turned back toward her mother.

Apple now in hand, Cat said mildly, "I don't know who he was."

"Then why did you not raise an alarm?" Fin demanded.

"Because he was well above me on that slope and shouted that he'd got lost trying to reach Nairn. I pointed northward, and he went on his way. Come to that, my love, I expect that someone on the ramparts heard us shouting and told you."

Fin nodded, frowning thoughtfully.

"How did you see him, Mam?" Katy asked. "I was not paying heed."

"The dogs alerted and cornered him," Catriona replied with a smile.

Katy relaxed. Argus and Eos knew Will and would not have treated him so.

Concern swept back when she realized that the man her mother saw might have been one of Will's brothers spying on them. De Raite had likely sent someone else to patrol the ridge while Will's ankle healed.

Still pondering, Katy returned her attention to her food.

She and Clydia headed for the garden that afternoon. Opening the shed where she kept her tools and pails, Clydia said, "We'll fetch water first from the stream."

"Aye, sure," Katy agreed, taking the pail she handed her. Leaving the courtyard, they walked down into the woods flanking the south stream.

When they reached the eddy from which they usually took water for the garden, Katy noticed a neat pile of stones that had not been there the day before.

"Clydie, Will has been here. That cairn is his signal. Usually, it means he will meet me at the Stone the next day, but it would not do to irk Da just when Will is back again. If he left this cairn this morning as he was heading south, mayhap I can meet him here on his way back."

"You must not come here alone," Clydia said.

"Nae, I'll bring the dogs. They will know he's coming before I will."

Will had made his escape the minute he could that morning, having concern only lest his headaches return or his ankle fail to withstand a whole day's patrol.

Within half an hour of leaving Raitt, away from his difficult family, he was pain free, alone with his thoughts in peaceful woodland, and grinning at a squirrel as it darted down a tree. It hesitated when it reached the ground to look at him and then ran across his path into the shrubbery beyond.

He had not gone as far south as usual, because it was his first day out. He had taken his time, and he wanted to be home in good time for supper.

He had also taken time earlier to leave a cairn of rocks by the pail-and-smack stream as a signal for Katy that he hoped to meet her the next day.

Nearing Finlagh, he decided to see if she had left a sign of her own.

Angling down the slope when he saw the castle, he wanted to end up just above the stream where he had met her twin.

The breeze blowing toward him was pleasantly cool, and the day was fine. Yet he saw no person outside the castle wall, nor any kerchief on shrubbery near the pool above the knoll. Still, she might have left a sign near his cairn.

Hearing distant yet unrecognizable feminine voices ahead, he slowed, taking care to move even more quietly. If one of them was Katy, the other was likely her twin, and he had no idea if that lass's opinion of him had improved since their first meeting. At least, he was upwind of them, so if they had Argus and Eos with them, the dogs were unlikely to catch his scent.

Minutes later, he halted, stunned, able to recognize both voices.

Katy was talking with Alyssa.

"Art certain of that?" he heard Katy demand.

"Aye, for Father said so just today," Aly said. "He sent a running gillie—"

Will heard no more, for heaving caution aside, he hurtled down through the shrubbery, making enough noise to alert both dogs. One made a snuffling noise, the other was silent. The voices had also fallen silent, for which he was thankful.

"I knew it was you, despite all the noise you made," Katy said with a grin when he plunged out of the bushes.

Will was watching Alyssa. "What are you doing here, Aly?" he asked, forcing calm into his voice.

"Looking for you," she said. "Meggie is in the clachan, but Father will not look for me today. He is talking with Hew and Liam and will not even miss me."

"You must not talk of things that you hear at home, lassie," he said gently.

"Och, how could you hear what I was saying when you were making so much noise yourself?"

"I began making noise because I *did* hear you. So might someone else."

"I forget how keen your hearing is," Aly said with a sigh.

"Is it not so, then, that de Raite means to offer reconciliation?" Katy asked. "I feared that it was not true. But, oh, how I wish it were!"

"As to that, we know only that he said he had sent a message to the Mackintosh. Until we hear Malcolm's reply, though, we must not speculate, so I beg you, Katy, to say naught of this yet. It could cause grievous harm if word of it gets out before any agreement occurs. In troth, the Mackintosh will likely come to Finlagh or send word of his decision to Sir Fin when he has made one."

"Aye, sure," Katy said. "I shan't speak of it. I would have to explain to my parents how I know of it, and I have told them naught of meeting you or Aly."

"I'm sorry, Will," Aly said dejectedly. "I did not know it was to be a secret. Father rarely says aught to me that he wants kept secret, so I thought . . ."

When she fell silent, he said, "I ken that fine. You do know better than to talk to others of what happens at Raitt, though. I am not angry, but mayhap you should start back now. I'll catch up with you, but I want a word with Katy first."

"Aye, sure, and if you take longer, recall that I go over yon pass and through the clachan. I've become gey deft at slipping in and out of Raitt whenever I like."

"Argus," Katy said. "Go with her. Eos, stay."

Aly grinned, patted the dog, and went on her way.

Will watched her depart and opened his arms to Katy.

"Oh, Will, she was so excited," Katy said as she snuggled into them and held him tightly around his waist. "I'm sorry you had to spoil her delight."

"I, too," he murmured. "But I distrust de Raite, and it will spoil her pleasure more if he decides he wants no part of reconciliation. Now, kiss me, *mo bhilis.*"

"But this is not our kissing stone," she murmured mischievously.

"Then I shall just steal one," he said, tilting her chin up with one hand while holding her close with his other arm. When his lips touched hers, he pressed harder, wishing he could do much more with her and realizing as he did how much he had missed her. He wanted to stay, not just to continue kissing her but to talk, too. "I do love being with you," he murmured.

"If your father means all he says, mayhap it will become easier for us."

"Perhaps." The word stirred strong misgivings, though he could not have said why it should. "I must go, lass, and we must continue to be cautious. Until we know more, I'd liefer not take the chance of anyone seeing us together."

"Very well, then, sir. When you catch up with Aly and Argus, just command him to 'go to Katy.'"

He smiled. "I'll tell him."

"I won't tell anyone about Aly or her news, Will, or about you."

"I know, Katy. I trust you."

He was gone on those last words, and Katy promised herself that, come what may, she would prove worthy of his trust. Taking time only to tumble the cairn and await Argus, she headed back to Finlagh.

Saturday and Sunday passed slowly, bringing her to a strong, unfamiliar realization that, for the first time in her memory, she was purposefully keeping secrets, even from Clydia, just because Will had asked her to do so. Guilt stirred, but common sense and her promise to him steadied her.

He was right, and while Clydia might disagree with her, Katy knew from experience how difficult it was to keep secrets in a castle, where every wall and floor seemed to have ears. One had only to recall how easily Rory had listened from behind the Stone, *twice*, to all that she and Will had said to each other.

If Bridgett should overhear her talking of such things with Clydia, Lochan would soon know and Fin and Catriona soon after that.

Katy shivered at the thought. Recalling how easily Catriona and Clydia seemed to read her very thoughts, she knew she would have to take special care to think of anything *but* what Aly had told her. She wanted to talk to Will, though, so Monday after the midday meal, she slipped away to the pool with Argus and left a kerchief with hopes that Will might see it and that she could meet him the next day.

Fortunately, she had no need to keep what she had learned to herself for long, because Gilli arrived late Monday afternoon with big news, which Fin announced to the family in the inner chamber just before supper that evening.

"Malcolm has had a message from de Raite, offering reconciliation due to their overwhelming losses at Loch Moigh."

"Mercy!" Catriona and Clydia exclaimed together.

Cat grinned at Clydia but said to Fin, "Do you think the villain means it?"

Katy kept her mouth closed and shifted her gaze from her mother to Fin.

"Who can know what that man thinks, let alone what he means by it?" he said. "I certainly don't trust him, but Gilli Roy says Malcolm is pleased. De Raite has invited him, your brother Ivor, and me, with our lawful tails, to join him and his remaining men at Raitt Friday for a grand banquet in honor of the new peace."

"But not your wives or daughters?" Catriona said musingly.

"Raitt is a household of men, my love. You and the twins would be most uncomfortable there. This will be more like the signing of a treaty than a *cèilidh*. In fact," he added, "until this agreement is signed and done, everyone here must take extra care when going outside the wall. If you see or hear aught that seems amiss in any way, be sure to return swiftly and report what you've seen."

"Will Donald of Cawdor attend, too?" Catriona asked.

Gilli Roy, sitting at Fin's right on a carved settle, leaned forward with a smile and said in a much more cheerful voice than Katy had heard from him in some time, "I dinna ken about that, m'lady. Likely, another runner went tae Cawdor, though. Tae me own mind, this be a welcome event!"

De Raite announced at suppertime that his messenger had returned with news that the Mackintosh had accepted his invitation. Then, ignoring the raucous cheers of his men, he returned his attention to his supper.

Will, watching him warily, wondered what he was thinking, and despite his walk that day, had little appetite.

Beside him, Aly was nearly beside herself with delight, but a look from him silenced any outburst she might have made. "Should I not tell him how happy I am that he has done this?" she murmured later as they arose from the table.

Will glanced at their father, noting that he had turned away from them to talk quietly with Hew.

Then, Will said quietly, "Silence might be wiser, Aly. I doubt he would receive your thoughts kindly but would just say again that this is men's business."

"And none of mine, aye," she said, her happiness visibly fading.

A short time later, Colley asked de Raite if he had invited anyone besides Malcolm to attend the banquet.

"Nae, for the Malcolmtosh and them will ha' some two score men wi' them, plus theirselves. This feud be between us Comyns and the Mackintoshes. Did the Thane come wi' his lot, they'd outnumber us and I canna have that."

CHAPTER 17

"Katy, I must find a way to see Aly," Gilli Roy whispered from below her on the stairs after supper that evening.

"Don't be daft," she whispered back, despite the fact that she meant to leave a kerchief on shrubbery near the pool early the next morning for Will to see in the hope that they might meet. "What if your father catches you or hers catches her?"

"But if we're tae ha' peace, certes we can—"

"Naught is certain yet," she interjected. "De Raite may have offered to make peace, but if you think he will let you marry his daughter—"

"Sakes, why would he not?" Gilli demanded.

"Let us go onto the ramparts," Katy said. "Someone may hear us here."

He muttered as they continued upstairs. However, he waited until they reached the parapet, with the guards too far away to hear him, to say pleadingly, "Katy, even kings arrange marriages wi' enemies after a peace. Forbye—"

"How would you get a message to her? How did you do it in the past?"

"I know a chap in Nairn, a cousin tae her woman, who can take a message tae her. I'd ha' tae go into Nairn tae find him, though. I couldna do that afore I delivered me da's message tae Sir Fin."

Katy nearly told him that Aly sometimes came to see her in the woods, but the thought stirred a gentle mental twinge that she was learning to heed. She had to think more about it first, lest such information lead Gilli to do something rash.

Instead, she said, "Gilli, the banquet takes place Friday evening, which is still four days away. Mayhap a chance of some sort will arise."

"Aye, perhaps, but me da will arrive Wednesday afternoon wi' his men."

"Then you must remain cautious," she said. "You know de Raite would condemn your meetings with Aly if he knew of them, and so would Malcolm. To hope that de Raite's invitation changes any of that will not make it so, sir."

He was silent, and she could tell that she had irked him.

At last, he sighed and said, "Aye, well, I'll be at that banquet wi' the others, Katy. Likely, Aly will be, too. At least, I can see her then."

Again the warning sense stirred, silencing Katy before she could remind him—since he seemed to have ignored Fin's description of de Raite's household—that the invitation had specified only her father, Malcolm, her uncle Ivor, and their lawful tails. As her mother had noted in the same conversation, de Raite had made no mention of wives or daughters.

"We should go back downstairs now, for my parents must be wondering where we are," she said tactfully. "Just do not do anything daft, Gilli. If you should spur de Raite to reject reconciliation, my father *and* yours will want your head."

He nodded, grimacing, and she led the way down the ladder and waited for him to precede her downstairs to the inner chamber, where they found the rest of her family. When Fin asked Gilli to tell him more about the battle at Moigh, Cat excused herself, taking Katy and Clydia with her back onto the dais.

Men were still moving about in the lower hall, either laying out pallets, playing cards, dicing, or just sitting by the fire and talking.

"We will shortly receive any number of guests," Catriona said quietly, pausing by the high table. "I shall need your help, both of you—Bridgett's and Ailvie's, too, as well as our other women, because I want to be sure that we do all we can to make our visitors comfortable for as long as they must stay."

"Likely, they will be here only overnight, though, aye?" Clydia said.

"I have learned never to assume such things where men are concerned," Cat replied with a smile. "I plan for whatever may come, but I have oft been surprised. You should both go along to bed now, though, for you must be up early to help."

The twins obeyed her and found Bridgett waiting for them in their chamber.

She was, Katy thought, looking rather smug. "You look as if you have just won a contest prize," she said.

Bridgett gave a slight shrug and smirked as she said, "Aye, well, I ha' just been told that I ha' the most beautiful eyes in Scotland."

"Marry, and who told you that?" Katy demanded. "Surely, not Lochan!" The stolid captain of the guard seemed a most unlikely type to wax poetic.

"You do have very fine eyes," Clydia said. "Right now, in the candlelight, they look dark, but one can still see the gold rings round your irises. In sunlight, they look bluish gray sometimes and pure blue or pure gray at other times."

"Aye, 'fascinating,' *he* said they are," Bridgett said.

"Never tell me that Lochan said any such a thing to you," Katy said. "I doubt that the man kens how to speak so prettily."

"Nae, he does not," Bridgett said with a grimace. "Though, tae be fair, he did say he liked the color o' *my* eyes better than his own. Nobbut what the man has the brightest, bluest eyes I ever did see, 'specially when they twinkle."

"Then who *did* say that your eyes are the most beautiful?" Clydia asked her.

Raising her chin, Bridgett said, "Bruce MacNab, that's who. The man be pure smitten wi' me. He said so."

Clydia frowned. "Bridgett, you do know that MacNab is Sir Àdham's squire and expects one day to become a knight. He has always seemed to be an honorable man, but he may be toying with you, or mayhap he . . ." She paused, then added gently, "One cannot know what he is thinking."

"Och, nae, I ken fine what he be thinking," Bridgett said with a chuckle. "But if his flirting can stir Lochan tae pay more heed tae me, 'tis all tae the good."

"That," said Katy, "sounds like a dangerous game for you to play."

Laughing, Bridgett turned to pour water from the ewer to the basin for Clydia and then helped Katy with her laces.

Exchanging a look with her twin, Katy shook her head.

Later that night, after Alyssa had gone to bed and the household servants had retired to their cottages in the clachan, de Raite sent for his sons, his nephew, and those of his loyal men-at-arms who were not already in the hall to gather there.

Wakened from a deep but much-too-short sleep, Will groggily donned his tunic, made his way down from the attic, and took his place at the high table.

"Colley," de Raite said, "see that the screens passage be clear and lock yon door there tae the kitchen. Liam, look intae yon minstrel gallery, the attic behind it, and the garderobe tae be sure nae one lingers, whilst Hew sees tae the stairways and solar. Hew, make certain Alyssa be asleep in her bedchamber wi' Meggie."

Silence fell while the three brothers did as he bade them.

When he was satisfied that he was alone with his sons and most loyal men, de Raite said, "I want ye all tae stand now and, one man at a time, tae take a solemn vow afore God wi' your hand on yer heart, tae say naught tae any person o' what I tell ye here. Ye'll thereby send your immortal soul straight tae hell an ye breathe a word of it tae any man, woman, or child outside o' us right here in this chamber, now or ever after, 'less I give ye leave. D'ye all ken the sanctity o' such an oath?"

"Aye, sir," they replied as one, getting to their feet.

Then, one by one, each man placed his hand on his heart and repeated the vow exactly as de Raite phrased it. Still only half awake, seeing no alternative despite a sense that he should refuse to make a promise without having some idea of what its consequences might be, Will recited the vow in his own turn just as his brothers and the other men had.

"Good then," de Raite said when the last man had spoken. "Ye can sit down now." When they had obeyed, he let seconds pass before saying in a confiding tone, "There be one detail o' this upcoming banquet o' ours that I failed tae tell ye.

"Fact is," he added, "I mean tae put an end tae the Malcolmtosh and all who come wi' him. I'll tell ye how I mean for us tae do it, but dinna forget, if ye repeat a word o' what I say tae any other person, ye'll not only imperil your immortal soul, but if I learn o' your treachery, I'll send ye straight tae hell, m'self."

"What aboot our Highland law o' hospitality?" Colley asked, tugging an ear.

"Bah," de Raite snapped. "When we visited Loch Moigh, did Malcolm observe our laws o' hospitality? He did not, so we'll be acting same as he did."

An icy chill slid up Will's spine, sharpening his mind and banishing any momentary urge to point out that Malcolm had not invited them to Moigh Castle.

What, he demanded of himself, had he just done? How could he possibly allow de Raite and the others to murder Katy's father, uncle, and granduncle?

For surely de Raite had just declared such intent.

Moreover, he had—however reluctantly—sworn the oath before God, making it one that he could not break without risking an eternity in hellfire.

Will's thoughts kept him awake for a long time, but he slept again at last, only to waken Tuesday morning from a pleasurable dream of Katy's beautiful bare legs and saucy grin to the mind-numbing memory of what had taken place the previous night.

As usual, he was the first to break his fast, but he had no sooner accepted a bowl of porridge than Dae joined him and sent the gillie to fetch warm bread.

"What brings you down so early?" Will asked him.

"I'm a-going wi' ye today," Dae said. "I need tae talk wi' some'un, and I canna talk tae any o' the others, so I'm a-going with ye."

Yearning for solitude to help him think and optimistically hoping to see Katy, even at a distance, Will said, "We can talk here."

"Nae, then, we can*not*," Dae said flatly. "Sithee, de Raite said Liam should go wi' ye. He said he didna want nae one from last night going about on his own the noo, but Liam said he didna *want* tae go. He's had his fill o' the ridge. So I said I'd be willing, and your da ordered me tae go wi' ye, so here I be."

When Will nodded silently, Dae picked up the meat platter, helped himself to several generous slices, and then thanked the gillie who returned with his bread.

Eating his porridge, Will wondered what his cousin wanted to say to him, but Dae held his peace until they were striding through the gray dawn light toward the top of Raitt's side of the ridge and well away from Raitt.

As the sun peaked over beautiful snowcapped mountains in the east, Dae said, "I must tell ye, Will, I could see that yer da's scheme stunned ye as much as it stunned me last night. Even Colley seemed perturbed, talking as he did o' Highland laws o' hospitality. What I ha' gleaned o' such be that ye owe safety tae any man under your roof, and if a man requests hospitality ye must give it. Then, having given it, ye must keep him safe. Or be I wrong about that, and the man hisself has tae *ask* for yer hospitality afore the law applies?"

"You are not wrong," Will muttered, aware that their voices could still travel far in the current silence, although they were above the tree line and had seen no one else. "If de Raite does as he says he will . . ." He sighed.

"'Twould be slaughter," Dae said. "I canna be party tae such villainy, Will. I ha' small ken o' Mackintoshes and nae quarrel wi' them. Sithee, though, I ha' me doots that de Raite will let me leave here and take me ken of all o' this wi' me."

Thinking that de Raite would likely kill Dae if the man said that he wanted to leave now that he knew of de Raite's secret plan, Will hesitated to say so and tried to think how he might express his own thoughts safely. The most important thing, though, was that they not continue discussing the subject in the open, as they were.

"Dae, I want to think about what you have said, but this is no place for private talk. I have overheard whole conversations of men below and above me on these slopes. When I travel this way, I go silently."

"Sakes, I ha' seen nae one or heard any voices," Dae said, looking around.

"I do have ken of a gey private place," Will replied. "But we must first make certain that de Raite does not send anyone to spy on us. He may have doubts about both of us now, and if any of the others should hear us talking . . ."

"Aye, sure, they'd betray us tae him straightaway, but I'll keep a-comin' with ye as long as de Raite commands us tae go in pairs. Mayhap ye could quiet-like point out some o' the landmarks hereabouts, though. When I came tae Raitt wi' Hew two years ago, we never came up this way."

Will quietly noted such places until they neared the top of the ridge. Then, he suggested that if Dae wanted to see wildlife other than birds or squirrels, they should henceforth keep silent. "We must watch for activity at Finlagh," he added, "but they ken fine that we're likely to be here, so from now on you must use your skill at moving silently through woodland."

"Aye, sure, I oft track and take deer in the Lowlands, so we'll no talk at all whilst we be on t'other side o' the ridge."

Nodding, Will led the way over the top. His thoughts lingered on Dae's concerns and his own as they went, but he saw only one solution for Dae. He must disappear before the banquet. However, if he left soon after walking a patrol with Will, de Raite would likely suspect collusion. And if—

Seeing Katy's kerchief draped on a shrub by the pool diverted his thoughts only until he realized that Katy would visit the Stone in vain that day, for he could hardly take Dae to such a meeting.

Nor could he face her himself with what he now knew, having sworn his solemn oath to speak of it to no one other than the men de Raite had informed. He could not bear to think about the heartbreak Katy would suffer at the loss of her beloved father and other close members of her family. Nor could he dwell on the loss he and Katy would suffer themselves as a result of such a betrayal.

Even so, much as he disliked de Raite, he had willingly agreed to return to Raitt Castle from Inverness when de Raite had sent for him and had served his duty with his Comyn kinsmen. Although he had never formally sworn loyalty to de Raite as his liege, the man was his father and had right and reason to expect his sons to be loyal to him and to their clan.

Also, and most important, he had sworn his oath of silence before God.

Tuesday morning passed swiftly for Katy and Clydia in a flood of chores and responsibilities. They took turns aiding the baker and helping with other such tasks generally left to maid- and menservants. Although Malcolm's men and Sir Ivor's would attend the banquet, Malcolm's party would arrive Wednesday, and Sir Ivor's late Thursday unless something unexpected delayed them. They would all return after the banquet, however, to spend one or more nights at Finlagh before returning home.

Katy soon rejected any thought of slipping away to the Stone that afternoon. She was certain, though, that in the hustle and bustle that would ensue after Malcolm arrived with his men she would be able to do so on Wednesday.

As Captain of the Confederation, Malcolm would bring his allotment of twenty men and likely a few more to leave at Finlagh. Her father and Sir Ivor, as knights of the realm, would take eight men each in their tails, so if Ivor chanced to arrive Wednesday instead of Thursday, Finlagh would become even more chaotic.

As Katy attended to her duties, her thoughts kept drifting to the kerchief she had left at the pool. If Will had seen it that morning, he would expect her to be waiting at the Stone that afternoon, but she dared not go without good cause to be away. On the morrow, she would have bread enough to take the cottars' portion to them, to share again with those of Malcolm's and Sir Ivor's men who would be sleeping overnight in the woods.

That meant more bread than usual, so Clydia would likely go with her, but she could still slip away long enough to meet Will at the Stone. Just not today.

It occurred to her that if Will had seen her kerchief the day before or that morning, he might take the chance of meeting her at the stream on his way back.

Accordingly, she sped through her tasks, setting a gillie to count pallets to be sure there would be enough for the men who would need them. Some of the men would sleep in the woods near the cottages, but others would sleep in the hall and the courtyard and would need pallets on their stones.

Soon after the midday meal, she was crossing the courtyard when Bridgett emerged from the kitchen and waved at someone a little to Katy's left, beyond her.

Turning her head, she saw the broad-shouldered figure of her cousin Àdham's squire, MacNab, descending the timber stairs from the great hall.

Bridgett had stopped where she was, and was smiling at the lanky squire.

Grinning back, he had begun striding eagerly toward her when another, more square-built, fair-haired, visibly angry figure interjected itself between them.

Katy stopped where she was, catching her lower lip between her teeth.

Planting himself between Bridgett and MacNab, Lochan faced the squire with jaw and fists clenched. "Bruce MacNab, I'm thinking ye ha' business enow tae take ye elsewhere. Would ye no agree wi' that?"

Eyes atwinkle as he gazed amiably from man to maidservant and back, MacNab said, "Aye, sure, Lochan, if that be your will."

"It be safer for ye is what it be," Lochan growled loudly enough for anyone in the courtyard to hear.

An odd feminine squeak then drew Katy's gaze back to Bridgett.

Her mouth was agape, but it snapped shut when MacNab turned away and Lochan strode purposefully toward her.

Clapping a hand to her mouth, Bridgett stepped hastily back.

Lochan quickened his step, scooped her up as if she were a featherweight—which she was not—slung her facedown over a shoulder, and strode off with her toward the main gate, which one of his lads hastily opened for him.

Tempted though Katy was to follow, she decided not to test Lochan's temper further than Bridgett had already. While everyone else watched the gateway, she went back inside and found Cat and Clydia taking their ease in the inner chamber.

"Is all in order outside?" Catriona asked her.

"I think so," Katy said, realizing then that she had neglected to check the outbuildings. "Lads are still sweeping, so I'll look again when we fetch water for the garden. As to that chore, Clydie, you have done more of the heavy chores today than I have. I can fetch the water and see to the garden on my own, if you like."

Clydia's eyes narrowed—as well they might, Katy thought, since she rarely made such offers. Then her twin said, "I would like that, for I mean to ask Bridgett to help me wash my hair this afternoon."

"If Lochan has not throttled her," Katy said with a grin before describing what she had seen.

Chuckling, Cat said, "I warrant both Bridgett and Lochan can take care of themselves. If you do not see her, Clydia, ask Ailvie or one of the other maids to aid you. As for you, Katy, be sure to take Argus and Eos with you."

"Aye, Mam, I will," Katy assured her.

Accordingly, an hour or so later, she set off for the woods with the pail, aware that she would have to make the trip at least twice, if not three or four times with a less-than-full pail, since it was still too early for Will to come by.

There was no sign of him when she made her first and second trips, but she knew that if he were walking toward Finlagh from wherever he traveled, he would likely see her moving back and forth and would wait for her at the stream if he did.

The third time she went to the stream, Alyssa stepped out of the shrubbery and greeted her with a smile. "Is it not wonderful?" she said. "For you must know of my father's offer by now. If we are to have peace, we can be true friends, aye?"

Returning her smile, Katy said, "Certes, we are friends now. Art hoping to meet Will on his return?"

"Aye, for he left this morning afore I was out of bed. Everything at Raitt is in a bustle now, though, in preparation for Friday's banquet. So, nae one will miss me. Father has even sent for musicians and jongleurs tae come from Nairn tae amuse the men. I do wish he'd let me attend, too. 'Tis most unfair that he will allow only men tae attend on such a grand occasion."

"In troth, Aly, I doubt that my father would allow my mother, my sister, or me to attend even if de Raite did invite us," Katy said. "Mayhap, after the reconciliation takes place, we can all celebrate together."

"I ken fine why Sir Fin might feel so," Aly said. "I may come here again tomorrow, or— Nae, nae, 'twould be best tae wait till Friday," she added, nodding. "All will be abustle then, too, and whilst they wait for Father's guests tae arrive, they will shoo me away, but I willna want tae spend the whole afternoon and evening alone in my bedchamber, even with Meggie tae bear me company."

"I must fill my pail and go back," Katy said, noting that both dogs had curled up near the stream. Their eyes had shut but all four ears were atwitch. "If you wait here, though, I can return to fill it again. One of the men on our ramparts did see me come into the woods and may be wondering what is keeping me."

She did not want anyone wondering about that before Will *did* come.

Aly shook her head. "I did hope Will would be here. But Father may send someone tae look for me, and whilst Meggie be skilled at diverting them for a short time, I should go. I'll come again Friday afternoon, though, if I can."

"I'll watch for you then," Katy said. "We do water my sister's garden almost every day now that it has grown warmer."

"I'll see you Friday then," Aly replied as she turned, headed back up the slope, and vanished into the forest.

Katy finished her watering, tinglingly aware that her kerchief still sat atop shrubbery by the pool. Will *had* gone out that morning, so likely he had seen it. Even so, she knew she dared not linger long enough to meet him on his return.

If he went to the Stone, he would know by the lack of cairn or kerchief there that she had not, and Aly would likely tell him that she and Katy had met.

Will had spent much of his day trying to reconcile his determination to protect Katy's family with his need to avoid sacrificing his honor by breaking the sacred vow of secrecy he had taken. Recalling Dae's objections to de Raite's plan, he wondered for a time if he might confide in the older man and seek his advice.

Aware as he was, though, that Dae was more Hew's man than de Raite's and, Lowlander or not, he was a Comyn and thus an ally, Will knew he dared not risk revealing his relationship with Katy to him, lest he speak of it to Hew or one of the others. He had known the man for too short a time to trust him that much.

He also realized that, since de Raite now insisted they go in pairs, he could not risk ridding himself of Dae to visit the Stone even to meet Katy and—even if he had to hold his tongue about the damnable banquet—at least take her in his arms one more time before then and tell her he loved her. He dared not let his thoughts dwell on what was to come, though, not with Dae moving silently behind him.

The man had been right about his ability to move quietly. The birds were singing and they had spotted several deer, including a young stag with a doe.

If only he might talk to Granduncle Thomas Cummings!

No sooner did the wish flit through his mind than he pictured Thomas leaning against a fencepost on a sunny morning, talking of honor and loyalty: "'Tis not mere learning about such traits that a lad needs, but the lad's ability to find courage and wisdom enough to remain loyal to a trust, not blindly, yet to act at once and fix his effort on doing what needs doing."

The one thing he knew about Granduncle Thomas was that he had always had a clear vision for himself of the difference between right and wrong.

To act at once and *do what needs doing*, Will mused, remembering Aly's accusation that he often took the easy road, that by the time he decided to do something it was often too late for it to matter.

Will fixed his thoughts on what, exactly, he had vowed.

He could think of the easiest way to go about warning the Mackintoshes, but how to keep his vow and act quickly enough to do what needed doing whilst de Raite insisted they go only in pairs he could not imagine. How, he wondered, could he leave Raitt only by taking someone else with him and still do the right thing?

He knew Dae was aching to talk about his own problem, for the man had mentioned it again when they stopped at midday to eat. Dae had guarded his language, but Will had pointed out that the Mackintosh men who patrolled the region were as skilled as he and Dae were at moving stealthily and likely had the same keen hearing of most hunters.

"Sithee, they must recognize me as easily as I recognize most o' them, but if one of them were to see us talking, he'd move close, Dae, and you ken fine what we both swore. I do have ken of a place of safety, though, where nae one will come upon us unexpectedly. If you come out with me again tomorrow . . ."

"Aye, sure," Dae said eagerly when Will paused, "I'd liefer avoid the others whilst I be trying tae keep me thoughts tae m'self."

Nodding, Will said, "I'll try to aid you. I have been thinking and I am nearly certain of what you must do, but I know not how best you might do it. If I can work out what I'm thinking, we can talk tomorrow afternoon at a place that few know exists and speak more freely."

Dae nodded. "I ha' wanted tae run like a deer. But I ken fine that this be nae time tae act in haste or out o' fear."

At best, Will thought, his half-formed solution might delay the banquet. At worst, God might deem it a quibble and condemn him to the fires of hell, whither his own, unbeloved father would surely send him if de Raite got the chance.

All of it would lie in God's hands but only if Will could eliminate or improve on the immediate imperfections of his plan.

Every fiber within him shouted that no such plan could possibly work.

The worst of it was that, once done, its result would fly beyond his control and into the hands of the Fates, long known by all to be capricious . . . at best.

CHAPTER 18

He was carrying violets again, but as she reached to take them, a large black dog stepped between them, looked at her, and moved on to the forest depths. When she looked back, the violets were gone, but Will held out his arms to her and . . .

At the familiar sound of the bedchamber door's latch, Katy grimaced, sat up, and rubbed her eyes.

Bridgett came in quietly, her expression sober, and Katy realized that she had not seen the woman since the previous afternoon, when Lochan had draped her over his shoulder and stormed out the main gate with her. Glancing at Clydia, who raised her eyebrows, Katy decided that her twin knew no more than she did.

As busy as everyone had been the previous day, they had not questioned Bridgett's failure to aid them in their preparations for bed that night. Such a thing had happened often enough when they were all busy that they had paid little heed.

Now, without comment or looking at Katy or Clydia, Bridgett carried her pitcher across the room to the washstand and began carefully to pour hot water into the ewer.

Clydia said, "Is aught amiss, Bridgett? You seem gey somber."

"Sakes, I thought ye'd ha' heard all about it," Bridgett said grimly. Looking at Katy, she added, "Ye saw what he did for yourself, aye?"

Clydia said, "She did, Bridgett, but we do not know what happened after Lochan carried you out of the courtyard."

Exhaling loudly and with a grimace, Bridgett said, "I expected that them on the ramparts would ha' told everyone. God kens fine they heard all he said and did tae me and I tae him, for we had a right royal row on the path by the castle."

"No one has said aught about that to us," Clydia said.

"Likely, Lochan ordered the men to keep quiet," Katy said.

"Aye, perhaps, but he didna just say aught tae me; he shouted tae me," Bridgett said, turning to open the kist that held Clydia's clothing.

"We will not ask you what he shouted," Clydia said gently.

"Thank 'e m'lady, for I'd no want tae repeat it, but when I tried tae slap his face for it, he caught me by the shoulders and shook me till me hair came unbound and said he did never want tae see me flirting again wi' men like that MacNab. So I said, 'And what d'ye think ye can do tae stop me, ye great lunk?' And what does he ha' the nerve tae say then but that he'll stop me by *marrying* me and putting me straight across his knee again tae make sure of it."

"*Again?*" Katy said.

"Aye," Bridgett said, reddening and rubbing her backside. "I did leave out that bit. That great handsome lunk. I didna think he cared near so much as that."

"It does sound as if he would like to marry you, though," Katy said.

"Aye, but he didna ask me or hear me say aye tae him, did he?" Bridgett said. "I ha' me doots the man will ha' courage enough tae ask me, as angry as he kens I be the noo and as shy as that man be when he's got his wits about him."

"We'll see," Katy said. After a pause, she said lightly, "Bridgett, what would Granny Rosel say about a big black dog walking between two people in a dream?"

"Treachery," Bridgett said. "Were ye dreaming o' two others or yourself?"

"I was one," Katy said, feeling a chill.

"Then treachery may soon cross your path is what Granny would say."

Katy stared at her but asked her no more questions.

Having put out fresh clothing for them and made their beds, Bridgett left with the sops bucket, and Clydia said, "I put no faith in dream predictions. Do you think she is pleased that Lochan may want to marry her or glad that he is shy?"

Katy smiled, remembering her own fury the day she had learned the truth about Will and her feelings afterward. "If she believes that Lochan lost his wits over a flirtation with MacNab, I think she wants Lochan as much as he wants her."

They went down to the hall then, broke their fast, and spent the morning supervising last-minute preparations for their guests. Fin would be going to meet Malcolm's party and would want everything in readiness when they returned.

Certain that Will would expect to find her at the Stone that afternoon, since he had not found her there the day before, Katy offered shortly after their midday meal to take extra supplies to the cottars for those who would need them, and Cat agreed, warning her to ask the baker if he had enough for everyone and to spare.

"We both know that he will," Katy said. Then, with a grin when Cat raised her eyebrows, she added, "*And* that he does like to be asked."

Catriona had not mentioned the dogs, nor did the men on the gate or any of the people she visited, so Katy decided that with peace in the offing, she need not fret about leaving them behind. That odd, niggling sense of warning stirred gently, but it merely made her glad that her father had already left to meet Malcolm.

Will had set a fast pace that morning, as much to deter Dae from talking about the forthcoming banquet and his dilemma as to think about his own. He knew what the right thing was to do. Right was to stop de Raite, to keep him from committing the cold-blooded murder of perhaps two score men. The easiest way— He scowled then, recalling Aly's accusation again.

Nevertheless, the easiest way, if the intended victims would believe him, was to march himself to the gates of Finlagh and warn them of de Raite's intent. Surely, if warned, Malcolm would forgo the banquet. That was the ideal solution.

However, Granduncle Thomas and a few priests had taught him in childhood that an oath sworn before God was sacred, that breaking such a vow meant eternal damnation. So, he could not tell any other person of de Raite's plan, making that route harder than it had seemed when his idea had thrust itself forward. If he broke such a vow, he could never tell Thomas, which meant not seeing him again, because Thomas could always tell when Will was keeping something from him.

So, what was the next possibility, and how could he see Katy alone that afternoon as she would expect?

The two thoughts collided, flinging an image into his head of the young rascal, Rory, concealing himself behind the Stone, not once but twice. Then Katy had done the same thing the day she had heard him approaching so clumsily, and had explained that she'd wanted to be sure it was he before emerging to meet him.

If she were to hear a stranger's voice . . .

Granny Rosel urged Katy to stay longer, demanding to hear the details of a rumored quarrel between her granddaughter and the captain of Finlagh's guard.

"I knew that word of that disagreement would spread quickly," Katy said. "But you must ask Bridgett for the truth of it, Granny. 'Tis not my tale to tell."

"How now?" the old lady snapped. "Ye like spreading news as much as the next body does, do ye no?"

"Not about family," Katy said staunchly. "And Bridgett is as much family as you and our Ailvie are, Granny. Forbye, Bridgett will likely *want* to tell you about it, but we have all been busy preparing for the Mackintosh, Uncle Ivor, and their men, who will arrive today and tomorrow. I will tell you that my da, Gilli Roy Mackintosh, and the two lads who traveled to Finlagh with Gilli left soon after our midday meal to meet Malcolm on the road and return with him."

"I ken all about yon grand reconciliation banquet," Granny said. "I dinna put much faith in it, m'self. That de Raite be a right villain whose word I dinna trust."

"Likely, Da does not trust him, either," Katy said. "But the

Comyns lost many men, when they attacked Moigh, so de Raite may *need* reconciliation."

"Aye, 'tis true, they did; so he might," Granny agreed.

Taking her leave then, and with the last loaf and parcel delivered, Katy walked eastward until she was beyond sight of Granny's cottage, then turned north to make her way to the Stone as quietly as possible through the denser shrubbery.

Earlier such visits, plus her fine sense of direction, soon brought enough of the upper part of the monolith into sight to make her go faster for several steps before stopping abruptly to take greater heed of the forest around her.

What exactly had stopped her, she did not know. On reflection, she became aware of an odd stillness. Nearby, a honeysuckle vine had wound its way up through the bushes, and its clusters of richly scented white flowers were drawing bees, but aside from their buzzing, the birds and forest creatures were silent.

Ears aprick now for any unusual sound, Katy eased her way through the shrubs toward the Stone. As usual, she was barefoot, her soles leathery tough but sensitive enough for her to test each step and avoid pressing down on any pebble that might rattle or twig that might snap.

She had reached the small open space some distance from the Stone where she had previously left Rory and the dogs. Certain that the boy was not following her now, she hurried on, still keenly aware of the unusual silence and taking care.

Suddenly, she heard a man's quiet, unfamiliar voice . . . then another, lower toned, both voices still too low-pitched or distant for her to be certain that either was Will.

Although she thought it unlikely that two strangers had carelessly wandered into these so-dense woods from the public road or the path to Finlagh from Nairn, she also doubted that Will would bring anyone else with him.

Even if he had, she could not risk meeting anyone who might talk of seeing her with Will. In fact, she decided, she wanted naught to do with any stranger.

On the thought, she pushed her way the last few feet through the shrubs to the Stone, hastily scrabbled nearby pebbles into a small cairn in front of it and slipped behind it, where Rory had hidden. As she burrowed into the shrubbery, she prayed that whoever they were, they had not brought any dogs with them.

"How much farther?" one voice asked, even closer than she had expected.

"Just yonder now." The second voice was Will's.

Impulse stirred to run to him, but her sense of caution toward his companion plus her strange dream of the black dog that morning overcame the impulse and made her decide to wait until Will had said more.

On reflection, she realized that the sensation she felt, though strong enough to cause wariness, was not strong enough to be the one her father had described as having made him duck and shift position, thereby avoiding being struck down by a warrior from behind. Nevertheless, the nature of the feeling kept her perfectly still.

She was directly behind the Stone, so she could not see the men, but she easily heard them cross the small clearing and stop in front of it.

They were so close and the woods so quiet now that she could almost hear the two breathing but dared not breathe herself until she heard Will speak again.

"As you see, cousin," Will muttered, noting the small pile of pebbles centered below the Stone and praying that the cairn meant Katy was there and not that she had come and gone, "this place is safer for private talk than anywhere else we have been today. These woods are too dense to invite casual wanderers and we are well off any useful path or road. The castle on its knoll sits to the south, high above us. Guards on its ramparts would see any large force moving toward these woods from the north, the west, or the ridge east of us that separates Raitt from Finlagh, but the woods are much too dense to attract such a force, and the thick canopy keeps those above from seeing or hearing us unless we shout."

"What about yon woods tae the west that we could see from the road?"

"They are full of Finlagh cottars," Will said. "The strath

beyond them includes Cawdor's land, four or five miles from here, and is home to Finlagh shepherds, cowherds, and other such tenants, whose charges have more sense than to push their way through the undergrowth here. We can talk safely, but quietly."

"Aye, for though this great standing stone may hear the whole, it canna repeat nowt," Dae replied. "But neither can a rock offer advice, Will, so ye must help me tae think what I must do."

"'Tis simple enough, Dae," Will said. "You must leave for home without a word or sign to anyone of your going. How to do it I will leave to you."

"Hoots awa'! Wi' that devilish banquet Friday night, I ha' only till then tae make good me escape, but I tell ye true, Will, I couldna sit there, let alone eat, whilst a-waiting for de Raite's fiendish toast tae send all his guests tae—"

"Whisst now," Will interjected. "It does neither of us any good to dwell on the details of that banquet. We have sworn a sacred oath to talk to no other person, which is why we came here, to talk to each other or, as you say, to the Stone."

"'Twould take God hisself tae stop the man," Dae said. "Sakes, but he told Malcolm and them there would be nae weapons, so they'll come unarmed, like sheep tae a slaughter. Your da does mean his own lot tae ha' weapons, though, and for each tae turn and kill the man standin' tae his left. I canna do that, Will."

"By my troth, Dae, I doubt that even praying to God could stop de Raite now. Not when he forced that vow of silence on us before telling us what, exactly, we were promising to keep secret. Sithee, he believes only in himself, in his power and his ability to control others. He ignores fairness, honor, and laws of hospitality, and he does not care who gets hurt. He cares only about beating the Mackintosh, gaining more power, and seeking more land for himself. In addition, he kens fine that the rest of us fear God too much to risk eternal damnation."

Dae was silent for a long moment, and Will tried to be casual about glancing past him, trying to see any further indication that Katy was there. If she was not . . .

"I must think more on this," Dae said. "I wouldna want your

da tae think ye'd aided me, though. Ye must take nae blame on yourself, neither, lad."

"I will think on your plight, too," Will assured him, clapping him on the back. "In any event, we should go now, for they will be expecting us soon. They may even come in search of us if we are later than usual."

As he spoke, he urged Dae back the way they had come, pausing when the older man went ahead of him to look back at the Stone and the shrubbery flanking it, hoping to see some sign that Katy had come in time to overhear them.

Just as he decided that his plan had likely failed, one leafy branch stirred and two slim fingertips darted out to steady it.

Relieved, and confident that she understood the danger that the banquet threatened and would at least try to warn the others, he strode quickly after Dae.

At first, Katy felt guilty for listening to what sounded like a private conversation, but curiosity and unwillingness to show herself to Will's companion held her motionless. After the man called Dae said that each Comyn was to kill the Mackintosh beside him, she had frozen in place. Scarcely daring to breathe, she could not have moved then had she wanted to.

Still in shock at all she had heard when Will told his cousin they should leave, she had shifted her position to see them. Realizing then that she had shaken a leafy branch and that, if she could see them, they would see her, she reached out gently to steady it, lest Will's cousin see her. Will's behavior had made it clear that he did not want Dae even to suspect that anyone else might overhear them.

The important thing now was to return to Finlagh as fast as she could to warn everyone of what she had overheard.

On the heels of that thought came a second one. She could hardly just tell them that she knew what would happen at the banquet as if the news had drifted to her from a cloud overhead or in a dream, black dog or none.

They would insist on knowing exactly how she had gleaned the information.

Grimacing at the thought, she waited until she was sure that Will and his cousin were well away before cautiously heading back the way she had come. Then, she walked slowly and thoughtfully up to the clearing below the castle knoll.

As she crossed the clearing, Clydia emerged from the woods by the south stream with a pail sloshing water over its rim. She saw Katy at the same time and waved with her free hand.

For the first time that Katy could recall, she wished that her twin could not read her expressions so easily. That wish brought their mother's image to mind. If anyone could read the twins better than they read each other, it was Catriona.

Today, Katy decided, would be the grand test of her long-doubted ability to think before acting and to keep her feelings and thoughts to herself.

The fact—for it was indeed fact—that she would be in trouble no matter how she proceeded should, she hoped, be motivation enough to delay telling anyone what she had heard until her father and Malcolm returned to the castle.

If she failed to do so, she knew she would face at least two if not three or four explosions of temper. Therefore, the best plan was to wait until she could tell Fin and Malcolm first, together, for they were the two most at risk and who would decide what to do.

Marry, Katy thought, *I am learning to think first and act afterward . . . if only Da and Malcolm do not delay too long in returning.*

Greeting Clydia with a smile, Katy asked if she needed help with her pail.

"I have made only one trip, so it is light, but you can help with the next if you like. Did you see Will after you took the bread round to the cottars?"

"Nae," Katy said, glad that the answer was truthful. "I visited for a time with Granny Rosel, though. She has heard the rumor of Bridgett's spat with Lochan and wanted me to tell her exactly what happened. I said she'd have to ask Bridgett."

Clydia chuckled. "Rory told me that Lochan has been touchy all day. In troth, the scamp said that Lochan's men are behaving as if they would tread across hot embers to avoid his notice."

Grinning, Katy said, "I do not know whether to hope he marries her or not."

"I think we know what Bridgett likely hopes. Why, though, would she want to marry a man who would beat her?"

Katy shrugged. "She loves him, I think. Not to mention that hereabouts, most any man we know is capable of doing what Lochan did."

"Aye, but they ken fine that their neighbors will tolerate only so much of that. Any Highland man who purposefully harmed his wife or children beyond mere correction of a fault would have to face a tirrivee from his neighbors and answer, as well, to his liege lord."

"Sakes, Clydie, do you think for a moment that Bruce Lochan would do Bridgett or any other woman true harm? He may be fierce with his men, but I have never seen him act violently toward any woman or bairn, or heard of such."

"I expect you are right, but you also know Bridgett, and she does seem to delight in teasing him. Were you visiting Granny Rosel all this time, then?"

"Nae, for I did go to the Stone, but I did not see Will, so I came home. I expected Da and Malcolm to be here by now."

"Mam said they will likely arrive before supper."

"In other words, Mam will delay supper until they get here," Katy said, thinking that if that were the case, the delay might be longer than Cat thought.

She could not imagine containing her news alone throughout a whole meal. If she had to face Fin and Malcolm, she would do so as soon as they arrived.

"I have been thinking about what you might do for your own safety if you leave," Will said when he and Dae reached the northernmost part of the ridgetop above Raitt Castle and could see for a distance in all directions.

In fact, he could see the crossing of the Inverness road with the path from Nairn to Finlagh and a company of men approaching it from the west. One redheaded man looked like Gil Mackintosh, the chap he had caught with Aly.

Nearly certain that he was seeing Malcolm and his men, Will wondered if Malcolm's youngest son might dare to attend the banquet in hope of seeing her.

"What ha' ye decided, then?" Dae asked. "Art sure it be safe tae talk here?"

"Aye, for we will talk quietly and only of your thought that you may return home soon. If you decide to go, you might bundle the plaid you have worn here with aught else you take and travel in your Lowland breeks, jerkin, and boots.

"Come to that," he added when the notion struck him, "just give your bundle to me and I'll take it right through the clachan to the north end of that wee loch with the forested islet southeast of Raitt. You do ken the one I mean, aye?"

"Aye, sure, I ken the loch well enow. My memories of it be painful ones, though, for 'twas there that a lass from Finlagh near broke me pate the last time I visited Raitt."

"After you collect the bundle and change into Lowland garb, you need only head east till you meet the road through Glen Spey. No one will trouble a solitary Lowlander traveling southward on that road."

Dae nodded. "'Tis a good notion, that, for I came and went by yon road on me previous visit." Lowering his voice he added, "Getting away safe be the worry."

"It need not be," Will muttered. "If worse comes to worst, ask Colley or Liam to go along . . . to Nairn, say . . . then slip off or choose an occasion to clout him over the head and escape. Once you're away, I doubt de Raite will send anyone after you. If he does, he'll spare no more than one man. You'd easily elude one."

"I dinna ken aboot that."

"Sakes, Dae, Hew already thinks you're a feardie, so he'll ken fine that you'd never risk your immortal soul by telling any other person about the banquet. He'll rightly assume that you wanted no part in such a wicked scheme."

"Art so sure o' that, Will?"

"I am," Will replied flatly.

Dae nodded, still visibly uneasy about the course he wanted most to take.

Will wondered if Hew was right to call Dae a feardie, but he dismissed his brother's opinion. Dae was likely just showing common sense.

By the time Fin, Malcolm, Gilli Roy, and the men with them arrived in the courtyard, Katy had tidied herself and changed into a pink kirtle with roses and daisies embroidered round the hem that she knew to be her father's favorite. Then she twisted her hair into two long plaits that she let hang loose, as she had before she decided she was too old to wear them so, and when the gates opened to admit the men, she was watching from the top of the timber stairs.

Descending the steps without haste, she went to them, made her curtsy, and arose with her right hand extended to Malcolm, "Welcome to Finlagh, my lord," she said with a smile. "I trust your journey was pleasant."

"Aye, lassie," he said, drawing her into his arms and giving her a hug and kiss. "Ye be as pretty as a pink rose in that dress."

"I thank you, sir," she said, trying to keep smiling as she moved to hug her father on tiptoes. "Da," she murmured as Malcolm turned away, "I must talk with you and Malcolm privately and straightaway, just the two of you. 'Tis important, sir, and for no ears yet save your own. Prithee, will you arrange for that?"

"Aye, sure," he said, meeting her gaze. "But I'm thinking your mother may disagree about its being more important than supper if she has delayed its serving."

"She has delayed it, but by my troth, sir, this *is* more important and you and Malcolm must hear it first and decide who else besides Uncle Ivor should know."

She nearly added that Fin would likely decide her punishment then, too, but thought better of it when he straightened, giving her a steady, measuring look.

Nodding then, he said, "I'll arrange it, lass, at once, in the inner chamber. You go on ahead now," he added, shifting his gaze to look beyond her.

Turning, she saw Catriona coming toward them with Clydia, so she stepped away and went quickly toward the timber stairs. By the time the others had finished their greetings and the men were ready to go inside, Katy was at the open doorway.

Glancing back, she caught her father's eye. When he nodded, she went in, crossed the lower hall and dais, and entered the inner chamber, leaving its door ajar.

Malcolm came in first and gave her a searching look but said nothing.

Fin followed him and told a hovering gillie that they would join the high table shortly, before he shut the door.

"Now, lass," he said sternly. "Tell us what this is about."

Having considered several benign ways of introducing her news, Katy said bluntly instead, "You cannot go to that banquet, Da. De Raite means to kill you all."

CHAPTER 19

Malcolm and Fin were silent for several moments before Malcolm said, "Be ye certain o' your information, lass?"

"I am, aye, sir," Katy said, keeping her focus on him but aware of Fin's grim presence between them. Despite her earlier resolve, she hesitated to continue.

Malcolm, smaller and at present less formidable than Fin, said, "I think ye must tell us more, Katy-lass. I ken fine why ye might fear that de Raite could be capable o' such madness, but . . ."

When he paused, Fin looked directly at her, so Katy said hastily to Malcolm, "'Tis not my fear, sir, but fact."

Glancing again at Fin to meet a heavy scowl, she took a breath, looked him in the eye, and said, "I overheard two men talking, sir. They were deep in the woods below the castle, near a huge standing stone. I do not know if you have seen it."

"I have, aye, long ago," he said grimly, holding her gaze. "The area where it stands is heavily overgrown and lacks a pathway. So, what were you doing there and who else overheard this conversation?"

His increasing anger urged caution. If he began shouting at her, everyone on the dais and mayhap throughout the great hall would hear him. Knowing better than to look away, Katy swallowed hard and said, "No one else, sir."

"By heaven, Kate, did I not—"

"Nae, nae, Fin," Malcolm interjected firmly. "Ye can scold her or take a tawse tae her backside later. What they said be o' greater import than the whys or how she heard it. Ye dinna doubt her word that she did hear two o' them, do ye?"

Fin pressed his lips together with a look that boded ill for Katy's immediate future before he said, "Nae, Malcolm. She may shade the truth at times but not with respect to aught of importance."

Just as Katy began to think she might still talk her way to safety, he added, "Who were those two men, and why were they, or you, near our standing stone?"

Fighting an impulse to chew her lip or do anything else that might reveal her tension, she said hastily, "They were Comyns, sir, and cousins, for one did call the other so. He said they had sworn a sacred oath not to tell another person and had come to that private place to talk, where only the rock would hear them. The second man even said that the rock could hear all they said but couldna repeat nowt of it."

Then, before Fin could ask another discomfiting question, she added, "He said de Raite told Malcolm there were to be no weapons, so you will be unarmed, 'as helpless as sheep to slaughter,' he said. Also, that their men *will* be armed."

"That villain," Malcolm muttered. "I feared we couldna trust him, but he did lose dunamany men, and I didna want tae fling away the slightest chance o' peace."

"So the two mentioned de Raite by name?" Fin said, eyeing her skeptically.

Hesitating, because Will's cousin had mostly said "your da," Katy recalled that Will always called his father de Raite, so she said, "Aye, sir, at least one of them did. I cannot recall if both men said his name."

"One be enough," Malcolm snapped.

"Aye, it would be if any of it made sense," Fin replied, still eyeing Katy sternly enough to make her squirm. "Sacred oaths and talking to a rock. You have yet to explain what took *you* to the standing stone, my lass, or how you came to recognize two men of Clan Comyn. Had you seen them before?"

When she hesitated again, he said dulcetly enough to send a cold chill up her spine, "You do recall that we are keeping the others from their supper."

Having no choice, she said unhappily, "I had met one of them before, sir, but not the other."

"I see that you and I must have a much longer talk," he said. "But, for now, tell me why you think this is not someone trying to make mischief with de Raite's banquet because that someone, other than de Raite, wants this reconciliation to fail. Just where were you when you heard all of this? Did they know you were there?"

"Nae, sir, for I had hidden behind the Stone when I heard two men coming. The one I know would have expected me to be there, though, because we had met there before. But, by my troth, Da," she added fiercely, "Will would do naught to spoil the peacemaking. He is a good man and I . . . I *know* he would never let harm come to me or my family if he could stop it. In fact, I think he persuaded his cousin to have their talk at the Stone with the hope that I *would* overhear them."

"Which one is this Will Comyn?" Malcolm asked. "I canna keep that lot sorted in my head."

"He is de Raite's youngest son, my lord," Katy said. "De Raite sent him to live with his granduncle, Thomas Cummings, near Inverness soon after Will's mother died. His brothers are years older. Then de Raite ordered him home again just before Inverlochy. Will did not participate in the battle, though."

"I know Thomas Cummings," Malcolm said. "He's a good man, and his lot, though still calling theirselves Comyns then, helped hold Inverness for me afore Lochaber when Alexander o' the Isles tried tae seize the castle and burn the town."

"Will did not tell me that," Katy said, recalling that Malcolm was Constable of Inverness Castle, appointed by the King soon after his grace's return from England.

"You know much about this Will Comyn, Katy, more than I like to hear," Fin said. "You seem to care for him and believe he cares for you, so I will discuss that further with you. I think we have heard enough for now, but you are not to discuss this with anyone else."

"He is right, lass," Malcolm said. "We dinna want word o' this flitting about, not afore we decide what tae do about it. Likely, not afterward either."

"I won't tell anyone," she said. "'Tis why I insisted on telling you both at once, but could you not ask to meet somewhere else, somewhere safer than Raitt?"

With a wry smile, Malcolm said, "Neither side would trust the choice o' the other any more than we trust de Raite in his place or he would trust me in mine."

"Off with you now, Katy," Fin said. "But heed my warning, lass, for when I said not to tell anyone, I meant *anyone* . . . not even Clydia or your mother. You will suffer my gravest displeasure if you disobey me in this."

"Then, may I tell Mam and Clydia that you have forbidden me to talk of aught that occurred in here, sir?"

"You will have no need to tell them," Fin said. "You are going to forgo your supper and go upstairs to await me in my chamber. I won't be long."

Making them another curtsy, Katy accepted her dismissal with mixed relief and trepidation. She had no wish to face questions from Catriona or Clydia, and she knew that had she emerged from the inner chamber and taken her place between them at the high table, they would have asked many.

Even so, the thought of waiting for Fin in his chamber made her wish that Malcolm had not mentioned the word "tawse." It had been years since Fin had employed corporal punishment with either twin. She could only hope he had not taken Malcolm's use of the word as a hint that he should do so now.

Having returned home with his cousin in good time for supper, Will tried to persuade himself not only that he had done the right thing but that Katy had understood all they had said and was wise enough to tell Fin, without raising a din to everyone else, even if she feared his reaction.

Dae said he would wash for supper and vanished to the attic chamber, so Will went in search of Aly.

Learning from Colley that de Raite had ordered her to keep to her chamber with Meggie for supper lest someone let slip a word of the banquet's purpose to her, Will followed Dae to the attic and found him there alone.

"Wrap up what you mean to wear home and set it in yon corner where I put my pallet," Will whispered. "Anyone who sees it will assume it belongs to me."

"I dinna ken if I can leave so," Dae replied. "I'm that scared, Will."

"Aye, but once you're away, you'll feel nobbut relief," Will said, knowing he had to continue to act as if the banquet were going to take place. After all, it was possible that Katy had feared to report all they'd said or had chosen her words so carefully to excuse her presence there that her father had failed to grasp the danger. "No one will be at that loch tomorrow or Friday, Dae. You need only choose your time."

"I were a-thinking I'd do yer route wi' ye and head east on yon road we saw coming home from Loch Moigh. The one as ye said led tae Rothiemurchus."

"We would put a noose round my neck if you did that," Will said. "If we went together, Raite would blame me for your disappearance. He might even think we had conspired to warn them at Rothiemurchus and mayhap at Finlagh, too."

Grimacing, Dae said, "I dinna want that. Still, I canna think a sensible thought about all o' this. That be plain fact."

"Then stop trying to think of *all* of it. You always wear boots, so just put breeks and a jerkin in yon corner, so I can take them to the loch for you. You do ken the boulders at the north end of the loch where we have oft built a fire, aye?"

"Aye," Dae muttered.

"I'll leave the sack amongst those boulders. Then, you need only go eastward till you reach the road south through Glen Spey that you have traveled before."

"Aye," Dae agreed. His tone remained dismal.

It was good that they had not counted on walking the ridge together the next day, for de Raite announced at supper that Liam and Colley would take that duty. "Nae one else is tae be on yon ridge the next two days save the pair o' ye, tae see that our guests ha' arrived and will no be coming here armed tae their teeth!"

Katy had not expected to enjoy her talk with Fin, nor did she. Within minutes of joining her in his chamber, he had extracted all that she could tell him about how she had met Will, their secret meetings, and what she had overheard that afternoon.

She felt as if Fin had wrung every last word from her physically but was glad she had forced herself to tell him the whole truth and relieved to have it over.

After he had expressed his feelings about her behavior in his sternest, most withering way, he added, "This man has been sneaking about behind his father's back, just as you did behind mine, my lass. If his family cannot trust him, why should we trust aught that he says or does, especially when he took such a torturous route to tell us instead of simply warning us not to attend the banquet?"

She had not tried to stem the tide of his anger while he directed it at her, but his accusations about Will brought her usual strength of mind surging back.

Blinking away tears but refusing to wipe away those that had spilled down her cheeks, she exclaimed, "Because Will believes as strongly in honor as you do, Da, and he risked his immortal soul to tell me! He is not one to do that lightly. You also believe in the immortal soul; I know you do!" she added angrily. "This was *not* easy for him, but he loves me and he knows I love him. He knows, too, that what his father means to do is a black sin and goes against every rule of hospitality."

"I see," Fin said when she paused for breath, and he spoke those two words much more mildly than she had had any reason to expect.

Had she not known him better, she might have thought that the look on his face then was a sympathetic, even a sad one. Whatever he meant by it, though, it told her that she had said enough.

The silence lengthened until he said gently, "Even if it is love for the pair of you, Katy-lass, it will likely prove fruitless in the end. You must know that."

"I can tell you only what I told Clydia. If I cannot have him, I won't marry."

"Now, lass—"

"You would like him, Da. I felt as if I had known him all my life after that first meeting on the crag. I think much of it is because he reminds me of you. He scolded me as you just have, albeit not as fiercely, for climbing that crag."

"I'd feel better about the man if he had put you across his knee for that," Fin growled. "I'm sorely tempted to do it myself, I can tell you."

Knowing that she had now said much more than enough, Katy bit her lip.

Fin smiled wearily and said, "You go on up to bed, lassie. Malcolm is doubtless impatiently awaiting me, and your mother will want to talk to me, too."

"Will you tell them both all that I said?"

"Nae, only what little they need to know and that they must not quiz you now. You must eventually tell your mother everything, though, yourself."

She grimaced at the thought but knew he was right and that, eventually, she would have to tell Clydia, too. Another thought stirred then. She said, "None of you can go to that banquet now, so what will Malcolm do?"

"I don't know, Katy, but I do want to say one more thing to you before I go."

When he did not immediately continue, tension flooded through her again.

Then he said gently, "I know it took courage for you to come to Malcolm and me as you did, lassie. You had to know that you would have to explain it all and that my reaction would be unpleasant at best, so the plain truth is that I'm gey proud to discover that you have that kind of courage."

New tears spilled down her cheeks then, but he opened his arms to her, and she went to him. When she felt them close warmly around her, she hugged him back as tightly as she could until he murmured that they should go.

She ran up to her bedchamber then and was relieved to find

it empty. Pouring water into the basin, she washed away the evidence of her tears.

Deciding that she did not want to talk to anyone until morning, she doffed her clothing, got into bed, wondered briefly what Will might be doing at that moment, and was sound asleep before Bridgett or Clydia came in.

Neither disturbed her and by the time she awakened Thursday morning, Clydia had already gone downstairs. Dressing quickly, plaiting her hair, and pinning the coiled plait up under a plain white veil, Katy soon followed.

Despite her father's assurance that he would forbid Clydia and Catriona to quiz her, when she saw that both of them were still at the high table, she feared that each would find a way to satisfy her curiosity.

"I thought you meant to sleep the day away," Cat said with a smile. "Do not forget that your uncle Ivor is coming with his tail of men. I think that we have all in readiness, though. Other than taking some meals here and the men sleeping in the hall, courtyard, or woods, Ivor's men and Malcolm's do look after themselves."

Katy nearly asked how long they would stay but realized where that question might lead. Deciding that the less she said, the less likely it would be that she might tread where her father had forbidden her to go, she nodded but held her tongue.

Having managed to take Dae's clothing to the loch the night before, Will had barely managed to inform his cousin of his success Thursday morning before de Raite ordered Hew to go into Nairn and see that the entertainers understood exactly when they were to arrive the next evening.

"Ye'll also take their leader a wee partial payment tae encourage them tae be early. Dinna go alone, though," de Raite said. "Take Will or your cousin with ye."

"I dinna need either one," Hew said. "I can take one o' my own men."

"Nae, ye'll take one o' them, so ye'll no talk o' aught that ye should keep tae yourself. Whatever ye tell your men, ye'll tell them just aforehand and nae sooner."

"Afore what, Da?" Alyssa asked as the stepped onto the dais, having apparently emerged from the tower in time to overhear the exchange.

"Nowt tae concern ye," snapped de Raite. "Which will it be, Hew?" he added as Aly, flushing deeply, stepped off the dais and hurried around to the other end of the table, evidently deeming that route a safer one than passing behind her father.

Meantime, de Raite awaited Hew's answer.

Dae gave Will a frantic look.

"I'll go if you like, Hew," Will said.

"Nae, if I've got tae have one o' ye, I'll take Dae. But dinna dally, cousin. Hie yourself, and dinna forget your boots, for I want tae be back here by midday."

Visibly reluctant, Dae gave Will another look and went to fetch his boots.

De Raite left the hall when Hew did, so Will, taking pity on Alyssa, nearly offered to walk outside the wall with her. Realizing where she might ask him to take her and that if he left the castle, he would likely draw more attention from de Raite than he wanted, he reconsidered and invited her to play Tables with him instead.

She fetched the board, disks, and dice, and they played in the solar until midday, when Meggie brought Aly's meal to her.

Will went downstairs then to have his meal and walked into an argument between de Raite and Hew, the latter having evidently just returned from Nairn.

"What the devil did ye do tae the man?" de Raite demanded.

His face scarlet with fury, Hew shouted back, "I did nowt, I tell ye! When we passed the harbor, going tae where ye'd said we'd find yon minstrels, a ship were about tae sail. Some'un said it be bound for Aberdeen, Perth, and mayhap Norway. They had cast off its lines and men were hauling the plank in, when that dafty Dae took off a-running and leaped on tae the plank whilst it were near six foot away."

"Blast ye, Hew, ye should ha' stopped him!"

"Sakes, Da, I expected him tae fall intae the water, but he did nae such thing. The ship were too far from the quay then for me tae jump, and men were setting the sail, heading east for the firth, so they couldna turn back. Likely, they'll throw him overboard, though. I dinna think he had one shilling wi' him, let alone more."

"Well, ye must ha' said summat tae irk the man."

"Nae! Like I told ye, Dae be a feardie. Likely he wanted nowt tae do wi'—"

"I see," de Raite cut in before Hew could finish the sentence. Then, catching sight of Will, he said, "Did *ye* ken aught o' this notion o' Dae's?"

"Nae, sir," Will replied. "He is not a talkative chap, as both of you must know. When he walked the ridge with me, we went hours without talking," he added, comfortably aware that every word was true.

It occurred to him that it was also now true that someone else would benefit from the clothing he had left at the loch. Dae was unlikely to return to Raitt.

Sir Ivor and his men arrived late Thursday afternoon, but Katy had time only to greet him before Malcolm and Fin took Ivor, Tadhg—the captain of Ivor's tail—Lochan, Malcolm's second in command, and a few other chosen ones into the inner chamber, where they talked privately until suppertime.

Although Katy studied their faces when they emerged, she could tell nothing from their expressions or behavior. When supper proceeded as always, her curiosity began running amok and her frustration increased accordingly.

Tempted to ask Cat a question that might glean information without breaking her promise not to talk of what she knew, Katy could think of no such question.

Catriona had not asked her about anything she had done, nor had Clydia. They talked to her as they usually did without revealing a hint of knowledge other than that the men were to go to the banquet as planned.

Although Katy was sure they would not go now that their leaders knew of de Raite's intended treachery, she had learned nothing to reassure her of that.

In fact, by every sign, Malcolm, Fin, Ivor, and their followers *expected* to go.

Catching Fin's thoughtful gaze on her more than once that evening, she took good care to say nothing to anyone that might suggest she knew anything that the other person did not. Consequently, she had learned nothing new by the time she and Clydia retired for the night.

The following morning when Bridgett entered with their hot water, she was smiling for the first time in days.

Clydia, at the washstand, using leftover cold water, said, "You are looking very cheerful for someone who is arriving later than usual, Bridgett."

"Aye, but I kent fine that ye'd manage without me, as ye usually do in such a case. I be late 'cause that Lochan came tae find me in the scullery. He said he wants tae make peace wi' me just as the laird and them mean tae make peace wi' that deevil, de Raite, tonight."

Stunned at that news and terrified that the men might still intend to go to the banquet, Katy nearly exclaimed that Lochan must be mistaken but managed at the last second to swallow the words. They *could not* still be planning to go unless . . .

Could Fin and Malcolm have just pretended to believe her?

Dressing in the first kirtle that came to hand, an old duncolored one, she twisted her plaits up under a veil and followed Clydia downstairs.

Both Fin and Malcolm sat at the high table with Catriona and Sir Ivor.

Katy went straight to her father. Bending close behind him, she murmured into his ear, "Da, may I ask you something . . . privately?"

"Aye, sure, lass. Shall we go into the inner chamber?"

Nodding, she let him lead the way.

"What is it, then?" he asked when he had shut the door.

"Bridgett just told me that all of you still mean to attend the banquet. Surely, sir—" Breaking off when he put a finger to his lips, she said, "I said naught to her, Da, I promise, but . . ."

"That was wise of you," he said when she paused. "Sithee, Malcolm means to give de Raite the benefit of the doubt. Nae, then," he added when she opened her mouth in protest. "We believe your friend told the truth as he knows it, and we *will* be prepared for trouble. It is essential, though, that no hint of our suspicion reaches de Raite. That means that everyone here must behave as if we mean to go to that banquet exactly as and when we were invited to go."

"But that means without weapons!"

The heavily lashed gray eyes that matched her own twinkled. "Have faith in us," he said. "Malcolm will quietly pass the word to hide dirks under our plaids."

"What if they search you?"

"They won't, because Malcolm would demand to search them first. Forbye, it would be an insult that de Raite won't risk, whether he is acting in honor or not, and in such circumstances, our dirks will suffice to protect us. More significantly, if meantime de Raite comes to his senses or your lad misheard him, he will never know we had dirks. I am telling you all of this, Katy, because by coming to me with your question as you did, you showed me that you deserve to know we will be safe. I'm placing much trust in you now, though, by telling you so."

"I know, sir, and I won't fail you. Just don't let anything happen to Will."

"I'll do my best, lassie. But, if violence erupts, I can make no promise."

"Da, you must!" she exclaimed. "You cannot let him die! I . . . I . . ." Her voice failed her, but tears welled into her eyes and trickled down her cheeks.

"What is it, Katy-lass? You said that he loves you and that you love him, but you have known him for so short a time . . . What have you not told me?"

"Do you remember Brother Julian?"

"Aye, sure, but what—?"

"I declared us married, Da. Will is my husband."

Fin stared at her, dismay plain on his face. He opened his mouth, shut it again, and then said, "Have you told anyone else about this?"

"Just Clydia." She saw no reason to describe her twin's reaction to the news.

"Katy, I do not know enough about marriage by declaration to know what its rules are, but neither can you be sure of them. I will do all I can to protect Will if the Comyns do attack us, if only because he managed to warn us. I cannot promise more than that, other than that you and I *will* talk more about this when I return."

Knowing she would have to be satisfied with that, she said only, "Does Mam know that you and the others will take your dirks?"

"Aye, she does, but you would be wise not to discuss the situation with her even so. You ken fine how swiftly rumors fly on merely a hint. Actions can speak much, too, so take care to act normally in all that you do, as if naught is amiss and we look forward to being at peace with the Comyns of Raitt."

"I will," she said solemnly. "Thank you, sir. I will not let you down."

He kissed her then and held her tightly for a long, welcome moment before they returned to the high table.

Katy and Clydia spent the rest of Friday morning attending to their chores. Clydia went upstairs to supervise the maidservants there, while Katy took her turn in the kitchen.

There, she watched over and often helped the scullery maid and the lads who cleared the high table, cleaned platters and other vessels used there, and swept the kitchen floor. Other lads replenished the wood in the kitchen fireplace.

After the midday meal, Katy headed for the stairway, meaning to change from her old kirtle into another one, when she met Bridgett coming down.

"Lady Clydia told me earlier that ye might like tae visit Granny Rosel wi' me this afternoon. She said Granny asked ye what happened betwixt Lochan and me t'other day and ye wouldna tell her. Ye might want tae hear when I tell her, though, for there be summat more tae the tale than what ye kent then."

"What more?"

"Nae, then, I'll tell me Granny first. Ye're welcome tae come, though."

Katy's curiosity stirred, but another of those odd senses followed as if something tugging at her that she ought to . . .

"Be ye coming, then?"

Blinking at Bridgett, Katy said, "I may have forgotten . . ." Pausing at the sight of Clydia heading for the hall exit in the apron she wore to work in the garden, Katy felt the teasing tug again, as if it were in her head. They would water the garden later, as usual, so if she were to linger at Granny's . . .

The thought of the garden and lingering elsewhere flung the image of Alyssa Comyn into her mind's eye, when she had lingered with her in the woods.

. . . all will be abustle then . . . so I'll see you Friday.

"I cannot go today," Katy told Bridgett. "I've just remembered a promise I made to do something else, but do give Granny Rosel a hug for me."

"Aye, sure, I could fair see your thoughts a-twitching," she said, grinning. "I may stay overnight wi' her, but I'll be back tae wake ye in the morning."

"Clydia might like to go with you. I'll ask her if you like."

"Aye, sure, I'd like her tae come."

Following Clydia to the garden, Katy explained. "Bridgett is going to tell Granny Rosel what has been happening with Lochan. I just saw Granny the other day, but Bridgett would like company. If you want to go with her, I'll take care of the watering and do some weeding for you, too, if you like."

Clydia gazed at her speculatively. "I know I am not to ask you what has been happening, but we could all three go and water the plants tomorrow."

"Da just told me to keep everything looking normal here, lest de Raite has people watching to be sure Malcolm doesn't lead an army to his banquet," Katy said. "So, I do think one of us should do the garden."

"Very well, then, I'll go with Bridgett. Do try to keep out of mischief, though, until I return. I ken fine that Da was in a temper the other evening, and I'd liefer you not fall into the suds with him again, so don't."

She waited, but when Katy remained silent, she shook her head and turned away, untying her apron as she went.

Katy made what she believed was a good show of weeding, while watching increasing male activity in the courtyard. When it was clear that the men would soon depart, she decided it was late enough so that she would not have to wait long for Aly. If Will was walking the ridge, he might turn up, too.

Smiling at the thought, she put the tools she had used in the shed, took the pail, and headed out the open gateway. As she hurried down the path and across the clearing, she glanced at the ramparts and failed to see anyone looking her way. The lack did not disturb her. With so many men about, who would dare harm her?

Moments later, she reached the pail-and-smack part of the stream, knelt to fill the pail, and was beginning to stand again when she heard someone coming. Straightening, she turned and saw Aly hurrying toward her with a big grin.

"This is such a wonderful day!" she exclaimed. "I do wish I could be at that banquet. Liam said there will even be jugglers. I have never seen a juggler," she added with a sigh.

"Mayhap you could stay here tonight, instead," Katy said impulsively.

"Nae, I couldna do that. I dinna want tae do aught tae irk Father. His banquet be too important tae him, and tae me, come tae that. When we ha' peace, you and I can be friends openly. That will be grand!"

Katy swallowed hard, wanting desperately to warn Aly that de Raite's banquet would lead to anything but peace, and to urge her to stay at Finlagh.

"Why do ye look as if ye've met your sorrows?" Aly asked, frowning.

Before Katy could answer, a chill of terror surged through her.

Spinning mindlessly toward the castle, she had barely moved a foot toward it when two men burst from the bushes, and her voice froze in her throat.

One man grabbed Aly, and at the same time, the second one grabbed Katy and clamped an arm bruisingly across her breasts, making it hard to breathe. When she tried to dig an elbow into him and opened her mouth again to scream, he shoved a dirty rag into it with his other hand before she could do more than squeak.

CHAPTER 20

Katy kicked, squirmed, and struggled to free herself from the arm clamped across her breasts and the equally hard hand holding the filthy rag in her mouth until the villain who captured her just lifted her off her feet and carried her so.

Though she tried to kick him, they were moving too fast, and it did not help.

"What were ye a-doing there, Aly, a-talking tae a maidservant, when ye must ha' seen that she likely belongs tae Finlagh?" the taller and darker of the two men muttered as they hurried along. "What did ye tell her?"

Hearing the question and hoping Aly would not correct his error in assuming from her clothing that she was a servant, Katy listened intently for Aly's answer.

"I told her naught, Liam! Only that I be excited about the coming peace."

"That be nae sort o' answer," the one called Liam retorted. "Did ye come here tae tell her summat about Da's banquet?"

"Just that he will have musicians and jongleurs and that I have never seen a juggler. What more could I tell her?" Aly asked earnestly. "I dinna ken more."

Liam glanced at the man carrying Katy. Then he looked right into her eyes.

Struggling frantically, Katy finally managed to kick her captor's right knee hard with her heel.

Grunting at the pain, the man tightened his grip until again she could barely breathe, and then he shifted a finger and thumb of the hand over her mouth to each side of her nose. "Behave yourself or I'll pinch your nose shut," he growled in her left ear. "Wi' this clout stuffed in your mouth, ye'll be dead in minutes. Ye be nowt tae us, after all. Ye only be alive 'cause it might upset our Aly did we kill ye."

"She is . . . she's my friend, Colley," Aly said. "Dinna be mean tae her."

"Ye shouldna ha' friends from that place, peace or nae peace," Liam said, still eyeing Katy but in a more measuring way that she disliked intensely.

"But surely," Aly protested, "if we are to have peace—"

"Haud your whisst," Liam snapped, coming to a stop. Then, to Katy, he said, "We dinna want tae carry ye all the way, so I'll give ye a choice. Ye'll go quietly or we'll kill ye here."

"Nae, Liam!" Aly exclaimed. "Ye canna do that!"

Liam slapped her hard. "Not one more word 'less ye want me tae tell Da where we found ye. Ye ken fine what'll happen then, aye, Aly?"

Tears trickling down her cheeks, Aly said, "Aye, Liam. I'll be quiet."

"Good. Now, wench, ye'll recall the choice I gave ye," he said to Katy. "Which will it be? I'll offer only once, and if ye dinna keep your word, that will be that for ye. Nod if ye'll behave yourself."

Lowering her gaze, Katy nodded.

"Put her down, Coll, and take that rag from her mouth." When Colley had obeyed, Liam said, "What be your name, wench?"

Although she disliked the demeaning term, Katy kept her eyes downcast, gave thanks that she had not changed her clothing, and muttered, "An it please ye, sir, it be Katy. They'll soon be a-looking for me, though. Ye should let me go."

"Nae one will miss one wench, not wi' all that must be a-going on there the noo. They looked as if they be ready tae depart, aye?"

Seeing no reason to lie about that, Katy said, "Aye, sir."

"How many?"

"I think some'un said they be nigh two score, sir."

Nodding, he looked at Aly. "How did ye meet this wench?"

"I'll tell ye, Liam, but prithee, dinna tell Father. Katy is the only new friend I have met for as long as I remember."

"Then mayhap we'll keep her for ye, lass," Colley said with a wink at Liam. "Liam would like that."

Aly looked stunned. Avoiding their gazes, she said hastily, "I walked this way one day, hoping tae meet Will on his way back from the ridge, and she were looking for wildflowers. I . . . I dinna recall why." She looked at Katy.

Katy shrugged. "The mistress wanted some for her chamber, is all."

Liam nodded and said, "She shouldna let such a pretty piece out alone. Ye canna ken who ye might meet. Aye, lassie?"

Katy thought it better not to react and kept her eyes downcast. To her relief, he merely gave her a push, and they moved on.

When, an hour or so later, they came to a tall archway in a long stone wall, Liam asked the guard at the iron gate where de Raite was.

"I dinna ken, sir, but he's likely inside," the guard said as he opened the gate wide. "Ye'll ha' tae ask Olaf where he be."

Nodding with a grimace, Liam led the way in with Aly beside him and Colley followed, gripping Katy by an arm.

Realizing with a start that she was seeing Raitt Castle at last and recalling bleakly how she had once risked climbing the crag to see it, Katy eyed it nonetheless curiously.

Despite the timber bridge leading to an entrance at least ten feet above the ground, with its pointed windows and doorway, she thought Raitt looked more like a kirk than a castle. Outbuildings dotted its courtyard, including one with windows similar to the hall that she decided must be a chapel. A round tower rose above the wall walk at the hall's far southeastern corner.

Liam strode to the timber bridge and up to the entrance, where he peered at a porter's squint and shouted, "Open up, Olaf!" When the door swung wide, he added curtly, "Where's de Raite?"

"He be shut up in his chamber wi' Masters Hew and Will, sir," the porter said. "Who be this wi' ye?"

"One o' Meggie's many cousins," Liam replied glibly. "She's tae keep Mistress Alyssa company during the banquet, since Meggie will be needed in the kitchen. Nae need tae tell de Raite she's here. I'll do that m'self."

With that, he urged Katy and Alyssa through the screens passage and great hall—already prepared for the banquet and bustling with minions—to the tower stairway. Putting a finger to his lips as they neared a passage with a closed doorway ahead to the room beyond, he urged them silently to their right and up the stairs, passing a second chamber with its door open, revealing a sitting room or solar.

At the top of the stairs, Liam pushed the door open, saying, "Ye'll stay here and say nowt, the pair o' ye. I dinna mean tae tell Da about your friend, Aly, 'cause I fear he'd hang her and take a tawse tae ye for meeting her. So, keep her out o' his sight. They'll be here soon. She can thank me for me benevolence after they leave."

He shut the door then, leaving the two young women gaping at each other.

When the Mackintosh and his party arrived, de Raite received them by the hall's impressive hooded fireplace and roaring fire. On the nearby dais, Will stood at the high table with Hew, Colley, Liam, and de Raite's captain of the guard.

Except for Liam at Will's far right, near the tower stair, each man had an empty space on either side of him. Will stood next to the space at the garderobe end with another between him and Colley, hoping to survive the night.

Below the dais, running lengthwise from each end of it toward the screens passage, forming a U shape from the dais, were two long trestle tables.

De Raite's men lined each side of the tables with spaces between them, waiting for men in the Mackintosh's party to take those places. The open area inside the U would accommodate the entertainers hired for the evening.

Assuming a stately air, de Raite stepped forward to greet the Mackintosh and—somewhat to Will's annoyance—Malcolm's youngest son, the redheaded chap Will had come to think of as Aly's Gil.

Sir Fin of the Battles followed with his good-brother and war leader, Sir Ivor Shaw-Mackintosh, their captains, squires, and the rest of the men in their tails.

Will wore his long dirk carefully hidden beneath his plaid and knew that his brothers had concealed their weapons, too. He failed to emulate their evident lack of concern, though, having all he could do to breathe normally.

Hew seemed oblivious of their guests. Standing next to where Malcolm would be seated between him and de Raite, with the wide space for serving carts and servers behind them, Hew quirked an eyebrow and smirked at Colley, who stood nearer Will. Colley glanced at Will then and gave an elaborate shrug. Only de Raite's captain of the guard, on the stair landing between the open door to de Raite's inner chamber and that end of the dais, looked as nervous as Will felt. The man's right hand twitched beneath his plaid near his sheath.

Will's mouth felt dry and his belly tight, making him doubt that he would be able to eat anything.

Watching Aly's Gil gaze about as if in search of her while Malcolm talked with de Raite, Will decided that she had been utterly mad to hope de Raite would allow such a marriage, even had he meant to make peace with Malcolm.

Will marveled, too, at Malcolm's serenity, as he watched him shake hands with de Raite. Was the man truly so trustful of de Raite's words, or had Katy failed to understand and convey the urgency of Will's warning?

Had she warned them? What if she had not even been there? Might what he had thought were her fingers been merely a trick of the ever-changing forest light?

Sir Fin caught his eye and gave a solemn nod in greeting.

Will could take no comfort from that gesture, though, because Fin had visited Raitt a few times since Will's return. Also, from all he knew of Fin, the man had honored the royal command to keep the peace even when de Raite had not.

Malcolm's expression remained mildly curious as he gazed around the hall before moving toward the dais, but, Malcolm, too, had visited the castle before de Raite had hanged the four Mackintoshes, albeit only once since Will's return.

In truth, such meetings often concerned complaints made or actions taken that Malcolm or Fin deemed objectionable, even illegal. Nevertheless, all three men had discussed those matters peacefully enough.

The other Mackintosh men soon took places at the trestle tables, alternating with de Raite's men. Gillies directed Malcolm and his leaders to alternate with de Raite's at the high table. When they had all taken their places, de Raite joined them and invited his guests to sit down so they might begin with some entertainment.

His captain of the guard stepped into the inner chamber and shut its door.

"I am Bruce MacNab, erstwhile squire tae Sir Fin's nephew, Sir Àdham MacFinlagh," the man to Will's left said, extending his right hand to shake Will's. "Sir Àdham be in the Borders with his lady wife, visiting her family, so Sir Fin said I should come here in his stead."

Giving his name, Will welcomed MacNab, who seemed as comfortable at de Raite's table as Will's brothers did, and then introduced himself to the stockier man at his right and learned that he was Finlagh's captain of the guard, Lochan.

Will wondered, even more, why de Raite's captain had appeared only to disappear into the inner chamber. Reassuring himself that he *had* seen Katy's cairn and more than likely those two slim fingers, as well, and that Katy was brave . . .

From the minstrels' gallery at the far end of the hall, two fiddlers, a piper, a harpist, and a lad banging a tabor began to play music and sing while gillies poured claret or whisky, as desired, for those on the dais. In the lower hall, jugs providing ale or whisky passed swiftly from man to man. Those seated facing away from the entertainers soon turned around with their filled goblets to watch them.

Shortly thereafter, a troop of acrobats ran into the area and began to perform, followed minutes later by a tall, skinny man who somehow produced handkerchiefs from his ears, whole eggs from his mouth, and juggled any number of odd things.

Their audience apparently had thoughts only for the entertainment, expressing their approval by stomping feet, cheering, shouting encouragement, or clapping. There was so much laughter that Will wondered if his brothers would all recall why they were there. Liam, for one, was ogling one of the female acrobats.

The fire in the huge fireplace burned and crackled cheerfully while torches flaming from sconces on the walls and flanking the fireplace hood cast flickering golden light across every wall.

At last, de Raite dismissed the acrobats and juggler with a wave of one hand and, with the other, signed to his chaplain to say the grace-before-meat, bringing the company hastily to their feet.

When they sat down again, the musicians in the gallery began a traditionally stately tune to announce the entrance of a cart bearing a great baron of beef with a ceremonial dirk plunged into its center. Surrounding the meat were spring flowers and foliage in which nestled rounds of haggis and baked oysters still steaming in their shells, with roasted, fresh-caught salmon framing the whole. Other carts followed with roasted venison, mutton, lamb, pork, chickens, and geese. Bread in baskets, pots of honey and mustard, and other sauce dishes graced every table.

While the carvers carved, gillies carried in tureens containing a thick pottage of chicken, leeks, and barley in broth. Two gillies served the men at the high table, while others carried tureens to the lower tables for those men to serve themselves.

De Raite signaled the entertainers to return, and the revelry continued, creating a lively din.

In the tower bedchamber, Aly moved from her favorite window seat toward the open door to the stairs. "It has become much noisier below," she said.

"Art sure we will hear anyone who comes up those stairs?" Katy asked.

"Aye, but nae one will now," Aly replied just loudly enough for Katy to hear her. "There be wine, ale, and whisky in jugs on all the tables, so the men will all drink too much and pay more heed tae the jugglers and acrobats than tae aught else. Even Meggie were ordered tae aid in the kitchen or the scullery."

Katy was sure the Mackintosh men would not be so reckless, but she knew that Aly was scared and did not want to frighten her more. Casually, she said, "Is the only way out of this chamber to go down the stairs?"

"Aye," Aly said flatly. "Our Liam tried once tae climb out my big south window there tae the roof, but the tower roof be like a stack of saucers with smaller and smaller rings of masonry making a peaked cone. He pulled some stones loose, which clattered tae the cobbles o' the courtyard and might have killed someone had they hit anyone. Father nigh had him flogged for that, so nae one else has tried."

"Mercy, were they able to repair the roof?"

"Aye, one of the men climbed tae it from the wall walk atop the hall and was able tae replace the stones. I think Liam and Colley will see that you get home safe, come morning, though. If they dinna do that, I'll tell Father who you are."

Katy realized that no one at Finlagh could possibly know where she was. If Clydia had gone with Bridgett as they had planned, others would likely have deduced that she had gone with them. When Clydia returned without her, she and Cat would worry but might imagine only that she had visited elsewhere in the woods and lingered longer than expected.

Since Fin was downstairs with the other men, she need not concern herself with him yet. But if aught went amiss with Malcolm's plan . . .

She shivered. Even if the Mackintoshes did prevent the Comyns from killing them, difficulties would surely arise. No matter how she explained . . .

"What is it, Katy?" Aly asked. "You look worried, but you needna be."

"Aly, no one at Finlagh knows where I am, and I doubt that my father will accept *any* explanation for my presence here," Katy explained. "It is also possible that if my mother becomes too worried, she may come looking for me."

"Faith," Aly said, putting a hand to her lips. "Certes, she wouldna come tae a household consisting almost entirely of men-at-arms without an invitation."

Since Catriona was known for both her intrepidity and her

impatience, Katy was not so sure of that. However, she could hardly tell Aly that the only reason Cat might *not* come was her knowledge of the treachery de Raite planned to carry out.

Even as that thought occurred, another followed, that Cat might hope that a mother turning up in search of her daughter would put an end to any plan of killing.

Aly had moved to the top of the stairway. "Just listen tae them," she said fretfully. "They get louder every minute."

Katy agreed. The noise had become a din. She was about to ask Aly to shut the door when Aly said, "I mean tae slip down far enough tae see what I can see. You hide in my bed till I return, lest someone sees me and follows me back up. I leave the bed curtains closed all day, so nae one will think aught of seeing them so."

Reluctantly, Katy obeyed. If de Raite saw his daughter, he would be angry, but if *anyone* saw Katy with her, they would both be in the suds.

The minstrels continued to play lively tunes from the gallery while their host and his guests enjoyed their food and the music. Wine, ale, and whisky flowed freely, and the banter at tables became merrier and more boisterous until the walls reverberated to the general carousing. Most of the servers and de Raite's chaplain had long since vanished from the hall.

Will's tension had increased, too. His heart was thumping so hard in his chest that he feared he might disgrace himself by losing what little food he had eaten. Since he sat at the end nearest the garderobe, he had consoled himself with the hope that if worse came to worst, he might make it to the latrine in time.

Then, at last, de Raite stood and raised both hands with his palms out, facing the minstrels' gallery at the far end of the hall.

The entertainers, noting the gesture, stopped their antics and proceeded with the few remaining servers, in a single line, out to the screens passage. The minstrels finished their tune, descended from the gallery, and followed the others to the passage, leaving de Raite's men and their guests alone in the great hall.

Waiting only until the castle's heavy main door had clanged

shut behind those departing, de Raite shouted, "All of us must now be upstanding, for 'tis time we make our final toast tae each other and this grand night."

Will's stomach lurched, but somehow he got to his feet and, as he did, he saw their captain of the guard, in a simple tunic and plaid like everyone else but bearing a silver ewer and goblet on a tray, cross the stair landing from de Raite's chamber, continue through the archway to the dais, and pass behind Liam, Sir Ivor, Hew, and Malcolm to stand directly behind de Raite.

Hearing MacNab, his own supposed victim on his left, clear his throat, Will experienced sudden mixed feelings of relief that the moment was at hand, guilt for his betrayal of his father and brothers, and a singular sense of sadness that his actions had been necessary. Drawing a breath and relying on his trust in Katy to steady himself, he looked past the sober Lochan, a visibly less sober Colley, and Katy's father, to de Raite at the center.

Lochan was also watching de Raite. So was Sir Fin of the Battles. Colley was watching Sir Fin.

Flanked by Malcolm and Fin, with his own guard captain behind him having poured fresh wine into a goblet and now holding the goblet ready for him, de Raite waited patiently until all the men in the hall had risen to their feet.

Will reached to touch his dirk, in case he needed to defend himself.

From his left, MacNab murmured, "Easy, lad, we ha' nae quarrel wi' ye."

Just then, motion on the landing below the tower stairway drew Will's startled attention to his sister peeping around the frame of the archway into the hall.

Raising his goblet, de Raite scanned the scene below from his right slowly to his left and back to the right again as he cried, "Tae all our departed comrades in arms . . . and tae all o' them . . . wha' will soon *join them*!"

At the high table and below, Comyns swiftly drew their dirks, but the Mackintosh men, anticipating them, were quicker.

Meantime, as de Raite was looking rightward again just before mayhem erupted in the hall, to Will's shock, Alyssa clapped a hand to her mouth, snatched up her skirt with the other, and whirled around to run back up the stairs.

De Raite had seen her, too, though. His guard captain, having cast his tray aside, stepped in beside de Raite to engage Fin. De Raite shoved Malcolm toward Hew and raced past them toward the stairs, bellowing, "Vixen! I kent fine ye'd been a-meeting someone, and now ye've betrayed your ain family tae that devil, whoever he be! I swear by God, ye'll pay a dear price for it!"

Shouting more epithets, he rushed through the still open door to his inner chamber, emerged seconds later with the great sword that had hung on the wall there, and dashed up the stairs after Aly.

Aly's redheaded Gil ran across the dais from the lower hall and followed them. By then, though, Will had closed the distance and was right behind Gil.

Katy, waiting impatiently in Aly's cupboard bed, heard chaos erupt below, then a deep-voiced bellow that echoed up the stairway in a sudden, brief hush.

Seconds later, Aly burst through the doorway, running toward the south window.

A big man with a graying beard and unbound hair, holding a great sword at the ready, filled the doorway, shouting, "By heaven, ye traitorous wretch, I'll teach ye no tae betray *me!*"

"I did nae such wicked thing, Father!" Aly shrieked, jumping onto the window seat. She turned to face him with her back to the big open window.

"Aye, ye did," de Raite roared, brandishing the sword menacingly. "I saw the guilt in your eyes wi' me own, Alyssa, so ye must ha' told yer damnable lov—"

"Nae, I did not!" she cried again, now so close to the open window that Katy clapped a hand over her mouth to keep from screaming, for she could not aid Aly one whit by making her presence known. Easily deducing that de Raite believed his innocent daughter had betrayed his plan, Katy feared that, as angry as he was, he would kill Aly or Katy herself, or both of them, and then Will, as well, if she shouted out that *she* had revealed the plan to Malcolm and Fin.

"Liar!" de Raite cried.

Through an inch-wide opening in the bed curtains, Katy saw tears trickling down Aly's cheeks.

"By my troth, Father," she cried desperately. "I swear on Mam's memory that I have done naught tae harm you."

"By God, ye'll nae swear such a lie on your mother's name," de Raite shouted, advancing on her until the point of his sword was inches from her breast.

Flinging the curtain aside, Katy screamed, "Nae, don't hurt her; it was me!" But a louder male shout from the doorway overwhelmed hers.

In one horrid second, she saw Aly teetering in the window with de Raite's sword slashing toward her, as another body hurtled forth, blocking Katy's view.

Gilli Roy, dirk out, grabbed de Raite by the arm with his free hand and tried to swing him out of his way.

De Raite whipped the sword toward Gilli, and Aly screamed again.

Determined to help Gilli fight the murderous de Raite, Katy leaped up from the bed only to be shoved back onto it and see Gilli stumble as a second male body shot toward de Raite.

The sword in de Raite's hand wavered toward the open, empty window.

With a startled grunt, de Raite collapsed, and Katy recognized Will only as he leaped to the window seat with his bloody dirk still in hand, peered down and then turned back toward the others, looking shocked and horrified, his broad shoulders slumping in defeat and tears welling in his eyes.

Gilli regained his balance only to cry out in dismay and gape at the open window. His dirk clattered to the floor. His face lost all its color.

Even before Will looked blankly at Katy, she knew what he had seen. "She's dead, isn't she?" she said, hoping he would disagree.

Visibly startled, he focused his gaze on her then, and his angry frown shot an icy shiver up Katy's spine.

Gilli said fiercely, "Ye should ha' let *me* kill that dastard, Will Comyn. It be wrong for ye tae ha' your own father's blood on your hands."

"But had *you* killed him, the tale would spread all over Scotland by sundown tomorrow that a Mackintosh had murdered Comyn de Raite. Not only would the feud resume but his grace might turn his fury on the Mackintosh," Will said gruffly, tears still glistening in his eyes.

"He is right, Gil," Fin said from the doorway. "This tragedy was de Raite's own doing. His thirst for vengeance did him in, so no one here or still standing below will blame Will for avenging his sister's death."

Starting at the sound of her father's voice, Katy turned toward him and met as fierce a frown as the one on Will's face. She opened her mouth to explain, but her throat closed against any words she might have said, so she shut it again.

Gilli Roy said, "I must go down tae Aly. I canna believe she is dead."

"There are cobbles below, Gil," Will said quietly. "Moreover, she fell nearly forty feet, so you must prepare yourself. I'll go with you, though."

Malcolm appeared on the landing behind Fin. "God ha' mercy," he muttered as his youngest son pushed past them.

"Is all quiet in the hall, my lord?" Will asked Malcolm.

"Aye," Malcolm replied. "MacNab followed ye and stood in the archway by the stairs tae keep everyone else away, so Sir Ivor, Lochan, and my own men have all in hand inside and outside, too. I fear, though, that most o' your Comyn men inside ha' perished. Only those on the wall walk, the guards at the gate, and innocent minions remain standing. I have offered forgiveness and peace tae all who admit defeat. Such men may choose tae bide here wi' ye, swear allegiance tae me, or join other Comyn factions elsewhere."

"I thank you for your mercy, sir, but pray excuse me now. The others will explain everything, but I must follow Gil. See you, my young sister has likely fallen to her death, but we must see for ourselves that she is not still suffering."

Malcolm gave him a steady look, then nodded and said, "Take MacNab with ye, lad, and dinna look too friendly, the pair o' ye. Though me own men be out there, doubtless some o' your lot will be, too, and some'un may wonder why ye be the only one o' de Raite's sons tae survive this night. 'Twould be best the question doesna come up an ye dinna stay here alone t'night."

"I do *not* want to live at Raitt after this," Will said flatly.

"Sakes, lad, it be too soon tae be sayin' any such a thing. 'Tis true that wi' de Raite gone, I deem Raitt tae be Mackintosh property again and doubt ye'll gainsay me, but I ken fine that this business tonight has been a great upset tae ye, and I'm thinking now that Gillichallum Roy be involved, too. We'll all talk more anon."

Nodding, Will hurried downstairs after Gil.

CHAPTER 21

Although, in her lingering shock over Aly's fall, Katy's first impulse had been to follow Will and see for herself if Aly had survived, not only did Fin and Malcolm stand between her and the door, but just thinking of that horrible fall brought the memory of Aly's description of the stones from the tower roof "clattering" to the cobbles thirty or forty feet below. Katy winced, unable to move, her stomach roiling. As she took a breath to steady herself, her gaze met her father's. Knowing that he and Malcolm still awaited an explanation, she braced herself and said, "I ken fine that you both want to know why I am here."

Fin nodded, but his expression had softened. "We do want to know that, aye, lassie, but we are very glad that you came to no harm here. Although you did not mention Will's sister when you told me of de Raite's intent tonight, I'm thinking that in the course of your friendship with Will, you came to know her, too, aye?"

"Aye, sir," she said sadly. "We . . . we became friends, too."

Malcolm looked about to speak, making her hope fervently that he would not ask her about Gilli Roy and Aly.

Fin looked at him, too, but Malcolm said only, "'Twas gey fortunate that ye learned the truth o' what de Raite meant tae happen here, lass, and we be that grateful ye were brave enough tae tell us. That canna ha' been easy for ye tae do."

"It would have been much harder for me to keep such news to myself, sir."

Both men spoke at once then, each one apparently trying to assure her that he understood her, but as they tried to defer to each other and otherwise sort themselves out, Katy thought she heard someone coming up the stairs.

Fearing that it must be MacNab coming to tell them that Will would be engaged below for the rest of the night, she missed what Fin and Malcolm were saying until Fin said, "Well, lass?"

"Forgive my inattention, sir," she said. "I thought I heard someone coming."

"Malcolm said that—with him, your uncle Ivor, and their men to see to everything here—I should be getting you home before your mam comes looking for us both. But I do think that Malcolm should first hear your explanation for himself."

"I'd like to hear that, too, sir," Will said clearly from the stairway.

Though Katy was relieved to hear his voice, his swift return told her as clearly as words could that Aly had died, and brought tears to her eyes.

When Will entered the room, he looked directly at her and said, "She's gone, Katy. I sent one of the lads to find Meggie and ask her to collect some of the other women to help her prepare Aly's body for burial."

Malcolm said, "I told my men earlier tae see tae proper burial for your people, lad. They can see tae poor Lady Alyssa, too, if ye'd like."

"Thank you, sir, but MacNab suggested having some of them carry her into de Raite's inner chamber, where the women can look after her more easily. I'll take the quilt from her bed down there to cover her."

Katy said, "You are right, Will, that it should be your womenfolk who tend to Aly. I would like to see her one more time, though, just to say—"

"Nae, lass," he interjected. "I ken fine that you think of Aly as a sister now, but you do *not* want to see her. 'Twould be much better for you to remember her as beautiful as she was before tonight. In any event," he added, holding her gaze, "we still want to know how you came to be here with her."

Katy's breath caught, but recalling that, for once, her predicament was not of her own doing, she swallowed and exclaimed, "It was not my fault! Your brothers caught Aly and me together when she visited this afternoon, Will. We had no—"

As one voice, Will and Fin said, "Were you alone or did you have the dogs?"

Aware that it would aid her with neither man to admit that she had not spared a thought for the dogs, Katy was silent.

Deciding that they could discuss that issue further at another time, Will turned to Malcolm and said, "I have not changed my mind, sir. With Aly gone, there is naught to keep me here at Raitt."

"Your brothers all be dead now, lad, so ye be your father's rightful heir."

"Then I must have the right to abandon Raitt or to hand it back to the Mackintoshes, have I not?" Will asked.

"'Tis likely so, but ye also have a right tae live here, if ye decide to, until his grace sorts out the legality o' my claim. Sakes, afterward, too, come tae that. I'd be glad tae have ye here, if what I suspect about your feelings for Katy be true, but ye'll decide naught o' such import now, as deep in mourning as ye must be."

Fin said quietly, "Whatever you decide, Will, you would still be wise to sleep elsewhere tonight. If you will agree to it, I'd welcome you at Finlagh. Sir Ivor and Lochan will stay here with Malcolm and enough men to see that all remains calm with your people."

"Aye, that be a good notion," Malcolm said. "Ye need make nae further decisions tonight, lad, and tomorrow ye'll find your head much clearer. I'll look after Gillichallum Roy, and taegether we'll see your sister in good hands."

"I'll stay here until Meggie and the women arrive," Will said. "In troth, although I know they will look after her kindly, I dislike leaving her here alone."

"In mine own experience, your women will be more comfortable if they *can* be alone with her," Fin said gently. "That decision is also yours to make, though. You can catch up with us easily enough if you decide to do so."

"I would like a few private words with Katy first, sir, if you will agree."

Fin nodded, and Malcolm said, "Aye, lad, ye should take her down tae the solar, where ye can say whatever ye want tae her. That will give Fin and me a few minutes more tae talk things over here, whilst the lads downstairs finish making a path from yon stairs tae the main door. He willna want tae take her through that slaughter until they tidy up a bit, but it willna take long."

Turning back to Katy, Will held out a hand. Although she seemed wary, as well she might, since he disliked her apparent lack of concern for her own safety, she took his hand, and with hers warm inside his own, he wanted nothing more than to be alone with her, if only to put the disaster of the night out of his mind for a few minutes and to ask her privately if, by chance, she had hoped they might live at Raitt to be near her family.

Taking the quilt from Aly's bed, he led the way downstairs, pausing at the open solar door to let Katy enter, and then followed her, shutting the door.

Lit by two cressets casting a golden glow onto the walls, the room seemed dark and cozy. His image of Aly sitting on the cushion in the window embrasure there was strong, though. She had left a pink wool shawl draped over a back-stool by the table where they had played cards and board games. Tears stung his eyes again.

Katy was staring straight at the south window, a twin of the one in Alyssa's bedchamber, though fortunately shut. Beyond the glass, pale moonlight glimmered on the shrub-laden hillside.

She turned from the embrasure and looked at him. "I can imagine her in here so easily," she said softly. "She must have spent much time here."

Nodding, he opened his arms, realizing that he wanted more than anything *not* to imagine Aly but just to hold Katy close again, breathing and alive.

Without hesitation, she came to him, resting her head against his chest as he closed his arms around her and breathed in the scent of her hair. After a long, quiet moment, she tilted her head back to look up at him. "May I ask you something?"

"Always," he said, looking into her eyes, bright with reflected cresset glow.

"Do you think that Malcolm could persuade you to live here?"

It was all he could do to keep the instant recoil he felt from stiffening his body, but he said as calmly as he could, "Do you mean that *you* would want to?"

"Never," she said firmly. "I would see Aly everywhere, and although you will not let me see her as she is now, I could not look at the big windows and their window seats without imagining your father threatening her with his horrid sword and making her fall to the cobblestones."

"I would, too, so we will hold firm against Malcolm," he said. "But, Katy-love, the others will be leaving soon for Finlagh, and I don't want to do anything more now than to hold you close and tell you how much I love you."

"Oh, Will, say that again."

He repeated his words and then stopped her reply with another kiss, as he stroked his hand gently down her back to her backside. When she moaned, he felt himself stir in response.

Moments later, although he was more than warm himself, he felt her shiver.

"You should have worn a cloak or a cape, *mo chridhe.*"

"It was nice out when I went to the stream," she said. "Kiss me again."

He obeyed, but his sharp hearing told him that the others were coming down the stairs. They had already given the two of them more time than he had expected.

"They are coming, Katy-love," he said. Then, seeing again the shawl over the back-stool, he released her, reached for it, and added, "We'll put this round you. Aly made it for herself, and I know she would be pleased for you to have it."

"I will treasure it, Will, but you should have something of hers, too."

He shook his head. "She had little to call her own, lass. Meggie and the other women who knew her will look after her things, in their own way."

As he spoke, he knew that there was one other thing he wanted. Wrapping Katy in the shawl and picking up the quilt, he urged her out onto the landing and downstairs, pausing only to put the quilt in the inner chamber to await Alyssa.

The hall was empty except for Malcolm, Fin, and MacNab on the dais.

Urging Katy toward them, Will went to MacNab and extended a hand to him. "Pray, sir, accept my thanks for all you have done."

"Sakes, lad, it be ye who deserves *our* thanks."

Shaking his head, Will said, "Tell Lochan I'm grateful to the two of—"

"Whatever it be, ye can tell Lochan yourself. That be him comin' yonder."

The square-built man was striding toward them from the screen passage. "Ye there, MacNab," he said. "Take yourself off tae look after our lot now. All be calm outside, but there be dunamany bodies tae bury, and I ha' business elsewhere."

"What business would that be?" MacNab asked him.

"*My* business," Lochan retorted. "What's keepin' ye, man?"

With a knowing grin, MacNab took his departure.

Fin said, "You mean to return with us straightaway, eh, Lochan?"

"I do, sir. Life be too short tae waste any more of it." After that cryptic remark, he added, "How many men d'ye want tae take with us?"

Fin looked at Malcolm, who said, "Five or six will do, Lochan. We'll head out now. Ye can catch up with us soon as ye choose who ye want."

Accordingly, Will put an arm around Katy's shawl-covered shoulders, and they followed Fin and Malcolm outside. As they moved toward the now-open gate, the two older men shifted position in a way that told Will they meant to shield Katy from aught she would liefer not see. Just then, Will noticed men carrying a covered shape on a long shutter toward the entrance.

Meggie walked beside it with two other women. When she realized that he had seen her, she waved him on.

Reassured then that Aly was in good hands for the nonce, he

nodded, and when Fin raised his eyebrows in query, Will escorted Katy through the gateway.

The half-moon was high, clouds few and scattered, making a pleasant night.

As they walked along behind her father and Malcolm, Katy said, "Do you mean for us to live at Finlagh, Will?"

"Nae, lass. I dinna ken where we'll go, but we might just run away as you suggested the day you married us." He turned to Fin. "Something occurred to me whilst Katy and I were talking about Alyssa, sir, and I would seek your advice as to my best course. See you, I still dislike leaving her alone at Raitt. Our mother is there, so Aly could lie next to her, but Aly was unhappy at Raitt."

"We have a graveyard, too," Fin said. "If you like, we can bury Alyssa there. We may be able to move your mother, too. Or we can leave her to rest in peace and have a stone honoring her memory placed alongside Alyssa's. You need not decide tonight about that, though."

Evidently overhearing the exchange, Malcolm said, "My offer o' Raitt will remain open tae ye, lad, but if ye ha' notions o' where ye'd liefer be, ye need only tell me, and I'll seek out what choices ye may have thereabouts."

"Thank you, my lord," Will said, as they reached the path to Finlagh. "Meantime, I would like to swear my allegiance to you, if you will accept it."

"Sakes, I offered tae accept it from any Comyn left alive at Raitt. I can hardly refuse tae accept a liegeman who likely already saved my life. I ken fine that ye fought tae preserve Inverness Castle for me some years ago, too. I'll no ask ye tae get down on your knees here in the road, but I would ask ye tae explain summat ye said whiles ago, though."

"Anything," Will said, wondering how he had stirred Malcolm's curiosity.

The older man cast a glance at Fin before turning back to Will and saying, "Fin told me ye'd met our Katy atop a peak hereabouts and became friends, but he didna mention any marriage tae me."

Memory of the fateful words surged back, and Will looked ruefully at Fin. "Did she tell you, sir?"

Nodding, Fin said, "To be precise, she said she had *declared* herself married to you but that she did it just as the Black Hour occurred, so I would understand if it caught you by surprise. If you do harbor a wish to ignore or dispute . . ."

Katy gasped.

Will gave her father a direct look and said firmly, "With your permission, sir, I would keep her."

"Since I am persuaded that you were truly as astonished to see her at Raitt tonight as I was . . ."

"You may be sure of that," Will said. "Moreover, sir, if I do keep her, I hope you will not object to my making it clear to her that she must have more care to her own safety than she oft seems to show."

"Sakes, lad," Fin said, "*if* you keep her, you won't need anyone's permission for that or to put her across a knee. I'll just pray you have better success than I did."

"Then by your leave, sir, I will keep her. But is it true then that a marriage by declaration is legal?"

"If there was a witness and you do not dispute it, it is," Malcolm said.

"A witness?" Will looked at Katy with an unexpected urge to smile.

"Rory!" she exclaimed. "Does Rory count? He overheard every word."

"Aye, lass, he counts," Malcolm said.

As their party turned onto the path toward Finlagh a half-hour later, they heard a shout from behind and waited for Lochan and five others to catch up with them before going on.

"Torches yonder," Fin said a short time later. "I fear that it may be—"

"Catriona with an army?" Malcolm suggested.

"If it *is* Cat, she had better have an army," Fin muttered. "What the devil is she doing out here at such an hour, and who is that with her?"

Hoping she was not flinging herself into the suds again, Katy said, "Mam is likely looking for me, sir. No one could have guessed where I'd gone, because Clydia went with Bridgett to Granny's, and I went out to water the garden."

When he continued to peer ahead, frowning, she added, "I do have a question to ask before they get here, Da, about what you call 'intuition.'"

"What is it?" he asked, still watching the approaching group.

"Just before those two men captured Aly and me, I felt that sudden jolt of true fear that you described. I tried to scream and to get away, but my voice froze, and then they were upon us. One shoved a rag in my mouth and lifted me off my feet. I don't understand how *you* could have ducked away as you did when the man already had his sword out and was swinging it toward you."

Fin looked at her then, frowning as if he were thinking of how best to answer her or simply recalling why her captors had been successful.

Malcolm said, "'Tis experience, lass, so likely 'tis age, too. The broader one's experience be, the better the chance be tae ha' the sort o' result your father described. He was a highly trained warrior even then. It was not his first battle."

Will said quietly, "Liam and Colley were also experienced, *mo chridhe*, not to mention much bigger and stronger than either you or Aly. De Raite had set them to watch Malcolm and his people depart, so they must have seen Aly and followed her. When they found you with her, they scooped you up, too."

"They mistook me for a maidservant," she said. "Aly let them think so."

"It *is* Catriona," Fin said in a tone that told Katy she might not be in as much trouble as her mother was. Then Will squeezed her shoulders gently, which reminded her that she no longer answered to Fin but to her husband.

"Will," Fin said then, "I should tell you that since I was not yet certain of the facts, I have told her mother only that Katy *thought* she had declared herself married to you. I'm thinking now that when her mam learns of this, she may insist that you have a proper ceremony before you consummate your union."

The thought that Will might do that *without* a ceremony stirred every fiber of Katy's body. Evidently, it stirred him as well, for he looked right at her as he said firmly, "If the marriage is legal, sir, I see no need to wait, though I would agree to let a priest say the words over us later if her lady mother desires it."

"So be it, then," Fin said. He pressed his lips together, but his eyes twinkled.

Will put his arm around Katy and she snuggled closer and heard Fin say, "Cat has Clydia with her, and Bridgett."

"She also has the dogs and two of the men I left at Finlagh," Malcolm said.

Lochan's voice sounded behind them. "Did ye say ye can see Bridgett, sir?"

"Aye, and Rory," Fin said.

Seeing the boy suddenly dart ahead of the others, Katy glanced up at Will.

He was watching Rory, who came to a stop when he reached Fin. "Lady Cat said tae tell ye she be glad tae see ye all safe and sound. She were worried about Lady Katy." Then, spotting Will, he added, "If ye hadna made such a song about forbidding me tae follow her again, I'd ha' likely made m'self more useful."

"If you want to discuss that further with me," Will said evenly, "we can do so as soon as we reach Finlagh."

"Nae, we can*not*," Rory said. "Ye've got our Katy tae look after, yourself, now, 'cause ye be holding her a mite too close no tae ha' Sir Fin's leave for such."

The others joined them then, and Catriona explained: "When we realized that Katy was nowhere to be found, I confess that I suspected she might have found some way to follow you to Raitt and run into trouble. We were coming only to discover if all was peaceful there or still unsettled."

"And if it had been the latter?" Fin asked her.

She smiled and put a hand to his cheek. "Then, sir, I would have created a great tirrivee. Sithee, I also sent to Cawdor for Donald to meet us there. Never think, though, that I lacked faith in you, for I was confident that you and Malcolm would prevail. My uncertainty was for Katy and what might happen to her."

"As you see, she is safe," Fin said. "I have more to tell you about that, too, so we will not wait for Cawdor, and I will walk with you. The others can follow."

"Begging your pardon, sir," Lochan said. "I ha' summat I mean tae say tae Bridgett, too. We can either go ahead o' ye, or follow everyone, at your will, sir."

Bridgett, beside Catriona, put her nose in the air and looked away.

Catriona smiled. "Do not beat her again, Lochan."

Lochan's mouth opened. "I *never!*"

"Unless she deserves it," Fin said with a meaningful look at Catriona, who grinned saucily back at him. Watching them, Katy smiled, too.

His mouth still open, Lochan looked from Catriona to Fin.

As Fin gestured for him to go ahead with Bridgett, Katy felt Will's arm tighten around her. Looking up at him again, she saw his teasing smile. "What?"

"Have you forgotten what your father said to me, little wife . . . earlier?"

Gaping much as Lochan had, she exclaimed, "You *wouldn't!*"

"Nae, not straightaway."

Katy breathed a sigh of relief.

"I want to hold you for a time and just feel you close to me, lass, so I'm for bed first, as soon as we reach Finlagh."

Will had long thought he was a patient man, but when hoofbeats behind their party a half-hour later announced the arrival of Cawdor, Wilkin, and their men, telling him that the "first" thing on his mind would have to wait, his impatience stirred. Although the newcomers soon learned that their assistance was no longer required, they did demand explanations.

Fin's was brief, but he assured Cawdor and Wilkin that he and Will would soon visit them and tell the whole tale. Lochan and Bridgett had disappeared by then, so Will urged Katy on as soon as he knew Cawdor would be departing.

The others soon caught up, and they all entered the castle together.

With a sympathetic smile, Catriona approached him. "I am so

sorry about your sister, Will. Sithee, Fin told me everything that I did not already know, including that my impulsive daughter married you without warning. He also told Cawdor and Wilkin. Cawdor agrees with me that you should have a ceremony and has offered his chapel for the service and his chaplain to perform it. I told him I would relay that to you but that you might have other plans. You will likely want time to send for your granduncle and cousins, if you would like them to come."

"I would like them to see us married in a kirk, mayhap even in Inverness, where Cawdor and my granduncle both have houses," Will said. "But whether it should be at Cawdor or elsewhere, I should like to consider for a time."

"Wilkin warned us that you might say something like that, and so did Fin, so that is what you must do," Cat said. "But you must both be exhausted by now, and Bridgett has vanished with Lochan, so I sent Clydia and two maids up to clear Àdham and Fiona's bedchamber for you. I also sent one of the lads to fetch hot water and take it up, so you can both wash or even have a bath if you like."

"A wash will suffice," Will said hoarsely. Having feared that she meant for them to wait for the ceremony, the news that she expected him to sleep with Katy affected him like an aphrodisiac.

Catriona nodded. "Then you should go straight up. Katy will show you the way. In the morning, you may break your fast whenever you like, for with all these men here, food is available whenever anyone wants it. Go now, though, before Fin or Malcolm thinks of something else he wants to discuss with you."

Tempted to kiss her, Will gave her a brief hug instead and urged Katy toward the spiral stairway. After all the chaos and slaughter at Raitt that had resulted in Aly's death, he could conceive of no better way to ease his sorrow than to hold his dearling Katy in his arms and consummate their marriage.

Clydia, meeting them on the stairs with two maids behind her, said, "You can tell me everything tomorrow, Katy." Slipping by them with a touch of a hand to Katy's and a warm smile for Will, she went on downstairs with her followers.

Relieved to have Katy all to himself at last, Will stood for a moment and just watched how the candlelight played on her face and gilded her hair.

"Do you want to wash first, or shall I?" Katy asked him.

"I think I will wash you thoroughly and put you to bed," he said, still watching her closely. "Never fear, though, for I shall join you there right speedily."

He could see that her body reacted instantly to his words, doubtless in ways she had not felt before, but she did not seem to be shocked or shy, merely intrigued.

"When you said that, I felt a thrill shoot right through me," she said, reaching for her laces. "Can you make me feel that again?"

"Willingly, and, I hope, often," he said, helping her out of the kirtle and the smock she wore under it. His notion of proper ablutions soon had her moaning and begging him to kiss her, so he wrapped her swiftly in a towel, dried her in a less leisurely way than he had washed her, scooped her up, and put her into the bed.

Tidying himself more hastily, he climbed in beside her.

He was a patient lover, and he found her to be a delightful partner: sensuous, delectable, and beguilingly responsive to his every touch. He liked being in charge, and although she was independent enough to challenge and stimulate him, in bed or out, he had come to recognize a certain vulnerability in her that would welcome his strength when she needed it.

Katy marveled at the sensations that Will stirred in her with every touch of his body or his hands, fingers, or lips. Any sensation she had felt before, or that Bridgett had described, seemed paltry by comparison with what Will was making her feel now. He was gentle with her and tender, though she knew he was also strong enough in mind and body to protect her from harm and her own foibles.

Her mother had warned her that one's first lovemaking could be painful, but the thought simply made her smile as she tried to imagine Fin and Catriona doing what she and Will were doing.

"What makes you smile so?" he asked.

"Only that when Mam explained this, I could not begin to picture her so with my father. But now—"

He chuckled. A few moments later, he said, "I think you are ready."

"Mam said it might hurt."

"I'll be careful."

"I know," she said. Though he was capable of conquering her and had not hesitated to express disapproval from time to time, he had never tried to bully her or change her in any meaningful way.

Just then, he touched her in a way that stopped her thoughts and focused her attention wholly on what he was doing. The sensations now put even the earlier ones to shame until he entered her, but even then he was gentle.

Kissing her on the mouth, nose, and each eye afterward, he said, "I will teach you all the pleasurable things we can do, and I promise you that from now on, you will be learning to enjoy everything about this particular exercise."

"Aye, Mam said the same."

He started to get up.

"Where are you going?"

"To get the cloth. Just stay where you are."

"But I—"

"Trust me, Katy."

She lay back, watching him, marveling at his splendid, muscular body. When he had attended to himself, he rinsed the cloth, dumped the basin water into the sops bucket, and poured warm water into the basin.

When he returned, he said, "You have the most beautiful legs, lass."

"How many have you seen?" she asked with a saucy grin.

"Not the thousands you seem to be imagining. I was referring only to ladies' legs, though I am perhaps unwise to mention that. Nevertheless, I would ask you to spread yours a bit, so that I can make you tidy again."

She stared at him for a long moment, but when he winked at her, she obeyed his request, and he taught her more quickly than she had anticipated that he did indeed have many more delights in store for her than she had imagined.

A short time later, he tossed the cloth into the basin and returned to the bed, standing beside it and looking down at her.

She scooted over. "Get back into bed, Will. Hurry, I'm getting cold."

His eyes twinkling, he said, "Do you mean to call the tune now, my love?"

Amused, she said, "If it becomes necessary, sir, I think I just might."

"Not, I hope, before you recall your father's suggestion earlier tonight of the rights I have acquired as a result of your declaration."

"You will not be so brutal, though," she said confidently.

"Nae, so as I am one who believes in keeping the peace, I'm thinking the best solution for us both would be to stay in bed until that fortnight ends."

She chuckled. "You are daft, sir."

"I am, aye. I married a wife now known by all to take liberties with the truth and be gey disobedient."

"I have not yet disobeyed you or lied to you, however."

"Aye, 'tis true, *mo chridhe*, but I expect it will not be long before you do one or the other. Then, may Heaven help us both."

With a gurgle of laughter at his so-falsely-woeful expression, Katy said, "You can always make me laugh, Will. I do love you so."

Dear Reader,

I hope you enjoyed *The Kissing Stone*. I based this story on the numerous versions of the legend of Raitt Castle's ghost. Readers acquainted with that legend will note that I did not follow the exact script for the "handless" ghost's death. However, the hangings, the seizure of Nairn, the prophecies, the total solar eclipse (including its likely corona), the lunar eclipse, the battle at Moigh, and the banquet all took place as noted. After the climactic event, Raitt remained uninhabited and is now a ruin. Details and dates in the many versions of the legend are sketchy or nonexistent, so the author's imagination filled in the blanks.

Finlagh Castle did exist on its knoll, the site also of an ancient fortress but may have been a ruin at the time of this story. It was well placed for Fin of the Battles, though.

Malcolm, Chief of Clan Mackintosh and tenth Captain of Clan Chattan, lived until 1457 and was Constable of Inverness Castle until 1452 when he said he was "old and unable for public employment" and resigned the castle to a Crichton, a less successful custodian than the Mackintosh chief. Three years later, the Earl of Ross seized the castle.

Marriage by declaration in Scotland remained legal after the union of that country with England. The Marriage Act of 1939 also continued to allow marriage "by cohabitation and repute" (common law) to continue. Scotland became the last country in Europe to disallow such marriages, in 2006.

Those of you who know that the outflow of Loch Moigh runs into the river Findhorn may be interested to learn that, in 1433, the Findhorn was known as the river Erne, and the town was Invererne. The town moved two miles west of its original location, after high water in the Moray Firth caused a flood that nearly demolished it. Global warming in the thirteenth and fourteenth centuries!

Those skeptical of a so-brief relationship resulting in marriage might like to know that my husband and I went out six nights in a row and got engaged on our next date two months later without seeing each other meantime (I was in California, he in Hawaii). When this book comes out, we'll have been happily married for forty-seven years.

On our second date, I said, "Remember the other day when . . ." He said, "Hey, we just met last night." We felt as if we'd known each other from childhood. Still do.

My sources for the Clan Chattan Confederation and Clan Mackintosh include *The Confederation of Clan Chattan, Its Kith and Kin* by Charles Fraser-Mackintosh of Drummond (Glasgow, 1898); *The House and Clan of Mackintosh and of the Clan Chattan* by Alexander Mackintosh Shaw (Moy Hall, n.d.); and many others.

Sources for Alexander, third Lord of the Isles, include *The Clan Donald* by Reverend A. MacDonald (Inverness, 1881); *The House and Clan of Mackintosh*; and "The History of the MacDonalds and the Lords of the Isles," by Alexander Mackenzie, *The Celtic Magazine* (v. 5, April 1880).

Many of you will have recognized characters from my Scottish Knights series: *Highland Master*, *Highland Hero*, and *Highland Lover*. If not, those books are all still available in stores and online.

A special thanks to Bruce E. MacNab for another generous donation to the St. Andrews Society of Sacramento, which allowed him to become a squire in *Reluctant Highlander* and reappear in *The Kissing Stone*.

I also want to express my thanks to Bruce and Bridgett Locken again for their 2016 donations to the St. Andrews Society of Sacramento. Bridgett provided the author with some wonderful suggestions for their characters.

I am also more than grateful to swordsman and battle choreographer Brian Dake and his wife, Patricia (board member of the San Francisco Area RWA), for their assistance in "choreographing" Will's swordsmanship at the Battle of Loch Moigh. These two have spent years as community fencing instructors and combat choreographers for local theater productions, including *Macbeth*, *The Scarlet Pimpernel*, and *The Three Musketeers*.

As always, I'd like to thank my long-suffering agents, Lucy Childs and Aaron Priest; as well as my amazing and insightful editor, Maggie Crawford; master copyeditor Sean Devlin; Editorial Director Philip Rappaport; Assistant Editor Annie Locke; cover designer Lesley Worrell; Senior Production Editor Megan Buckman, and everyone else at Open Road Integrated Media who contributed to this book.

I also extend a special thanks to all of you, my readers, who have so strongly supported my books over the years. You are brilliant and wonderful people. I love hearing from you, because I could not have done it without you.

Meantime, *Suas Alba!*
Amanda Scott

www.amandascottauthor.com
https://openroadmedia.com/contributor/amanda-scott
www.facebook.com/amandascottauthor

ABOUT THE AUTHOR

A fourth-generation Californian of Scottish descent, Amanda Scott is the author of more than sixty romantic novels, many of which appeared on the *USA Today* bestseller list. Her Scottish heritage and love of history (she received undergraduate and graduate degrees in history at Mills College and California State University, San Jose, respectively) inspired her to write historical fiction. Credited by *Library Journal* with starting the Scottish romance subgenre, Scott has also won acclaim for her sparkling Regency romances. She is the recipient of the Romance Writers of America's RITA Award (for *Lord Abberley's Nemesis*, 1986) and the RT Book Reviews Career Achievement Award. She lives in central California with her husband.

THE HIGHLAND NIGHTS SERIES

FROM OPEN ROAD MEDIA

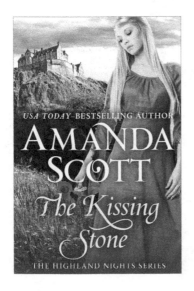

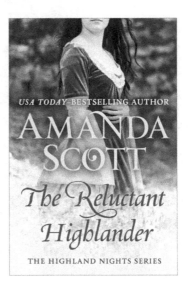

INTEGRATED MEDIA

INTEGRATED MEDIA